Also by Stell

DECE

Introducing Black Raven

Praise for *Deceived*:

"Stella Barcelona's stunning debut, *Deceived*, has it all. Mystery-check. Action-check. Romance-check. A heart pounding must read." – Cherry Adair, New York Times Bestselling Author

"*Deceived* brings history to life in a suspenseful, contemporary tale that sends the protagonists on a research trip to a past close to their hearts. Barcelona's debut book brings an excellent author to the fore; the intrigue blends beautifully with the romance." – Heather Graham, New York Times Bestselling Author

"Barcelona has written a story that grabs you from the beginning and sucks you right in." – The Reading Café, Review Blog

"Must read for romantic suspense lovers." – BCWAB, Review Blog

"A weaver of words, Ms. Barcelona creates a story that draws you in from page one, keeps you on the edge of your seat, and leaves you wanting more. The plot is original and the research and historical facts make *Deceived* an excellent and intriguing read. Not only the main characters, but the supporting characters as well, are interesting, believable, and loveable. ...*Deceived* is a fast paced, heartwarming, maddening, and enjoyable book all rolled up into one terrific package!" – InD'Tale Magazine

"Finally – Someone gets New Orleans right!" – La. Family Historian, Amazon Review

"The weather may be chilly outside, but a few lines into local author Stella Barcelona's debut novel, *Deceived*, will have you working up a sweat as you unravel a mystery, follow some interesting plot twists, and revel in a steamy romance." – Tangi Lifestyles Magazine

"2 A.M. page turner. ...A great 'history mystery' that doesn't get bogged down in details." – S. Harris, Amazon Review

"If you enjoy a little suspense and intrigue with your romance, I would definitely add *Deceived* to your reading list. Stella Barcelona is a great new voice in romantic suspense!" – Smart and Savvy with Stephanie, Review Blog

SHADOWS
A Black Raven Novel

Praise for *Shadows*:

"[A] smart techno-thriller with a steamy and surprisingly touching love story between two characters who are both torn between duty and desire. The stakes are high throughout, but the sacrifices that the hero and the heroine have made for what they feel is right makes their relationship that much more meaningful and offers a safe haven in the midst of a tangled, dangerous and well-plotted escapade." – Romantic Times Book Reviews

"WOW! *Shadows* is a highly polished, gritty, suspense-packed tale that will have readers hanging on the edge of their seats! Brilliantly written, this story with profoundly unique characters will leave readers gasping while refusing to lay the book down. – InD'Tale Magazine

"Terrifyingly possible, *Shadows* is romantic suspense on steroids. It starts with a bang and never slows down. Not for the faint of heart, but definitely for fans of the genre, this book was just amazing." – Long and Short Reviews, Review Blog

"[F]asten your seat belt because you're going to have the ride of your life!! ...It's fast paced, with a high amount of violence, sex scenes and death. What more can you ask? Highly Recommended!!!" – Romorror Fan Girl, Review Blog

Shadows has "lots of plot twisting, double crossing, passion, rage, violence, oh just about a bit of everything that makes this a very, very good read. ...I loved that we get to hear from Skye and Sebastian, but what absolutely made this book for me, is we get whodunit too! In all his warped, twisted mind's glory!" – Archaeolibrarian, I Dig Good Books, Review Blog

"Riveting from the very first paragraph, the reader barely has time to buckle up before the ride begins! And it is an amazing ride...." – Between My Bookendz, Amazon Review

"[M]ake it your business to pick up this book today. . . . Barcelona takes inspiration from true-life headlines and the abrasive talking heads on cable news programs, but she does an excellent job boiling down the big picture while making the chase for the secrets extremely emotional and personal. The plot twists and turns, trust is a theme, graphic violence is prevalent, and sisterly love is a beacon of sanity in a frightful situation. Once the action slows down for a breath, the sizzling attraction between Skye and Sebastian explodes, but even their initial love scene unfolds with a few surprises." – History Repeats, Amazon Review

JIGSAW

Stella Barcelona

Jigsaw is a work of fiction. The people and events in Jigsaw are entirely fictional. This story is not intended by the author as a reflection of historical or current fact, nor is the story intended as an accurate representation of past or current events. Any resemblance between the characters in this novel and any or all persons living or dead is entirely coincidental.

To everyone who has read my books and taken the time to write a review, reached out to tell me they liked them, or simply found a few hours of enjoyment in my writing. I'm grateful for each and every one of you. Thank you for allowing me to tell you a story.

To Bob - Thank you for encouraging my dreams. And about that beach vacation...I'm ready. Always.

Prologue

The White House, Oval Office
Saturday, January 1

"Bring me Andre Maximov's severed head." President William Cameron's dark brown eyes were intense, his photo-perfect, handsome face mottled in shades of pink and red as he sat behind the intricately carved Resolute Desk. At the commencement of his first term, his full head of brown hair had made him look young and handsome. Now in his second term, his hair had silvered. Thin lines extending from the edges of his eyes and slight shadows underneath revealed the strain of the job and nights with little sleep.

"I want Maximov and his damned killing organization decapitated. ASAP," the president said to his friend and confidant, Judge Theodore O'Connor, for the moment the only other occupant of the Oval Office. "After last night's bombing, I'll gladly parade down Pennsylvania Avenue with his head on a pike, so everyone sees what happens to terrorists who dare to operate in this country. I'm done being politically correct. Let's nail the bastard and make his punishment public."

Fists whitening as they pressed into the surface of his desk, the president leaned forward. "The Vegas strip on New Year's Eve, for God's sake! Intel tells us terrorist cells that declare an affiliation with Maximov are celebrating the attack." While redness faded from his cheeks, his tone remained harsh. "Use the International Terrorist Tribunal to deliver Maximov to me, and you'll have whatever is in my power to give you."

The judge let the momentary quiet of the office settle around them as he gave his friend time to rein in his rarely-seen temper. When he did speak, he was careful to keep his tone as cool and calm as possible. "I'd like nothing more than to deliver Maximov to you. The ITT could possibly make it happen. But I caution you, if you tell the public that the end result of the ITT proceedings will be capturing Maximov, you're setting yourself up for possible failure, because we don't have him. Yes, the ITT proceedings are determining whether there is a link between the Maximov organization and the terrorist acts at issue. Yes, every participant in the proceeding knows that finding Maximov, in person, is a goal. But reality is he's as elusive as a phantom."

His friend's growing frustration was evident in the grim look in his eyes. Yet the president needed to be reminded of the unfiltered facts. "Also, even if we capture Maximov, you'll never have his head on a pike. That's medieval. If he isn't killed in the capture, at best he'll be sentenced to a lifetime in Ultimate Exile." The judge referred to the prison ship where all convicted by the ITT were to be imprisoned. "We agreed to forego the death penalty to get the U.K., France, and Colombia on board, and we needed their participation in the ITT to get the other countries, and economies, to agree to follow the verdict."

"That concession was necessary, no matter how much we regret it now." Distaste for the compromise evident in his marked frown, the president walked around the wide desk, past the flag of the United States that flanked the right side of it. He leaned against the edge and faced the judge. Four and a half years in the White House had only chiseled his resolve, which was apparent in the firm jaw, squared shoulders, and steady gaze. He strode to a table where a silver decanter and morning pastries were laid out. "I can tell you, a bomb ripping to shreds Americans who were doing nothing but celebrating New Year's Eve in Las Vegas damn well makes me regret allowing the death penalty to be taken off the table. Coffee?"

The judge shook his head. The president filled his mug, then returned behind the desk and settled into his big leather chair. "Osama was a challenge," he said, expression set. "But we met it. We're beating China in the cyber war. We have an international task force of operatives on the hunt for Maximov. The best of the best. Not to mention the legions of bounty hunters looking for him. Maximov is only a man. Why the hell can't we find him?"

"I don't have an answer." The judge shifted in his chair. "But I'm not letting you hang yourself on this one. At this morning's press conference, do not promise that the ITT proceedings will result in finding Maximov. In the end, if it works out, claim credit. Revel in the fact that you've persuaded eighty-five percent of the world's economies to agree that the verdict of this ITT will be enforced. The strength of this coalition is unprecedented."

The president leaned forward in his chair, coffee forgotten. "Before the press conference, I want your assurance that the International Terrorist Tribunal will not fail in establishing a link between the terrorist acts that it is investigating and the Maximov-in-Exile organization."

The judge had never been one to give false assurances, especially when sitting in the Oval Office. Even so, he gave a slow nod. "Yes. A link between Maximov and the terrorist acts at issue is a baseline goal. I've studied the stipulations, analyzed evidence, and looked at preliminary findings. I've worked with Amicus Curiae counsel—"

"Stanley Morgan." The president frowned as he referred to the lead attorney on the Amicus Curiae team. "Is he on board with our objectives?"

Confident that he could control Morgan, the judge didn't bother his friend with his misgivings about the man. "Yes, sir."

The president flinched. "You call me sir when you're worried about something."

Judge O'Connor chuckled. "At least I didn't call you Mr. President."

"Yes. You only do that when we're truly screwed. Come on, Ted. Shoot straight with me."

Reality was that the judge shared the president's misgivings about Morgan, who had been the top pick for the position of U.S. Amicus Curiae to the ITT. Amicus meant friend in Latin, and in ITT proceedings Amicus Curiae counsel was the official friend to the court. In private, the president had expressed misgivings about Morgan. The president believed he was too opinionated. Normally, that would be a great trait for a lawyer, but in this proceeding, with the world hanging on the decision of the ITT, Amicus Curiae counsel needed to be malleable. Stanley Morgan was brilliant, decisive, and a passionate advocate.

In no way was Stanley Morgan malleable. In Morgan's last briefing memo, he'd expressed concern regarding the lack of direct evidence reflecting a link between the terrorist acts and the Maximov organization. He'd recommended more expansive data gathering and a delay in the trial, set to start at the end of January. A delay could prove fatal to the consensus of the countries that had created the ITT.

"Don't worry about Morgan," the judge said. A private conversation with Morgan would reorient the man's views. No delay in the proceeding was necessary. The ITT record had enough data, and direct evidence wasn't important when there was enough circumstantial evidence to hang Maximov and his damned organization. The judge intended to remind Morgan of that fact. "Even at this early stage, I'm confident that the verdict will be that the Maximov organization was responsible for each terrorist act the ITT is analyzing. Even without Maximov in custody, with the other countries agreeing to enforce the verdict, we'll cripple the Maximov organization financially. He'll have nowhere to do business. He'll have no money to pour into the hands of the cells that are doing his work. Terrorist acts that are attributable to the Maximov organization will stop."

"All right. I'll focus on that in public. The Prime Minister and the French and Colombian presidents will be arriving shortly." The president glanced at his watch. "The conference starts in one hour. Let's fine-tune my bullet points."

The president picked up his briefing papers. Back erect, with a steady, authoritative tone, he said, "The International Terrorist Tribunal, an arm of the International Court of Justice convened with the express purpose of combatting terrorism, will begin proceedings in Paris on Monday, January 31. Four terrorist acts that were committed in the last year are at issue. One, the January metro bombings in France. Two, the February bombing at the trade show in London. Three, the February drone attack on the cruise ship in Miami."

He glanced into the judge's eyes, his harsh look underscoring his reaction to the homeland attack. "Four, the March courthouse attack in Bogata. Together these terrorist acts killed more than two thousand people. Innocent people. Preliminary proceedings have been conducted in each country. Hundreds of suspects have been apprehended. Many have already been convicted through guilty pleas. Only a handful will actually testify before the ITT. Most evidence will be considered by the tribunal based upon stipulation."

"It's a shame the proceedings can't be expanded to include last night's bombing in Vegas," the judge said. "But it can't. It would cause too much disruption. Make sure you cover that point with the press and that what we uncover in the proceeding may shed light on what happened in Vegas. Also emphasize that the proceedings provide the defendants who will testify an opportunity to mitigate their punishment. We need to give something to appease the civil liberties unions."

The president made a note on his briefing papers. "Any progress in getting information on Maximov from those in custody?"

"They all know information buys leniency. Defense counsel Robert Brier has consistently advised them of that fact. None are talking. Silence is pervasive."

"And torture is now illegal." The president's distaste for the concession was obvious in his frown.

"Watch that frown. The nightly comedians are using it in their parodies."

"Not running the country for their approval."

"They influence public opinion, and we need the public behind the ITT. I wouldn't express your personal views on the gentle nature with which ITT interrogations are taking place."

"Of course not." The president reached for his cup of coffee, took a sip, and studied his papers before resuming in his press-conference tone. "The ITT proceeding is a hybrid of U.S. federal judicial proceedings. The procedures that we are following are the product of a consensus of the forum countries. There is no privilege against self-incrimination. There is no appeal."

"Yes. Mention all of that."

"Punishment will be swift and permanent," the president continued. "There is no death penalty, but there is the possibility of a lifetime of imprisonment. Ultimate Exile is a method of imprisonment that the world has agreed upon. A prison from which there will be no appeal and no escape." The president paused, leafing through papers. "I'll give more details about Ultimate Exile. The press loves the prison ship." He looked up. "How much do you advise I say about Maximov?"

"As little as possible," the judge said. "State that the ITT is examining whether the Maximov organization, or any other international terrorist group, was involved in the four terrorist acts. With a guilty verdict that establishes any link in the terrorist acts, economic sanctions against the parties involved will be imposed by eighty-five percent of the world's economies. All assets of complicit parties will be seized. The ITT has defense teams, we have prosecution teams, and we have Amicus teams. Tell the public about the role of the Amicus Curiae counsel; that the lawyers on the Amicus teams act as a friend to the court. They're not prosecution or defense. Not for or against. They're simply looking for the truth and acting as advisers to the judges. They assess the evidence and facilitate the proceedings, which resemble an adversarial process as much as possible. There is no need for you to suggest at the beginning that we know or believe Maximov is responsible for all of these acts."

"But even the general public believes the Maximov organization was involved."

"I know. But we need to avoid the appearance of prejudging, because, in reality, we aren't. The dragnet could very well pull in other terrorist organizations. The U.S. prosecution teams have been culled from upper echelon Department of Justice attorneys. We were fortunate to get Robert Brier to head the defense team. The U.S. Amicus Curiae team, led by Stanley Morgan, is more than capable of tying the ends together and presenting a persuasive recommendation."

The president nodded. "Understood."

"One final caution. The press is using the term '*witch hunt*,' which they've picked up from the defense teams. Dissuade them from using that term. This will be a fair trial. The end result will be unassailable. '*Witch hunt*' implies prejudging. Prejudging makes the other countries nervous, and it gives human rights activists fuel."

Red flared in the president's cheeks. "Witch hunt?" He ground his teeth, shook his head, and straightened his shoulders. "Could be good and bad, but after last night's bombing in Vegas, I'd say Americans won't give a damn about that label. For now, I'll let the press run with it. I haven't forgotten history. Americans love a good witch hunt." His dark eyes flashed with hard-as-steel resolve, "As long as the goddamn witch is caught."

Chapter One

Ana slipped her small hand into her father's. Her soft touch pulled Zeus Hernandez from his conversation with two senior Black Raven agents, reminding him that the purpose of this gathering wasn't work. He and Ana were on a father-daughter trip to New Orleans, Louisiana, away from their home in Miami, Florida, to attend the wedding of Zeus's best friend and business partner, Sebastian Connelly to Skye Barrows.

"Daddy, hurry," she said, pulling on his hand. "They're getting ready to cut the cake. Come *on.*"

Zeus looked down into velvety-brown eyes shining with the unfiltered excitement of youth. He bent to one knee and planted a soft kiss on her cheek. With his free hand, he straightened the bow on her red hair ribbon. Loose tendrils of silky black hair had escaped from her ponytail and fallen across her face. He pushed the wayward hair back, gently tucking the strands behind her ear. She let go of his hand, draped her arms over his shoulders, and pressed her forehead to his so that their noses touched.

Inhaling her sugary sweet, girlish scent, he stared into her eyes, as she asked, "Don't you want to see?"

"Of course, my sweet angel."

He let Ana lead the way through the courtyard of New Orleans' City Park, towards the Pavilion of Two Sisters. As Zeus opened the door, his eyes scanned the wedding guests before resting on Sebastian, who talked to Skye and her younger sister, Spring.

Zeus was happy for his friend. Barely eleven months earlier Sebastian had been on the operating table, having life-threatening brain surgery following a week from hell. The Black Raven job that had involved Skye and her father was complete before Sebastian went under the knife. But even while Sebastian was down, the world remained filled with bad guys. In the ensuing months, London, Miami, Bogotá, and Paris had been rocked with large-scale terrorist acts, leading to the inevitable conclusion that the terrorists were winning, and that was before New Year's Eve was marked with a bombing on the Vegas strip, resulting in the deaths of hundreds of innocent revelers. Television cameras had been primed for the New Year's Eve festivities. Instead, the cameras caught a bloody massacre.

Now, thirty days after the New Year's Eve bombing, economic markets remained in turmoil. The global fall-out was great for Black Raven's security business, but not for one other damn thing.

Sebastian had recovered from his surgery with none of the troubling aftereffects they'd all dreaded. He was back to normal, at the helm of Black Raven with his partners where he belonged. Guests at Sebastian and Skye's Sunday afternoon wedding celebration were the inner circle of Black Raven agents, partners, and friends. Partygoers gathered at one end of the reception hall, where cakes were on display.

"Daddy, I can't see." Ana tugged at his hand as they stood at the edge of the crowd.

He lifted her, and settled her on his hip. At six, almost seven, she'd soon be too big to hold like this, and too old to want her father to carry her, but today, her skinny arms wrapped around his neck as she held on. "How's this?"

"Wow," she said. "I've never seen so many flowers on a wedding cake. The colors are weird, aren't they? But it's beautiful."

The father of the bride, computer software genius Richard Barrows, the man whose kidnapping from prison had brought Sebastian and Skye together, had walked his daughter down the aisle. Upon his official release from prison, Barrows had started work with Black Raven at their Denver headquarters. Zeus worked with him, along with Ragno, the head of their data analysis unit. Zeus and Ragno had concluded that Barrows was brilliant when focused. His ordeal had done nothing to diminish his brainpower, and they were damn glad he was now working for Black Raven instead of a competitor.

Zeus watched Sebastian bend to his bride and give her a lingering kiss. At this wedding, the groom revealed none of the hesitation that had marked Zeus's own wedding day. No second thoughts. Not one bit of doubt. Zeus had pretended to be just as happy as Sebastian really was. Now, watching Sebastian's genuine, heartfelt reactions to the moments that marked his wedding day, Zeus wondered whether he'd fooled anyone.

Skye led her sister to the cakes for photographs. For a moment, Spring looked overwhelmed by the attention, but she managed a smile. Sebastian, who was hanging back and allowing Spring to bask in the attention given to the cakes she'd created, approached Zeus. His eyes changed from happy groom to serious

Raven. "How are operations going?"

"Not today. You've got a gorgeous new wife to focus on." His gaze fell on Barrows, who stood a few feet from the cake tables, smiling at his daughters. "A ready-made family. Besides, things are fine. Nothing unusual."

Zeus and the other Ravens who were at the wedding reception were mic'd to Ragno, who was at headquarters in Denver. Sebastian was not. For the last two hours, in deference to the celebration, Ragno had maintained radio silence.

"Zeus," Ragno's voice came through the mic, as clear as if she was standing next to him. "You spoke too soon. I'm talking only to you, and it can't wait. Understand?"

"Got it," he said after Sebastian stepped away from him to return to his new wife. The band picked up their instruments, a signal that soon he wouldn't be able to hear Ragno. "Give me a second."

Zeus walked over to Agent Victoria Martel, the Black Raven agent who had full-time duties over Ana, whether Ana was with Zeus or with her mother. When Zeus could, he worked from home in Miami, but most of his time he was based at Denver headquarters. From time to time, he worked as an on-site problem shooter on high-profile jobs. Due to the global reach of Black Raven's business, and the frequency with which jobs became volatile, at any moment in time Zeus could be anywhere in the world. He was lucky if he got a few weeknights and a couple weekends a month with his daughter.

Agent Martel was Nanny Vick to Ana, a beloved sitter, friend, disciplinarian, and confidant. To Zeus, Agent Martel was a caregiver with a Glock, his insurance for Ana's safety. Overkill? He hoped so. With his daughter, there was no such thing as being too careful.

Used to Zeus's sudden transitions to business mode, Ana wriggled out of his grasp and stood firmly on the ground next to Agent Martel. Eyes on him, she asked, "Want me to get you a piece of cake?"

"If one of those cakes is chocolate on the inside," he said, touching her cheek, "absolutely. I'll be right back, baby. Stay with Vick." He turned from them and walked outside. "Ragno, I'm all ears."

"Stanley Morgan, Chief Amicus Curiae Counsel for the United States, at the newly convened International Terrorist Tribunal, died six hours ago in Paris. His death looks like insulin overdose in a diabetic. Initial reports suggest it was accidental."

"Okay," he said, walking across the brick courtyard, the lone person outside of the reception hall. Bright sunlight shone on the courtyard's bordering gardens, filled with pink, red, and white azaleas in full bloom. Fountains in sparkling water gardens trickled and splashed. The water noises grew louder with each step he took away from the reception venue and the sounds of the band.

In a world without peace, the courtyard with its fountains and flowers welcomed guests with a glimpse of what life could be like if one managed to forget the evil that was now everywhere.

Zeus never forgot.

He was the Raven in charge of operations. Managing partner of an international company in the business of protecting clients from threats of all kinds. Black Raven was the go-to company for state of the art security systems and manned details at upper echelon businesses and private residences. The company handled special assignments in far-flung destinations, and government contracts with varying degrees of secrecy. Black Raven had blossomed into a company that was synonymous with safety, protection, cyber-systems security, and skilled investigations. They were an elite, private army for hire.

"You're up to speed on International Terrorist Tribunal proceedings, correct?" Ragno's words were fast and efficient, her tone businesslike.

"As much as I've needed to be. ITT for short. Trial starts in Paris tomorrow. The world's watching. Good people want to see someone punished. Terrorists want to see the proceedings fail. The ITT has one month to conduct four proceedings in four countries, then reach a verdict regarding last year's terrorist acts in France, the U.S., Columbia, and the U.K." He took a few more steps across the courtyard as he talked. "I think the current ITT proceeding is too ambitious, convened too hastily, and promises to be a clusterfuck of epic proportions, fueled by the media's feeding frenzy on the public fear of terrorism. Terrorists, whether affiliated with an established group or random wannabes, will find targets among the proceedings. Media's thirsty for the first shots to be fired. How's that assessment?"

"Accurate," Ragno said. "Although there's no indication of foul play, Stanley Morgan's death has caused shockwaves about security concerns in at least one person, and he's made a hiring call to us for personal security for the person stepping in to fill Morgan's shoes."

"Isn't there government-agency security in place for the

judges and participating parties who are there on behalf of the U.S.?" He stopped walking when he reached a pond that was the centerpiece of the courtyard. His eyes drifted over flowering water lilies, with pink and purple petals and dark green, waxy leaves. He looked past the foliage, into clear water where shimmering gold koi lazily swam.

"Yes. Marshals. DHS. Plus, the ITT has its own security forces in each country."

"So, someone is trying to circumvent the security that's already in place?"

"Yes. The person making the hiring call claims that Morgan's death was not accidental."

"Any evidence of that?"

"No credible suggestion so far." Zeus heard Ragno's fingers clicking on her keyboard as she talked. "Having low confidence level in existing security, he wants Black Raven. Specifically, he's requested that you personally provide on-site protection to Morgan's replacement."

"Did you mention that I no longer do field work or bodyguard details?" It was midafternoon, and the January sun had warmed the mild winter chill out of the air. He pulled off his suit jacket as his eyes followed the fattest koi in the pond.

"I explained that, but he won't take no for an answer. By the way, we provide extensive, on-site and off-site security at his personal residences and several of his business properties. His companies have been existing clients of Black Raven for some years."

Oh fuck.

"Answer's no. I don't care who he is, so don't tell me. We've got more than enough work right now. If he doesn't like it, he can take his business elsewhere."

"You're the originating partner on his files. Over the years his companies have paid us millions. High millions."

Zeus paused as he considered Ragno's information. The fattest koi's scales shimmered with crimson red and sunlight gold. It was speckled with white and black spots. When smaller fish crossed its path, it swam fast and nudged the others out of its way. Zeus bent down, picked up a few pebbles off the path bordering the pond, and dropped one near the bully as he started an attack. "That doesn't change my answer. I don't care how much he's paid us. Tell him we have a number of highly qualified agents who can handle the job. I'll oversee the operation and be personally involved from afar, but I'm not going to be on-site, day in and day out."

"He told me you wouldn't say no, even after I had accounting provide a rough estimate of the daily fee, which included a ridiculous rate for you. It's an enormous job. Multiple countries. High profile. I'm estimating you'll need twenty agents. Minimum. Worldwide transports. We factored in high profit levels on every conceivable contingency."

"Like I said, manpower is taxed." Though he was getting damned curious.

"I know, but we can handle it, especially given the profit factor." As Ragno rattled off astronomical numbers, Zeus dropped another pebble, wondering if the aggressive fish was smart enough to learn that his own actions were creating the threat. "Even with that kind of figure thrown at him, and a warning that the estimate will only go up, he said no one other than you is acceptable as lead agent on site. He insisted that I call you, tell you about the job, and ask you to do it. So that's what I'm doing." After a pause she continued in a gentler tone. The one they used when talking about personal issues. "Zeus, I'm thinking you won't tell him no."

Son of a bitch.

"Okay. I'll bite. Who is he?"

"Samuel Dixon."

The name carried an out-of-the-blue gut punch. He'd trained himself to react with equanimity to almost every conceivable situation, yet the adrenaline rush that came with hearing Dixon's name jolted his very being. Zeus looked up at the bright blue, cloudless sky, and waited for the words that would seal his fate. The sun's heat warmed his exterior, while internal trepidation chilled his insides.

No was the only answer that made sense, but he knew he wasn't going to say it. *No* was not a word he was going to articulate, because Samuel Dixon would only be making this request on behalf of one person, knowing that, like a goddamn moth driven to flame, for all the reasons his answer should be no, Zeus was going to say yes. He'd been on a road leading away from her for years. It was a painful turn he'd taken willingly, resulting in a sharp, regret-filled detour that could never be undone.

Ragno continued, "Dixon believes she's in grave danger and insists that you lead the protective detail. You saved his life once. He has the highest respect for your capabilities. No one else will do."

Let me be wrong.

"She?"

"Morgan's replacement is Dixon's granddaughter. Samantha Dixon Fairfax."

Fuck!

He'd given her the nickname Sam, and it had aggravated her to no end. To him, she was way more than a pretty woman with a nickname. To him, she was the one.

The one—though I've never told her that fact. How could I? I didn't realize it myself, until it was too late. It made sense that Dixon was making this request on behalf of his granddaughter, his only heir. Zeus knew from the first job he'd handled for Dixon that the man was more like an overbearing parent to her than a distant, adoring grandparent. He also knew from personal experience that not only did the man love his granddaughter, he was a Machiavellian meddler in her life.

Cunning and crafty, Dixon was capable of pulling strings from afar in order to assure that his granddaughter took the path of his choosing. Zeus had seen that dark, manipulative side of Dixon. He didn't know whether Sam had. It hadn't been his business then, and he didn't see why it would be now. The man's relationship with his granddaughter mattered not to Zeus. What did matter was that Dixon believed she was in danger and was willing to pay Black Raven a shitload of money to make sure she survived and was unharmed.

His gaze rolled over the fishpond, then bounced up to the clear-blue sky, coming back to rest on the trickling waterfall.

Dammit.

He tried to think of a way out. He couldn't.

Of all the variations of hell Zeus had confronted in his life, this one would be the hardest to navigate. It was a hell that defied reason—a scorching, internal inferno that he'd created. He wasn't a man who walked away from anything or anyone without closure. Except her, and now it was coming back to bite him in the ass.

Embrace the suck.

Over the years, the phrase had become a Black Raven mantra. When the going got tough, Black Raven agents powered through—any way, anyhow.

Embrace the suck and do the job. Get. The. Job. Done. Any way, any how.

This job, though, wasn't going to be just a job. Walking through this fire-filled cauldron was going to test him in ways he didn't want to think about, and that was even without worrying about the risks the job would present. While his thoughts raced with legitimate reasons he should refuse, adrenaline played tricks throughout his body. His dick had long ago sworn an oath of allegiance to her that produced a hard-on whenever he dwelled on what sex with her had been like. His dick rejoiced by hardening as his mind raced through the possibilities that lay in store. His palms became clammy. His heart pounded.

Hell. Hell. Hell. Hell.

"Zeus?"

"Dixon's right. I'm in."

"Maybe you should think about it."

"Don't sound so concerned. I can han—"

"If you say it's just a job. That you'll keep personal issues out of it," Ragno retorted in a tone that was more worried than teasing, "I'll strangle you next time I see you."

"With you, I won't even pretend." He chuckled, though the sound came out more like a choke. "You're damn straight it's personal."

The silky feel of Sam's long blonde hair, the coolness in her ice-blue eyes, and the warmth of her ivory skin on his fingertips had been immediately imprinted into his psyche. On the outside, she was more ice than fire, but once he chipped away the icy coolness, the fire within burned so hot he'd never been able to get her out of his system. Memories of her urgent, demanding style of making love—a surprise at first, and positively addictive within seconds—had haunted him for years.

It's well past time for those memories to die.

He'd do the job he was paid to do. She'd be safe. Personal issues wouldn't interfere with that. Somehow, he'd make amends for what he'd done in their past. Not that she'd ever acted like she gave a damn, but his gut regretted what he'd done to her. His gut told him all kinds of things, and he had to figure out if he was right.

As his mind clicked into gear, he shook off the feeling that a freight train was bearing down on him. "Occurs to me this job could provide firsthand exposure to information for Jigsaw."

Jigsaw was the code name for an intelligence gathering and assimilation program that Barrows designed, which Zeus and Sebastian had, in turn, marketed to the Department of Homeland Security and National Security Agency. In a rare move, DHS and NSA had acted together and hired Black Raven to use Jigsaw to assist them in their joint goal of defeating terrorism. The hiring decision—made just six months earlier—was top secret. With the off-the-record hiring decision made, Jigsaw was now more than a computer program; it was a highly lucrative, top-secret intelligence gathering job for Black Raven. Only a handful of people in the government—or even in Black Raven itself—knew the job existed.

"I thought of that as well," Ragno said. "The more puzzle pieces we have, the better off Jigsaw will be. Right now we have no links in the data that can pinpoint where the next terrorist attack will be, or who it will come from."

Puzzle pieces was Ragno's term for cyber data, which Jigsaw accumulated, dissected, and manipulated, until the program made order out of seeming chaos. Jigsaw collected data of U.S. intelligence agencies, and also analyzed European, Asian, South American, and African intelligence gathering efforts. It didn't ask for permission. It simply scrolled through cyber-data and took. The program didn't limit its cyber-assimilation to intelligence agencies, either. It scrolled through world-wide networks and assembled cyber data without being detected. Personal phone calls, banking records, emails, text messages—in short, anything was fodder for Jigsaw. The data became pieces to the largest jigsaw puzzle ever conceived, with the pieces cyber-enhanced and sorted through by the brilliance of Barrows and his ability to engineer computer code that assimilated raw data into meaningful information.

The puzzle pieces would one day fit together. Not one minute too soon, because the goddamn terrorists needed to be stopped.

Zeus turned towards the reception hall. "Ragno, on top of the business aspects of the ITT job, I need your help with a personal issue. Keep this between us. Help me figure Sam out. I really only know the things about her that she told me, or that Samuel told me. I want to know everything about her that makes her act the way she acts, like she's encrypted code. This time, I'm damn well going to crack it."

Chapter Two

Paris, France
Monday, January 31

"Samantha? President Cameron would like to speak to you."

Samantha Dixon Fairfax's finger hovered over the send button on her laptop as the words registered. She was sitting on the corner of the couch, papers spread to her side, with her right foot tucked under her left leg.

She glanced into the dark eyes of Charles Beller, who bent towards her with the cell phone that he used for the business of the Amicus team. Charles gave her an arched-eyebrow nod. "His secretary is holding for you to accept the call." He silently mouthed, *Wow*.

My thought, exactly.

The U.S. Amicus team of lawyers to the ITT consisted of Samantha as the newly appointed chief, with two lawyers—Eric Moss and Abe Smith. Samantha and her team were facilitators for the judges so that the trial proceedings ran smoothly. They were to make recommendations regarding questions that arose during the trial, and as the proceedings drew to a close they were to ultimately make a recommendation to the judges regarding what their ruling should be. Her recommendation to the judges of the U.S. needed to be persuasive enough that it won the vote of all the judges, not just those from the U.S.

With the first official day of ITT proceedings concluded, Samantha, Charles, Eric, and Abe were working together in the Hotel Grand Athens, where they were staying.

Sudden silence, heavy with the same expectation that accompanied the flash of time existing between lightning and thunder, filled the hotel suite's living room. All eyes were trained on her.

Samantha had met President Cameron several times at social gatherings and fundraisers. This was her first official call from the White House. E-mail forgotten, she slid the laptop from her lap, deposited it on the couch, and stood out of habit. Her legal training had taught her that important conversations were best conducted on her feet.

She gripped the phone as she stepped forward in a slow pace. "Samantha Dixon Fairfax."

"Ms. Fairfax, please hold for President Cameron," a male

voice said.

Heart quickening as she waited, she drew a deep breath.

Calm down.

Act like you've been here before.

She was determined her legal career would take her important places. If things went as planned, this was not going to be her last official call from the leader of the free world. She walked forward five steps, between the table and the couch, turned, retraced her steps, and turned again.

"Good evening, Ms. Fairfax." President Cameron's unmistakably deep voice held a hint of a Northeastern accent. "I know it's late in Paris. I hope I'm not disturbing you."

"No, Mr. President," she said. Feet now glued to the floor, she glanced at the Eiffel Tower from the sixth floor of their hotel in the Seventh Arrondissement area of Paris. Floor to ceiling windows provided an unobstructed view of the tourist attraction. In the dark, winter night, lights turned the iconic structure into a soaring golden beacon. "Not at all."

"I'd like to thank you for accepting the appointment. I know that you have, for several years, worked closely with Stanley Morgan. Please accept my condolences."

"Thank you."

"You were highly recommended by the ITT judges. In particular, Judge Theodore O'Connor. I'm calling to underscore the importance of your position. Our country needs to be the leader in this trial, and the judges will depend on you to assist them in making this proceeding a success. I trust you will hold your own when you advocate to the other judges for France, Columbia, and the U.K. I have every confidence you will succeed. The world is watching," he said. "I'm watching. If you need any assistance from me, please do not hesitate to ask."

"Thank you for this opportunity, Mr. President. I assure you I will not disappoint you."

"Goodnight, Ms. Fairfax."

He clicked off the call. She drew a deep breath as she returned the business phone to Charles and lifted her laptop from the couch. She sat down again with the computer on her lap.

"Well?" Charles asked, his dark brown eyes questioning. He had a neat, cardigan-wearing look that reminded Samantha of an old-time librarian. His conservative clothing and calm demeanor gave him a knack for blending into his surroundings.

She reminded herself that she was leading a team and their

reaction would feed off of hers. Though her insides were shaky with the impact of the official call, she kept her voice calm as she repeated the substance of the short conversation to Charles, Eric, and Abe.

"Now..." she paused. "Back to the briefing memo."

Eric, who became second chair attorney of the Amicus team when she became first chair, Abe, now third chair attorney, and Charles, who multitasked as her paralegal, secretary, and personal aide, had been waiting for her to press send on the email that would deliver the memo to the judges. Their work wasn't over for the day until the daily memo went through. Their security detail, a team of U.S. Marshals, stood in the hallway, outside the closed door.

Whether Stanley Morgan's death the evening before had been a heart attack caused by an accidental overdose of insulin, whether he had intentionally overdosed himself, or whether someone had forced an overdose upon him were open questions. Samantha's job didn't include figuring out the answers, because the ITT proceedings wouldn't pause, and she had no time to take a side bar to investigate.

Her name had been on prior nightly briefing memos, but safely tucked beneath Morgan's. Position in the signature block meant everything in the legal world. In ITT proceedings it meant ask the guy on top the hard questions.

Now, I'm the guy on top.

As President Cameron had just reminded her, the world was watching. Instead of pressing send, she pressed print, giving herself an extra few seconds. The last protection from the antacid she'd eaten an hour earlier—in the bathroom, away from the watchful eyes of her team—had worn off with the phone call. With one month to conduct proceedings and reach a verdict, a twisted knot of trepidation had formed in her belly and wouldn't loosen. President Cameron's call torqued the knot even tighter, yet she kept a calm expression on her face.

"Charles, would you get the memo for me? I'd like to proofread it one more time."

Charles stood, crossed the room, lifted the document off the printer, returned to her side, and handed it to her. She flipped the pages and scanned it, searching for errors that she knew were nonexistent.

The judges would reach a verdict on March first. One short month away. Her stomach knew the task was mission impossible, despite her assurance to President Cameron that she wouldn't disappoint him. Like everyone else, she pretended everything was under control.

I can handle this. I can.

In keeping with protocol, the nightly briefing memo went to the U.S. judges, the three sitting on the panel and the one alternate. It was sent directly from the email account of the chief Amicus Curiae counsel, with a personal note. Her personal note of the evening thanked the judges for offering her the position.

In the memo, the Amicus team provided a short summary of what had been accomplished in Monday's trial proceedings. Forensic investigators from France had testified, explaining the minute details of the metro bombings. One issue that had been avoided by the French investigators was an analysis of how the bombings compared to known attacks by the Maximov-in-Exile organization. The answer to that was simple and direct, and one that Samantha and her team could sum up in a few short words. The metro bombing wasn't similar to prior attacks, which had been linked to obvious political motives. The Amicus team also took the official trial plan for the next day and provided the American judges updates on what should be accomplished with each witness, based upon proceedings thus far.

Samantha also provided the position of the Amicus team on the latest discovery issue—the French investigative teams had drawn their discovery requests narrowly and the evidence they had produced to support their conclusions seemed scant. When the French forensic investigators testified earlier that day, they concluded that there was a link between the metro bombing and the Maximov organization, but Samantha didn't see it. Neither did the defense lawyers, who went to town attacking the conclusions.

Essentially, the French team wanted the teams from the other countries to accept their conclusions, without providing evidence. The lack of direct evidence had been a concern that bothered Morgan. It was now her worry, and the first order of business of the court on Tuesday morning was going to be argument regarding whether the French had to produce the full contents of their files.

She put the paper down, drank from a bottle of lukewarm water that she'd opened hours earlier, and hit send.

"Done."

"Congratulations on officially concluding your first day as our chief," said Eric, combing his fingers through his perpetually unruly red hair, his serious green eyes showing the strain of the day.

"Bittersweet, but thank you." She glanced past Eric through the large window into the dark Paris night. As her gaze took in the beauty of the Eiffel Tower and the crystal-clear night, strobe lights erupted into a glittering and blinking show, prompting her to glance at her watch.

10:30.

Perfect timing for the end of day memo from the Amicus team, which was expected to be delivered to the judges between 8:00 and 11:00 p.m. Not bad timing at all, considering that Morgan had died less than thirty-six hours earlier. She felt a lingering twinge of sadness at his death, accompanied with a moment of trepidation over the responsibility that had fallen into her lap.

Shortly after Morgan's death on Sunday evening, the judges from the United States decided to offer Samantha the lead position. When Judge Theodore O'Connor made the call, she'd accepted immediately. Now, with the whirlwind of the first day of ITT proceedings behind her and the nightly briefing memo on its way, she finally had a moment to ask herself whether she was up to the task of taking his place.

"The system is slow." With a frown, Charles straightened his navy blue wool cardigan, bent forward, and clicked at his laptop's keyboard. "You cc'd me, right?"

"Yes. I cc'd all of us." As she waited for the email sent notification, her moment of self-doubt dwindled away. *Am I up for the task of being chief?* Absolutely. She'd been born for opportunities like this and had worked hard to ensure that when chances for advancement came her way, she could capitalize on them. Law school had been grueling, but she'd finished number one in her class.

Obtaining her masters in international law had also been tough, but she'd excelled in that program as well. She'd been with Morgan and Associates for five years and she'd become Stanley Morgan's right hand, the associate he went to with the tough assignments. He'd been respected throughout the world as a brilliant jurist, and the opportunity to learn from him was something that many of her contemporaries coveted. Her next move would be a federal judgeship.

Being the chief—rather than simply Stanley Morgan's second chair—would put her in a better position before a judicial review committee. President Cameron's call underscored that fact. But, as ambitious as she was, she'd gladly give up the lead position if relinquishing it would mean that her friend and mentor was alive to take the reins. Capitalizing upon the death of someone she had respected, admired, and grown to love was not how she had planned to achieve her career goals.

"The email isn't in my inbox yet," Charles said with a frown.

Samantha glanced up. "Even something as simple as email delivery can't be left to chance. Let's make sure it goes through before we shut down."

"I'm starving." Eric stood and stretched. He walked from the conference table to the wet bar, grabbed a handful of nuts from a silver bowl, and munched on them.

She'd looked forward to the French fries and roasted chicken she'd ordered. Plus, she wanted her nightly glass of crisp sauvignon blanc. She was trying to keep with the civilized tradition that Morgan implemented for ending the day. When traveling for work, the team sat down for dinner and discussed something other than the projects that had consumed their day.

It gave perspective, he'd said.

"I know this isn't the way you anticipated becoming first chair, but I can't think of anyone better qualified to lead the team." Abe Smith, seated at the table, glanced at the screen of his open laptop and shook his head. "Damn, but this email is slow. I don't have it yet."

Previously, Abe had been in charge of their stateside team. He'd arrived in Paris only an hour earlier, called in to deal with the manpower shift necessitated by Morgan's death. Abe had blue eyes, brown hair, and tortoise-shell glasses that made him look almost as smart as he was. While Eric had the look of an L.L. Bean model, Abe was all Brooks Brothers-style polish. His clothes were crisp, his hair smooth, even after a transatlantic flight.

"That Morgan isn't here still seems surreal," Abe added. "I'm sorry for the circumstances, but I'm thrilled to be here."

"You'll be great," she said, glancing into his brown eyes. "Thanks for mobilizing so quickly." Samantha's attention returned to her laptop. Until the email was actually delivered to the judges, her job wasn't done. Servers failed. It had inexplicably happened once over the weekend while they'd been in France, and twice the week before when they were using the ITT email system in the U.S., in preparation for the trial.

There was a gentle knock on the door and the muffled announcement, *"Service de chambre."*

"I'll get it." Eric crossed the room to open the door.

"We'll have just enough time to eat before Black Raven arrives for the transfer at 11:15," Charles said.

"Still not sure why we need to move tonight," Eric said as he opened the door.

"We can discuss that with the agents when they get here." Samantha knew from prior experience with Black Raven that no progress would be made in altering the course the security company had chosen. Still, they were all tired. They needed to rest and be ready for proceedings in the morning.

She nodded to Lorenzo, the room service attendant, who she recognized from their previous two nights at the hotel. Lorenzo smiled in return as the door shut behind him. He wheeled a gleaming cart into the room. Crystal glasses clinked as he proceeded to cross to the smaller table near the window that they used as a dining table.

"*Mlle Fairfax, j'ai fait que les frites soit chaud ce soir,*" Lorenzo said.

He'd made sure the potatoes were hot. Samantha returned his smile. "*Merci beaucoup.*" The night before, her fries had arrived barely warm and she'd sent them back to the kitchen. She continued in French. "I really appreciate the effort."

"Charles, should we try to send again?" Eric asked.

"Give it a minute," Samantha said. "If I send two emails, I'll get questions regarding which attachment is the one to look at."

Lorenzo efficiently floated a white tablecloth on the table, and set napkins and silverware. Gleaming silver domes covered their plates. The aroma of fresh baked bread and roasted meats filled the room.

Working with Morgan had made her see the benefit of having an official end of the workday, and marking it with a nice dinner. She was determined to keep the tradition going, so when they'd returned from court at 6:30, she gave the team a fifteen-minute break to change into comfortable clothes and make personal calls. She'd taken out her contact lenses and put on glasses, slipped into jeans and ballet flats, and pulled a black cashmere cardigan over her white dress shirt. Then it had been back to work. It was late for dinner, but given the upheaval caused by Morgan's death, she was glad she'd been able to send the memo and end their workday before midnight. Besides, their bodies were still operating in the Eastern time zone. It didn't feel nearly as late as it actually was.

"This is ridiculous. Damn email still hasn't gone through." Eric plopped onto the couch, lifting his laptop, and clicking at keys. "We're working on the most important international tribunal ever convened, and the network is less sophisticated than something from the 1990's."

"Sophistication is what slowed it," Samantha answered. "State of the art firewalls, encryption devices, and filters make it secure and unhackable and for that, we all should be grateful. Otherwise we'd be slipping paper memos under the doors of the judges each evening. Absolutely that would be a job for someone other than first chair." She gave Eric a pointed look and a smile, indicating the job would be his, not hers.

Knock. Knock.

The rap of hard knuckles fueled by a powerful arm on solid wood resonated through the room, stealing any laughter from her joke.

"Has to be Black Raven. Marshals wouldn't have let anyone else up," Charles frowned. "They're early."

Black Raven wasn't supposed to arrive until 11:15, and the transport to their next hotel was to occur shortly thereafter, assuming it was going to occur that evening. Eric, Charles, and Abe exchanged a glance, then their attention turned to her. She had explained what Black Raven-style protection entailed, and their eyes revealed more than a bit of unease. She didn't blame them.

Knock. Knock.

The solid sound, coupled with the early arrival of the security team, when the security company normally worked with the precision of a Swiss timepiece, sent a shudder of sudden uncertainty through her.

"One minute," she called, adjusting her eyeglasses as she stared at the computer screen. Whoever was on the other side of the door would have to wait until the email went through, just like the rest of them. Having a private security company was not her choice, and the agents would have to learn they weren't going to interfere with work.

Samantha had encountered few people as stubborn as she, who chose a course of action and followed it as though it was chiseled in granite. Her grandfather was one of those people. To the rest of the world, he was Samuel Dixon, the ballsy, eccentric leader of multiple Fortune 500 companies. Within minutes of Morgan's death, her grandfather had called. In his typical controlling fashion, he'd steamrolled her protests as he insisted Samantha and the rest of the Amicus team from the United States have their own security detail.

It didn't matter to her grandfather that there was nothing alarming in Morgan's death. At 65 years old and an insulin-dependent diabetic, with a history of cardiac events, reality was that Stanley Morgan had health issues that could lead to sudden death. Once the judges offered Samantha the position of chief, Samuel became even more adamant.

Black Raven was her grandfather's go-to security company, and he'd already made the hiring call by the time he first told her his idea. With steadfast insistence, and continued reference to the horrors of terrorist acts that the ITT was examining, he'd worn her down in repeated phone calls. She'd given her grandfather one stipulation; she'd agree to Black Raven protection, but she did not want Jesus Hernandez to have anything to do with her on-site security detail. She didn't want to see him or hear from him, and she damn well expected her grandfather to make this happen without it becoming an issue.

Jesus Hernandez.

Zeus to anyone who knew him.

Once, years earlier, she'd known him well. Or so she'd thought. Turned out she hadn't known him at all. She focused her gaze on the intricately cut crystal water pitcher that the waiter placed on the table. In the last twenty-four hours, she'd been too busy with work to worry about whether her grandfather had truly understood the gravity with which she'd made the stipulation. She hadn't intended her demand as something her grandfather could consider and reject.

Now, with the hard knock marking the arrival of the private security company and the literal changing of the guard for the team, her stomach twisted into a hard, nervous ball. Samuel, the larger-than-life man who had raised her after the death of her parents, had taught her to be self sufficient, disciplined, ambitious, and successful. From a young age, he'd treated her as an adult and an equal. He'd always insisted she call him by his first name. Never Grandpa, or Gramps. Yet even with his no nonsense attitude towards everything in life, Samuel knew the reasons why she didn't want Zeus there. At least he knew some of the reasons why. Surely her grandfather had damn well listened to her?

Knock. Knock. The email notification finally flashed that the message and the attachments were sent. The cc copy that she'd sent to herself appeared in her inbox with an accompanying ding, just as Lorenzo put a vase of fresh flowers on the worktable that he'd transformed into a dining table.

"Done," she said, shutting down her laptop and standing. "Thank you for all your hard work today." As Lorenzo stepped away from the table, she said, "Lorenzo, the table is beautiful. *Merci beaucoup.*"

Knock. Knock. Knock.

She walked across the room as Charles signed for the room service. She opened the door. Zeus, arm lifted and fingers curled together as he prepared to rap on the door again, towered over her five seven by a good ten inches. Dropping his arm to his side, he gave her a cool nod, his brusque manner suggesting a nod was all that was needed to bridge the gap between his decision to leave her and the intervening seven years. "Hello, Sam."

Chapter Three

I'm never speaking to Samuel again.

Samantha swallowed her shock and composed her features. She was a world-class litigator, for God's sake. She'd practiced the look of composure in the mirror. She gave Zeus the kind of look she used in court when she knew she was on a losing side of an argument. It was the kind of look that revealed nothing about inner turmoil, and she thanked God she'd practiced how to reflect confidence when she felt none, because right now she needed every bit of cool she'd ever deposited in her considerable reserves.

A brick wall of a man, Zeus stood still and erect, shoulders broad, muscular arms loose at his sides. Waves were evident in his cropped, thick black hair, which matched the midnight-black of his eyes. In the intervening years since she'd last seen him, she'd had plenty of occasion to remember what he looked like, because her mind played the cruel trick of never forgetting anything about him.

Time hadn't diminished his smoldering good looks, or the gravity in his jet black eyes, set off by high cheekbones, thick eyelashes, and dark brows. His gaze had an intensity borne of constant, carefully measured thoughts he typically left unspoken.

There's no way out of this. Requesting Zeus's removal from the job will mean Zeus will know why. He probably would've figured it out even if the request came from Samuel, but now he'll have no doubt that the request came from me. He'll know how much he got to me. Gets to me. Oh hell. He does not get to me. That happened seven years ago, remember?

A neat evening shadow accented the hard set of his jawline and hollow cheekbones. Some men wore that style facial hair as a fashion statement. He was the kind of guy the others were emulating. Ribbing on the sleeves on his black polo shirt stretched over muscular biceps. Black pants were pulled taut over his muscular thighs. A gun was holstered at his hips, on a low-slung belt that carried extra ammunition clips and a stun gun.

Flanking him were four men, dressed exactly as Zeus, almost as tall, all muscle bound, and all looking serious. Testosterone came off them in waves. If there hadn't been variations in hair, eye color, and skin tone, she'd have sworn Black Raven was a clone factory. Each agent carried a black bulletproof vest. The two marshals who had been on duty in the hallway stood to the side, their navy-blue blazers and gray dress slacks seeming ordinary in comparison to the blatant show of brawn and power the Black Raven agents displayed.

"Are you and your team ready?"

"No. The plan was Black Raven would arrive at 11:15, even though we'd prefer to do the move in the morning."

Without heels, looking Zeus in the eyes required her to tilt her chin up, and that action brought flashes of fragmented, dormant memories—lips parting for a kiss, his powerful arms reaching around her while her body yearned for his, gentleness becoming heated, frenzied desire, his rugged body covering hers, their limbs tangled together, a palette of contrasting skin tones in soft candlelight, his tawny, hers ivory. Samantha gave herself an inward, mental shake, immediately irritated that these visions remained in her memory bank. Outwardly, she did nothing but blink, breathe, and square her shoulders.

He had a world-series-worthy poker face, and he wore it now. Although she'd once glimpsed that he was a man of deep feelings and great passion, he typically showed the world only what he chose to reveal—that he was tough, powerful, capable, and smart. Decisive.

Damn him and his decisiveness.

She wished that Zeus had declined the job. He was a mercenary, though. By definition, he was a man who could be bought, and God knew her grandfather had enough money to buy people. That's why Zeus was there, darkening the doorway of her hotel room. She wished it were a trait that made her dislike him, yet she understood ambition of any kind, even ambition fueled by economic desire.

She had enough other reasons to dislike him.

She only needed one, actually.

"We left a message. Plan changed." Zeus glanced at the two agents to his right and almost imperceptibly flicked his head. They walked into the room, and set the vests they were carrying on the couch as Lorenzo pushed the cart out of the room. One agent stood with his back to the far corner, his eyes crawling over every inch. The other went to the windows and shut the drapes.

Samantha had a business phone and two personal phones. One of her personal phones was used solely for phone conversations with her boyfriend, U.S. Senator Justin McDougall. She hadn't touched either personal phone in two hours. She'd been too busy focusing on work and in particular the nightly briefing memo. When she focused, she had tunnel vision. Anyone involved in ITT work needing to reach her would have gone through Charles, who monitored her business phone. The only call that had come through on her business phone had been from President Cameron.

"You called on my personal number?" She knew how Black Raven operated. She didn't plan on relinquishing both of her personal phones to Zeus, so she pretended to have only one.

Dark-as-night eyes glanced at her. Hard. Assessing. "On the number you provided."

She turned in the doorway, half in the room, half out of it, and glanced at Charles. Neither of her personal phone numbers should have been put on the Black Raven questionnaire. Charles's eyes met hers with a silent apology. He'd answered most of the questions for her. The more probing, personal questions she'd directed him to leave blank. From firsthand experience with the company, she knew the questionnaire was only a formality. Black Raven had ways of knowing things about the people they were charged with protecting. Much of it involved taking full advantage of insecurity in cyber data that people expected to be private.

"In the future," she said, her eyes returning to Zeus, "please go through my business line." It wasn't his fault that she'd missed the message, but she was still annoyed.

"From here on out we won't be communicating by phone," he said, his tone conveying confidence in his ability to dictate the circumstances of their interaction.

"Smoke signals? Carrier pigeon?" As her blood boiled with frustration at her grandfather for putting her in this position, and with Zeus for signing up for the task, his dark eyes met hers for a second.

The barest twitch of a smile, at the left corner of his lips, disappeared as fast as it almost materialized. "Unnecessary. We'll be only a few feet apart, at most. For the duration."

Undercurrents?

His flat, dark eyes, told her nothing. Sharks revealed more personality in their fathomless eyes. Perhaps he'd never felt the tug and pull of forces that she'd been powerless to control. Perhaps he'd never wondered, *what if.* If he had, he gave no indication that any memory of their time together existed.

Bastard.

His eyes slid away from hers. He looked over her shoulder and into the hotel room as he touched his ear, holding his fingertip on an almost invisible transmitter. "Repeat."

Seven years earlier, she'd learned to read him. Or so she'd thought. The to-the-ear gesture reminded her he was in constant communication with other Black Raven agents, both onsite and off. As he listened, he was stiller than still. His eyes focused on hers as he assessed the information that he was receiving, conveying with a flat, focused look and the hard set of his square jaw a message that didn't need words. He was there early for a reason.

Something was wrong.

"Jesus Hernandez." His attention shifted to her team, who stood behind her. His self-introduction came in the usual brisk, to-the-point manner that Samantha hadn't forgotten. "Call me Zeus. Compliments of Samuel Dixon, Black Raven PSC is now in charge of your security. Each of you has a primary agent. Eric." Zeus's eyes went directly to Eric, confirming that introductions weren't needed. "Meet Agent Stan Lewis. Abe, Agent Brad Lambert is yours. Charles, meet Agent Zane Axel."

Zeus glanced at Sam as each bodyguard shook hands with their charge. He didn't need to identify her primary agent, nor did he offer to shake her hand.

"We'll provide more details on logistics upon arrival at your new hotel. Each primary agent works with other agents on a team dedicated to your personal security. You'll meet your team members later. This," he glanced again to his left, at the lone agent who remained at his side, "is Mark Small. He and his team handle logistics, analytical support, and backup. You each have a Kevlar vest. Custom fitted vests are on their way, but for now these'll do the job. Wear your vest in all business meetings, whenever we're in transport, and whenever instructed to do so. The only time you won't wear the vests is when you're secured in your hotel rooms."

Mark Small handed Sam her vest. The weight of it carried a reality that chilled her. Before she could voice the question, Eric asked, "Are vests necessary?"

Zeus glanced at him. "Yes."

Had she never been around Zeus, had she not personally witnessed him taking a bullet for her grandfather without hesitating, she'd have argued with his high-handed, imperious style.

He glanced at her. "Put the vest on and let's go."

"We need to have dinner first," Samantha said, forcing her voice to be low and equally as authoritative as his. "And we need to discuss why we need to leave tonight. We'd prefer to make the move tomorrow morning."

"Departure time isn't up for discussion." She'd never met another man who could convey so much with so few words, while his expressions and body language filled in the blanks. He remained in the hallway, slightly to the side of the door, suggesting he expected them all to walk out in single file on his order. "No time to eat."

She glanced over her shoulder at her team. Charles stood in shocked, open-mouthed silence and Abe met her glance with a puzzled look in his blue eyes and a frown line bisecting his brow. Eric, who was the furthest from her, was focused on Zeus, and he was giving him a slow negative headshake. When she resigned herself to her grandfather's demand that she have Black Raven protection, she'd given Eric, Abe, and Charles an option to take it or leave it.

The conversation had taken place as they were focusing on trial exhibits of the metro bombings that were the subject of the Paris ITT proceedings. Abe had been in the States, Eric and Charles had been with her. The grisly photos had acted as persuasion devices more than anything she could have said. Though she had warned Eric that Black Raven transfers could be abrupt, she could tell by his narrow eyes and flushed cheeks that Eric was only now grasping the reality.

"This is ridiculous," Eric said. "I didn't agree to being manhandled. We've worked all day. Our dinner was just delivered. Let us eat while we discuss how this will work."

"I agree with Eric," Abe said. "Aside from our preference that we leave in the morning, we were all set to leave at 11:15."

"Actually, I'm not sure moving makes sense at all," Eric said. "This hotel is crawling with security because the judges are here. We've got a team composed of marshals and DHS agents." He shrugged. "Plus, the French military is providing security."

"Zeus, if there's a reason for the urgency, it would be best if you explain it," Samantha said. Explaining himself wasn't something he did naturally, but perhaps in a business capacity he'd be more transparent.

He didn't hesitate. "Thirty minutes ago the ITT prosecution team from Columbia was leaving a restaurant." Zeus's tone was calm and matter of fact, while the faces of the Columbian prosecution team flashed through her mind. "A car bomb detonated as they approached their vehicle. One dead. Two critical." He glanced at her. "If you had answered your phone when I called, you'd have known this."

"Aw, hell," Eric said, collapsing onto a chair at the dining table.

Sam turned from Zeus, her attention on the marshals who had been overseeing their protection and who were now hovering near Zeus in the hallway. "Why weren't we apprised of this?"

Marshal Robert Smith shook his head. "French authorities are investigating, along with ITT forces." ITT security forces were made up of law enforcement personnel from the four countries. "We're not sure yet that the Columbian prosecution team was the target. It happened at a crowded café on the Boulevard Saint-Germain, known to be frequented by American tourists."

"The fatality?" she asked.

Marshal Smith shook his head. "Don't know."

Zeus turned to her, his jaw set. "Enrique Gutierrez."

Enrique, one of the younger members of the Columbian prosecution team, had dark brown hair, caramel colored eyes, and an intense courtroom demeanor. Sam swallowed. Behind her, she heard Charles gasp.

"Son of a bitch," Eric said.

She glanced at Abe, whose horn-rimmed glasses sat starkly dark against his face, which was devoice of color. No doubt he was rethinking his position of jumping on a plane earlier that day and joining the on-site Amicus team.

"I won't tell you how to do your jobs. Don't tell me how to do mine." Zeus's hard gaze focused on Eric. "Because the American and Colombian judges are here, this hotel is an obvious target. Black Raven doesn't control the premises. The reality is that with the existing security at this hotel, the judges take precedence over your security. I'm sure you all recognize the value in being top priority?" He said it as a question, but the flat look in his eyes indicated he wasn't expecting a response.

Eric's cheeks were flushed, but he remained silent. He reached for the crystal pitcher of water on the table and filled a glass.

"On security matters," Zeus continued, "this is not a democracy. There is no room for argument. There is a reason for everything Black Raven does. Sometimes it will not be apparent to you. Do not put us in a position where questionable judgment on your part causes us to take unnecessary risks with your lives and our own. Put the vests on and move out. Agent Small will handle transportation of personal and business effects."

"We have computers and iPads with sensitive information,

not to mention files, trial binders, and other documents," Charles said, straightening his shoulders as he adjusted his cardigan. "I need to personally oversee the transportation of our work product."

Zeus directed his ironclad gaze at Charles. "Souls first, bullshit later. Your life is our number one concern, and because you don't seem to understand the urgency of the situation, let me explain it further. Until we know differently, we're assuming Stanley Morgan was murdered."

Eric said, "Now that's just plain ridiculous. He had a heart attack. No one has suggested that."

"Zeus," Samantha said, worry that matched Eric's indignation sending blood pulsing through her veins. "At the request of Judge O'Connor, the autopsy was expedited. The report just came in and indicates death due to cardiopulmonary event, precipitated by severe hypoglycemia, with a suspicion of insulin overdose. To our knowledge, the investigation has not revealed foul play. Do you know something we don't?"

"Sudden cardiac arrest in a diabetic could be a natural death," Zeus nodded. "It could also be the result of an intentional insulin overdose, which could mean suicide, or it could be foul play."

"He didn't commit suicide," Samantha said.

"No way," Charles agreed.

Zeus gave them a nod. "So given that he was a key player in a proceeding that is being threatened by every crazy wannabe terrorist and damn legitimate ones, I'd say an accidental death is unlikely. If you want a security company that looks at the world with rose-colored glasses, you've got the wrong one here."

"No terrorist group has claimed responsibility," Eric pointed out, rubbing his hand through his red hair, shaking his head, and reaching for the glass of water he had poured.

"Lose the clichés," Zeus retorted. "Terrorists don't always claim responsibility."

"Maximov does," Eric said. "Through the cells that operate on his behalf."

"Maximov isn't the only game in town," Zeus retorted. "You're in a position to know that. For now, we assume foul play. Black Raven also assumes the Colombian team was the target of a terrorist act. So right now, you're in an unsecure environment, it's a potential target, and threat level is high. No more debate. You're leaving. Now. All possessions and work items will be at your next destination within the hour. Let me repeat: on security issues, this is not a democracy. If you choose not to leave immediately, I will consider that you have chosen to forego Black Raven protection and our employment contract, which each of you signed, will be void." He glanced at Samantha. "Not an option for you."

Eric stood, his cheeks flushed red. Instead of arguing, he gulped down the water, slammed the glass down hard enough to rattle the covered dishes on the table, and gave a headshake of frustration in Zeus's direction.

"Put the vests on over your clothes by loosening the side straps and pulling it over your head," Zeus instructed. "Adjust the shoulder straps so the bottom of the vest sits above your navel. We're taking stairs, going through the kitchen, and exiting through service doors. We'll direct which car you're to go into as we exit."

As she undid the Velcro side straps, Samantha glanced at each member of her team. Abe and Charles were complying. Eric stood still, his face red, his breathing rapid. *Dear God, is he going to continue to argue with Zeus?* She slipped the vest over her head and gave him a pointed look. "Eric?" she asked. "It's a waste of time to argue." *Zeus is immovable.* "I need you to comply."

Her second chair attorney gave her a frantic, panicked glance as he clutched his throat with both hands. His knees buckled and foam spittle flew from his mouth. He gagged a harsh, rattling breath. Yellowish, foamy liquid gurgled out of his mouth.

Horrified, Sam started across the room to grab Eric before he crashed into the table.

"Ragno, Eric Moss collapsed. Fast-acting poison, I suspect. Call 112 and get our medics here ASAP." Zeus's commands came fast, but his tone was level and calm. "Alert marshals and ITT security. Lewis—stay with Eric. Communicate with our medics. Small—find that waiter. Sam—stop."

An ironclad grip on her forearm jerked her to a halt as Eric fell half across the dinner table.

"Lambert. Axel. Get your clients out of here. Move!"

Food and plates jettisoned in the air. He hit the carpeted floor with a jarring thud as plates, food, and silverware landed around and on top of him. His face and neck flamed red and his eyes rolled back as he struggled for a gurgling breath, his hands on his neck.

Her mind registered Agent Lambert pulling Abe past her

and Agent Axel pushing Charles through the doorway, but her gaze was focused on Eric. His feet flutter-kicked, as his body bent and contorted with the effort of trying to breathe. Zeus's grip had tightened on her arm to the point of pain. He was turning her in the direction of the doorway. She struggled to break free from his grasp, slapping at his hand that had a death grip on her right bicep. Not loosening the grip, he stepped in front of her. His body became an impervious wall of solid flesh, blocking her vision of Eric.

Dark eyes held hers. "Walk out."

"No."

He placed a firm hand on her left shoulder, strong-arming her in a restrained push. If he had wanted to push her six feet into the hallway, he could have, with a fraction of his strength. "Go now."

"I won't leave him."

He bent at the waist, crouched into a squat, gripped her wrist with his right hand, and slung her over his shoulders. As he stood, his left arm folded over her calves, pressing her legs against his chest and down his body. Her eyeglasses fell on the floor with a soft thud.

"Let. Me. Down." His shoulder dug into her belly with each step he took. Her left hand was her only limb that was free. She punched him in the back, the action as effective as punching a steel wall. There was no sign he felt her hammer-fisted punches while her wrist screamed from the strain. Her effort didn't slow his pace.

He went down the hallway and to the stairs. "Small and Lewis, keep talking. Teams for Small and Lewis. Sixth floor, now. Medic team?"

"Let me down," Samantha said, landing a punch on Zeus's spine as he opened the door to the stairwell. From what she could tell, he was impervious to her hit.

"Will you walk down the stairs without argument?"

"Yes."

He slipped through the doorway without letting her down, and took the steps at a jog.

"I said yes, dammit," she said, barely able to get the words out as his shoulder dug into her midsection with each of his downward steps.

"Don't believe you."

"I'm. Going. To. Vomit."

"Go ahead."

"Seriously."

He paused at the next landing, pulled her off his shoulder, and stood her so that her feet touched the floor. He held her up, his hands under her shoulders. Without glasses or contacts, her vision blurred. The stairwell spun from the quick movement. Agents ran past them, on their way up. Black eyes looked into hers as she leaned against the wall for support. He was virtually leaning into her as he assessed her. He smelled of a fresh forest after a rain, of slightly aromatic soap, of musk. So goddamn much like the man of her dreams—if she admitted to herself that such a man or dreams existed—that she could feel herself melting just from breathing the air that surrounded him. "Stop crowding me."

"Did you eat or drink anything from that table?"

She shook her head. "No."

"Feel okay?"

She nodded. Above them, a door opened and shut. The agents who were running to the upper floors had apparently made it there. "Eric?"

"Don't know yet." Dark eyes, devoid of optimism, studied her. He drew a deep breath. Quiet in the stairwell told her that for the moment, they were alone. "You sure you're okay?"

"I'm fine. The upside down jogging down the stairs got to me. Plus, I really need my glasses," she said. "And that was totally unnecessary. You don't need to manhandle me like that."

"Glasses will catch up to you. Sam, look—"

"Samantha. Not Sam."

He shrugged. "Sam to me. Let the rest of the world call you Samantha." With a jerk of his chin, he gestured to the stairs that led down. "Keep going." She pretended like climbing down the stairs without her glasses wasn't problematic and got moving, despite her blurred vision. He fell in step next to her. "When I say leave a room, leave the fucking room. Don't let our past interfere—"

"Don't mention our past, Hernandez. Not now. Not ever again."

"I'm not playing that game. I'm giving fair notice—we will talk about it. I'd prefer sooner, rather than later. I will wear you down, if you insist on pretending it never happened—"

"Oh, it happened. There's no pretending involved," she said, careful to keep her voice calm. "It just doesn't matter now. If it matters at all to you, just think about your wife and your child for perspective. Or," she gave him a sideways glance as they reached another landing. By her count, they were on the second floor. Even with her pathetic, blurred vision, as he turned to her she saw his jaw was set and his cheeks slightly flushed, "However many children you might have by now."

"Only one, and about my—"

"That wasn't a question. I don't want details."

"Look, there's some—"

She put her hand on his forearm, interrupting him as she shook her head. "I repeat. Not interested in details. Decisions were made. We've both moved on. There is nothing more to say. Our past is irrevocably behind us and irrelevant to today. We're professionals. We both have jobs to do here, and my job today is way more important to me than what happened between us seven years ago. Since my life is your job, I certainly hope you're taking yours seriously as well. Leave the past in the past. It can only amount to a minor distraction that neither of us needs. Don't waste time on it."

She turned and continued down the stairs, this time at a jog. No matter how fast she went, he kept up.

Damn him.

Chapter Four

"Get my granddaughter's ass on a jet back to the States before sunrise. Persuade her to resign from the ITT proceedings and get her the hell away from there." Samuel Dixon's normally calm voice crackled through Zeus's earpiece, concern and fear over the evening's events elevating his decibel level to just below a yell.

Zeus glanced at his watch. 0120. Tuesday. Sunrise was a mere five hours away. Considering the enormous mobilization effort Black Raven pulled together in the last thirty-six hours, the idea that the job could end this abruptly was almost laughable.

He perfectly understood the man's about-face.

The problem was that Dixon's granddaughter had grown into an accomplished attorney, who was operating on an international stage while building a reputation for her future. Even seven years earlier, when she still faced a rigorous year of post-graduate school and hadn't yet passed the bar exam, she had unflagging determination and absolute certainty of her capabilities. She hadn't been a quitter then, and Zeus doubted she'd become one.

"Give me a few minutes." Zeus jogged up the stairs to the third floor. "I'll have her call you, and I'll back you up on getting her to resign."

The likelihood of Samuel's demand being met before sunlight broke the horizon, or at any time, was pretty damn slim. Black Raven was in the security business. Miracles were someone else's forte.

"Bring her home, Zeus. Make it happen," Samuel continued. "I'll pay Black Raven's full fee, as though you did the job in its entirety, through the verdict reading in Brussels on March first. Understand?"

"Yes. Understood." Zeus clicked a button on his watch that controlled phone reception, breaking the connection.

Resignation? Not going to happen.

While he had worked the job of body guarding her grandfather, before he acted on his feelings for her, he and Sam had shared many late nights in the office of Dixon's home with their laptops open. She had studied. He had dealt with security issues for Dixon's team and Black Raven management issues. They'd had hours and hours together and many quiet conversations, where he had learned that she, who came from immense wealth, planned to work as hard as he, who came from relatively humble beginnings. Her determination to navigate and excel in the arena of prestigious legal work based on her capabilities and hard work—as opposed to the leverage that came with her grandfather's name—was one of the many things he had loved about her.

They'd shared their dreams and ambitions. Sam's goals were to become partner at a prestigious firm, then become a federal judge, first on a district court, then in an appeals court. At the right time, she wanted to be considered for a seat on the U.S. Supreme Court. Zeus had respected such lofty ambition and the willingness to work hard to meet her goals. Even years earlier, her goals in life didn't include Malibu mansions, townhomes in New York, and long days of shopping with other high-society ladies, all of which she could have with the snap of her well-manicured fingers. If she had dreamed of having a family with a husband and children, that was one ambition she hadn't voiced. At most, she talked about finding a hard-working man who understood her commitment to long hours of work, who would enjoy watching sunsets, and who would help her raise Golden Labs. Maybe, he now thought, the omission of wanting children or more of a family life should've sent up a red flag. It hadn't, at the time, or afterwards.

Back then, he'd wanted her to succeed, and he was happy for her that she held such a powerful position today. Which was why he wasn't looking forward to telling her she should resign from the prestigious position.

The idea is goddamn laughable.

Sam was unlikely to follow her grandfather's orders. Zeus knew it and he guessed Samuel knew it as well. That's why his tone had been near the far horizon of desperate.

As he reached the third floor hallway, two agents stepped to the side to allow him into the suite that he and Sam were sharing.

"Good to have you in the trenches, sir," Jenkins said.

Hand on the doorknob, Zeus glanced at the younger man. Todd Jenkins. Two years with Black Raven. Solid. Dependable. Eager.

"Thanks."

As Zeus turned the doorknob and shoved open the door, he heard John Miles, the second agent, say under his breath,

"Impressive one of the bosses is pulling guard duty himself, right?"

There were no easy tasks in Black Raven. What the younger agents had no way of knowing was that being managing partner, especially in recent months with the uptick in terrorist attacks, had been one hell of a wild ride. Guard duty for Sam now, with what had happened between them in the past? A different kind of ride. Not one for which there'd be a long line among his agents, or any other man who'd made a mistake with a woman that haunted his nights and days.

Rewind? Redo? Try again?

Fuck.

He'd learned the hard way that some moments in time were etched in stone and were meant to be carried every day, every step, every moment, with every breath. Fortunately, God had given him oversized shoulders to carry the burdens that had been thrown his way.

He stepped into the living room that divided his and Sam's bedrooms. His bedroom with its private bathroom was on one side, hers on the other. Both bedroom doors were shut. The living room, a beige and impersonal space, smelled of jasmine and rose—the fragrance in her soaps, lotions, and perfumes. His pulse quickened. Dammit.

Embrace the suck.

Hell, enjoy this suck because—he inhaled deeply—she's here. A hell of a lot closer than she had been for seven years and now, instead of dreaming remotely about what being with her had once been like, he could at least lay eyes on her in person. Through her closed bedroom door, the whir of a blow dryer confirmed his guess that she wouldn't have fallen asleep so fast after the bad news that Eric Moss had died, which had come as they'd arrived at the safe house.

They were in the Sixth Arrondissement, in a large three-story residence on the Avenue Saint Lorraine. Black Raven had used the home before as a safe house. View? Irrelevant. Floor to ceiling drapes would remain closed for the duration of their stay in Paris. The living room, with soft light and neutral tones, was designed for work and relaxation. There was a desk, a comfortable couch and chairs, a television, a small dining table, and a wet bar. Strategically placed lamps cast pools of warm light on polished wood and soft furnishings.

He carried his iPad, a new phone for Sam, and a first aid kit. The kit and its contents would only be necessary if she decided to stay on the job.

Black Raven had stripped the Amicus team, Sam included, of their telecommunication devices. At least he had tried to take Sam's phones. She'd given him one personal one and her business phone. He needed to have a conversation with her about the phone she hadn't relinquished.

He'd now give her the new phone, which she'd use for personal and business calls. The phone was not smart, in the conventional sense of the word, but genius, in the Black Raven sense, designed for monitoring incoming and outgoing communications and scanning communications for interference. It was tailored to keep her, and her team, secure.

He turned on the TV to see what the media was feeding the public. News shows were focused on the scene at Café Cliquot, where yellow tape kept the public out and red and blue lights lit the night. As he punched passwords into his iPad, his ears stayed tuned to the muffled whir of the hair dryer. He'd give her a few more minutes.

Ragno's team had re-routed the phone numbers that Sam used for business and personal phone calls through Denver headquarters, and he now had a list of callers for her. In addition to her father, others also had gotten the news of the Boulevard Saint-Germain bombing. The media immediately connected the dots between the ITT's Colombian team of prosecutors and the bombing. Those in the know had received news of Eric's poisoning, though that info hadn't hit media outlets. Yet.

With prior knowledge coupled with the constant intel received in the last twenty-four hours, he recognized many of the names of callers on the list. Chief U.S. Judge Theodore O'Connor—the most powerful voice on the ITT's panel of judges. Defense Counsel Robert Brier—a forceful advocate and formidable presence in every proceeding he appeared. A few lawyers from the firm of Morgan & Associates.

Also, on the phone Samantha pretended didn't exist, the one that she hadn't turned over to him, he knew she'd received calls from Senator Justin McDougall—her boyfriend. Soon to be fiancé, if media speculation was accurate.

McDougall was a blue-eyed, tall, first-term U.S. senator from Massachusetts. He was one of three brothers, part of an American dynasty that was built upon oil. Each brother routinely made headlines, always with a photograph. They were that good looking. Justin's twin, Jared McDougall, was a star NFL quarterback. The older of the three brothers ran the oil company with their father and starred in the oil company's feel-good television commercials, wearing a hard hat, a million-dollar smile, and shaking hands with brawny roughneck oilfield workers as he persuaded the American public that McDougall Oil was the next best thing to God and country.

Given the considerable wealth and business holdings of the McDougalls, and Sam's vast wealth as her grandfather's only heir, high society gossips and people in the know painted their likely engagement as a pending power merger, not a marriage.

He didn't blame Sam for holding a grudge against him, but Zeus admitted that Senator McDougall was an impediment to Sam being receptive to him. To an apology or any attempt by him to make amends for what he'd done to her. To anything. Which reinforced exactly what she'd told him in the stairwell—maybe their past really was irrelevant to today.

Beautiful. Fucking beautiful. I've spent seven years thinking of her, while she forgot me the moment the door shut.

The list of Sam's callers was growing. It was time for her to have a phone, otherwise he'd end up being her goddamn personal secretary. The blow dryer was still going full steam, though, so Zeus sat on the couch, placed the first aid kit on the coffee table, and put his feet up beside it. He'd give her a few more minutes of privacy to pull herself together. Sam didn't like anyone knowing she was vulnerable. Eric Moss's dramatic death had clearly shaken her to the core, and if Zeus hadn't slung her over his shoulder and gotten her out of the room, it would have been worse for her.

Cyanide.

Holy fucking hell.

Right now he could be struggling to deal with Sam's death. It had been that fast, and that goddamn easy for someone to get to her team.

Everything on the room service cart had been contaminated with lethal doses of poison. At least Eric's death hadn't been bloody. If there had been blood involved, Sam would have been out for the count. Tough as she was, the sight of blood was her Achilles' heel.

When he'd received confirmation of Moss's death, he'd relayed the news to Sam and her team. They'd been on the first floor of the safe house, having an orientation to the reality of Black Raven-style protective detail. For a second, on hearing the grim news, Sam's crystal-clear green eyes had shown unfiltered fear and grief. If they'd been alone, he doubted he'd have cared one goddamn bit about the steels walls that past decisions and time had erected around them. Consoling her would have come naturally and he fucking-well touched people when he consoled them.

Fortunately, she didn't need or want his consolation. Didn't need him for a thing that mattered, which had been—and always would be—their reality. She'd composed herself fast, turned away from him and to Abe and Charles, and comforted them with a hand on their arms and gentle words. She had braced herself for a phone call to Eric's wife. Zeus handed her his phone for the call, stepped discreetly away, yet listened as she handled the difficult task with compassion, grace, and dry-eyed dignity.

By twelve forty-five, she'd retreated to her own room. She hadn't looked like she was about to break down as she climbed up the stairs. He'd left her at the doorway of her bedroom. He'd asked her whether she was okay, and her one-word reply had been, "Fine."

On the emotional side of things, she was a mirror image of him. It was damn plain unsettling to watch her in action.

"Ragno?" he asked as he scanned secure intel on his iPad. The Boulevard Saint-Germain bomber had blown up with the bomb. Shrapnel had flown for a city block. Bomb mechanism disintegrated. Eighteen confirmed deaths. Many others injured.

"Yes?" Her crisp, steady voice in his ear greeted him.

As long as Zeus worked the Dixon-ITT job, Ragno was his. She and the team of Denver-based analysts working on security for the Amicus team would operate in real time with him. Their time zone would be the time zone where he and the team were located. They would process and analyze a steady stream of information deemed necessary to keep Sam and the Amicus team safe. They'd discard the clutter, organize the need-to-know data, and pass it to Zeus. "Can't fucking believe we started this job by losing one."

"If you hadn't followed your hunch and gotten there earlier than planned, you'd have lost four," Ragno answered. "One went down, but you saved three."

Two minutes later and they'd all have been dead. Ragno was right. He pushed his frustration aside, parking it far away. Personal frustration would only get in the way. "Tomorrow's proceedings are still a go?"

"Despite the Boulevard Saint-Germain bombing and Moss's death, tomorrow's ITT proceedings have not been cancelled. Media's showcasing the bombing. There's an upsurge in internet chatter among various groups, some credible terrorist organizations, some not so credible, targeting the ITT proceedings." Ragno rattled off some familiar names. Zeus mentally filed them.

"If Dixon has his way," Zeus informed her, "we won't have to worry about this for long. Job's over if Sam re—"

"You just can't call her Samantha, can you?"

"No." She'd always be Sam to him. In a move that was out of character for him, and for reasons he hadn't realized at the time, when he first met her and she introduced herself as Samantha, he had shortened it to Sam. A pet name only he had used, apparently.

Privately, she was his Sam. Though in reality, not his any longer, and probably never had been. Seven years earlier, her all-American patrician good looks had stolen his breath. With one turn of her head, a glance from eyes that revealed intelligent curiosity, and a quick flash of her natural, easy smile, she'd claimed a large chunk of his heart.

Not that he knew it at the time. It took him years to understand what had happened, because he wasn't a man who was used to letting things like feelings filter into his life.

"Don't worry, Ragno. I'm fine. I'll be even better once she resigns." Except Zeus knew Sam, her ambitions, and the root of them, and he didn't need new intel from Ragno to tell him those things.

"You sound hopeful."

Hopeful?

Ragno had a way of hearing things that others didn't and she knew him better than anyone. Since saying yes to the job, each passing moment tightened an invisible tourniquet on his chest and he didn't doubt that Ragno knew that, as well. The feeling of impending personal doom wasn't going away as long as he was near Sam. If she resigned she'd be out of harm's way and there'd be no reason for them to be together. He'd be able to breathe without the breath-stealing pressure that came with being so close to his biggest mistake. *Hell yeah, I'm hopeful.* Hope wasn't logical under the circumstances, but he was hopeful, nevertheless.

"Do authorities have any leads on the Boulevard Saint-Germain bombing?"

"Not that we can tell."

"What about the cyanide killing?"

"The investigation at the Hotel Grand Athens remains a

scene with too many one-feather Indians and not one chief in sight. French counter-terrorist military forces, U.S. Homeland Security, and U.S. marshals all are vying for the lead. Agents Small and Lewis report that the kitchen and wait staff have all been detained and questioned. No one knows anything. The waiter who delivered the dinner was found at his station and professes to be shocked at the incident. Small and Lewis are no longer in the interrogation rooms, so we don't have real time information. Investigative and security forces for ITT proceedings have a closed circuit communication system with heavy encryption."

"We aren't in their system?"

Black Raven had finely honed infiltration capabilities, and their skills had increased exponentially over the last year. "We're in some aspects of the ITT system, but not security. Hold a second. Let me check with Barrows."

Barrows. The reason why their cyber skills now rivaled, and in many cases, surpassed, the finest intelligence agencies.

"Zeus, we're almost there."

"Great. Let me know when we're in."

"Sebastian and other Ravens have picked up most of your management duties since you're orchestrating on-site protection and not in the office. Of course, you still have Jigsaw monitoring, but Sebastian and I will keep you informed on developments with that. Your partners have left insurance matters to you, since you've been handling those negotiations."

"I saw that in one of Sebastian's earlier emails. I'm talking with the final broker tomorrow. We're probably only one of the few businesses right now that doesn't need business interruption coverage due to terrorism and I'm asking that she take that out."

"Will they strip out the terrorism clause?"

"I'm trying to figure that out, because the fee for it is exorbitant. With all the extras they're slapping into the policies, the self-insurance option is looking more palatable." He drew a deep breath. "You talked to Samuel Dixon lately?"

"Right before he called you," Ragno said. "Good God, but that man is tough."

"And?"

"Black Raven is built for this mission. The job's highly profitable, so that's a consideration as well." She paused. "But, in reality, the only sure-fire way of keeping Samantha safe is by keeping her away from ITT proceedings. Our client wants his granddaughter to resign and we're committed to helping him.

This isn't a case where the client has no choice. Samantha Fairfax has a choice. We have to help her make the correct one."

"Okay." He fell silent, listening. The blow dryer was still going full steam.

"If you had to make a bet, what do you think?"

He made a prediction to himself, one that resulted in his chest tightening further, but he answered, "I don't bet."

"Maybe not out loud." Ragno was quiet for a second. He heard her fingers on her keyboard as she multitasked. "But I bet you just made one. I'm betting yes. She'll resign. Her grandfather is damn powerful. As you well know, Mr. Bodyguard."

Ragno was right, but Zeus wasn't pulling the bodyguard detail for Samuel Dixon, nor the money. Given that he now had Ana, who valued the life of her father as much as her next breath, very few people in the world could have gotten him to return to paid bodyguard status. Plus, he was more valuable to Black Raven at the helm rather than in the field for extended periods. In fact, he could think of only one person for whom being a bodyguard was worth all the risks and headaches the job entailed, and she was on the other side of the door, blow-drying her hair while Rome fucking burned.

"All right," he said. "It's show time."

"Here if you need me," Ragno said.

Leaving his iPad and the first aid kit on the coffee table, he stood, crossed the room, and rapped on the door loud enough for her to hear over the blow dryer.

Chapter Five

Even with no makeup and slightly damp hair, she was so goddamn pretty the zing-zap in his chest that came with looking at her hurt. Sleek and thick, her blonde hair framed her face in soft waves and fell a few inches past her shoulders. Long, dark brown lashes fringed her green eyes. High cheekbones accented her lean face, which was flushed from the heat of the hair dryer.

The rectangular, matte black-framed eyeglasses that had fallen off when he'd thrown her over his shoulder in the hotel room were perched on her nose. As promised, the bulky glasses had caught up to her with the transfer of personal effects. On anyone else, they'd have been plain old eyeglasses. On her they were sexy.

She was ivory-skinned, slim, and had a long-limbed, athletic build. Her lean, angular figure was accentuated by form-fitting leggings and a snug black hoodie that she'd zipped to cover most of a cream-colored, lace camisole. Only the top ridge of lace peaked through. It was enough to make him remember the first time he'd bent his head there, brushing his mouth over the jasmine and rose-scented valley and the pillow-soft skin of her breasts.

Dammit.

He could pretend that what she looked like didn't matter one damn bit, but pretending didn't change that she was who he dreamed of, from the moment he first laid eyes on her, until, well, *fuck*. Until now.

"You should eat something."

She shrugged, a cool expression in her eyes. "Not much of an appetite after what happened."

"Food is fuel." *And you never sleep well on an empty stomach.* Only one of numerous pieces of inane trivia he'd remembered about her, and one that he'd actively tried to forget in the last seven years. "With the high stress you'll be under for the duration of the job, eating shouldn't depend on appetite. If you're too scared to eat now, you shouldn't stay."

Making no move to walk out of her bedroom, she folded her arms and faced him, the open doorway separating them. "Shouldn't stay? Meaning what?"

"Resign from the job."

She cocked her left eyebrow in a gesture that spoke volumes.

As in *you don't get to tell me what to do.*

"No. I'm not a quitter. Shouldn't be a newsflash to you."

"Isn't news. But you need to discuss your decision with your grandfather. Call him. He wants to talk to you now." He handed her the new phone. "You'll use this for the duration."

She reached for it with her left hand, flipped up the cover with her thumb, and looked at him with an irritated glance. "Seriously? This isn't a phone. It's an antique."

"Think of it as a portal. Your calls will be filtered through Black Raven. Don't make calls from any other devices, even the phone that you're trying to hide from me."

Her eyes flashed with anger. "I only call Justin through that one. U.S. Senator Justin McDougall. My boyfriend."

"I know exactly who he is."

"Our phone calls are priv—"

"To do this job the right way, I get to decide what's my business. What I access."

"As I was saying, my calls with Justin are secure and encrypted and..." She paused, eyebrows lifted. "Absolutely none of your damn business."

He knew to concede the point. After all, Ragno was going to listen, anyway, and the reality was they had to be mindful of McDougall's position. Nothing McDougall said in phone conversations with Sam could be leaked by Black Raven. Zeus knew better than to gratuitously piss off a sitting U.S. Senator. One day he'd need Senator McDougall's vote on a hiring contract, or any number of matters. Crap popped up all the time, like the Barrows debacle for which the company had been raked over hot coals by a Senate review committee.

"Press any button and tell the person who answers the number you want. They'll connect you. If it's a text, dictate it. They'll send it."

"Black Raven will monitor calls? Business and personal?"

He shrugged. "We're providing security. Not privacy. Threats come from within and the people you may contact, as often as from other sources. You know that. You can still use the ITT server for your inter-court, official emails."

Her eyes searched his. "Please tell me Black Raven hasn't hacked into the ITT servers."

He stared at her, gridlock focus meeting his gaze.

"Answer enough," she whispered, with a knowing nod. "That's a felony—"

"Which will never be detected or proven."

"I should report it."

He shrugged. "Go ahead." If others found a trace, Black Raven would get out, leaving no cyber footprint. They'd get right back in when the heat was off. It was Chinese checkers, twenty-first century style.

"Black Raven dodged a bullet last year with the senate subcommittee hearings after the Barrows incident."

Yeah. You have no idea. And we came out more golden than ever. A fact you will not learn.

The Barrows case and explosive fallout had cast the national news spotlight on Black Raven, and the resulting senate subcommittee hearings had kept the lights on them. "There were no adverse findings."

"Yes, but it could have gone the other way."

"Didn't, and wasn't likely to."

"Still, Black Raven is on the radar of many powerful people."

"Yes, and they hire us. Constantly. On jobs like this—"

"You can't deny you have detractors." She underscored her comment with a slight smile.

What she was saying was true. For now, though, in the power offices in Washington, Black Raven's supporters were outweighing and outnumbering the detractors. "In fact, we received accolades and commendations for how we handled the Barrows job. It's been a boon to business, which we now have to turn down on a regular basis."

Her eyes flashed with anger. Her cheeks became more flushed. "I never would've agreed to this, but for my grandfather's insistence."

With that statement, she folded her arms as she dropped one argument and took on another. If she had broken down over Moss's violent death once she'd been alone, there was no sign of it. Her eyes weren't red. She looked more irritated than grief-stricken.

"If by this, you mean Black Raven protection, it may be short-lived. Your grandfather wants you to resign." Her cheeks and eyes burned with an instant flare of disagreement as he added, "I agree with that course of action. It is the only foolproof way to keep you safe."

She squared her shoulders, unfolded her arms, glanced again at the flip phone that fit squarely in her palm, and shook her head. As her flush faded, she leveled a cool glance on him and pressed zero with her right index finger. She gave the Black Raven operator her grandfather's name and number. After a moment's pause, her eyes burning with steady resolve, she said, in a firm voice, "Samuel?"

She held the phone to her left ear, listened for a few minutes as she shot Zeus an arched-eyebrow glance. "Does this thing have a speaker?"

"Ask for it."

Another flash of irritation waved through her eyes. "Someone's listening now?"

"Yes."

"Please enable the speaker function." She paused, eyes on Zeus, feet firmly planted inside her bedroom, as though planning to end the conversation and shut the door in a matter of seconds. "Samuel?"

She held the phone in front of her, midway between the two of them. Samuel's voice boomed through both rooms. "Are you listening to me? I said—"

"Yes, I'm listening. You're on speaker and you don't need to yell. Zeus is here. You two are echoing each other. I'm only going to say this once." Her tone was calm and authoritative, but her green eyes flashed with determination as she drew a deep breath. "Resigning isn't an option. And just so that you're perfectly clear on this, Samuel, I made one request of you. Only one, in recent memory. You didn't listen to me. After this phone conversation, which will be short, I'm no longer speaking to you. From here on out, if you wish to speak to me, go through Black Raven."

"Fine. Zeus." Dixon snapped both words out in a strong, powerful voice. He managed to sound exactly like what he was— both a frantic father-figure and a decisive, powerful businessman, who was used to having his every demand met. "Talk some sense into my granddaughter, would you please? She was one goddamn French fry away from being killed." Zeus had given Dixon the details of the cyanide poisoning, and the man's summation was accurate. "It is high time for her to give up this endeavor and return home."

Zeus met her steely-eyed gaze. He should've done a videoconference from his iPad, so that Dixon could draw some of his granddaughter's ire face to face. "I'm trying. Don't think we're going to move her."

"I'm standing right here," Sam reminded them. She held the phone in one hand, but her steady determined focus was all on Zeus. As though he was the damn reason why anything was wrong in her life. "I have an important job to do, now more than ever, and I refuse to be intimidated or controlled. I'm not an idiot. I'm well aware of the danger, nevertheless I will not resign, and I won't leave. I received a phone call from President Cameron tonight. He personally underscored the importance of the job. I'll be hyperaware, I'll listen to Black Raven's instructions, and I'll watch my back. But no matter what either of you says, I'm not quitting."

Sam brushed past Zeus as she stepped through the doorway and into the living room. He tried not to smell the jasmine, rose, and natural musk that drifted from her body in a tease that had no business occurring, because it wasn't intentional. Yet he couldn't help breathing in, deeply, and relishing the scent as she crossed the room, her back to him. She hadn't changed her nightly ritual of a hot shower, shampooing her hair, and applying body lotion in the same fragrance that she wore throughout the day. On other women, he knew the scent was Chanel No.5. On her, with her body warm from her shower and the heat of the hair dryer, the classic fragrance became something that couldn't be bought at a department store. It morphed into an aphrodisiac that, combined with the sudden flood of memories of what it felt like to make love to her, brought blood-rushing arousal.

When she reached the dining table, she turned to him, eyes blazing with determination. "Save your breath, and stop trying to persuade me to quit. That isn't happening."

I've got the message. Loud and clear. Doubt your grandfather does, though.

"Honey," Samuel said, "the reality is the ITT proceedings are nothing but an ill-conceived, and very dangerous, dog-and-pony show. No one would blame you if you resigned after what happened tonight."

"Bullshit. My resignation would be the first thing thrown in my face by a judicial review committee when I get nominated for a federal judgeship."

Zeus walked to where Sam stood and, picking up on the thread that Samuel had started, added, "The ITT is a hate party with a guest list that includes the usual jihadists, Islamic terrorist groups, Al Quaeda splinter groups, Maximovists. Ragno?"

"Yes?" She'd been monitoring the conversation, but had stayed silent.

"Get in on this."

"Hello, Samuel," she said, her voice now coming though the speakerphone, which Sam held in her left hand, elbow at her waist. "Samantha, I'm in charge of Zeus's Denver-based analytical and data support for the duration of the job. If you need me, just ask for Ragno. Night or day."

"You're agreeing with Samuel and Zeus?" Sam asked.

"Yes," Ragno answered.

"Answer is the same for all three of you," Sam said, holding the phone so that she spoke directly into it. "I. Am. Not. Resigning."

Impressive. She's being triple-teamed and she isn't flinching. That's what I love—her rock-solid will. Unwavering determination. Courage to stand by her convictions. Gridlock focus on things most people wouldn't give a rat's ass about.

Whoa. Wait. Love?

Loved. Past tense. Remember? You blew it. Bad. In just about the worse way possible.

"Ragno," Zeus said, trying to keep his mind on task, "who else is at the hate party?"

"The list is extensive. Right now I'm looking at a U.S. homegrown group called TRCR that so far has been flying under the radar. Intel indicates they're experimenting with drones." Sarcasm filtered into her voice. "Drones seem to be the next best thing to the pressure cooker bomb as foolproof methods of creating terror in urban situations."

"TRCR. An acronym for what?" Dixon asked.

"Texas Rebels for Civil Rights. Intel has them in a compound in rural Texas, but we're not certain if that's their headquarters. North of El Paso. Could be a terrorist training school. Satellite images aren't revealing much, though. Intel suggests approximately one thousand loyalists and they're importing AK variants from China, selling them in the U.S. and elsewhere. Typically, they're quiet. Off the cyber grid. But recently they started recruiting on the dark net. They're calling for the ITT to stop. Their logo combines the initials KKK, swastikas, a lone star, and barbwire. Seems like their view of civil rights doesn't quite match what our forefathers had in mind when they drafted the U.S. Constitution."

"They're new to me," Dixon said.

"Where is the intel coming from?" Zeus asked, though he knew at least part of how Ragno had gotten it—Jigsaw—which he knew she wouldn't mention.

"Department of Homeland Security. Tracking their source now. Unfortunately, DHS data on this is incomplete. I'm having to figure this out the old fashioned way—on the telephone, talking to the person who interviewed the source."

Great. More information for Jigsaw.

Walking around the table to where Sam stood, he watched her place a stem of purple grapes on a plate without breaking one off. With her eyes leveled on him, he said, "It has become impossible to keep up with the faces of the threat. New groups appear every day. When they make an appearance, like the TRCR, they do so with a solid set of followers, a bankroll, an agenda, and an impressive cadre of weapons. Someone, somewhere, is bankrolling these groups. No one has figured out who, though everyone blames Maximov. Until the real culprit is identified, any attempt to stop these small cells—like the ITT proceedings—will be a minefield."

"Now tell me something I don't know," Sam said, holding the phone at chest level, shoulders square.

"You shouldn't be walking through it," Zeus answered. "That's what you obviously don't know. Your presence here isn't necessary."

"Like I said, not an option," Sam retorted, shifting her attention to the plate. She pulled a few grapes off the stem with her left hand.

Zeus watched her toy with the grapes. Was her hand trembling? Maybe. She didn't eat them. Instead, she removed a few from the stem and pushed them to the side of the plate, making a neat pile.

"Ragno, any link between the TRCR and Maximov?" Zeus used the shorthand name for Maximov-in-Exile, the group that for years had been the culprit behind terrorist acts around the world in retribution for the destruction of Praptan, Chalinda caused by the 1986 meltdown at the Chalinda Nuclear Power Plant. Given the established nature of the organization, and the considerable wealth attributed to it, Maximov-in-Exile was the strongest contender for bankrolling the startup terrorist groups and pop-up cells that were currently wreaking havoc around the world.

"Some of their recruiting on the dark net suggests an affiliation with Maximov," Ragno said. "But there is no affirmative link between the two groups."

Sam pulled three more grapes off the stem. He was right. There was a slight tremble in her left hand. The stress of the night had gotten to her, even though she was doing a damn good job of not revealing it.

"Wait. Isn't it an established fact that Maximov is funding most of these start-up groups?" Dixon asked.

Zeus answered, "That might be reality, but as far as we

know, it hasn't been established. There aren't money trails to follow. At least none that anyone has been able to detect."

"That is one issue we're analyzing in this ITT proceeding." Sam used a fork to lift thin slices of ham and two slices of bread onto the plate with the grapes. With the utensil in her hand, the trembling was more evident.

"Oh, come on," Dixon asserted. "The U.S. government has seized millions upon millions of dollars belonging to Maximov and his group, and forensic analysts have long opined it's just the tip of the iceberg for the organization."

"Well, it's suspected that Maximov is the culprit, but so far no one has proven he's the power behind the blossoming groups. And frankly, no one has even proven that the money that was seized belongs to Maximov. As you know, no one has been able to find Maximov, despite the bounty that's been on his head for years now," Zeus said. "The last time anyone saw Maximov in person was during the 2006 raid at Belmarsh. When he escaped."

"Goddamn Brits," Dixon said. "They should have relinquished custody of the bastard to us. His ass would be rotting in solitary confinement in a supermax, and the world would be a better place."

Zeus watched as Sam slipped the phone to the table.

"Aside from the difficulty of having to rely on evidence, and getting four countries to agree to anything, the ITT proceedings have a really big problem. Operating in the face of terrorist acts. Acts." Dixon's voice was clearly audible through the speaker function. "Not threats."

"Your grandfather's assessment is one hundred percent accurate," Zeus said. She ignored him as she spread a neat, thin layer of mayonnaise on each slice of bread, and assembled her sandwich. He continued, "The bombing and poisoning tonight revealed vulnerability in the proceedings. There is blood in the water. Terrorist acts will be ramping up."

"#IAMMAXIMOV and #MAXIMOVINEXILE are trending worldwide right now," Ragno added. "Believe it or not. Maximov and his organizations are cult heroes."

Sandwich apparently forgotten, Sam looked up, meeting his glance with eyes that flashed with anger. "Seriously? As though Maximov is a war hero. Do these people even understand what Maximov has done?" She stood straighter. The light in her eyes intensified.

Dammit.

Like dark storm clouds on the horizon, her resolve was building. But when she looked at her plate of food, her hands still trembled. She shook her head, as though willing the fear out of her. Reaching for a glass of water, she lifted it, and became pale as she raised it toward her lips. The glass thudded when she placed it on the table next to her phone, without drinking any of it.

Son of a bitch.

She had all the motivation in the world to continue the job that she'd started, but she was too damn afraid to eat or drink. It was a fact that would have given her grandfather a fucking heart attack and a fact that he knew was royally pissing her off. Though she was just as vulnerable as anyone, Sam didn't like to appear weak in any way. He had figured that out about her before, and assumed that was why she hadn't acted hurt when he told her goodbye.

She drew a deep breath as she picked a few pieces of ham off the sandwich. Watching closely, he bet none of the morsels would make it to her mouth. She had every reason to be afraid. The scene with Moss had been brutal, but if she stayed, there could be more scenes like that one. More close calls. She'd never make it through the next month if her recovery time wasn't shorter.

"Ragno. Zeus," Sam said. "This new American group—TRCR—you mentioned they talk of drone attacks. Is your intel establishing a link between them and the cruise ship bombing in Miami? Or any of the other bombings the ITT is looking at?"

Damn.

The sandwich was now pulled apart, and not one morsel of anything had made it to her mouth. Food and water on a dining table inspired hand-shaking terror, but her question proved that she had the tenacity to use Black Raven for intel. Zeus bit back a smile of admiration.

"Sam, you're the one with the overview of the ITT evidence," Zeus said. "Why don't you give us the answer to that question?"

She didn't respond. Ragno and Dixon waited in silence.

"As a matter of fact," Zeus pressed on, "at this point, of the four of us, only you know how the proceedings are faring internally. Will the result of the ITT proceedings be worth the effort and risk that you're pouring into it?"

He studied her gaze. Steady. Solid. Nothing.

Not giving one damn thing away.

"Your silence is answer enough, sweetheart," Dixon said, his tone serious and firm, yet placating. "The ITT proceeding was a great idea for the politicians, but it will ultimately be a waste of time. For every person who might be convicted in these proceedings, hundreds more will rise up and take their places. I can't have you risking your life for this."

Sam gave a hard headshake. "My life, my decision. At a minimum, the proceedings will set new precedent for handling those convicted of terrorist acts."

"Ideally, yes. But that assumes success," Dixon said. "And also assumes that the proceedings result in some kind of a verdict, which assumes that the proceedings aren't bombed, that everyone associated with the proceedings—including you—isn't killed. Too many assumptions. A hell of a lot can go wrong in thirty days. Right, Zeus?"

"That's right. An ungodly amount can go wrong. Surely you don't want me to list the possibilities? ITT proceedings are a galactic-style clusterfuck, in an era where terrorists have morphed into super-villains. There's just no way to anticipate where the threat will come from next, except to know it can come from all sides, at all times." He leveled his gaze on Sam. "Even in the French fries."

She folded her arms with the phone poised on her shoulder. "I repeat. Resigning is not an option."

Dixon harrumphed, his anger and frustration evident. "Dammit, Samantha. Why don't you ever listen to reason?"

"Your reasons aren't my reason. I'm serious about this, Samuel. Back. Off. I've told you before, I don't want you interfering in my life. You obviously haven't gotten that message." She glared at Zeus as though he was a stand-in for her meddling grandfather. "And I don't want you interfering in my professional life. I don't want your help, your guidance, or your opinion. I mean it. I said earlier I'm not talking to you any longer, and if Zeus weren't standing in front of me, I'd sure as hell expand on all the reasons why. I mean it. You have no idea how outraged I am. If you try to control my professional decisions..." She drew a deep breath. "I promise I will cut you out of my life. I've told you a million times, I don't want or need your money, nor do I want your love if you can't rein in your desire to control me."

The back of Zeus's neck itched. He'd heard that exact tone before. Calm, controlled, decisive, and lethal—exactly how she'd sounded seven years earlier when she'd refused to listen to his apology. Seven years earlier, he'd wanted to talk things through.

She hadn't. There'd been no shock from her, even though he'd been shaken to his very core by the news he'd had to deliver. She'd nodded, processed it, and *fuck*, she'd shown him the door and not looked back. He chalked up her lack of visible emotion to pride and composure and not wanting to appear weak. She was, after all, a woman whose competitive streak knew no bounds.

He'd been heartbroken, and that had been a shiny and new, un-fucking-pleasant experience for him. He'd also been spitting angry that he felt so fucking obligated to do the right thing—the thing that required turning his back on Sam.

At the time, he'd understood the depth of how much he'd hurt Sam, even if she didn't show it. In the intervening years he'd felt like shit every time he thought about her, and he'd felt guilty for breaking her heart—when he wasn't feeling sorry for himself for breaking his own. He'd been so goddamn miserable, he hadn't given much thought to context, how his walking away from her could've possibly factored in her overall life, which had been guided by her grandfather's extreme meddling.

Hell. He hadn't thought it through.

Watching her now, he realized she was capable of shutting off personal feelings if those feelings interfered with her job trajectory. He recognized and respected that capability. He had it himself. He wouldn't be at the top of Black Raven in the competitive, dog-eat-your-own-sweet-mother world of private security contracting if, for years, he hadn't had the ability to employ gridlock focus on his goals and look at every decision through filters that kept his goals at dead center.

Now, as she threatened to cut her grandfather—her closest living relative—out of her life if he interfered with her career, he wondered...

Through his mic, Ragno's voice, calm and even, provided a welcome interruption to the thought that was so half-baked he didn't want to acknowledge it. "Zeus, your ears only. I've dropped them from my line. You wanted me to dig deep into her life, and I've started that process. Reality is Dixon has controlled every step she's taken since her parents died. He can't control her now. He knows it. She knows it. Even if she wants to quit, she wouldn't. Just to prove to him or to herself—hell, it doesn't matter—she's proving that he isn't in control. You and Dixon are going to lose this battle."

No shit.

As a stand-off ensued between grandfather and granddaughter, Zeus decided not to intervene. Instead, he assembled another sandwich for her. He didn't have to think of how she liked it, nor did he need to mimic what she'd just done.

The ingredients and assembly method were just more inane trivia about Sam that he hadn't been able to purge from his brain. White bread. A thin layer of mayo. About a third of an inch of thin slices of ham. A layer of barbeque potato chips on the sandwich. Not off. Slices of bread lightly pressed together. Ends removed. Cut in thirds, so the sandwich became neat, rectangular finger sandwiches. He poured a fresh glass of water from the pitcher.

As she watched him, he took a bite from one of the sandwiches, chewed, and swallowed. He reached for a few grapes, ate them, then the glass of water that he poured for her and took a sip.

She studied him, seemingly holding her breath, as he didn't start frothing at the mouth and drop to the floor. He whispered, "See? Food's fine." He set both the plate and the glass down in front of her.

Warm gratitude flooded her eyes and told him thank you in a way that words never would have. Her open, honest eyes conveyed everything that needed to be said, and for a moment she looked exactly like she did before their detour to lives without each other—trusting, honest, and without a filter over what she was really thinking.

Goddammit. If he could just step back in time and go to the point where he'd made the wrong turn, he'd do it in a heartbeat.

"Zeus," Ragno said. "Tell them that with the escalation of threat caused by the Boulevard Saint-Germain bombing and the cyanide poisoning, and the increased chatter, Black Raven will need double the manpower originally anticipated. Maybe that will help her make her decision."

Zeus repeated Ragno's warning and threw in numbers. High numbers. They'd break seven figures a few times. Easily. The simple reality was that Black Raven ran a business for profit. Risk was up, so manpower needed to increase. Every hour of manpower, for each agent, cost hundreds, if not thousands, of dollars, depending on agent skill level and task. Not to mention the safe houses they'd need, the transports, and the dedicated analytical support that Ragno's group would provide. Samuel understood that fact, and so did Sam.

Still, the numbers were daunting. He added the caveat that Black Raven always provided. "And this is only an estimate. The number will go up as circumstances evolve."

Sam shrugged, took a bite of the sandwich, chewed slowly, and swallowed. "Budget issues are between you and my grandfather. I didn't hire Black Raven, and I especially didn't hire you." She took another bite, and drank a quick sip of water. "I'm not resigning, even if my grandfather decides not to pay you, even if you decide to quit the job. I'm doing the job..." She leveled her eyes on his, ate a grape, and added, "With or without you or Black Raven. Understood?"

He nodded as he watched her eat more of her sandwich. *Got it. Loud and clear.*

"Threat level of every country participating in the ITT– United Kingdom, United States, France, and Colombia– Hell," Dixon said, breaking his silence. "The terrorist threat level worldwide is critical right now. I don't want you in the goddamn bullseye, Sam. Bring her home, Zeus."

Is the man listening to his granddaughter?

"Bring me home? As though I'm a package? Or a suitcase? He will not. I will not quit. The. Answer. Is. No."

Zeus held his breath as he waited for an explosion from Samuel Dixon.

"Well, fine," Dixon said, tone calm. "Zeus and Ragno." His voice switched from concerned grandfather to thoughtful and steady businessman. "Spare no legitimate expense on the security detail for the Amicus team."

"Absolutely," Ragno, back on the line with the three of them, answered.

"There's been a ten-million dollar bounty on Maximov for years," Dixon said. "Is Black Raven pursuing it?"

The off-the-wall question had Zeus's gaze riveted on Sam's eyes, because the surprise he saw there matched his. Not just surprise—he also saw worry as to where this was going.

Hell.

Zeus knew where it was going and there was plenty of cause for worry for Black Raven. He could almost see the giant fucking flashing neon sign yelling, "conflict of interest." In all caps. Underlined.

He maintained his poker face, unable to acknowledge that such a Black Raven job existed. An honest answer to the question required he reveal Jigsaw.

Not gonna happen.

Chapter Six

Jigsaw was still in its relative infancy and Zeus, of all people, knew how sensitive it was. Two years earlier, Black Raven's cyber division had been hired by the DHS on a project-by-project basis. At the same time, the NSA hired Black Raven's cyber division on other projects. The DHS and NSA projects were unrelated, but shared a common objective—gathering information about terrorist threats. As with other outsourcing conducted by the governmental agencies to Black Raven's cyber division, the existence of the projects was strictly confidential.

One year after being hired on the separate DHS and NSA projects, the prison break involving Barrows occurred. Black Raven's search for, and ultimate hiring of, Barrows resulted in an infusion of classified, sensitive information into the company. One result of the prison break and hiring Barrows was that Black Raven became privy to Shadow Technology—the top-secret data collection and assimilation program Barrows had designed for the government.

Zeus and Sebastian, working with Barrows and Ragno in the months after Black Raven acquired both Barrows and Shadow Technology, believed that Shadow Technology could enhance the pending DHS and NSA projects. Every bit of brainpower possessed by Barrows and Ragno, and others in Black Raven's cyber division, had resulted in Jigsaw—a program tailored to DHS and NSA concerns. Meanwhile, terrorist activities were escalating. Zeus gave Barrows a couple of months of lag time for research and development, then personally pitched the project to the Secretary of the DHS and the Director of the NSA, who were under increasing pressure from President Cameron to damn well do something about terrorism. Zeus and Sebastian gave the new project the code name Jigsaw, the name of the Barrows-designed program that ran it. Forming a collaborative, top-secret task force, the DHS and NSA hired Black Raven for Jigsaw.

With funding secured, and with Barrows having free rein on the job, Jigsaw blossomed into a wide-ranging project that had the potential to throttle the terrorists who now held the world in a chokehold. Jigsaw was tasked with the wide-ranging, lofty goal of a safer and more secure America. The program compiled, assimilated, and assessed data from intelligence agencies worldwide. The objective was to predict behavior and defeat organizations like Maximov and others, who managed to succeed in coordinated terrorist acts like those the ITT was investigating and the recent bombing in Las Vegas.

Barrows was working out kinks, performing upgrades, creating shortcuts, and analyzing output. The Vegas New Year's Eve bombing had produced shockwaves for Barrows, Ragno, and Zeus—because the program hadn't predicted it. Barrows now assured Zeus the program was almost operating at a level where answers could be produced. Answers to burning questions, like where the hell is Maximov.

Damn program should have an answer.

There were other questions, as well, such as the questions the ITT was investigating, whether there was a link between the terrorist acts at issue in the trial, whether the Maximov organization was funding the current wave of terrorism, and what terrorist organization was behind the Las Vegas New Year's Eve bombing.

If answers aren't produced soon, we'll be skewered.

Jigsaw's level of secrecy was the highest Zeus had ever known. Now, six months after Black Raven had been officially hired by the DHS and NSA on Jigsaw, only a select few were even aware of the breath and scope of Black Raven's Jigsaw. Even some of the agencies that were collecting and compiling their own data regarding credible terrorist threats—Maximov being one such threat—weren't aware that Black Raven was using their information.

A point that brought Zeus back to Samuel's question. *Is Black Raven working on the bounty hunt for Maximov?*

"No," he lied easily. "We're not pursuing the bounty."

True answer—hell yes.

If Jigsaw produced information that would lead to the apprehension of Maximov, Black Raven would have the terrorist nailed to a fucking wall in a matter of hours. They'd happily claim the bounty, even though Jigsaw's fee far surpassed anything that could legitimately be charged for a mere bounty hunt. As it was, clues as to Maximov's whereabouts were starting to come in. Teams of elite agents had been mobilized.

"Why not?" Samuel asked.

Here goes. This is why I get paid one hell of a lot of money. I'm damn good at the creative lying that comes with top-secret government jobs.

"We're not bounty hunters. We're paid for our services. Expenses for a team of elite agents searching the world for

Maximov, with the kind of dedicated analytical power that team would require, could quickly rival and surpass the value of the bounty."

Sam raised a brow. "Ten million is a lot of money."

"I agree," Dixon said.

"Yeah. If we had the time to search for him. But time is money, as you well know. Black Raven requires a client to bankroll the job, because without someone paying us, well, once we netted out our expenses, ten million dollars is not a significant sum of money."

"Well, you've found your client for the job," Dixon said. "Your fees and expenses, of course, plus you get to keep the damn bounty when you find Maximov and hand him to President Cameron. Consider it bonus money."

Shit! Talk about double dipping. Samuel wants to bankroll a job on which I'm already working.

When Zeus didn't immediately respond, Samuel continued, "I want to hire Black Raven to find Maximov. To be perfectly clear, Zeus, your job is to protect Samantha. Your eyes are to be on her at all times, but I want you to monitor and direct the team hunting for Maximov. Put your best men and women on it."

"That's crazy," Sam told her grandfather, her face pale. "An international task force with military expertise is looking for Maximov. Let them do their job."

"Won't be the first time I'm called crazy," Dixon said, his voice sharp. "I didn't get where I am by running from risk or sitting around, waiting for the government to get a damn thing done. The world is scared right now. Terrorists have created a humanitarian disaster and an economic disaster and it's time to teach them a goddamn lesson. Maximov might be a phantom, but he's only a man. If he's gunning for the ITT proceedings, and my granddaughter is front and center, he won't get away with it. Find Maximov, Zeus, and the world will make headway in the fight against terrorism, compliments of Dixon Enterprises."

Sam slowly shook her head, her lips parted, a frown line bisecting her brows. She held the phone in a white-knuckled grip as she glared at it. "Samuel, you can't do—"

"I can, and I will. If you're fighting terrorists, I don't see why I shouldn't as well. We'll try to tackle these sons of bitches from both sides. One of us is bound to hit them on their blind side. Goodnight, honey. Let's talk after you've slept."

Dixon clicked off the call. Zeus and Samantha stood in surprised silence.

"God," Ragno said. "I love that man."

Zeus chuckled. Ragno, he was sure, had enjoyed what had just transpired. Together, he and Ragno would have to come up with a method of creative accounting that didn't cheat Samuel out of his money. Black Raven routinely bent laws to satisfy the needs of their jobs, but the almighty dollar—the oxygen on which the company thrived—was always treated honestly and with the respect it deserved.

His chuckle faded as Sam drew in an exasperated breath. Her eyes were strained, as though her argument with her grandfather had worn her out, and his decision to hire Black Raven to lead a bounty hunt for Maximov was only icing on the cake of a day that needed to end. "Ragno, give me a few minutes."

Ragno clicked off, and he and Sam were alone.

"You okay?"

"My grandfather is picking a fight with the most feared terrorist in the world, two people who were close to me have died in the last forty-eight hours, and"—she glanced at her watch—"I need to function in less than seven hours on the most important trial in which I've ever been involved. Why wouldn't I be fine?"

"If it's too much you could re—"

"Don't go there." She drew a deep breath and squared her shoulders. "I need to be up at seven, at court at eight forty-five. Proceedings start at nine."

"I'm aware." He didn't think he needed to explain to her that for the next thirty days, his every breath would revolve around the details of her life. He wouldn't be doing his job if he didn't know her schedule intimately.

"Would you please make sure my grandfather is secure? My involvement here, and now the bounty hunt." She drew a deep breath, and exhaled slowly. Her eyes were worried, revealing that even though she put up a tough front and had just threatened to cut the man out of her life, she loved him. "He could become a target."

Samuel Dixon was in residence at his Orange County home, in one of the most exclusive guarded and gated communities in the world. The house itself was a fortress, made impenetrable by Black Raven, and exactly where Zeus wished Sam would run to. "We'll evaluate. Your grandfather will be fine," Zeus said. "His security isn't anything you need to worry about."

As she walked towards her bedroom, he said, "One more thing."

She glanced at him. "What?"

He walked to the wet bar and washed his hands, gesturing with his head to the coffee table, where the first aid kit waited. "Microchip."

For a second, her jaw dropped. "Like I'm a dog?"

"More like a car. It's a GPS system we can monitor remotely." He stepped to the coffee table. Before opening the kit and pulling out the syringe, he paused. "Blood phobia is still bad, right?"

"With movies, photos, and evidence, I'm fine. Otherwise I couldn't do my job. Real life?" She shook her head with a slight blush on her cheeks. This was another sign of weakness that she hated. "I still can't look at one drop without passing out. Once I come to, if I look at it again, I get nauseated. That's almost as bad as passing out."

"I'll work around it. Come here," he said. "I need your left arm."

"You didn't do this last time." She didn't move from her position right outside her bedroom.

"It's been seven years. That's light years in technology. We started using chips last year, and we've recently developed a stealth mechanism. The chip is almost undetectable."

"Almost?"

"Yeah. Almost."

"I've counted at least twenty agents tonight. Chances of anyone taking me away are slim to none. I have to admit, I find this pretty damn offensive. So explain why it's necessary."

"Remember that part about listening to my instructions? The promise you made to your grandfather?"

"Yes. And by the way, I said I'd listen to Black Raven. Not necessarily you." Arms folded and eyebrows arched, she didn't look like she cared one damn bit about the promise she'd made.

"Same thing."

"Whatever." Despite her nonplussed tone, something cracked in her composure. As her eyes flashed with emotion that he couldn't quite read, he realized she was more bothered than she was letting on. Whether it was Eric's death, the stress of a long day, or...

Oh hell. "You knew Black Raven was hired. You didn't know I was coming. That's why you're so pissed at your grandfather."

A mask of cool calmness fell over her face. "Stay on task, Hernandez. I'll follow instructions related to security, but the instructions have to be logical. Chipping me like a dog doesn't seem logical, when I know you and your agents are going to stay glued to me."

"Logic? How's this for logic?" He didn't bother trying not to sound irritated, because, dammit she'd just irritated the hell out of him by ignoring his question. "Reality is I have no clue what the next thirty days will bring, but we're preparing for the worst. In the unlikely event you get separated from Black Raven, this chip could help with search and rescue. The chip isn't foolproof, but it's the best we've got. If you're taken, you'll be praying—"

"So you're God, and the chip will enable you to answer my prayers?"

"Stop being such a fucking smart ass. Save that for other lawyers. God's busy. Black Raven doesn't wait for him to answer prayers, when our clients are begging, pleading, and yes, praying for their lives. I wasn't going to give you a visual, but since you're being hard-headed, go ahead and imagine there's a machete at that slender neck of yours, the cameras are turned on, and this chip might be the only thing that lets me find you. Now stop arguing."

She frowned, giving him a glance of disgust as she approached him. "Understood. You said it isn't foolproof. What do you mean?"

"If you're in tall buildings, or a congested city area, or mountains, or underground, it's hard to get precise data. And there's always the chance the people who take you are smart and have signal jammers or advanced scanners that can find this. If they do, they'll cut it out of you. Or send your arm to your grandfather. Or kill you. Dammit, Sam." He softened his voice as she stepped closer. "On security issues, don't ask me to explain myself."

When she sat on the couch, he sat down heavily next to her. She worked on pushing up the snug sleeve of her sweatshirt. "Just do the things I ask. There won't be many answers you like. What you're doing isn't logical. If you want logic, resign. Go home and practice law. And your sleeve isn't going high enough, so take your sweatshirt off."

"I'm not wearing much under here."

"Not a problem." He ground his teeth together. In his peripheral vision, she shrugged out of the sweatshirt and let it fall to the side of her. She hadn't been the shy, modest type seven years before. In fact, she'd been happy to walk around naked. He hadn't minded.

He forced his focus on the contents of the first aid kit. "If I couldn't handle looking at you for thirty days, I wouldn't have taken the job. Despite our past, I'm a professional, and you're a client. That's it."

And I'm a lying motherfucker, because you will never be just a client.

He might want to make love to her with every fiber of his being, but even with Sam, he had some degree of willpower when on the job. Fortunately for the two of them, stars were in alignment for extreme willpower, because not only was he on a job, he was facing a woman who didn't want him. And she was practically engaged to someone else.

"This goes inside left elbow. Lie down. That way, if you pass out, you're already down. There shouldn't be much blood, but if you're staring at the injection site, you'll see some."

He glanced at her as she swung her legs up on the couch, lay down, and squeezed her eyes shut. *Dammit.* Not wearing much was an understatement. The lace camisole stretched so tightly that pale pink nipples were visible and *fuck it*, they were hardening to nubs. Cold? Desire?

Hell. Wishful thinking. He was goddamn hallucinating. *Don't look.* Not at her small, high, near-perfect mounds with the slight up-tilted peaks. His mouth watered as though he was staring at a feast and starving. Both were true, when she was the offering and when he thought of how much he wanted her. *Fuck. Don't look at the way the camisole hugs her taut, flat belly, and tapering waist.*

Fuck me to hell and back. Sexual thoughts on night one were only going to ensure thirty long nights of torture.

"Hurry," she said, left arm extended to him, eyes closed, oblivious that his mind was playing out a far different scene than the one she expected.

In silent hell, he ripped open the alcohol packet. He bent to his knees on the floor, then found her pulse by running his index and middle finger along the impossibly soft skin of her inner arm, above her elbow. After swabbing her arm, he pulled the lid off the syringe.

"Big stick." *Hah.* Joke was on him. Given his erection, his words would have been amusing but for the desire that had his body on fire and his balls aching.

She flinched as the needle went in. "Ouch! Son of a gun, Zeus. That hurts."

Hurts? You have no idea. Me worse than you.

He pushed the plunger, pulled out the needle, and gritted

out, "Don't open your eyes." After swabbing the blood and bandaging her arm, he waited a second. When he was sure she wasn't going to bleed through the bandage, he sat down next to her. "All done."

She drew a deep breath, opened her eyes, and sat up.

"Go slow," he said, watching for signs that she'd faint. Remembering, though, that when he'd last seen her pass out it had happened so quickly there'd been no advance warning.

She stood, waving off his concern as she shrugged back into the sweatshirt, engulfing him with a fresh waft of perfume as the material covered her. "I'm fine. I won't pass out if I don't see blood."

"Most of the time," he whispered. She glanced at him with a startled look. God, but he'd missed her. He'd dreamed about her, and yes, he remembered every damn detail about her, every moment that they'd been together. "Sometimes you pass out from sudden standing after lying down. It happened when the lightning storm came up, when we were on the beach." He left out the part about what they'd been doing on the beach, and the reason why they hadn't noticed the thunderclouds building. They stood up to run for shelter, and she'd passed out. He'd caught her in the split second before she fell face down. He had to carry her off the beach.

Now, from the raw look of pain in her eyes that she quickly concealed, he'd bet his life that she remembered exactly what he was talking about and what they'd been doing. "Still a problem?"

"Hasn't happened since." As she turned from him, words he'd never had the opportunity to say suddenly needed saying. Whether she wanted to hear them or not. Before she disappeared into her bedroom, dammit.

He jumped to his feet and started after her as she wordlessly headed for her room. Once she closed that door the window of opportunity might be lost.

Now or never, asshole.

He wanted—no, needed—the first night of being near her to end with one fact clear between them. He stopped a few feet away as she stepped through the doorway and turned to shut the door. Her eyes widened in surprise to see him standing so close.

Now.

"I'm divorced. My marriage didn't work."

He'd intended for those words to come out smoother. But in the moment, there really was only one way to say what needed to be said. She froze, hand on the door handle, seemingly as shocked as he was that he'd blurted out the words. Damn, but it was impossible to read her, and that was new. When they'd been together before, she'd been hard to read, but he'd managed. It was part of what he'd loved about her. She was a challenge. Now? Not a chance.

Dammit-to-hell, ask me why. He now knew why his decision seven years earlier had been the right one for the time, but the wrong one for his eternity.

Having Sam give a damn why was more important than anything. *Ask me why, because that's what I need to tell you.* But she didn't say anything, and after making the first overture, he sure as hell wasn't going to beg her to open the lines of communication.

Instead of responding, she did what he'd have done when faced with such a potential emotional nuclear bomb from anyone other than Sam. She looked at him with eyes that didn't reveal a goddamn shred of emotion or thought, without even an eyebrow arch, and shut the door in his face.

The solid *thwap* of the door brought a harsh reminder of an inescapable truth. There had been two people at his detour, and they'd both decided that going their separate ways was the correct course of action. He'd chosen the sharp turn leading away from her, but Sam had let him. She'd easily let him go, without a fight, without trying to change his mind, and she was a woman who damn well fought for what she wanted.

The niggling half-baked thought, the one that had materialized after she threatened to cut her grandfather from her life, rose up. He tried, and failed, to squelch it before it fully materialized.

Face facts, buddy.

Maybe his decision to leave her hadn't haunted her at all for the past seven fucking years. Maybe everything that had passed between them, all the things that meant so much to him, had amounted to nothing but forgettable moments to her.

Maybe the only heart that had been irreparably broken had been his.

Chapter Seven

Samantha hadn't seen that one coming. Zeus's flat announcement had stunned her into silence. He wasn't the failing—or quitting—type. With those words, her heart boomed the illogical beat of a hopeful fool. Yet her logical brain fired caution flares through the swirling fog of doubt that engulfed her.

He was the reason she'd learned to use logic over her heart's desire. So his marriage hadn't worked out? Damn him for bringing it up.

When had his marriage fallen apart? How long ago? Six years? Four? Yesterday? At any time between then and now he could've picked up the freaking phone to check to see if the information might have an impact on her life. But he hadn't. He'd taken the opportunity to share the information only because the bastard was here. Hired by her grandfather. If Samuel hadn't paid him to come to France to provide security, she'd have never known Jesus Hernandez's marital status—one way or the other.

Samantha tamped down her anger the second it started simmering. *Do not react. Don't let him know how much he gets to you.*

Shutting the door on him, a move dictated by instincts of self-preservation and brain-powered logic, was the only action she'd been capable of, though the simple move took all her strength.

Door locked, she leaned against it, powerless. She exhaled. Inhaled. *Don't go there. Do. Not. Go. There.* Their shared history produced three simple truths, each bringing varying degrees of hurt and resolve.

One—he hadn't chosen her and he never would. It was a painful truth, but a truth nonetheless. Sure, there had been exigent circumstances, the kind that made his decision logical. Reality was she wasn't the kind of woman with whom he'd stay, and she'd never be that kind of woman. She wasn't needy, and he damn well needed to be needed.

Two—he'd been the first true love of her life. The job that he'd been hired for back then had provided enough time for them to get to know each other, before they acted on what they were both feeling. She had learned that he was strong and stoic, brave and considerate, and as determined and smart as anyone she'd ever met. She had loved to make him smile—which was something he didn't do often. Loved to challenge him, and when she'd been in a room with him, loved the way he seemed aware of her, even when his dark eyes weren't on her. She'd watched him fearlessly cover her grandfather when a would-be assassin fired a barrage of bullets. She had wanted him more than anyone. What he'd done after those three weeks, when the job was over, had proven that he wanted her just as badly.

Damn.

She shook off the heat that came with the memories of when they had first made love, without even a word. He'd just shown up at her door, unannounced. Next thing she knew, they were in bed, and they'd kept at it.

For days.

She shook her head, pushing those thoughts to the side. There was nothing to be done about the fact that he'd been the love of her life, except to make sure that wasn't still the case. She didn't have time for that kind of distraction.

Three—he had used his only chance to break her heart. She was stronger now. More focused. He would only be a distraction, just as he'd been all those years ago. Thank God this third truth was empowering, because it cancelled out the pain that came with one and two.

One plus two plus three equaled being as impersonal as possible with him.

Focus on the job and I'll get out of here with my heart intact. Life will resume. I'll be who I am, without the distraction that inevitably comes with allowing a man to take over the precious real estate that is my heart.

Excel, remember?

Let your brain-fueled logic rule your life.

Don't be like your mother.

Memories of her mother, and the weakness that defined her mother's life, gave her willpower.

Zeus's marriage status? *Irrelevant.* Shutting the door between them was as explicit of a statement as she intended to give him.

Back pressed flat against the door, she breathed a few times before the dull ache in her arm where Zeus had injected her registered more than the turmoil caused by his announcement.

She turned sideways, pressing her ear towards the sound of his deep, low voice from the other room. Words weren't decipherable, yet the deep timbre of his voice had a magnetic pull. *God help me.* Listening to the calm authority with which he spoke, she fought the urge to open the door and let him envelope her in warmth, strength, and all the in-the-moment, mind-numbing passion he was capable of offering.

Yes, offering. Because she wasn't stupid, and the statement *"my marriage didn't work,"* while Zeus stood on the threshold of her bedroom, looking at her with an honest, intense, and hungry gaze, had nothing to do with the face value of the words. It was an invitation that screamed *let's make love.*

No. Not love. Lesson learned, remember?

Her body didn't care how the invitation was worded. When Zeus looked at her with those dark eyes, a simple "Let's fuck" would do, because sex with him had been incredible.

The best I've ever had.

The best she was ever going to have, because sex with him was in the past.

She stayed there, listening to his voice on the other side of the door, until she gathered enough energy to pull herself away. *There will always be a reason he'll leave you. Don't give him the opportunity. Again. Never again. Do. Not.*

Clearly, by the tone of his words, he wasn't talking to a friend to unburden his heartbreak at her response to his earthshattering announcement. It sounded like a business call.

Wow, and ouch.

It had taken him all of a minute to get back to business as usual. There was a lesson to be learned there. Samantha crossed the room, sat on her bed, picked up the flip phone that Zeus had given her, and speed dialed one.

"Hello, Ms. Fairfax. I'm Agent Lenore. How may I help you?"

She opened her laptop. "You have messages for me?"

"Yes. We've let your callers know that you're fine. Any other details, we thought it best if you provided." He continued to other people who'd left messages or numbers in the last five hours. There were twelve. Checking the private phone that she and Justin used for their personal conversations, Samantha saw that he'd called three times.

She glanced at her watch. It was 2:30 a.m. in Paris. 8:30 p.m. in Washington, D.C. Because the callers knew she was fine, she decided only Justin needed a return call.

She and Justin didn't live together. Yet. Unless he had an event that she didn't know about, he'd be home from work, probably sitting in front of the television, watching news shows while he read through the piles of work he brought home every evening.

He answered midway through the first ring. "Holy shit, Samantha! I've been worried sick. It's about damn time you called. I've got the pilots on standby and was headed your way if you didn't call in the next fifteen minutes. Figured I could have breakfast with you, or at least see you at the lunch break. Just wanted to make sure you're okay."

The concern in his deep, smooth voice brought a sudden and overwhelming reaction to Eric's death, coupled with grief-stricken longing for Stanley Morgan's wisdom and guidance. Her hands shook and her stomach twisted. She struggled for composure.

If she broke down, Justin really would fly to Paris to check up on her. He was, after all, her best friend. She wasn't a crier, but hearing his voice made her eyes sting. She'd had to swallow back tears at different times during the day. Stress, sadness, and Zeus had made it a cry-worthy freaking day.

"I'm fine," she whispered.

"Is that so? You don't sound fine."

"Can never fool you, can I?" Tucking the phone under her chin, she winced as a slight bit of pain from the chip-placement shot zinged up her arm as she stripped off the leggings and sweatshirt. Wearing only the camisole and panties, she slipped into the king size bed's linen sheets and nestled under the thick comforter. Lying on her side, head resting on the soft pillow, she pulled the covers over her shoulders. "I know this line is supposed to be secure. You've made sure on your end?"

With his position as senator, and her high-profile job now being even more high profile, neither wanted to take chances that their phone call could be compromised. Still, whenever they talked about anything sensitive they used their own kind of shorthand. Just in case.

"Always. Tell me, because my mind is now going in a hundred directions, and I want to be winging my way to, apparently not so gay, Paree, right now."

"No. Don't come. I'd love to see you, but there's no need. Seriously, Justin. Here's what's happening..." They talked for a half-hour, covering Eric's death, the Boulevard Saint-Germain bombing, President Cameron's call, and her grandfather's insistence that she resign. Justin's smooth, deep voice soothed her as much as his words.

When he was caught up, she raised a worry that was starting

to fester, one that she wouldn't admit to anyone else. "What if Samuel is correct—what if this is nothing but an ill-conceived, unproductive dog and pony show? What if the ITT proceedings become such a debacle it becomes a black mark on my career?"

"If that happens, we'll figure it out. Some risks you take will pay off. Some won't. Just do what you think is right. You're the smartest person I know. You'll figure this out." He paused, "As always, I'm here to help you with anything you need."

"Thanks," she said, her heart swelling with gratitude. It was comforting to know Justin would walk over hot coals, both literally and figuratively for her. And she'd do the same for him. She paused for a moment, debating whether to tell him about Zeus. "There's more."

"What?"

"We've made the shift to Black Raven security."

"Okay."

"Remember I mentioned that I asked my grandfather to make sure Zeus Hernandez wasn't involved with the job?"

Justin drew in a deep breath. "He didn't."

"He did. Hernandez is here, front and center. He's not only in charge of the detail, he's heading my personal team. Body guarding me, for God's sake. I'm furious." She and Justin had few secrets from each other. They'd met in law school and known each other for eight years. They'd been study partners and the best of friends before she'd met Zeus the first time. She'd told Justin some of what had happened with Zeus at that time. Actually, she had told Justin most of what had happened, because it had taken her quite a while to get back to normal, and her good friend had insisted on knowing what the hell was wrong with her.

"Well, tell me about him."

"Not in the mood."

"Because?"

"I'm exhausted." Partially true.

She turned on her back and stared at the ceiling, gripping the phone tight, as Justin's voice became a lifeline, pulling her to a mental space where she had strength, resolve, and the ability to resist.

"I can't say that I blame you for that. Wish I was there to give you a neck rub," he said. "You sure you don't want to talk more about him?"

"Positive."

"Come on, Samantha. Now that you've seen him, is there

anything still there?"

"Meaning?"

"You know what I mean. You. Him. Close quarters. Thirty days."

"Honestly?"

"Of course, honestly."

"As much as I can pretend it never existed, there will always be our past. There will never be a future, though. I don't want or need him." She gripped the phone tightly, trying to keep her voice calm. "When I have you. I guess the big news, at least for him, is that apparently he's now divorced."

"Well, that is big news." Justin's voice sounded steady, tempered, and even. "What'd you say when he told you?"

"Nothing at all. I shut the door on him."

"Not your usual way of confronting adversity head on." His voice was dry, but filled with concern. "From what you've told me about him, that was just his opening salvo. With the fact that he's divorced, you know he wouldn't be there if he wasn't interested in revisiting the past."

"I hope not. I'm so tired I can't even think about it," she said, not giving Justin the one-hundred-percent honesty she typically did. Reality was, she couldn't stop thinking about Zeus being free. Because the more tired she became, the more she thought of his dark eyes, and his low, steady voice. His square jaw, with his high cheekbones, and the set of his serious lips. His broad shoulders and muscular chest, tapering to his narrow waist. The way he smelled of fresh-scented soap and underneath that, a slight hint of musky male, like a wooded forest on a crisp Fall day.

More terrifying than the lure of his physical attributes was the remembered comfort of his arms, and his innate fortitude that whispered a siren's song of strength, safety, and stability. Those traits reactivated a deep-seated longing for what they'd once shared. Back then, she'd believed she'd found the one man who would love her passionately, yet be strong enough and secure enough not to suck her life blood—her ambition—out of her. That belief, once forgotten and now simmering into her consciousness, was what made Zeus Hernandez a dangerous man, because she couldn't handle a heartbreak-inspired detour. Not now, and never again. She didn't have time to waste on the hope and a prayer that a relationship would work, that someone would live up to lofty expectations inspired by emotional love.

Besides, she'd set a course of action for her life and didn't plan on deviating from it. After Zeus had walked out, she had decided to abandon all notions of romantic love. The heartbreak Zeus had caused had made relationships based upon platonic love seem like the only intelligent, logical option for her. While any observer assumed that Samantha and Justin shared a sexual relationship, the truth was their relationship was non-sexual. For the closest of emotional contact, and the bonds that came with deep love and respect, she and Justin turned to one another. For sex, she and Justin both went elsewhere. Discreetly. Only Samantha and Justin knew all the reasons why, and they both planned to keep it that way.

"Should I be worried about you? Personal turmoil dealing with Hernandez, plus the business stress the trial is producing, plus your grief over Morgan and now Eric; this could all be too much to handle."

"I'll be fine," she said, squeezing her eyes shut, trying not to see Zeus. "He won't produce personal turmoil. Don't worry."

Worry. Be very worried.

"Go to sleep, honey," Justin said. "You know I love you to the moon and back, don't you? No matter what."

"I love you too," she said, breaking the connection.

Chapter Eight

"We couldn't have orchestrated a better opportunity if we tried," H.L. said, his focus on three large screen TVs. Each featured a different news show with views of crowds that had gathered for the arrival of judges and lawyers at the Gothic-style, eighteenth-century buildings housing the International Terrorist Tribunal proceedings on the Ile de la Cite. It was a cold, gray, drizzly Parisian morning. He and his two partners were in an apartment on the Ile St. Louis, a short walk from the ITT proceedings.

Adrenaline rushed through him as they observed the jostling crowds. From toes to fingers, and chin to scalp, his skin crawled with excitement. Worldwide fear would multiply exponentially with each of their attacks on the ITT, and today they'd unleash more than one news worthy event.

They were far smarter than the two-bit thugs that now called themselves terrorists, and they'd been successful throughout the years. Like vampires fed off blood, he and his partners fed off fear. Everything they'd done until now had merely been the appetizer course. "This will be easier than shooting fish in a barrel."

"And a hell of a lot bloodier." The words came from the partner in their fear enterprise known as J.R., a tall, thin man with gentle brown eyes that belied the darkness of his soul and the staggering body count the man was capable of establishing with his go orders.

Like H.L., the initials J.R. bore no resemblance to the man's real name or anything about him. They'd simply chosen initials that provided private humor, and they changed them periodically. H.L.? A memorable villain from the sad tale of very silent, very slaughtered lambs. J.R.? The scheming leader of a notorious fictional family from Dallas that made a fortune in oil.

Sitting on a couch, laptop perched on the arm of it, J.R. sucked one of his perpetual cigarettes. The man wore a two-thousand-dollar business suit and smelled like an ashtray. He was impeccably groomed, with not a hair out of place, yet the stench of his cigarettes invaded everywhere the man was.

The other partner present, M.C., adjusted his tortoise-shell glasses as he focused on the TVs. His initials weren't taken from a fictional character in a megadrama, but rather from his role. Master of Ceremonies. M.C., their operations manager, made sure the infrastructure was in place to fulfill their goals.

M.C. and H.L. tolerated J.R.'s cigarette stench. He was an integral cog in their machine of terror, the genius who designed their attacks with an engineer's precision.

Waving away a plume of J.R.'s smoke that had travelled to the table where he worked, M.C. said, "I'm pleased." He was well versed at understatement, his mind, no doubt, moving on to implementation concerns for their next task.

The thousands of people gathered on the island in the Seine River were not admiring the order and precision reflected in the Parisian architecture, nor were they focusing on the tourist attractions of the Cathedral of Notre-Dame or the St. Chapelle Church.

On Monday, January 31, day one of the ITT proceeding, onlookers had been a mixture of protestors and supporters. Protestors claimed the ITT was a violation of basic human rights because the trial had few of the safeguards utilized in the judicial systems of civilized countries. Supporters believed the tribunal was the correct tool to combat terrorism—a last ditch effort that needed to succeed. The people outside of the proceeding held signs, but the gathering had been, for the most part, quiet.

News of the Monday night Boulevard Saint-Germain bombing and the cyanide poisoning of Eric Moss, an American lawyer on the Amicus team, hit the airwaves early Tuesday, February 1, day two of the ITT proceeding. The crowd outside of the proceeding had multiplied and grown more vocal, with protestors and supporters exchanging angry words.

This morning, day three of the proceeding, protestors had multiplied and outnumbered supporters. The media focused on the more extreme protestors—the extremists—in the restless crowd. H.L. and his partners cultivated extremists like farmers cultivated cows. There was selective inclusion in their herd, with careful feeding and years of nurturing. Calm indifference at the slaughterhouse was a prerequisite to success in their cause and, on a more fundamental level, to their sleeping well.

H.L. slept very well.

In fine linen sheets and cool, climate-controlled air, he slept the sleep of one in the arms of angels, without a thought for the people killed on his order or the abject fear he'd instilled in individuals. People were simply a tool for H.L and his partners to manipulate as they plotted and implemented their heinous acts in cigarette-smoke filled rooms. Most of the time, however, they mingled with the power brokers of the world—upper-echelon men and women who had no idea of their secret lives.

On the sidewalks and in the courtyards around the Palais de Justice and the Conciergerie, the building that housed the prison where Marie Antoinette was incarcerated, protestors jostled each other for space behind barricades. Women wearing headscarves and burkhas, and men wearing turbans, were interspersed throughout the crowd.

People held signs that read, in various languages, *Remember Chalinda*, and *I am Maximov*, the battle cry of terrorists who followed Maximov. *ITT=Star Chamber* and *Stop Ultimate Exile* were popular messages. A young woman with long dark hair bent her upper body against a barricade, holding a sign that read, in jagged, black handwritten letters, *ITT=Witch Hunt.*

Cameras and recording equipment were not allowed inside the courtroom. However, reporters were in the gallery and terms that were used by the lawyers and the judges had made their way out the doors and into the world through the media. On Monday and Tuesday, defense teams repeatedly accused the prosecution of being on a witch hunt, in arguments geared to persuade the judges and the reporters sitting in the gallery.

Because the United States was perceived as the driving force behind the ITT, anti-American sentiment became a popular theme among the protestors. A young man with a blonde crew cut held a sign that said, *Stop American Greed.* The man next to him carried a sign with a message that wasn't so benign. It said, *Behead Americans.* When a camera focused on a close up of the man, his steady, unwavering blue eyes, suggested he was capable of the task and would not flinch.

"Find out who he is. Interview him," he said, eyes on the TV screen, but nodding in the direction of M.C.

"Our recruiters are in the crowd. I'll direct one to him," M.C. replied, eyes trained on the T.V. screen.

"What are the plans for today?" H.L. asked.

M.C. removed his glasses and wiped them with a microfiber cloth before settling them back on his face. "We're operating on three fronts," M.C. answered, meticulously folding the cloth before returning it to his pocket. "First, a public show. Second, continued stress on the judges and lawyers. Third, the prisoners."

"I'm aware that we have access to the prisoners. We will only implement that as needed, though. Right?" H.L. asked.

"Correct," M.C. responded.

"I do not foresee today," H.L. said. "Agreed?"

M.C. nodded.

J.R. blew out a plume of cigarette smoke. "Yes."

"What is the plan for stress on the judges and lawyers?" H.L. asked.

"He's the plan." J.R. jutted his chin at the middle T.V. screen. A news show focused on one of the judges from the United States as he stepped out of a black sedan and was immediately surrounded by U.S. marshals and ITT security. Judge Kent Devlin was tall, lean, and fit. Gray hair at his temples, on an otherwise dark head of hair, gave him a distinguished look. His face remained calm, giving no indication that he heard the crowd's yells, though screams of "*executioner*" were captured on the news audio feed.

"What will happen to Judge Devlin?" H.L. asked with a smile.

"We're starting with our plan to pressure families of ITT participants. McLean, Virginia. This morning, Doctor Patricia Devlin will leave their home and drive to her office where she does whatever dermatologists do to wealthy women for a shitload of money." J.R. paused as he lit a fresh cigarette off of one that he had smoked to the filter. "Dr. Devlin will not make it there. Maximovists will leave a simple, to-the-point love note with her body. *I am Maximov. Stop ITT Proceedings.*"

"Of course, her murder will not stop the proceedings," M.C. interjected, a gleam of enjoyment visible in his blue eyes. "But we'll be getting closer to that goal. For now, an alternate judge will fill Judge Devlin's role if he is too grief-stricken to proceed. Her death, will, however, cause stress and among the other judges and lawyers. It will also ratchet up the chaos factor."

As the T.V. showed Judge Devlin disappearing inside the stately building, H.L.'s palms tingled with excitement. He glanced at J.R. and M.C. Their eyes were trained on him.

"Should I give the go order for the demise of Doctor Devlin?" J.R. asked.

H.L. nodded. "Yes. Absolutely. The public show?"

"We've ruled out an interior attack," J.R. replied, exhaling a fresh plume of smoke. As always, his matter-of-fact tone suggested he was discussing an agenda for an ordinary business meeting. Which he was, as they were in the business of creating chaos and terror, measured by blood and horror and the amount of economic disruption they caused. "Security is too effective on the inside of the building and, given the ban on cameras inside, exposure would be insufficient. Capitalizing on the crowds on the sidewalks, the narrow walkway between barricades that the judges and lawyers are using, and the placement of the media cameras, we've settled upon two possibilities—bombs and snipers. We're ready to implement either on my go order."

"Any particular target?" H.L. asked.

"Judges and lawyers would be best, but we don't need to be too selective at this point." J.R. shrugged. "Collateral damage is inevitable, no matter who we hit." He looked at the monitors as he spoke. "That being said, any of the American judges would be a home run."

"At this stage, a bomb will create the most chaos. Save sniper attacks for later, when it may become our only option," M.C. said.

"Then let's go with a bomb," H.L. said, his eyes on the left TV screen, which showed Samantha Dixon Fairfax's arrival. After yesterday's proceedings, she'd become the media darling.

Leading a team beset by tragedy, she was well educated and unafraid to be vocal and opinionated. She also had a beautiful, all-American look with which the public identified. In the proceedings, she continued to underscore the doubts that her predecessor, Stanley Morgan, had regarding the evidence, and the media caught wind of that theme in last night's news reports.

As she stepped out of a dark sedan, her blonde hair caught what little sunlight the morning offered. Their source had told them that Black Raven Private Security Contractors had taken over security for the Amicus team, compliments of Fairfax's grandfather, Samuel Dixon. H.L. knew that Black Raven had become synonymous worldwide with a simple message: "Don't fuck with us." For this job, Black Raven wasn't using subtlety. Fairfax was immediately surrounded by a four-man team of security personnel, their dark overcoats hanging loosely over their business suits and, no doubt, weapons. Security in place, Fairfax was concealed by a wall of flesh and brawn and barely visible to the cameras.

"Man to Fairfax's immediate left," M.C. said. "Black overcoat. Sunglasses. Taller than the others."

H.L. glanced at the man who walked step in step with her. Jaw set, with barely an inch between his side and Fairfax's arm, he was glancing at the crowd. "Yes?"

"Not just a bodyguard. Our sources indicate some

interesting intel on this one. Jesus Hernandez. A partner at Black Raven," M.C. said. "It's noteworthy that he's on site. He is well known in the world of private security contractors. Brilliant. His reputation is a leader, a strategist, and a big part of why the company is so successful. Had his own company that thrived in the Middle East after September 11, 2001. Joined forces with Sebastian Connelly at that time. He has high profile clients, Samuel Dixon, grandfather of the new chief Amicus Curiae counsel for the U.S. being one.

"Hernandez isn't typically front and center on jobs. From what I know, his job in recent years has been running the company and being a behind-the-scenes cleaner for some of the trickier situations they've gotten into."

"He should be sending us a thank you note for all the business we've created for them," J.R. said.

H.L chuckled. "I doubt one is in the mail, given that no one knows of our existence."

"We need to watch him," M.C. said.

Detecting unease, H.L glanced at M.C. "Why?"

"I'm now getting inside intel from the joint task force that the ITT countries have looking for Maximov," M.C. said. "The task force has integrated some of the more credible bounty hunters that are on the search for Maximov. Overnight I learned that Black Raven has joined the bounty hunt."

J.R. gave a low whistle, grinding his cigarette into the ashtray and for once not lighting another.

"Who is paying Black Raven?" H.L. asked.

"None other than Samuel Dixon," M.C. answered. "I've long thought that the task force is a loose cannon and with Black Raven on the hunt, even more so. Black Raven is unencumbered by governmental allegiances and red tape that have slowed the task force. They're sleek, efficient, and have the capabilities of a SEAL team, with the best analytical brain power in the world behind them."

M.C. shifted in his seat. "Richard Barrows works with them. Yes, *the* Richard Barrows. Creator of the most sophisticated cyber data gathering and assimilation technology in the world, working for a company that is known to have cyber hacking capabilities that rivals the best intelligence agencies. All of this means we have to keep them on our radar. Having Hernandez"— his eyes focused on the camera as Samantha Dixon Fairfax and her entourage slipped inside—"on the inside of those proceedings and privy to ITT information is also something to concern us."

"Who says he's privy to ITT information?" H.L. asked. "Black Raven is providing security services. They're not participants."

"And he'll be in the proceedings, day after day. Trust me, he'll be getting intel from the ITT communications. Plus, Black Raven penetrates data systems. That's how they operate. Their analytic and investigative department is based upon hacking technology," M.C. said, his tone admiring. "Their agents in the field have direct access to some of the best intel in the world, gathered by world class hackers."

"Stay on top of it," H.L. said, M.C.'s unease infecting him with a niggling bit of concern. When M.C. nodded, he continued. "Any complications arising from Morgan's death or the cyanide poisoning?"

"No," J.R. replied, lighting another cigarette.

"The Boulevard Saint-Germain bombing?"

J.R. drew a deep drag on the cigarette, then exhaled. "Nothing we need to worry about." The man's gentle brown eyes were steady and focused on him. "You should know that at this point, my go order requires six hours to reach zero. Do I have your approval for a bomb this afternoon?"

A rush of excitement ran through him. In their world, zero meant show time. Impact. Bombs exploding. Fear escalating. He asked, "Terror quotient?"

J.R. gave a humorless smile. "On scene, the usual pandemonium."

"Off scene?"

"Given the nature of the ITT proceedings, and the media coverage that's already in place," M.C. said, "we anticipate worldwide repercussions."

"Give the go order," H.L. instructed, reaching for his overcoat and umbrella. A few minutes later, looking forward to the day's ITT proceedings, he started his slow, leisurely walk to the Palais de Justice.

Chapter Nine

"You've never been to a Maximov training camp, have you?" Robert Brier, lead defense counsel for the United States, asked the accused, Alain Duvall. His voice boomed through the large courtroom where the ITT trial was taking place. The lawyers from the defense teams of each country had pooled their representation of all the accused. Brier was questioning Duvall, the twenty-three year old alleged mastermind behind the grisly bombings on the Paris metro that had taken place in April the year before.

An imposing man, Brier had silver-gray hair and brownish-green eyes. He was no taller than Sam, but what he lacked in height he more than made up in muscle, brawn, and bravado. He'd made a name, and fortune, representing criminal defendants in trials that garnered worldwide attention. Over the last two decades, that meant terrorists. This ITT case, spotlighted by the Klieg lights of the world stage, would cement his reputation as the go-to attorney for every kingpin, every drug lord, and every terrorist in the free and not-so-free world.

"Objection," four voices called before Duvall could answer, the tone of the speakers indignant.

Samantha ground her teeth in frustration as the lawyers readied themselves for argument. Glancing at her watch, she saw that it was 3:30. Precious little was getting accomplished on day three of the proceedings, making day three no different than days one and two. Rustling papers accompanied creaking chairs as members of the prosecution teams rose to their feet and headed to the podium shared by the prosecutors.

The courtroom was designed for proceedings with multi-judge panels, numerous advocates with interests in the cases, and large audiences of interested parties, media, and the general public. Sixteen black-robed judges, four from each country, sat in the front of the room on a dais in high-back, leather chairs at a crescent-shaped, wood-paneled table. Three judges from each country were voting judges. An alternate judge from each country was present in the event one of the three needed to step down. All the judges had a place on the dais. Ten votes were required for a verdict. Only nine were required for a mistrial.

Law clerks, secretaries, stenographers, and translators sat in front of the judges at a lower table. In front of that crescent-shaped table was the witness chair and three podiums, one each for the prosecution, defense, and Amicus teams. The lawyers sat at four long tables that each seated sixteen, one table for each country. Surrounding the proceedings on three sides was a two-story gallery, where media, security, and politicians from each country sat. It felt like the Romans were watching the gladiators in the arena.

Movement to Samantha's right, in the gallery, caught her eye as onlookers shifted in their seats. A man wearing press credentials stood and walked out.

Zeus, sitting in row three of the gallery and two seats down from the now-vacant seat, gave her a barely perceptible nod when her eyes rested on him. He'd handed his overcoat to one of the agents who stayed outside of the proceeding, the agent who was the designated keeper of the overcoats. Zeus had also removed the jacket of his charcoal gray suit. His white dress shirt would have looked ordinary on most men. On him, the crisp white of the shirt, stark next to the burgundy necktie, was a marked contrast to his olive skin, black hair, and dark eyes. The fitted shirt showed off his broad shoulders and chest.

Brain-fueled logic had Samantha keeping their exchanges cool and impersonal, yet logic and self-preservation instincts could only do so much. Proximity to him, virtually twenty-four seven, had her wanting to touch where his chest met his neck with her lips. She remembered curling into him, flesh to flesh, the feel of his large arms holding her close, and the delicious male scent of his skin in the hollow of his throat.

Acknowledgement that his eyes were on her was about the extent of their communication since the wee hours of Tuesday morning and the bombshell he'd dropped.

"I'm divorced. My marriage didn't work."

In the intervening day and a half, he'd spoken few words directly to her, and most of those had been related to his job, which was her security. *"Here's your custom-fitted vest. Wear it. Should fit under your clothes."* He'd given her a soft, guiding touch on her shoulder as they departed the safe house. *"Second car. When we arrive, step out. The team will surround you. Walk. I'll be your shadow."*

On a break in the proceedings at midday on Tuesday, he'd stopped her as she headed into the bathroom, placing an impersonal hand on her upper arm. He'd given the team a nod and told them to search it, before muttering, *"Wait, Sam. My men will clear it, then I go in with you."* At least she'd been able to pee with the stall door closed and he'd sent the other team members out.

After she'd washed her hands at the sink, he'd watched her open a pack of antacids and pop three into her mouth. *"You okay? You're barely eating, and most of what you eat is crap."*

She'd shrugged off his comment as she chewed and swallowed the chalky tablets.

Undeterred, he had continued with, *"I need to know if you're not feeling well. We have medics here, with a doctor. I can call him."*

Her answer had been, *"No, I feel fine, thank you, and you can spare me the commentary on the quality of food I eat."*

The left side of his lips had lifted in that almost way of smiling that he had. Almost, but not quite, and the twitch was gone as soon as it materialized. No light ever made it to his eyes. He was either the most guarded man she'd ever met, or he didn't actually feel a thing. He was exactly as he'd been in the first few days that he'd been on duty with her and her grandfather. Full of intense, focused awareness, and seemingly impervious to emotion.

When her heel stuck on a crack in the pavement as they'd departed ITT proceedings the evening before, he steadied her by gripping her forearm. *"You need to wear shoes that are more practical. Won't be able to run in high heels, if necessary."*

Business-like. That was how she wanted it between them, and that's what Zeus was giving her. He'd gotten her keep-your-distance message when she shut the door on him. He knew her well enough to know that her boundaries were not lines drawn in sand. Rather, her boundaries were impenetrable fences, with glistening razor wire at the top. When she drew a line, she meant stay-the-hell on the other side of it.

They both had enough work to keep them busy. While sitting in the gallery, his iPad was open. Cameras and phones were not permitted by the general public in the courtroom, but there were so many exceptions to the rule everyone in the proceeding seemed have ready access to phones and internet. All the lawyers and their aides used phones, tablets, and laptops that were scanned each morning. While photographs were prohibited, the media had internet access for real-time reporting of the proceeding.

Sanctioned security teams were allowed to carry tablets that had been scanned. They also were allowed to wear communication devices and carry firearms. Black Raven was a sanctioned security team. As the ITT proceeding marched forward at a slug's pace, Sam guessed that Zeus was making use of his time, communicating with other agents via text message and email. As her grandfather had requested, Zeus's eyes were on her, but Zeus was also orchestrating the bounty hunt for Maximov.

God knew he had enough time to multitask while sitting in the ITT proceedings, because precious little was getting done.

As Zeus's eyes drifted to the iPad on his lap, Sam refocused on the proceedings. Alain Duvall. Skinny. French citizen. Black hair. Dark brown eyes that expressed no remorse for the 130 people he'd murdered and the hundreds others he had injured. Crude tattoos crept up his neck, above the white-collar of his shirt. Over his Adam's apple were the words, *Je Suis Maximov*.

I am Maximov.

This young man was not Maximov. Although no one was certain as to Maximov's appearance or age, intelligence agencies believed the terrorist to be in his mid-50's.

Duvall had been in the witness chair for two and a half hours, apparently long enough to learn that there was no need to answer questions immediately, because most questions drew objections. Objections meant arguments, and rulings took time. As the lawyers gathered at the podiums and readied themselves for argument regarding the pending question—whether Duvall had ever been to a Maximov training camp—hatred oozed from Duvall's eyes, becoming more intense as he stared at the lawyers. His lips parted in a sickening, sarcastic smile. He was enjoying the show.

"Before we proceed with the argument regarding objections to Defense Counsel Briers' pending question," said Judge O'Connor, Chief ITT Judge for the United States, "with the indulgence of the other judges I'd like to ask Amicus counsel for the U.S. to provide a short statement of evidence against Mr. Duvall."

As the other judges of the panel nodded, Samantha stood, bringing her iPad with her to the podium in the sudden, hushed silence of the courtroom. The prosecution teams had asked very little of Duvall, instead choosing to rest on stipulated evidence. Samantha appreciated Judge O'Connor's effort to put clarity into the trial record.

Her file for Duvall was open as she placed the iPad in front of her. She focused on the panel of sixteen judges. Thirteen men. Three women—alternate U.S. Judge Amanda Whitsell, French Judge Bridgette Tambour, British Judge Melinda Glendin. All the judges were members of the judiciary of their own country, with varying degrees of experience. Bronze nameplates identified the judges, but they all wore the same black robes.

One day, Samantha thought. *One day, I'll be the one in the robe.*

For now, though, she relished the opportunity to be a lawyer in front of so many esteemed jurists. Having been a practicing attorney working closely with Stanley Morgan for the last five years, Sam had several appellate arguments under her belt. Those had been before three-judge panels. She also had litigated a few trials. Facing sixteen judges at one time was a new experience for her.

Daunting? Perhaps. She'd have loved working through this trial with Stanley Morgan's wealth of experience and quiet guidance. God, she missed him. On the other hand, she could handle it. Chin up, shoulders squared, she rested her palms on the corners of the podium and leaned slightly towards the mic as she recounted the most important evidence they had on Duvall.

"Evidence establishes that Mr. Duvall was a participant—if not the ringleader—in a coordinated, timed explosive attack on the Paris metro."

"Continue." Judge O'Connor, a black man with short, close-cropped curly dark hair that was peppered with gray, nodded. When not an ITT judge, he sat on the United States Second Circuit Court of Appeal. He'd been a participant in key rulings regarding the Patriot Act and other post-911 efforts by Congress to combat terrorism. Widely known as President Cameron's best friend and confidante, he was on the short list for the next appointment to the U.S. Supreme Court.

"Six bombs were carried in backpacks onto five trains and left there. Between 8:45 and 9:00 a.m., five of the bombs detonated. Authorities suspect that six individuals carried the bombs on the trains. Of the suspected six bomb carriers, only Mr. Duvall and Mr. Tombeau have been apprehended." She drew a breath. "Neither has been cooperative with the authorities, though Mr. Tombeau has provided more helpful information than Mr. Duvall."

"Will Mr. Tombeau testify, or are we proceeding on stipulation with him?" Judge O'Connor asked.

It was a good question, as the vast bulk of ITT evidence was being entered into the record by stipulation, without live witnesses. "He is testifying following the testimony of Duvall."

"What led investigators to Mr. Duvall?" Judge O'Connor

asked.

"Initially he was a suspect because he'd been on the terrorist watch list of French authorities prior to the event due to involvement in anti-government rallies. As the investigation ensued, it was discovered that metro station cameras caught him the morning of the attack and authorities rounded him up for questioning."

"In preliminary proceedings, has he admitted any involvement in the crime?" Judge O'Connor asked.

"He denied involvement, but Mr. Tombeau implicated him. He has not provided any information regarding motive, other than to say the crime was done on behalf of Maximov-in-Exile." Samantha glanced at her iPad, swiping through the pages of files, before refocusing on the judges. "However, considering the evidentiary conclusions we have from the French investigative forces, Mr. Duvall's personal involvement in the metro bombing is without question."

"Why is he considered a leader?" Judge O'Connor asked.

"The one backpack bomb that did not detonate contained explosive Goma-2 ECO, a powerful explosive used by Oticatech, a Spanish mining company. Traces of the same explosive were found in each of the trains where the backpack bombs detonated. French and Spanish investigators apprehended Paulo Barreca, a miner who stole the explosive material. He is in custody and is on the trial schedule to testify after Tombeau. Though we do not have the reports themselves, French investigators have reported that Mr. Barreca, the miner, identified Mr. Duvall as the negotiator of the purchase."

"What is the evidence establishing a link between Mr. Duvall's terrorist cell and Maximov, if any?"

"French Investigative forces have linked Duvall with Maximov."

"Based upon?" Judge O'Connor asked.

Great question. Correct answer? Hell if she knew. Which she most definitely was not going to say, because her job—and decorum—demanded more diplomacy. "Your honor, Mr. Duvall declares he was operating on behalf of Maximov-in-Exile. While French investigative forces may have more data that establishes an affirmative link, that data has not been produced to the ITT—"

Judge O'Connor interrupted her with, "Yes, counselor." The interruption meant, *enough said.* "I'm aware of yesterday morning's ruling of the ITT that the data produced by the French was sufficient." His voice reflected a twinge of sarcasm.

He had dissented from the ruling. Ten judges of the twelve-judge panel had voted in favor, though, so the ruling stood as the law of the proceeding. In a private conversation with Samantha, Judge O'Connor had predicted that the ruling had the potential to cripple the proceedings, because each country would now claim that their investigative analyses were proprietary and did not need to be produced.

Which meant they had diddlysquat to connect Maximov or any other large, established terrorist organization to Duvall's decision to plant bombs on the Paris metro in busy rush hour traffic on a workday. They didn't even know how Duvall had scored the Euros that he had used to purchase the Goma-2 ECO.

Countries of the ITT had agreed to harsh terms of imprisonment for anyone convicted of terrorist acts, but they'd also agreed to no torture. The Americans had agreed to the no-torture condition unwillingly.

What was playing out before the ITT was a lesson in the ineffectiveness of simple questions posed to a recalcitrant witness. Trial rights set forth in the U.S. Constitution were not applicable to the ITT proceedings, so Duvall didn't have the option of staying silent based upon the Fifth Amendment right against self -incrimination.

Duvall was happy to talk. Problem was, he wasn't talking about anything helpful and his comments typically weren't responsive to the questions that were asked.

Judge O'Connor nodded. "Thank you, Ms. Fairfax. The question that is pending to the witness, posed by defense counsel Brier, is 'You've never been to a Maximov training camp, have you?'" The judge's sharp eyes focused on the prosecutors. "Counselors, present your arguments. On behalf of the court, I admonish you to be brief."

"The question is irrelevant, leading, and pointless," Daniel Beaumont, the lead prosecutor from France argued, in perfect English, the official language of the proceedings. For those who couldn't speak English, translation was provided through earpieces. "Presence at a Maximov training camp is not a prerequisite for working with the organization. The insinuation defense counsel is making is preposterous. We know Duvall was operating on behalf of Maximov-in-Exile, whether he went to one of their training camps or not."

"You know that," Brier retorted, his tone indignant and loud as he turned from the microphone to face the prosecution podium and the lawyers gathered there. "We know no such thing, because the French teams have not produced their investigative materials. If these ITT proceedings are designed to determine who is truly behind the terrorist acts that are at issue, we must have access to your investigative materials."

"That issue has been decided by the court." Beaumont's face was mottled. He was almost yelling.

"I'm just trying to establish a fact," Brier said.

"Which you may do without asking leading questions," Beaumont retorted, his tone imperious and high-handed.

"You don't get to tell me what to do, or how to ask my questions," Brier snapped. "There is no rule against leading questions in ITT proceedings. As a matter of fact, the Rules of Practice and Procedure explicitly permit leading questions."

The resonating sound of a wooden gavel snapping hard onto marble silenced the bickering attorneys. "Counsel, you must address the court," said Judge Jean-Paul Ducaisse, the chief judge from France, and the wielder of the gavel. In ITT proceedings, the lead judge from the forum country was the decision maker for evidentiary and procedural questions. "Stop arguing amongst yourselves."

"Your honors." The lead prosecutor from the United States, Benjamin McGavin, was short, chunky, and soft-spoken. He reached for the microphone and pulled it down so that his voice would carry through it. "While there is no rule against leading questions in ITT proceedings, the taking of evidence should have some basic decorum. Questions as conclusory as those asked by defense counsel are a waste of time. We're midway through the week that was allocated to the French proceedings and not nearly halfway through the business of the court for France."

An instant message blipped on Sam's iPad as she stood at the podium for Amicus counsel, ready to break into the argument if needed. The IM said, *I've got access to the French investigative materials if you want it. All their backup. Z.*

No doubt Z was Zeus, and his capability of sending a private instant message to an iPad that was supposedly purposed only for ITT files and ITT communications was something new and disturbing. But what was more disturbing was the content of his message.

Without turning to look back at him, she reached for the iPad, moved her cursor to the reply option, and typed quickly, *Seriously? B.R. hacked into the French investigative files? That's a felony. And by the way, how the hell did you manage that?* She pressed enter, zinging her IM to him.

"Objection sustained," Judge Ducaisse said. "Rephrase your question, Mr. Brier."

"Your honor," Brier interjected, "I'd like to point out to the court that the ruling is not consistent with the ITT Rules of Practice and Procedure. Rule 12.2 (a)(2) provides that leading questions are permissible for securing background information."

Zeus's responsive IM appeared on her screen. *Don't ask how. Just know I have it. And it isn't a felony if you don't get caught. Trees falling in woods. Silent, unless someone is there. Yours if you want it.*

Samantha tore her eyes from Zeus's instant message in time to see Judge Ducaisse give Brier a curt nod. "Objection noted. Rephrase your question, counsel."

"I'd also like to point out that this proceeding is rapidly devolving into a travesty of justice," Brier said, "becoming closer to the witch hunt label the press is—"

Another gavel snap silenced Brier. "You may save your argument, and your opinion of this proceeding, for closing argument in Brussels. For now, we are in examination mode. Do you have any other question of Mr. Duvall?"

"No, your honor."

"Any other questions from the defense teams?" Judge Ducaisse asked.

"No, your honor," the lead defense attorney from France said. "The prosecution has proved nothing through the witness. No further questions are necessary."

After the lead defense attorneys from Colombia and the U.K. indicated they had no questions, Judge Ducaisse said, "Amicus teams?"

As usual, the Amicus teams from the other countries waived their questions. Samantha was the only Amicus counsel at the podium, even though France, England, and Columbia each had their own teams. No one but the U.S. team was willing to take the lead this early in the proceedings and given that Eric's death by cyanide was now public, she couldn't say that she blamed them for hanging back. There was plenty enough work to do in the background.

Zeus's cavalier admission that he had hacked into the files, and his offer of them to her, raised a sea of professional and ethical questions. It would have been damn nice to have the French materials before examining Duvall, but she couldn't very well use something that had not been ruled into evidence to formulate her questions.

Could she?

She'd work her mind around that dilemma later. She shook her head, clearing her thoughts as she leaned into the podium and looked into Alain Duvall's dark brown eyes, consciously softening her expression to one that imparted a message of interest and receptiveness.

You can talk to me.

Chapter Ten

"Mr. Duvall, I have just a few questions for you." Samantha focused on Duvall with tunnel vision, as though he was the only person in the room. "First, would you tell me why you have the tattoo that is on your neck?"

Since his neck was covered with multiple symbols and words, she lifted her chin and gestured with her finger on her own neck to the tender area over her vocal cards.

As his eyes followed her gesture with a leer that almost sickened her, she clarified, "I'm referring to the tattoo that is to the right of the swastika. The one that says '*Je Suis Maximov.*' Am I reading that correctly?"

Duvall gave her a nod. In English, he replied, "Yes. You've read it accurately. *Je. Suis* Maximov. I am Maximov." His dark eyes held hers with a mix of venom and scorn.

The preposterousness of such a bald claim could have been humorous, but for the fact that around the world there were many men and women who had the same tattoo on their necks, in precisely the same spot. The universal claim was translated into multiple languages on untold millions of people in search of a cause.

German—*Ich bin Maximov.*

Spanish—*Soy Maximov.*

Italian—*Sono Maximov.*

English—*I am Maximov.*

Like peace signs and smiley faces, the statement had become ubiquitous. Unlike peace signs and smiley faces, the popularity of the sentiment that it stood for—anarchy at all costs—was not uplifting. Rather, it had turned the civilized world into a victim, because it wasn't just inscribed on necks and left there.

It was painted in blood at crime scenes. Social media statements of credit for bombings contained the battle cry. While mourners wept for the loss of loved ones, the world of people who claimed to be Maximov tattooed that identity on their skin to celebrate the anarchy they created.

I am Maximov.

A drumbeat of hatred and death, the oft-repeated statement was an epidemic, perpetuated and spread by social media outlets. It was robbing the world of peace and hope. It was no wonder the world was desperate for this ITT proceeding to end the existence of Maximov.

But there needs to be concrete evidence that Maximov was involved. Something more than supposition by the French investigative team and the bold claim of a thug.

"You do not mean that literally, do you?"

"Yes. I do."

"What is the name on your birth certificate?"

"My birth certificate is in evidence." He pursed his lips together and furrowed his brow. Sarcasm flooded his eyes. "Surely you can read it."

A prosecutor stood up. "Your honors, if it would save time, we will stipulate that this man is not Andre Maximov. The witness is correct. His birth certificate is in the record and the name on it is Alain Duvall."

"Why is that tattooed on your neck?"

He shrugged. "I believe in the Maximov cause."

"What is it?"

He shook his head, arched an eyebrow, and snickered. "What do you mean? Don't you know it?"

She smiled gently at him, trying to give the impression that she appreciated his great wit and her lifelong goal was to have a meaningful conversation with him. She wanted him to believe that she was enjoying her time with him. "I'm pretty sure I do, but I want to know your understanding of it."

"The Maximov-in-Exile organization is led by Andre Maximov. It was originally formed to seek revenge for the destruction of Praptan, Chalinda as a result of the meltdown at the Chalinda Nuclear Power Plant. It now serves as a tool against government oppression."

Well, at least he knew that much. "When did the meltdown occur?"

Silence.

She shrugged. "I forget dates as well. Does 1991 sound correct to you?" She chose a date before the twenty-three year old was born. Not knowing whether he was a history buff, she was gambling on the premise that dates before his birth blended together into ancient history.

He nodded. "If you say so."

"It isn't for me to say. We need your testimony, Mr. Duvall." She put on her best trust me face, and said, "I need to know if 1991 sounds correct to you. Did the nuclear disaster at the Chalinda Nuclear Power Plant occur in 1991?"

The nuclear disaster occurred in 1986. Samantha was trying to establish that Duvall had no idea of when the event occurred.

Behind her, from the direction of where the teams from France were sitting, she heard a lawyer groan, no doubt a prosecutor. There was nothing objectionable in her question though, so the restless lawyer remained silent.

"I'm not sure of the exact date," Duvall answered. *Well, he may have been caught red-handed, but he wasn't a total fool.*

An IM appeared on her screen from Abe, her second chair counsel. Together she and Abe had developed her questions for Duvall, and he was prompting her with a reminder. *Looks like a good time to try the cause/contact/connection questions. Now, rather than later.*

She gave a slight nod over her left shoulder, in Abe's direction. She agreed with him. "Why do you believe in the Maximov cause?"

Before answering, Duvall sneered. The right side of his upper lip drew up so high, Sam could see his slightly yellowed teeth. "Because governments are oppressive tools of the rich."

"Who is your contact in the Maximov organization?"

"He has no name."

"What does he look like?"

"I've never seen him. No one ever sees the leaders. Surely you know that."

Well, that was the rumor. Someone had to see the leaders. "Mr. Duvall, has defense counsel informed you that if you give this court helpful information your sentence will be mitigated?"

"Yes."

Samantha leaned forward on the podium, capturing his gaze. "Would you like to tell the court the identity of the people with whom you worked in the metro bombings?"

"No."

"Would you like to tell the court how you came into possession of Euros with which you paid for the Goma-2 ECO?"

"No."

"Would you like to tell me how the killing of innocent people, people who are simply using the metro station to go about their normal business, relates to the Maximov cause?"

"No."

She narrowed her eyes. "Can you?"

"Of course I can."

"Then do it."

Duvall smiled, with a gleam of humor in his eyes. "No."

Judge O'Connor leaned forward in his seat. His eyes were trained on Samantha in a manner that indicated his focused attention was on her. He gave her a slow headshake, but he remained silent. She could guess what the headshake meant and she bet she was going to hear it from him later. She refocused on Duvall.

"If you're convicted, your sentence in Ultimate Exile is potentially for a fixed term of 100 years. For each piece of helpful information you provide to the court, years will be subtracted. Do you understand that?"

"Yes."

"Do you understand that because you have provided no helpful information," she paused, "so far your sentence—from which there is no appeal and no possibility for release—remains at 100 years?"

"Yes."

"I will ask you one more time. Would you please explain how the metro bombing that you orchestrated relates to the Maximov cause?"

"No."

Two U.S. marshals entered the room through a door behind the judges. Their faces grim, they stepped up to the dais. One walked to Judge Ducaisse, another to Judge Devlin. A few words were exchanged.

Judge Ducaisse slammed the gavel on marble. "Let's take a fifteen-minute recess."

With a flurry of black robes, the judges exited the courtroom. Sam turned from the podium and walked straight to the gallery, in the direction of Zeus. He stood and walked into the aisle, meeting her at the railing, his dark eyes dead serious.

He opened his mouth to speak, but she didn't give him the chance. "You cannot be breaking into the investigative records of foreign countries," she said in a low voice so no one overheard her. "You were here for yesterday's ruling. You know the judges have not ordered the production of those records to the ITT. If the French think the Americans are breaking into their records, they'll—"

He shook his head, his eyes dark and cold. "The French will never know, unless you tell them. And even then, I'll deny it."

"You'll lie?"

"No. I'm getting the job done and I'm not using the data for anything other than accomplishing my objective. As with all Black Raven jobs, it boils down to a simple choice. We can play by the rules others have created, and possibly fail." Disdain flashed in his eyes, but otherwise his expression gave no indication of how little he thought of the failure option. "Or we can create our own rules and pull in as much data as possible, analyze it, and use it if we need to. The data's there for the taking—"

"Only by world-class cyber-theft."

He shrugged. "It isn't as complicated as you think. In protecting the Amicus team, and in the search for Maximov, I choose to create a world with my own rules."

"It isn't a matter of choice for me. I'm working in parameters where ethics and integrity dictate my actions, and last I checked..." She drew a deep breath. "Lying isn't a permissible option."

A slight eyebrow arch and a twitch at the left corner of his mouth let her knew what he thought of ethics and integrity. "In my world," he said, his eyes scanning the room before his gaze returned to hers, "ethics and integrity mean get the job done."

"We're not operating in your world, and the ITT isn't operating with the convenience of such a result-oriented approach."

"So you say."

"Countries have agreed upon the procedure the ITT has implemented, and—"

"We can continue the discussion later."

"Don't interrupt me. And it's an argument, not a discussion," she said.

The cold look in his eyes shifted to something different. He touched his hand to his ear, listened for a second, before refocusing his attention on her. "Right now we've got bigger problems."

Heart in her throat, she braced for more bad news. "What?"

"Judge Devlin's wife was murdered. Earlier today. Someone left a note with her body claiming to be Maximov. They're demanding that ITT proceedings be stopped."

"Oh, dear God," she said, struggling against the breath-stealing panic that stole her voice.

"News just broke, right as the marshals came into the room."

Her gut twisted with fear. "They're going after our families?"

Zeus's curt nod sent shock waves down her spine. "We're stepping up security at your grandfather's house. And working with the security team that provides protection for your fiancé, as well as the family members of your team. Anyone else?"

Fiancé?

It took her a second to realize he was talking about Justin.

Who was not yet her fiancé, but that didn't matter for this purpose. The media had painted him as almost at the on-bended-knee stage with her, which was accurate. Some reports indicated he had already proposed, and they were waiting until after the ITT proceedings to announce their engagement. Neither of them had attempted to dispel the reports. If a terrorist wanted to kill someone close to her, second to her grandfather, Justin was as close as anyone.

"No," she said. "That's it."

Judge Ducaisse stepped back into the proceedings and slammed his gavel down for attention.

Sam turned from Zeus and rejoined Abe and Charles at the table, standing at attention while the room quieted. Without the other judges of the ITT panel flanking him, Judge Ducaisse seemed, somehow, diminished in power—a lone, middle-aged man in a black robe with a worried expression on his face. The chatter in the room ebbed slower than usual, because the bad news was being disseminated in emails and instant messages. Some of the lawyers were already on their phones.

"We are in recess for the remainder of the day," Judge Ducaisse said. "Proceedings will begin tomorrow at the usual time." He paused, as though considering whether to say more. The grave expression in his eyes was enough for everyone in the room. No more would be said until later. He nodded, then departed.

Zeus opened the gate on the railing, and was at Sam's side in a matter of seconds. "Let's go."

With those words, she knew to scoop her materials into her briefcase, turn, and walk. If she delayed, a firm hand on her arm would pull her along and her iPad with its sensitive data would catch up to her later. She preferred to have it with her.

One Black Raven agent helped her into her overcoat, while another reached for her briefcase. Zeus and his agents escorted her and her team members out into the day that was only marginally brighter than it had been in the morning.

They had about fifty yards to walk through the courtyard, between the wide doors of the courthouse and the line of cars that waited for the judges and the lawyers.

"Hell," Zeus muttered.

"What?" she asked.

"Cars are pulling in and blocking the second lane," he was saying into his mic. He wasn't talking to her, but he was answering her question anyway. "We need two lanes. One for people to step in," Zeus said into his mic, "another to drive away. Procedure was followed yesterday. What, for fuck's sake, are they doing today? There are now two lanes of virtually parked cars. Our cars are wedged into the lane that can't get out."

His hand gripped her arm, slowing her as he and his agents assessed the situation. They were ten yards out from the cars, between barricades of screaming protestors, with a crowd of lawyers, clerks, and judges behind them.

"This is how the ITT and the French military steps up security? You got to be kidding. Fucking idiots. We'll be goddamn sitting ducks while we wait for cars to move."

Five yards out from the cars, almost blocked from view by Zeus, Samantha got a glimpse of Judge O'Connor getting into a car with his security team. One of the French judges climbed into a car behind him.

Zeus, gripping her left arm, pulled her close, and sped up his pace. "Teams. Plan B. Drivers. Get in your cars. Move when you can. Sam—walk fast."

Behind the barricades, bystanders were yelling, "*Witch. Hunt. Witch. Hunt. Witch. Hunt.*" Inside the barricades, there was stoic calmness, yet the urgency in Zeus's short orders was contagious. Still, from what Sam could tell with the partial glimpses that she had of the judges, lawyers, and security charged with escorting everyone to their cars, Black Raven seemed to be the only security team acting as though the situation was off kilter.

For Zeus, it was a fast walk. For her, it was a jog in five-inch heels and a tight pencil skirt. It didn't matter whether she could balance. He and the agent on her right each had strong hands on her arms and practically carried her along.

"Which car?" she asked.

"We're not."

He guided her down the sidewalk, to his right, past a black sedan as a driver climbed into it. The driver gave Zeus a curt nod as they passed. She recognized the driver as a Black Raven agent. She also recognized the next driver, and the next. All Black Raven agents.

"Drivers, proceed out as you can, when you can. Stay in your cars." Zeus said into his mic. His tone was calm, yet his eyes were grim as he scanned the crowd. "I repeat. Plan B. Walk away from this clusterfuck. Exit Ile de la Cite via Boulevard de Palais, or any clear way, cross the river at Pont St. Michel and head towards Boulevard Saint-Germain. Lambert and Axel, you copy?

Perimeter agents, meet us along the path. Start talking to me."

Even with the Black Raven cars ten yards behind them, Zeus didn't slow his pace or loosen his vice-like grip on her arm. "Drivers and all agents. Rendezvous points to be established when you manage to get the vehicles moving."

He glanced back quickly at the line of cars. Samantha barely heard the boom before he crushed her in his arms, pushing her to the ground and covering her body with his.

Chapter Eleven

Plan-fucking-B did not mean the client suffered injury instead of death. Neither option was acceptable.

She isn't moving.

"Sam, you okay?" Zeus said, in the split second post boom, post shrapnel whizzing past him, in the pause before pandemonium would erupt in the crowd. He'd cocooned her in his arms, his hands cradling her head, her body tucked under his. His lips were against her head, touching the soft, silky blonde strands. His elbows supported him and she was nestled against his chest, with his legs on either side of hers for support. Jenkins and Miles pressed against him, one on each side. The fourth agent on Sam's team, Brad Deal, was to the side of Miles.

They'd hold the position until Zeus decided it was time for them to move, based on his mental crapshoot of whether there'd be another bomb blast in the near vicinity.

But for the overcoats he and Sam both wore, the position he was in was classic for activities that had nothing to do with saving her life. Her pelvis was right below his. If they were naked, he'd be able to slip inside her with a few micro adjustments and one powerful stroke. Easily. He lifted his body a bit, giving her a few inches to breathe. Giving him the physical distance needed to fucking-well forget what it was like to do the things he'd dreamed of doing for seven long years.

"Zeus, you okay?" Ragno asked, in his ear.

The same type of chip that was embedded in Sam was also in his arm. This meant, unless there was interference with the signal, she knew his position, relative to Sam.

"Fine."

"Samantha?" Ragno asked.

"Sam?" He lifted his chest slightly, taking more of his weight on his elbows, then lifted his hand so he could use two fingers to feel the uneven pulse at her temple. Her skin felt sweaty and cold. Shock. "Blink once if you're alive," he muttered.

Her lashes fluttered.

"Great bedside manner, Hernandez. News shows were focused on the departure from the proceeding," Ragno continued. "The blast occurred about twenty yards behind you. Closest to the car of Columbian Judge Exekial Calante as he entered the vehicle. He and his security detail are down, as are onlookers in immediate vicinity, and throughout the crowd."

He listened, but his whole focus remained on Sam. "Sam? Open your eyes now, dammit." His heart was in his throat, where it had no business being. She couldn't be hurt. Stunned into silence, maybe, but not hurt. He'd acted fast, and Jenkins, Deal, and Miles had been in protective formation on the way down. "Answer me."

She lifted her chin. Wide, scared, clear green eyes looked into his. Her nod accompanied sudden, teeth-chattering, full-body trembling. Fear emanated off her with each shake, while relief coursed through him. "Fine. I'm f-f-fine." She drew a deep breath and lifted her arms. He thought she'd push him away. Instead, she gripped each of his biceps, holding on, and said, this time stronger, "Fine. I'm fine."

Brave. Courageous. The woman of his dreams was also brilliant, and someone as smart as Sam knew that this situation was horrifying. She was also trying hard to overcome her fear.

"Teams," he said, his eyes locked on hers. "Report."

"Sir, Agent Axel. Charles is fine. We were far back. Team is fine. We're down. Waiting on your order."

"Lambert?" Abe's team, led by Lambert, had been behind Zeus, closer to the blast.

"Yes, sir. We were ten steps behind you at detonation. Abe has an injury to an arm. A cut. Appears minor."

"Your team?"

"Tannen has something that looks like metal in his left thigh." A pause. "He says he can walk. Otherwise, minor scratches. Waiting on your order, sir."

The scent of Chanel No. 5 mingled with the smell of gunpowder, smoke, and her fear. The surreal, slow-mo action suddenly picked up speed, launching him into real time.

"One minute since detonation," Ragno said.

When in similar situations, Zeus had imagined he could smell the collective panic that was ready to erupt from the bystanders. This time he had no doubt. He breathed deeply, finding strength as spectators converged on the scene. People started screaming. Situations that were fearful to others drove calm logic for him, and now, as Sam's bodyguard and the leader of the protective detail for the Amicus team, there was only one logical course of action: get Sam and her team out of harm's way, away from the masses of people. Odds were most meant well.

It only took one, though, to kill.

Lifting his head, Zeus scanned the crowd. The worst was behind them, just past the Black Raven cars. Bodies and parts of bodies littered the street and sidewalk, which had become painted red in splashes and growing puddles. By the carnage, he knew some were dead. Those that could were stirring. A woman nearby cried in gulping sobs as she looked around with tears running through the blood on one half of her face. Some near him were on the ground. Others stood still, dazed. A man, five feet to his right, lay on the ground, moaning and clutching what was left of his tattered leg. Crimson blood oozed between his fingers.

Zeus did a quick inventory of the agents who were at the scene, assessing how many could be left behind to assist the injured and directing them to do so. "Ragno, reposition agents who can be spared from safe-house operations over here. Plenty of people need help."

Screams were building to crescendo, mingling with yells of excitement of those who came to help and those who came to gawk. Given the number of protestors in the crowd who had carried signs of hatred and support for the Maximov cause, he guessed more were there to gawk than help. High-pitched sirens cut through the sounds of pain and fear. There'd soon be pandemonium. Or worse. Time to roll the dice.

This one was in hands other than his. *Please God, don't let there be another fucking bomb. If there is one, make it far away from Sam.* "Teams. Fall out. Plan B. Now."

Jenkins, Deal, and Miles stood.

Zeus shifted to his side. As he moved, he shielded the side of Sam's face, using his right hand as a blinder from the people that surrounded them, while using his left hand to cover the cut that he now felt on his forehead. "Close your eyes. I'm carrying you out of here."

"No. I can walk," she said, with a firm headshake. She pushed his hand off her face as she used her other hand to lever herself off the ground. "Or run. I'm fine."

"We're in a scene from hell."

"I've seen bad sights."

"In pictures and evidence. You're in this one in real time, and I don't think you want to carry this with you for the rest of your fucking life. Close your eyes and relax. I'm carrying you."

"No, I'm walk—"

"Shut the hell up." An over-the-shoulder carry would work best for a run, but that would leave her too exposed. Whether there'd be a second and third explosion was still anyone's guess. Cradling her in his arms was the best way to protect her until they were a safe distance away. "Close your eyes. Arms around my neck. Head against my chest."

She did as ordered. Almost. Unfortunately, as she wrapped her arms around his neck, her eyes were open. Something in the distance snagged her attention. Following her gaze to a point a mere twenty-feet away, he saw a woman clutching what remained of a tattered, mangled arm.

"Eyes closed, dammit."

The very last bit of color drained from her face as she looked slightly above his eyes. Her body went limp as she passed out.

He'd known he was bleeding near his hairline. Sticky warmth trickled down his temple. Whether the foreign object remained in him was irrelevant to the task at hand. He doubted the injury was significant, but there was no time for assessment. He lifted Sam and got moving.

"Perimeter agents have three cars," Ragno said. "They're en route to the Pont au Change. Security forces are closing bridges to vehicular traffic. From what we can tell from camera feeds, crowds are shifting. Barricades are down. Get to the bridge as fast as you can to rendezvous with our cars."

"Understood," he said, weaving through people who were also running for the closest bridge off the island. His team was in step with him. Sam's legs were over his right arm, her shoulders at his left, with his forearm under her left armpit. Her head lolled back, eyes closed.

"A newsfeed just caught you," Ragno said. "It's quite an image. Jesus, Zeus. She looks dead."

"Call Samuel. Tell him she's fine. He'll have a fucking fi—"

"He's calling now. Okay, you and Samuel are patched together."

"Zeus?"

"She's fine, Samuel. The sight of blood got to her. Mine. Not hers. She has no injuries."

"It's dripping down your forehead," he said.

Great. The media must have zoomed in on them. "Minor scrape."

"Have Samantha call me when you get her situated. Make her do it. I'm damn tired of her silent treatment."

"You hired me to keep her safe. Not make her do things she doesn't want to do. If she doesn't want to call you, there isn't a goddamn thing I can do about that."

No fucking answer.

Zeus had learned from Ragno that Samuel repeatedly tried

to call Sam on Tuesday and Wednesday mornings. She wasn't returning his calls.

"He's gone," Ragno said. "At least he's smart enough not to bother a busy man for too long. Theresa has called headquarters."

Theresa was his ex. Ana's mother. "Call her back and update her. Agent Martell has probably alerted her, but make sure she understands what happened here and with Judge Devlin's wife. Tell her to keep Ana from watching television. This will be in the media cycle for a while." Glancing at Sam for a second, he saw that her eyes remained closed. "Tell Theresa I'll call her later."

"Will do. They closed the bridge to vehicles. You'll have to cross on foot. How are your legs holding up?"

"Fine," Zeus said, stepping into the street, dodging a group of ten or so people who had stopped in the middle of the sidewalk. "Just because I've mostly been in the office for the last few years, doesn't mean I'm not in shape. Tell me about our drivers and the cars on the scene."

"When you implemented Plan B, they each got in their cars a few seconds before detonation."

"And?"

"Our driver closest to the blast is down. Agent Pitts. Rear window blew from force of flying debris. Good thing no one from the Amicus team got in that car."

Fuck. "Extent of injuries?"

"Serious enough that Pitts will need a surgeon. Mostly limbs. No visible head injury. He managed to get face down on the front seat before the debris reached him."

"So much for bulletproof and bomb resistant vehicles," Zeus muttered, though he knew that true bomb resistance was hard to accomplish in a car, if not impossible. That was why he hadn't steered Sam into a car when his instinct told him that things were off. He'd felt that something was going to happen. He just hadn't known what, where, or when.

Sam stiffened. He looked down. *Shit.* Her eyes were open and on him for a second, before she squeezed them shut.

"Please stop. Put me down. I'm going to be sick." Eyes closed and watering, she clasped a hand over her mouth. She looked even paler than when she'd been in a dead faint.

He and the team stepped onto the bridge. He'd been to Paris before, on this exact bridge. A few times for work. Once for a honeymoon that should've never happened. He'd looked at the murky, green-gray water of the Seine River more times than he could count. With Sam in his arms, he knew this was the most important time he'd ever visit the city.

The wide expanse of the bridge, crowded with people running from a bomb blast that wasn't even a mile behind them, left them too exposed to stop so she could catch her breath and fight her nausea. "Lean into me. Shut your eyes and focus on breathing. Breathe in through your nose. Hold it, three counts."

Her head pressed against her chest, her eyes shut, but she shook her head. "Breathing techniques don't work."

"Dammit, Sam, try. Trust me. This'll help. Breathe in. Hold it—one, two, three. Now purse your lips and breathe out, as slowly as you can."

"Zeus!"

"Sorry. No way in hell are we stopping. If you puke, you'll do it on both of us, and I still won't put you down. Inhale, through your nose. One, two—"

"I won't faint again. I faint once," she whispered, "then—"

"You vomit if you see blood again due to stress-induced nausea. You're going to see it, Sam." Damn. His legs were burning and his arms were starting to ache. Ragno had planted the seed with her teasing, and now he was feeling the exertion of running while bleeding from a couple of wounds. Sam's weight, slight as she was, wasn't helping. He guessed that she didn't weigh more than one twenty-five, but cradling her in his arms at the same time he tried to run, while trying to keep from jarring her too much, was awkward and straining muscles in his back, his shoulders, and his arms. Talking to her was making it worse. "I can't stop blood by force of will. You're going to vomit. Just go ahead and do it. Won't be the first or last time that happens to me as I work."

Eyes shut, head against his chest, with a hand balled into a fist between her mouth and his chest, she said, "I hate being sick."

"I know." He focused on the buildings across the river, breathing deeply. "We've got at least five more minutes before we're in the clear."

"Hate, hate, hate being sick."

Yeah, he knew. "Breathe in, through your nose. One—two—three—"

Sam leaned into him and wrapped one arm over his right shoulder and around his neck, and the other under his left armpit. She pressed her face into his overcoat and clasped her hands behind his back. As she inhaled and fought through her weakness, he realized he had a chance at redemption. She perceived her blood phobia and subsequent nausea as signs of uncontrollable weakness. He saw it as something that made her human. Remembering that she was human, and therefore not the perfect goddess his memory had created, made him feel hopeful.

Today was the second day of February. He had a month until the verdict reading in Brussels on March first to tell Sam what he was trying to tell her when she'd shut the door in his face. Even the most stubborn human could change her mind, and he was nothing if not patient.

"Now exhale. Slowly," he said, glancing down, his heart melting at the sight of her trying so hard to follow his directions. He dragged his eyes back to the buildings of the Right Bank and picked up his pace. "That's it. You're doing great. Breathe in. One—two—three—as slow as you can. Almost there. Hold your breath. Hold it. Hold it, okay, now start a long, slow, exhale. Through your lips. Slow." He'd find a way, around whatever bombs got thrown at them, around the bounty hunt, and around the ITT proceedings. He'd find a way to make her not only listen, he'd find a way to address the mistake he'd made.

The mistake she let me make.

He'd do it the only way he knew how—he'd find a way to take them both back to the few days of absolute bliss that they'd shared, before life threw a curve ball that he'd hit the wrong fucking way. Once there, they could decide where to go. Her almost-fiancé was an obstacle, but Zeus knew obstacles were just something to figure out. None were insurmountable. Justin McDougall was only going to be an insurmountable problem if Sam wanted him to be one.

"Now breathe in again. Slowly. One—two—three—"

"Hope you're helping her, Zeus. You have me so relaxed I almost fell asleep. God, I like this new, softer version of you. By the way, the tracking devices merge when the two of you are so close together," Ragno's voice grounded him. "Samantha's chip produces a red blip on my GPS. You're blue. When you're smashed against one another, the two of you are one small purple blob. How is she?"

He glanced down. "Fine. Hanging on for dear life, face buried in my coat, and, I'm damn happy to report, not puking," he said, "Breathe in, long and slow."

"Yes, sir. Oh. You're talking to her, aren't you?" Ragno said, before switching from her friendly, slightly concerned yet teasing tone, to the clipped one she typically used for business. "We've got open communication with ITT Security Forces. They're getting ready to shut the bridges and seal the island to foot traffic. Theory is the person who left the bomb could still be on the island. Hold a second, Zeus."

Ragno went off mic, but didn't mute her connection. Zeus heard her talking to other agents who were on-site in Denver with her and heard her keyboard clicking. "I'm back. We're communicating with ITT security, but don't know if what we're telling them will filter down to the boots on the ground at the foot of the bridge. If you don't want the hassle of a roadblock, hurry."

"We're fifteen yards from stepping off the bridge," he said.

"I've got you," Ragno said. "When you step off, the very first street is Quai des Grand Augustins. Go right."

"Zeus." Sam's voice was muffled in his overcoat, because her mouth was still smashed there. She didn't attempt to look up.

"Yeah?"

"Need to think about something pleasant. Tell me about the sunset from your Keys house."

"What?"

"Your Keys house. Sunset."

"How'd you know I got it?" Five yards from the edge of the bridge. Deal, Jenkins, and Miles were in step with him. Road wasn't blocked.

"Seven years ago it was a dream." She buried her face deeper. "Know you well enough to know you made it happen."

Turning right on Quais des Grand Augustins, eyes constantly moving to spot danger, he said, "It's on Islamorada. On the Florida Bay, which leads to the Gulf of Mexico. It's a raised house. Sits on an acre and a half. I was lucky to get the property."

"The sunset, Hernandez."

He thought through words that would give her a visual of the specialness of the place, which was oriented for sunset views. "It faces west. Sunsets are spectacular from the deck, which I've set up like a kitchen and living room, with a giant outdoor television."

Gripping his coat tighter, she shook her head. "Sunset. Colors. Tell me."

"Patience, Sam." He chuckled. "I'm getting to it. No matter what I'm doing there, whether I'm working or doing things with Ana, I settle in about fifteen minutes before and wait for the show. I've got these chairs—I swear time stands still when I sit in one." He drew a deep breath. "The sunsets are wonderful."

"The colors. Tell me about the colors."

"Zeus. Take your first left," Ragno said. "Small side street. Rue Git-le-Coeur. Vehicles are waiting for you in the first block."

He exhaled, having to think hard about the colors. Describing a sunset while running from a bombing was a new one for him. *Hell.* Describing a sunset was a new one for him. "When the sun first touches the horizon, pinks, oranges, and reds shoot through the sky. The colors reflect off the rippling water. It's one of the prettiest sights I've ever seen."

Aside from you.

Chapter Twelve

Thirty minutes later, the Amicus team was at the safe house. He and Sam stripped off their coats at the door. Cheeks burning bright red, she climbed the stairs to their third floor bedrooms, eyes averted from everyone so that she wouldn't risk seeing blood. He followed her into the living room that separated their bedrooms.

Before she slipped into her room, he asked, "Are you feeling okay?"

Her back to him, she nodded and answered, "Humiliated, but fine."

He thought about telling her it was okay to be human, then decided she wouldn't want to hear it. He turned to enter his own bedroom to do a quick clean up before a Black Raven medic worked on his wounds.

"Thank you, Zeus."

Turning back to her, he saw that she was leaning against the door to her bedroom. She didn't face him and he knew why. The blood had stopped flowing, but he hadn't cleaned it off his forehead, and the wound from his arm had bled through his suit jacket and shirt sleeve. "No need to thank me."

"What about you?"

"Me?"

Her face was to the side, but she still didn't gaze at him. Her attention focused on a lamp, she lifted her hand to smooth her hair. His arms ached to once again feel the weight of her. "Your forehead. Are you okay?"

He shrugged, even though she couldn't see it. "It's minor."

"Your agents?"

"One serious. Others will be okay." He watched her shudder. "I'm waiting on reports."

"The whole thing was horrific. If you hadn't moved us away from there..."

Whichever Amicus team member had gotten into the rear seat of the Black Raven car closest to the blast would've been severely injured, if not killed, along with the Black Raven agent in the car. He tried not to think about Sam being in that rear car, but the thought haunted him. Until he implemented Plan B, that had been his plan.

"Best not to think about it."

"Your job sucks, but you do it well. Regarding that instant message that you sent to me while I was at the podium?"

"Yes?"

"Your offer of the French investigative files and their analyses still stands?"

"Of course," he said, though the trepidation that he'd felt when he made the offer came back to him with a pang that twisted in his gut. Giving Sam the information Black Raven was uncovering for the bounty hunt would result in Sam wanting to use the information in ITT proceedings. He and Sam would be able to put their heads together and figure out a way to use the evidence without Black Raven's acquisition tactics being highlighted, so that wasn't the real sticking point. The bigger problem in giving her access to Black Raven data was that he didn't want to create a reason for her to be front and center. Didn't want her there at all, much less at the forefront of controversial arguments.

He just didn't believe he could keep the information from her. Sam had lectured him on ethics and integrity, and what she didn't realize was he operated on a higher plane than most other individuals. Her grandfather was paying for the information. Her grandfather wanted Maximov captured at all costs. Accomplishing that goal didn't mean keeping potentially relevant information from Sam.

"I want the files. I want everything you're uncovering for the bounty hunt. Free access." Her tone had hardened, making his gut twisted even more. "Regardless of how you've come across the data."

"What happened to your concern about Black Raven breaking laws? I believe you accused me of committing a felony. With a capital F."

"Today." Even with only her profile showing, he could see that she set her jaw. "Today happened."

He wished they were facing each other. The partial view of her face told him the resolve there was a beautiful thing. She didn't need to say more.

"This is all wrong," she continued, quietly. "Morgan—dead, under circumstances that could be viewed as suspicions. Eric—a murder, by cyanide. The Boulevard Saint-Germain bombing. Judge Devlin's wife—murdered," she added. "This afternoon— another bomb. I don't understand how this can be happening."

"No one does."

"But my job is to try to make sense of this proceeding. Stanley Morgan was bothered, and so am I. The world wants a conviction of something bigger than the two-bit thugs who engineered each of the individual attacks, but the evidence isn't adding up. I feel as though I'm trying to put together a puzzle, without all the pieces."

Tell me about it.

Through Jigsaw, Black Raven had been trying to do the same thing. Jigsaw was privy to any data obtained by the U.S. government—through any intelligence effort. It was also privy to data that the government didn't have, because Black Raven analysts who were working on Jigsaw followed prompts that led elsewhere. It was strict company policy to do anything and everything needed to get the job done. Even if it meant bending a law or two to do it. Even if it meant hacking through private networks without authorization and breaking encryption codes.

Jigsaw spied on citizens and law enforcement alike. Any cyber-data it collected became puzzle pieces that led to more puzzle pieces. Jigsaw took information, dissected it, analyzed it, and used it continually, over and over, until seemingly random bits of information made sense. It detected human behavior by analyzing co-existing relationships in cyber-data. With its ability to trace and follow co-existing digital devices, it found human connections in the proximity of digital devices. Privacy was a quaint, nonexistent concept for the program.

There was one big problem with Jigsaw. Data-gathering techniques used by Black Raven for Jigsaw would outrage anyone who believed in old-fashioned notions of privacy, and that was most Americans. Exposure of the job to the public and to governmental agencies, who were unknowingly providing the pieces to the puzzle, would, no doubt, end it.

"Or maybe all the pieces are here, somewhere in the record, and I'm just not seeing it," Sam continued. "No one is seeing it. If I'm going to make any sense of this at all, I need more puzzle pieces, and frankly"—she drew a deep breath, and her cheeks became a little less pale—"after today, I don't care how I get them. I'm done following the rules. I want to see whatever information you're using for the bounty hunt. My grandfather hired you. He'll direct you to share that information with me, if you need him to do that."

"We can share bounty hunt information with you, but Black Raven intel cannot be integrated with ITT files. You're correct. There are sourcing issues." He laid out the only condition he thought was a legitimate prerequisite, given the fact that her grandfather was funding the bounty hunt and the information-gathering effort that went with it.

"Of course not," she said.

"And there will likely be some files we cannot produce." Because he couldn't produce to her the bulk of the information that Jigsaw had acquired. She didn't have clearance to know the job even existed. "Information exchange results in confidentiality agreements that sometimes cannot be breached. We don't give our word, then break it."

"Good to hear. Do you think this could be one person, orchestrating all of these attacks?"

"Don't know yet."

"Seems to me that if this is one person who is trying so hard to stop the ITT, something in the ITT record should give us a goddamn clue as to who it is."

His heart beat harder in his chest. She'd gone from zero to sixty—scared to determined—in just a few minutes. "Couldn't agree more, and that is exactly what we're looking for. We're working on the theory that somehow we'll find a clue that will lead us to Maximov."

"I want it all."

He thought she was going to say more, but she didn't. She opened her door.

"Sam, your grandfather wants you to call him."

"You've told him I'm fine, haven't you?"

"He'd rather hear it from you than from me or Ragno."

"I'm not talking to him, and he knows why."

"Isn't the silent treatment tactic a bit juvenile?"

"I've learned to communicate with people in a manner they can understand, and my grandfather evidently doesn't understand more adult forms of communication. By the way, you, of all people, should stay out of this one." She stepped in her bedroom and shut the door behind her.

As the door closed, he decided it was best if he did exactly as she said. Her refusal to talk to her grandfather was none of his business, particularly when he was still working on getting closer to her good graces. Turning to go into his own bedroom, Zeus shrugged off his concern for Samuel.

The bomb blast had scared her to death, and rightly so. But she was more determined than ever, and she recognized a valuable asset when she saw one. Black Raven investigative files on the bounty hunt were going to be a treasure trove of information. Sam was brilliant enough to know that she should have the information, because something, somewhere, could be relevant to her task with the ITT.

"I'd say she's a damn effective communicator, and she's nothing if not tenacious," Ragno said in his ear as he stepped into his bedroom. "You know you can't tell her about Jigsaw, right? She doesn't have clearance."

"Yep. Don't need that reminder."

"You're having a medic look at you, right?"

Zeus chuckled. As usual, Ragno's timing was spot on, her sentence ending as an agent walked in his room with a first aid kit. "Rix is here."

"Good. While he works on you, I have Sebastian on the line."

"Zeus," Sebastian said. "Good call on implementing Plan B outside of the courthouse. Would have been worse for you guys had you gotten in the vehicles. Still, that was a hell of a lot of blood running down your face."

"Thanks for the concern, and I'm fine. Aren't you supposed to be honeymooning?"

"I am," Sebastian said. "But that doesn't mean I'm not working."

Sebastian and Skye hadn't planned a post-wedding trip. Rather, given how busy the company was, his friend had opted to delay an extended trip and simply spend their first few post-wedding days at his new wife's home in Covington, Louisiana. Zeus knew his friend enough to know that given the bombing outside of the ITT proceeding, Sebastian was now maintaining constant contact with Ragno.

"I have more intel on TRCR," Ragno said.

Texas Rebels for Civil Rights. The group Ragno had mentioned as being new to the hate party, when they'd been trying to persuade Sam to resign. Zeus stepped into the bathroom with Rix, leaning over the sink as Rix prepared to wash the wound on his forehead.

"Info I talked about the other night came from DHS files," Ragno continued, recapping for Sebastian that the TRCR was a new terrorist group that intelligence had revealed was operating in rural Texas. "I didn't know the source. Zeus, you asked me to find it. I did. Had to use Jigsaw-level clearance, and now I fully understand why. If this gets out, there'd be a war on the U.S.–Mexico border."

"Who is it?" Sebastian asked.

"It's coming from Protectors of Peace."

Protectors of Peace—known in shorthand lingo as the Protectors—was a motorcycle gang operating primarily out of West Texas, with members numbering seven hundred to a thousand. They were notorious for anything but peace along the Mexico-U.S. border. They'd been a steady source of income for Black Raven for years. People and businesses on both sides of the border needed protection from the Protectors.

Zeus winced as Rix sprayed alcohol into his forehead wound. As fresh blood and liquid dripped into the sink, he shut his eyes to prevent the liquid from going there. "You're kidding."

"Nope," Ragno answered.

"Never have known them to run with law enforcement for anything," Zeus muttered.

"Remember a few months ago that video that exploded on social networking sites of one of their gang members being decapitated?" Ragno asked.

"Yep." Even in Zeus's world, where violence and bloodshed was commonplace, a beheading was hard to watch.

"Certainly enough of an impetus," Sebastian said.

"Yes," Ragno said. "The Protectors said to the Department of Homeland Security—and nowhere else I can tell—that the TRCR was responsible for the beheading. Jigsaw hasn't identified a source for the beheading. Yet."

"Can't trust a damn thing the Protectors say."

"Agreed, and government intel only goes so far. Good enough for government work doesn't mean good enough for us," Ragno said, repeating a phrase that had been used so frequently in Black Raven it had become a cliché. That was why the government came to them for projects like Jigsaw. "For Jigsaw's sake, seems like we should probe further. It might lead us somewhere."

"Well..." Zeus pressed gauze onto his forehead, glanced at Rix, saw that his hands still held the bottle of antiseptic, and prepared himself for another burning squirt. "We certainly don't have any friendlies in or near the Protectors."

"Agreed, and this is coming from the tip-top."

Zeus shook his head, and not due to the fresh sting of alcohol that Rix was applying. "You're fucking kidding me. Blaze?"

"Yes."

Shutting the toilet lid, Zeus sat, and leaned his head back so Rix could assess the wound.

"A stitch or two will help a butterfly bandage," Rix muttered, squinting at the cut.

"Fine."

"Fine what?" Ragno asked.

"I'm talking to Rix. Go ahead. Stitch it."

Rix shook his head, a worry line bisecting his brows. "Sir, this could result in a scar. I can do stitches okay in places where people don't care about scars, but this is your forehead. I'm not a doctor. He's downstairs, with Abe. I'll see if I can get him up here before he heads to the hospital to assess Pitts' injuries."

"No." Pitts, the driver who'd been injured, needed a Black Raven doctor more than Zeus. "Don't delay him. A scar won't kill me. Close it however you need to and bandage it," Zeus said, his mind more focused on Ragno's intel than his forehead. The man known as Blaze was the alleged mastermind behind the motorcycle gang's network of alien smuggling, heroin dealing, and arms smuggling. He was also legendary for keeping members of the Protectors of Peace out of the orbit of law enforcement and out of prison. "Ragno, Blaze is probably just snitching on TRCR because they've encroached on his territory. Which gets me back to the point—we can't trust a damn thing he says."

"Agreed, but I think he's worth talking to for Jigsaw, because from what Jigsaw is now pulling up on TRCR, they're claiming affinity to Maximov. Plus, Jigsaw is fingering TRCR as a potential source of credible terrorist threats."

"Them and about a thousand other home-grown criminal gangs," Zeus said. "Not to mention the lone wolves Jigsaw is fingering."

"Still, Blaze snitching to Department of Homeland Security is just too interesting to pass up," Ragno said.

"I'm agreeing with Ragno," Sebastian said.

"I'm always hopeful that a few more puzzle pieces on the table might lead Jigsaw to something," Ragno added. "Problem is— Wait a second while I try to figure something out."

He heard her fingers clicking on her keyboard. Rix made the first jab with the needle into his forehead. Zeus clenched his jaw as he felt the thread pull through his skin.

"Ah. Got it." Ragno said. "By my estimate, in the last five years, we've caused a body count of eight members of the Protectors of Peace on Black Raven border jobs in South Texas and Mexican territories that are near the border."

"Too bad it isn't higher," Zeus muttered.

"Sounds high to me, considering you want Blaze to talk to you," Ragno said.

"Yeah, but I'm not sure eight is high enough to have Blaze's respect," Zeus said over Sebastian's chuckle. "The Protectors killed two of ours, correct? From the Allied job?" The metals transport job had turned ugly once they'd crossed the client into Mexico. Hindsight told them that Black Raven never should have agreed to the job, but due diligence at the time hadn't raised red flags.

"Yes. We've always attributed the kills to them, but there were multiple gangs on site. Mexican, American, and Colombian."

"Arrange for me to talk to him." Zeus glanced up at Rix, who had the needle poised for another jab into his forehead.

"Information from Blaze will cost us." Ragno kept typing as she spoke.

"Jigsaw's budget will cover it," Sebastian said.

"Correct." Ragno's fingers picked up speed as she multitasked. "My worry is, Blaze won't be asking for money. Not sure we want to be beholden to the Protectors of Peace."

"Let's decide when he asks," Zeus said. "Depends on what kind of information Blaze offers. If anything."

Chapter Thirteen

Behind the closed door of his bedroom, after Rix was through, Zeus worked on agent repositioning. Agents who weren't essential to Amicus team protection, for the moment, were tasked to the bombing aftermath on the Ile de la Cite. Their job was to provide assistance, keep their ears open, and report in. Once Black Raven medics took care of the minor injuries on the team and the Black Raven agents who'd been on-scene at the bomb blast, they'd provide assistance wherever needed. After agent logistics, he talked with Barrows about the best way to share information from the bounty hunt with the Amicus team.

Head wound treated, showered, and dressed in clean clothes, he stepped out of his bedroom into the sitting room that separated his room from Sam's. Her door remained shut. Jenkins or Miles, both positioned at the door of their suite, would notify him if Sam left her room.

The first floor of the safe house had a formal sitting room in the front, where most of the agents worked when Sam, Abe, and Charles were in the house. There was also a kitchen and a dining room, a laundry room, and, in the rear of the house, a large library that spanned the width of the building. The second floor had bedrooms for Abe and Charles and their lead agents. All the remaining agents, when not on duty, were housed in a hotel down the street. Most of the time, the house was full of agents on the inside and watched by agents on the outside. After today, more agents from the States were on their way.

The library had large windows that would have overlooked a garden and the evening dusk, but the drapes were tightly drawn. There were two tables in the room and two seating areas. A fire crackled cheerfully in the large stone fireplace. A sideboard had bottles of water, a tray of fruit, and other snacks.

In front of the drapes, four large-screen television monitors stood on pedestals. Two monitors, tuned to news, showed repetitive loops covering the ITT bombing and aftermath. The image of him carrying Sam, with her head back and her eyes closed, her blonde hair draped over the arm of his dark overcoat, was part of that loop.

The other two screens focused on financial news channels. Repercussions of the bombing—a direct, lethal attack on the tribunal that was supposed to be stopping such attacks—were rippling through the economic sector. Worldwide financial markets were in turmoil. The blast had occurred at 1100 in New York. The Dow tumbled so badly, stop mechanisms were implemented, and the markets were closed for the remainder of the day. President Cameron was scheduled to address the nation in a few minutes.

It was now 1900 in Paris. Miami was six hours behind, so it was 1300 there, which meant it was almost time for the video call with Ana that Ragno was putting together for him. It was parent-teacher conference day at school; Ana only had a half-day of classes. Ragno had checked in with Vick, the Black Raven agent assigned as Ana's nanny, and informed Zeus they were almost home. He loved talking to his daughter each day when she got home from school and any other chance he got.

As he waited, he worked at one table, with Agents Axel and Lambert on either side of him. The second long table was dedicated to the Amicus team.

Abe's wound, a superficial shrapnel cut, had been stitched and bandaged. Charles hadn't been injured. Abe and Charles were working on their laptops as they waited for Sam.

Zeus sipped black coffee and scrolled through his iPad, looking at information that had been provided by Black Raven Agent Michael Gabriel Hernandez. Zeus's younger brother. The lead field agent in charge of the bounty hunt.

"Ragno?"

"Yes."

"Gabe's intel looks problematic. Not his conclusions, but where the conclusions are taking him."

"Agreed. This is concerning, and you know I don't often use that word when describing assignments for field agents." She drew a deep breath. "It's been less than 48 hours since he was put on task," she said. "Perhaps Angel will come up with a safer option."

"Let's hope," Zeus said, yet he didn't have much. He'd never been able to break Ragno of the habit of calling his younger brother Gabe by the nickname she'd given him immediately upon his entry into the company. She'd developed a soft spot for his oversized little brother at first sight—just like everyone else who ever met him. Gabe reciprocated by taking everybody under his protective, meddling wings, with warm smiles and a disarming, innate joy that masked cunning instincts and a fight-to-the-death protectiveness.

"ITT Task Force is executing a search in Turkey tonight," Ragno said. "We should know something by morning. After

Turkey, there's a lead in Syria. Top secret, by the way. Angel's idea could all become moot if either of those lead to Maximov."

"If Gabe thought the task force was going to be successful tonight, he'd have figured out a way to be there."

"Agreed. He's skipping Turkey, but working on getting in on the Syrian mission slated for tomorrow night."

"Assume Gabe will have to move forward with going into Praptan. Gear up the intel for a search. I want as much detail guiding his team as possible." When hired for the bounty hunt, after Sam shut the door on him, Zeus had strategized with Sebastian and Ragno on how to proceed. Gabe had been the ideal candidate to lead the team, not only due to his tactical skills but because he was the type of field agent who naturally cultivated contacts. Some of the people with whom Gabe had become friends over the years were also on the joint task force of the ITT countries who were on the hunt for Maximov.

Gabe had been on a job in Afghanistan when output from Jigsaw started pointing to Chalinda. Samuel Dixon's decision to hire Black Raven for the bounty hunt gave them a great cover for operations, because if their motives were questioned, they could finger Dixon's project as the impetus and not Jigsaw.

Zeus pulled Gabe off the Afghanistan job, conferred with him about team members and logistics, and gave him the green light to mobilize quickly. Currently, Gabe and his team were operating out of a private airport in Germany, with analytical support on site and more provided by Ragno's team in Denver.

Zeus followed the threads that led Gabe to believe that Maximov could be found in the ghost city of Praptan, Chalinda. If Maximov was easy to find, he would've been found by now. Gabe's latest email indicated Praptan seemed like a leading contender by default. Maximov hadn't been found in any other place and, in recent years, very few reputable teams had made searches there. So far, Zeus agreed with Gabe's assessment of the intel. "Do we have intel from the other searches of Praptan?"

"Yes. But no one from the outside knows that city like Maximov and his people, and no one from the outside wants to stay there very long, due to radiation levels. I'm sending you recently taken drone footage of Praptan. It's from high-level intel. Gabe has it, along with everything else I'm able to find that shows views of the area."

Ragno's email with the drone footage pinged on his iPad as Sam walked into the library with Jenkins at her side. Zeus gave his agent a nod. "Jenkins. Take an early dinner break."

"By the way," Ragno said in his earpiece. "Samantha just had one hell of a phone conversation with Judge O'Connor. He thought her questions to Duvall were going too far in exposing weaknesses in the case against Maximov."

Sam's examination of Duvall had been fascinating, and everyone in the courtroom had been focused on it. He'd bet she didn't like being reined in by the judge. In a low voice, he asked, "Her reaction?"

"I'm paraphrasing. Something about integrity, evidence, and intellectual honesty. She very nicely, in a beautifully articulate and cool way, told the judge to fuck off and let her do her job. I love her."

Great. That makes two of us.

Sam now wore tight black exercise leggings, a white sweatshirt with night-glow strips, and running shoes. Her still-damp hair, pulled into a tight ponytail, exposed her slender neck and firm jawline. Her laptop was in a shoulder bag, slung over one shoulder. She carried a pair of lightweight gloves, an exercise belt with lights for nighttime running, and a wool cap. The frightened, sick-to-her-stomach woman was gone. In her place was the cool, controlled leader of the Amicus team.

"She still hasn't called her grandfather, by the way. Her silent treatment of him continues. Oh. One more thing," Ragno said, tone low and fringed with an underlying concern, the tone she used when acknowledging that the job was both business and personal to Zeus. "When the team transitions to London this weekend, Senator Justin McDougall, aka her boyfriend, almost fiancé, is meeting her there for dinner. I'm monitoring the private line she uses with him, and it seems like they know it. Their conversations are almost shorthand. Samantha has requested that we coordinate logistics with the senator's staff and security."

"Fine," Zeus said, though his gut twisted with the thought of having to bodyguard her while she was having dinner with her boyfriend. He put the thought out of his mind. Work was work was work. He was, first and foremost, a professional. "McDougall uses EDGE International for security. I had a conversation with them earlier about upping McDougall's security, in light of the murder of Judge Devlin's wife. I'll coordinate with them for Sunday."

"Just thought you'd want to know what is in st—"

"Understood." *Stop worrying about me.*

Sam placed her laptop on the table where Abe and Charles

sat, and tossed the running gear beside it.

"Sam," Zeus asked, "your plan for the evening?"

"Work for an hour or so while news comes in regarding what happened today. At this point I'm not sure whether proceedings will be taking place tomorrow. Do you or Ragno know?"

"No word yet."

"I just talked to Judge O'Connor." She gave a slight frown. "Aside from a few shrapnel cuts, he's fine. The other U.S. judges are as well. One of the marshals on Judge O'Connor's security team was outside the car." Her eyes flashed with pain. "He died upon arrival at the hospital. That is all I know. I have no word about personnel from the other countries. Do you?"

"Judge Calante suffered extensive injuries," Zeus said. "That's been reported on the news, and my agents on site have confirmed it. There are three fatalities from Calante's security personnel."

More pain flashed in her eyes. "The people in the crowd?"

He shook his head. "Don't have statistics yet. Numerous injuries. My agents are telling me five deaths. Numbers are likely to change."

Zeus eyed Sam's exercise gear as she sat at the table with Abe and Charles. A vigorous five-plus-mile run through the streets of Paris, in the cold night, with Sam at his side, would be heaven. Another piece of Sam-related trivia that he'd tried to forget was that she was a fast, long-legged runner with a competitive streak. She'd always tried to outrun him. Once he'd let her, before he realized that she could pick up her pace to a six-minute sprint and finish stronger than she started. When he realized she really was capable of kicking his ass in a five-mile run, he stopped pulling back. She was a gracious loser of a race, but also a beautiful winner. Back then, he hadn't known which version of her he liked better. He just liked being with her so much it had—hurt.

Fuck. Let it go. Now's a different time. Stop thinking about what happened. Start thinking about what you're going to make happen, while she's planning dinner dates with her almost fiancé, or whatever the fuck he is to her.

Zeus wasn't looking forward to telling her she couldn't have her outdoor run. He knew she needed the stress relief, but it was too risky. He considered positioning for a moment, then sent a message to Miles, the agent in charge of logistics. *Two treadmills. Put them on third floor, in the living room of Sam's suite. Stat.*

Sam sat at the table with Abe and Charles. Her voice was low, but with an authoritative tone. He listened with half an ear as he opened the file that Ragno had sent of the drone footage from Praptan. Sam was telling Abe and Charles they should go home, giving them advice that she wouldn't take herself.

On all the television screens around the room, President Cameron took the podium, and Zeus upped the volume. The speech was short, and to the point. "We will catch the perpetrators. We will determine who is at fault. We will stop these acts of terror." The camera switched from the president to the pandemonium outside of the ITT proceedings, and included within the footage was the image of Zeus carrying Sam away from the scene. She was passed out and oblivious to the mayhem.

In the video footage, he glanced down at her, and looked up again. He hated that there was so much raw emotion on his face. Eyes deadly serious, he looked like a man who had been to hell, and promised the devil there'd be a rematch. His expression was one of steely determination, but there was also a softness to it, heartfelt concern for what he held in his arms, as every few steps he glanced down at her.

Observing her now, he saw that her eyes were riveted on the same screen.

Well, nothing to be done about what that video shows. Does she see what I see? How I'm looking at her like I'd rather die than see her hurt?

Without glancing at him, she took her attention off the television screen and opened her laptop.

Answer enough.

Zeus shifted in his chair and stretched his legs. "Ragno, start the Praptan video."

"I'm watching with you," Ragno said. "You're looking at the once-bustling, once-modern downtown area of Praptan. The city itself was only two miles from the Chalinda Nuclear Power Plant. You can't tell from this footage, but on April 17, 1986, the city was a beautiful, thriving metropolis. It was a jewel of a city and the capital of Chalinda, a leading powerhouse in the Soviet Union. Praptan was known for its museums, parks, and education system, until the incident. The nuclear meltdown is still the largest in nuclear history."

Zeus studied the footage on his iPad. He'd seen photos of the ghost city of Praptan before, but this footage, taken on a bright, clear day, was stark and eerie, thanks to the close-up capabilities of drone technology.

"How many people were evacuated?" he asked.

"The meltdown resulted in the sudden and permanent evacuation of almost 500,000 people and resulted in the instantaneous closure of businesses, universities, and museums. It forever altered the lives of the people who once thrived there."

He pressed pause. "Sam?"

She stopped in midsentence and glanced at him.

"Want to see drone footage of Praptan?"

She nodded, gesturing to Abe and Charles to walk over to where Zeus stood. He shook his head and pointed to one of the four television monitors that they'd hung on the wall, sending the video feed from Ragno there so they could all see it.

"Zeus," Ragno said. "This is high-level intel. It would be damn hard to explain how we have it. I'm not sure we should be sharing—"

"Understood, but I believe it's necessary to complete the job."

"How so?"

"Trust me on this. Just like I knew we had to get the Amicus team out of that hotel earlier than planned, just like I knew we had to exit on foot, I know the Amicus team needs to know what we know." He pressed a button on his watch. "Ragno, you're now live. Talking to the conference room, which includes the Amicus team and Black Raven agents."

He replayed the footage from the beginning. As it rolled, he stood and went to the sideboard. After picking up an apple, he cut it into quarters, peeled each quarter, and removed the seeds. Zeus knew the dark red peeling had nutrients. The apple was for Sam, though, and nutrient levels didn't seem to guide her eating.

New shots picked up with derelict high-rise buildings with broken windows, streets that were reclaimed by greenery, and dark shadows of animals running through what had once been a square.

"You're sending agents there?" Sam asked, wide eyes on him.

"It's an option," he said. "Unless someone finds Maximov first or we come up with a better idea."

"Are those dogs?" Charles asked.

"Some may be. Mostly they're wolves," Ragno answered. "There are thousands of them."

"I thought Praptan was a ghost town. With no life at all," Charles said. "What is there for so many of them to eat?"

Zeus glanced at Charles, whose wide brown eyes were glued

to the monitor. "Rats. Roaches. Each other. There's life. Just not as we know it. Ragno, medics are providing rabies vaccines to the team in advance?"

"Yes. Among others. Because timing is a factor, and prophylactic measures likely won't be fully effective, doctors are working up a post-trip protocol, which includes radiation detection and decontamination."

The drone banked left, over an amusement park with a tall Ferris wheel, frozen in time, its bucket seats in yellow, red, blue, and white, with streaks of rust dripping down the buckets.

"The amusement park was to rival Disney World. It was going to open in June 1986. Past the amusement park, the drone will get to a university," Ragno said.

The drone flew slower. A caption at the bottom of the screen indicated the area was Praptan University of the Liberal Arts and Sciences. There were no people. Building after building appeared empty. Trees and shrubbery had overgrown what might have once been a manicured campus.

"Ragno," Zeus said. "That's where Maximov went to college?"

"Yes."

He brought the apple to Sam, along with a bottle of water. Her eyes on him, he took a bite out of one of the pieces and took a sip out of the bottle of water before placing it in front of her. The fact that she hadn't eaten or drank anything without him first sampling it wasn't lost upon him. She reacted powerfully and viscerally to real-life situations, and she was still dealing with the cyanide poisoning. Her blood phobia had materialized after being in the car crash with her mother and father. It had been a bloody and violent head-on collision, and thirteen-year-old Sam had been in the car with them as they died.

Years earlier, Zeus had only known that Sam's parents had died in a car crash and that Sam had been in the car. Now, with Ragno's investigative skills focused, in part, on figuring out what made Sam tick, Zeus knew much more about her father and his struggles with alcohol. The car crash occurred because her father, drunk at the time, had veered into oncoming traffic.

He touched his watch, muted his mic, and bent to her ear. In a low voice, intended for her ears only, he said, "If you don't want me to kick your ass when we run, you should eat a few bites."

Eyes unreadable, but with a smirk that he recognized as a challenge, she reached for a piece of apple. "I'm not racing you." Eyes on him, she took a delicate bite. "But if I did, I'd win."

"Would university records provide information on people who may now know his whereabouts? College professors? Fellow students?"

"Zeus, the disaster happened in 1986," Ragno said, responding to his question as he walked away from Sam while keeping his eyes on the monitor. "The university was large, with over twenty-five thousand students. University records weren't computerized back then."

"There have to be paper records," Zeus said.

Sam answered before Ragno. "Access is a problem. Stanley Morgan and I thought of that a few months ago. We wondered whether anyone had gone there for intel. Research indicates that the university area, which is between the city and the nuclear power plant, is a radiation hot spot."

"Meaning?" George asked.

"Meaning no one is going there to study or retrieve paper records." Sam took a sip from the bottle of water he'd given to her. "Throughout the contamination zone, some areas are worse than others. The university is the worst of the worst. Radiation never dies, and everything in that area is toxic. If the answer to Maximov's whereabouts is in paper records in the university files"—she shook her head—"no one will ever find it."

The drone flew over sprawling neighborhoods, with swings that no children had touched in years, streets on which no cars drove, and houses where no one lived.

"Sam is correct," Ragno said. As the drone did one more fly-over of the city, Ragno continued, "People of Chalinda believe the disaster was intentional. In the Soviet era, Chalinda and other Soviet states were competing for supremacy. Needless to say, after the disaster, Chalinda wasn't a competitor for anything, except on the A-list of the world's creepiest places."

No shit.

"Conspiracy theorists blame the Russian Federation and the block of countries that had sent scientists to assist the nuclear facility in implementing safeguards," Sam said. "That includes the U.S. and England."

"What are radiation levels in the city itself?" Zeus asked.

"We don't have reliable measurements. Some areas are believed to be minimal. Other areas are considered hot spots." She paused. "Zeus, your video chat will begin in two minutes. About Gabe. I talked to him a couple of hours ago. He isn't worried about the radiation levels. He says he'll hire guides to take him around the hot spots."

"Hell. Like he's a freaking tourist."

"You know Gabe. Fearless."

Yes. Fearlessness was a trait that ran in the Hernandez family, and Gabe had more than a healthy dose of it.

"That is all the drone footage," Ragno said as the monitor went dark.

"Ragno," Zeus said, as Sam turned back to Abe and Charles. "If I know my brother at all, he's looking forward to going into Praptan."

"He's assembling the necessary equipment, including radiation suits. Odd thing is there are people who live there, off the grid, and they seem to be fine. The Times did an article on the people who live there—just a handful, of course. I'm sending it to you now. They live there without electricity, without internet, without anything. Communication with the outside world is nonexistent, except for satellite phones, and not many people there seem to have them. It's like being on a prairie in the Wild West."

"Without the hope of a better life," Zeus added, as he scanned the articles that Ragno sent to him. "Alert Gabe that I need to talk to him. Arrange the call for nine my time." Two minutes had elapsed. "Is my video chat with Ana ready?"

"Yes. Here you go."

"Give me a second."

He stood, picked up his iPad, and almost made it to the door of the library before his daughter Ana, dark hair pulled into a loose ponytail, wearing a T-shirt with two Minions on the front, appeared on his iPad. "Daddy! You won't believe what happened at school today!"

As her voice carried through the room, his heart swelled at the sight of his beautiful girl. Her wide smile lit her almond-shaped, dark brown eyes. He had Ana most weekends. His workweeks were typically spent at Black Raven's headquarters in Denver, and weekends were with Ana in Miami or at his house in the Keys. One month on the road on the ITT trial meant he was missing four weekends with his girl.

He should've muted the call, but he thought Ragno would listen to him when he said to give him a second. Hand on the doorknob, he glanced over his shoulder at Sam, whose eyes were on him. Something flashed there, but what, he didn't know. The look struck him with the intensity of lightning, before disappearing fast. In its place, he saw a cool woman, who was determined to ignore his personal life.

As she turned her attention again to Abe and Charles, he stepped through the doorway and focused on Ana. "Hello, my sweet angel. Tell me all about it."

Chapter Fourteen

"I'll hit the six mile mark before you," Zeus said, stepping out of his bedroom.

Sam was on the carpeted floor of their third floor living room, stretching on a towel. Positioned near the two treadmills that had been set up in that room, with her nose on her knees, she remembered what he looked like when they ran together. She braced herself before glancing in his direction.

Mental brushstrokes of her memory had painted his physique as a marvel, a sculpted body that had once been a wonderland for her to enjoy. While part of her—the part that had her remembering what his arms felt like as he'd held her just that afternoon—hoped reality wouldn't disappoint, the logical part of her fired caution flares with the message, "Don't look."

If you do look, don't pay attention.

She glanced in his direction as he draped a towel over the back of a chair, then turned to her. Bare-chested, wearing nothing but running shoes and shorts that fell to mid-thigh, the reality of him didn't disappoint her memories.

When God handed out brawn and muscles, he'd blessed Zeus with quality and abundance. The man had built upon what God had given him, honing his body to sculpted, toned perfection. Tawny, naturally tanned skin stretched taut over well-defined muscles, accentuating broad shoulders, tight pecs, a narrow waist, strong arms and long legs. His considerable height added leanness. There was no bulk. No fat. Nothing soft.

Abs? Yes. *Dammit*, but each one was still there, visibly ridging his taut torso. A memory, for years repressed but now vivid, zinged through her mind. They'd been in bed. She'd run her fingers and lips over his abdomen, from his heart down and counted out loud as she moved down his body. She'd told him she only counted four. He'd insisted on a recount. Four, she had lied again, pretending that she couldn't feel or see more. *Correct the first time*, she'd said, and added that his paunch got in the way. He'd laughed as he'd made her pay for that joke. His way of making her pay had felt unbelievable, in ways she'd never forgotten.

If it wasn't for the bandage at his left bicep, and the small strip of flesh-colored first aid tape barely visible at his forehead, his body could have made her forget he was mortal. Oh—there were other scars. One on his right arm, in the middle of his bicep, was faded. It was a reminder of a bullet that had been intended for her grandfather, the one Zeus had taken instead. The scars added to his aura of indomitableness. His physique made him worthy of his nickname—a brave, powerful god who was known for many things, including erotic prowess.

Stop. Right. Now.

"Good to see you've been taking care of yourself," she said, carefully keeping her tone cool as she straightened her legs and then bent her nose to her knees.

"I try. Performance sometimes counts in my line of work."

Performance? Dear God, don't let my mind go there.

Sitting up, she tucked her legs into a cross-legged position. He bent at his hips for a palms-on-the-ground stretch. She tried hard not to stare, but the wide expanse of shoulders and back, tapering to a narrow waist, was beautiful. She let her eyes linger over the ridges and ripped muscles, before refocusing on her own warm-up.

Damn him.

Where was she? Sit-ups? No. Done. Legs. Oh yeah. She stretched them in front of her and touched her toes. Her legs felt ready for a vigorous run, but the tension in her neck was killing her. As she slowly rotated her head, she winced at the sharp pain that emanated down her spine and through her shoulders. Left, back, right, front—no.

Ouch.

Job-related tension. The events of the day. Bombs. Murder. The look of hatred in Duvall's eyes as he said, *"I am Maximov."* The chastising phone call from Judge O'Connor when she had returned to the safe house. Zeus's daughter's gleeful greeting to her father. All tension builders, and her neck was telling her she'd had too much.

Shake it off.

She tried to rotate her neck again, but she kept hearing, *"Daddy!"* The sweet voice zinged straight into the raw place in Samantha's chest that, after Zeus, she'd learned to protect with hard-edged resolve and mental armor. The evening was now officially a macabre joke, where the thing that troubled her most was innocent and sweet and had nothing to do with the turbulent storm of bloody terror the world was suffering. His daughter's greeting was the only occurrence of the day that shouldn't matter to her at all.

Yet it did.

He's just a man. A man with a life. A life that didn't include me.

She'd let him go to that life, and he hadn't looked back.

He'll do the same thing again. Remember? He's here because he's getting paid.

Get the hell over it.

With neck muscles screaming in protest, she tried to bend her head. She exhaled, inhaled, and tried again.

"Neck's tight?"

She nodded. "It'll feel better after I run."

He walked across the room and stood in front of her, giving her a view of well-defined calves and beautifully muscled thighs that made her sorry he wore anything at all. He had just the right amount of dark black body hair, an amount that reminded her of what his skin felt like as he rubbed against her. Male. Pure male, fueled by a sensual nature that had blown her mind.

"That's a bad way to start a run."

"I'm fine," she said.

He bent to his knees on her towel, right in front of her. "Take your sweatshirt off and lay on your stomach. I'll massage out the kinks."

Please don't. My hormones are doing somersaults. I can barely keep my hands off of you. I don't want the memories you'll stir with your touch, nor do I want the reaction that is certain to come with the feel of your fingers on my neck. "If I needed a massage, I'd call a masseuse."

"No time for that." He rubbed his palms together, warming them. Heat emanating from his body carried wafts of clean, fragrant soap. He wasn't the type to wear cologne.

Get a grip.

"We've got lots to do. So lie flat and let me get to work on your neck. We—"

"We?" She folded her arms.

"We have a race to run. Dinner to eat after, and since it seems to me that you're not eating a damn thing without me testing it for poison first, that involves me and you, which equals we. Plus, I know you want to look at some of the material Black Raven has gathered in connection with the bounty hunt, and we'll have a data-sharing mechanism in place in an hour or so. You need a full night of sleep, and so do I. So that's also we. So let's get started. You need—"

"Stop telling me what I need."

"Security isn't a democracy, remember?"

"Your definition of security is way too broad."

He shrugged. "If it has to do with your well-being over the next twenty-seven days—".

"You're counting the days till the job is over?"

He nodded. "Aren't you?"

No. Right now I'm doing nothing but thinking about the last time we made love—or whatever it was—because this towel isn't enough real estate for us to be sharing when you're almost naked.

Eyes dark, rapid pulse at his temple, jaw set so hard he was almost grimacing. Oh, yes, he was thinking about the two of them together, too. The sex hadn't just been good. It had been fantastic and, she clenched her jaw—*go ahead, admit it*—positively unforgettable was an understatement.

Crap. *What was his question?*

"Yes." She exhaled with her answer, glad that she hadn't let the sexual tension between them completely fry her brain. "Verdict. Twenty-seven days." She frowned, dipping her eyes to his bare chest, before dragging her gaze to his face. "I'll have a recommendation formulated by then, and your job will be over."

Payment due. Black Raven moves on, and I'll never see you again.

With that thought, reality hit her so hard she almost gasped.

Holy mother of God.

Why hadn't she seen it before?

He was going to move on at the end of the job.

Which meant sex with him was exactly what sex needed to be. Sex. That was it. Nothing more than body parts and glorious release. Praise Jesus—*no, not Jesus*—praise Zeus, in all of his mortal and muscle-bound, half-naked, testosterone-driven glory.

She wanted it, he could give it.

He'd move on. For a million reasons, mostly because she wasn't his type. History proved that. But also because she'd make damn sure that he did.

Unencumbered sex sounded great. Problem was, could she be one hundred percent certain that she'd be able to move on without a second thought? Niggling doubt kept her from jumping on him as her brain rejected the win-win scenario by screaming, *bad idea.*

Bad, bad idea.

Kneeling in front of her, oblivious to the epic game of tug-of-war playing out in her mind, he said, "As I was saying, if it has to do with your well-being over the next twenty-seven days, it is security. Let me rub the kinks out of your neck, so I can race you without pulling back."

His hands on her? Now, when she was fighting with herself? Probably not a good idea. "I didn't say we were going to race," Samantha equivocated.

That almost-smile, the twitch to the left of his lips was there and gone. The twitch told her he was fighting a smile, but he wasn't giving in. A fresh reminder that even in the smallest things, Zeus had unbelievable willpower.

Years earlier, he hadn't touched her while on the job. Hadn't even acted like he wanted to touch her, and that was one of the reasons she was so drawn to him. It was only after the job had ended that he appeared at her doorstep and showed her how wonderful a large dose of pent-up frustration could be. "You didn't have to."

Damn. Resentment flared from deep within. He knew her too well.

"Sweatshirt off. Flat on your belly. I remember how much you love a good neck rub." His voice deepened. Yes, she remembered his style of neck rubs as well. "No using your neck as an excuse when I beat your ass."

"Never going to happen, Hernandez," she said lightly. Easier not to argue. Besides, her neck really did hurt. She pulled her sweatshirt over her head and placed it on the floor. As she shifted to lay face down on the towel, his eyes lingered over her black exercise shirt. It was barely larger than a jog-bra, and it left her midriff exposed.

Their eyes met. Held. A glimmer of raw hunger flashed in his dark eyes.

Would he act on it?

Samantha sucked in a breath. Would she stop resisting and give in to what they clearly both wanted? She wasn't afforded the chance to see where that look could take them. He knelt at her head, leaned over her, and pressed his hands flat on her shoulder blades.

"You're really tight. Does that pressure hurt?"

She almost groaned, for a second wishing he was talking about a different part of her anatomy, one that was craving as much release as her neck. Yet relief at her neck came from his warm touch, and she forced herself to focus on those muscles and tendons, ones that didn't raise a host of underlying issues. "Oh God, that feels great."

"When you passed out today, your head fell back." His voice was almost a whisper. She recognized that tone, remembered what they'd been doing when she last heard it, and felt like telling him not to stop at her neck. "I tried to run without jarring you too much."

Keeping his palms on her shoulder blades, he spread his fingers out and pressed them into her flesh while using his thumbs on either side of her spine, inch by inch working out the knots. "That. Feels. Soooo. Good," she said, breathing in deeply, and relaxing as he probed at her pressure points. After long minutes where he worked magic on her neck, she added, "It wasn't the run."

"Recurring problem?"

Face still down on the towel, she nodded. "Seems to be lately. My job has gotten more and more stressful. End-of-day runs or swimming help. But I've missed too many exercise sessions in the last couple of weeks."

He lifted his hands, using the base of his palms for pressure for a few minutes, and started over with his thumbs, probing and rubbing along her spine, concentrating his effort on the area where her neck joined her back. *God.* What the man could do with his thumbs should be bottled and sold. He ended the massage by flattening his hands and spreading his fingers over her neck and shoulder area, applying gentle pressure.

"Sit up," he said, removing the warmth of his hands. She enjoyed his touch far more than was wise. Damn. She shouldn't have let him put his hands on her. His touch sent muscle memory zapping though every single fiber in her being. The resulting desire didn't give a damn about logic, nor did her aching need for him care about the gut-wrenching hurt that had overcome her when he'd made his decision.

"Do a range of motion rotation," Zeus instructed when she sat up. His husky, quiet tone indicated he'd rather be telling her to do something else. He gave great instructions in bed, where she loved to give a few herself. *Hell.* She sat up, squared her shoulders, and met his eyes. "Tell me if your neck's better."

Sitting cross-legged, she shut her eyes, and rotated her head. Opening her eyes, she glanced up at him, and gave him a thumbs-up signal when she was through. "You knew it would be better."

He nodded as he drew in a deep breath. "I hoped."

He made no move to stand. He stayed on his knees, right in front of her. Because of his height and her flat-on-her-butt position, she had to look up to meet his glance, but not more than a foot of space separated their faces. Unfiltered, pained honesty suddenly flooded his eyes. It was the same look he'd worn after telling her his marriage hadn't worked out, right before she'd shut the door on him the other night. It was a look that said he wanted to have a conversation that would dredge up painful emotions and feelings. The conversation that would only end one way—with them being sure that no matter what they felt for each other, they weren't right for each other. There was no point to the conversation, because she already knew the outcome.

Please God, don't let him go there. There is no point rehashing our past.

Instead of talking, he stood, but that look spoke volumes. He wasn't going to let it drop forever. For now though, he stayed silent.

Good. Because that's a conversation I'm never going to have.

He walked over to the treadmill. "Ready when you are."

"I'm not really up for a race," she said as she stood. "I just need a good, solid run."

"Suit yourself. Six miles. I'll finish before you, whether you race me or not." He bent into a lunge to stretch his quads, before starting his machine at a slow walk. "Waiting on you."

Trying to ignore Zeus, she started at a six-miles-per-hour pace, keeping her attention focused on the glowing dots tracking her progress while she thought about the next day's proceedings. There was still no word as to whether the proceedings would be cancelled for Thursday due to the bombing, or whether it would be business as usual.

"You're behind by an eighth of a mile," Zeus said, interrupting her thoughts.

"I'm not racing," she said. "Thinking through some things."

Judge O'Connor's phone call had been short. After confirming that the Amicus team was fine, he'd gotten to the real point of his call. He hadn't liked her examination of Duvall, because she'd hit too hard at weaknesses in the ITT case against Maximov. His directive was simple and explicit: "*For now, take more of a low profile approach.*"

She had responded that her integrity wouldn't be compromised, because the job of Amicus counsel was to honestly represent to the court an accurate summation of the evidence.

His response: "*No, your job is defined by the tribunal, and I'm telling you not to highlight the weaknesses in the evidence. We've got to find a solution to the problem that this proceeding is becoming."*

The conversation had continued, politely, from there, but Sam hadn't bent. If the proceeding itself was becoming a problem due to the lack of evidence tying the terrorist acts to Maximov or any other terrorist group with international reach, it was her job to make that clear to the judges. If conclusions weren't based on hard facts, the record needed to reflect that the conclusions lacked foundation. Her job was to make sure the record accurately reflected the evidence. At least that was how she perceived her job. Judge O'Connor was making it clear he had other thoughts.

She hadn't felt good about Judge O'Connor's call when it ended, and it now served as a reminder that the job of Amicus counsel required diplomacy.

Diplomacy wasn't a strength of hers. It was usually her way or go-the-hell-down the highway.

She'd work on it.

She set her pace to a nine-minute mile. Zeus reset his pace to match hers. They were both competitive to the nth degree. In everything. Not just in runs. *In bed, too.* She put that thought to the side, and shot him a glance. "Aren't your legs tired after running this afternoon?"

He chuckled. "Not at all."

At the two-mile mark, she lowered her pace. He didn't reset his, no doubt assuming that she wouldn't keep up the eight-minute-mile pace for long. She almost smiled. He had no idea what was in store for him.

"Still," she said. "You're injured, and you were carrying me. I weigh one hundred twenty-three very heavy pounds." She paused, focusing on breathing. "Carrying me had to be a bit of a strain on those leg muscles. Plus, you're built for endurance. Not speed."

"Talk trash all you want." Zeus adjusted his pace. "You'll only lose your breath."

Bastard.

She hit the two and a half mile mark as he did, and reset her pace, dropping it to the fastest sprint she could maintain for two-minute interval. Justin was a serious runner. He'd taught her how to shave time for distance runners. Her runs were now solid, fast, and steady, and punctuated with interval sprints. It was a world-class workout, and she was going to leave Zeus in the dust.

Starting now.

"You can't keep up that pace," he said.

"Watch me."

She focused her legs on her run and her thoughts on her work, and not the man running next to her. In response to Judge O'Connor's call, she had toned down the nightly briefing memo, explaining the problem to Abe and Charles. The internal proceedings of the ITT for that day were minimized in comparison to the bombing. She turned the memo into a bland, but accurate, summation of the day's proceedings and gave a snapshot of what was planned for the next day. If the proceedings were taking place at all. After six more sprint intervals, with short, slower-paced intervals between the sprints, she hit the six-mile finish line thirty seconds before Zeus. She slowed the treadmill to a fast walk, gasping for air.

"Holy shit." He drew a deep breath, stepping off the treadmill.

She wiped the sweat off her brow, enjoying the rush of feel-good endorphins that came with the strenuous run. "Pretty good, huh?"

Palms on his knees, he inhaled and exhaled. "You're even faster than before."

"Justin runs." She stepped off the treadmill, pulling in deep breaths as she reached for the towel. "Marathons. Getting faster was a matter of self-preservation if I wanted to keep up. Or win."

He walked around the room. On his second pass, he lifted his towel from the back of his chair to wipe his forehead, neck, and shoulders. If the mention of Justin bothered him, he didn't show it. Nor would he. His world-class poker face was focused on nothing but regaining his breath. After a few long minutes, as she did a standing stretch, palms flat on the floor, he asked, "When's the wedding?"

Ahhhh. So he was paying attention.

"We haven't set a date. Justin isn't my fiancé. Yet."

As she straightened and stretched her arms overhead, he stopped walking. He was only a foot or so from her, less than an arm's distance away. She wanted to run her fingers down his muscles, over the light glisten of perspiration on his stomach, and feel the rise and fall of his chest as he breathed.

Damn.

She wanted to lick all the way up. Or down. Direction wouldn't matter, when his chest rose. And fell. Like that.

Stop looking.

When she dragged her eyes back to his, he gave a convincing *whatever* shrug. "Media reports paint a mixed picture, but the consensus seems to be that the two of you are engaged. They say it's a merger, not a marriage."

She ignored the press, but it was hard not to be aware of their rife speculation. All of which was becoming irrelevant as her body reacted to the nearness of Zeus and the possibility of having him. He stood so close, she felt his body heat. Or maybe what she was feeling was her own rising temperature.

Eyes on her, he toweled perspiration off his chest, and slung the towel around his neck. With his hands balled into fists, he pulled at both ends of the towel, as though he was giving his hands something to do rather than reach for her.

Her therapist had said she needed to persuade herself that Zeus wasn't as good as she remembered. From the intense fire in his eyes, the way he was looking at her like he was ready to pounce, her opportunity to be persuaded was coming soon.

Do me. Now. Hard. Fast. Deep. Like you used to.

Evidently not a mind reader, he gave her a slight frown and kept his distance. "I saw the two of you together."

"When?"

"June second. Last year. Ten thirty in the evening."

That was pretty damned specific. She thought back. June second was just a date in the past. Nothing special came to mind. "Where was I?"

"D.C. Walking into Dixon Tower."

One of her grandfather's high-end real estate developments. Offices filled the lower three floors. Condos filled the upper floors. She lived in a penthouse. Black Raven provided on-site security on her grandfather's properties, including Dixon Tower. The security company employed thousands of people. She'd never seen Zeus there.

"You were there for work?"

"No," he said. "It was the day my divorce was final. I went there to talk to you."

Her heart pounded harder from what he was saying than from the exertion of the run. She'd assumed he hadn't bothered trying to contact her before showing up in Paris this week.

Assumptions? Very, very dangerous things.

She'd made quite a few with him seven years earlier, and they'd been lethal. Foolish people made assumptions, she reminded herself. *Do not assume anything.*

"What did you want to talk about?"

"I wanted to have the conversation I tried to have with you the other night, when you shut the door in my face."

"I don't want to have that conversation. Not now," she said. *Because there are hard truths that even I haven't faced.* "Not ever."

He gave her a slow nod. "Message received, loud and clear. But I'm not going to honor it. We will have that conversa—"

"June 2. Last year. You went to D.C. to have a conversation with me. You saw me. Why didn't you say something?"

"When I arrived at eight, I figured out that you'd left for the evening. I have an in with the security personnel in the building." He shrugged, lifted the towel from around his neck, and let it fall to the floor. "I waited for you to return. You left alone, but returned with McDougall. You were wearing high heels. A black dress. It fit you like a glove. He was in a tuxedo."

She shrugged. "Sounds like just another night in D.C. We attend events constantly. Why didn't you say something?"

"The two of you got out of a cab together. He talked to you for a few minutes. I wasn't even twenty feet away. He sent the cab away and went in with you. For the night."

She reached for her own towel, which she'd left hanging on the treadmill. It gave her a chance to look away from the honest pain in his eyes. She wiped perspiration off her neck and chest.

If I start telling you about hurt, the pain will consume us both.

June 2nd. Last year. She didn't remember the exact night, but she had no doubt that Zeus was right. She and Justin frequently slept at each other's places. They were, after all, a couple, and though their relationship was platonic, through observing how others behaved Samantha believed that she and Justin were closer than many traditional, long-term couples.

When sexual desire had them going elsewhere for satisfaction, they exercised the utmost discretion. At most, she and Justin told other sexual partners that their relationship was open, that they did not practice monogamy. The reasons why were kept private. No one other than she and Justin knew. They both chose their sexual partners carefully. Discretion was a paramount prerequisite.

Samantha had found that in-depth conversation wasn't necessary with her sex partners. In D.C., people who mattered understood discretion. Still, toys were typically easier than men. After all, toys were equally forgettable, but more dependable, and she didn't have to worry about discretion from her favorite vibrator. It didn't much matter who or what her sexual partners were, because for years, no matter what was happening between her legs, she'd close her eyes and imagine that Zeus was making love to her.

Something he'll never know.

"I've wanted to talk to you forever, but I wasn't going to call you while I was married. There was no point to it. When I saw you with him, I realized you had a life," he said. "I didn't have the right to interfere in it."

Dear God, on top of everything else, why did you have to give this man such a healthy dose of integrity?

With Zeus, she knew she'd have to tell him about the understanding that she and Justin had. Her past with Zeus told her that he had old-fashioned morals, the kind that might keep him from having sex with a woman who was almost engaged to another man.

As her mind searched for the words she needed to tell him of the arrangement, she acknowledged the truth in his statement. "Of course I have a life. Without you. I have a great one."

"I fully realize that. I just thought—"

"That I'd care that you were divorced?"

His shoulders slightly lifted in a shrug. His eyes were intense, honest, and proud. He was laying out his thoughts with strength and giving her the solid message that she could take it or leave it. "That was my hope."

"Why the hell didn't you say something?"

"Dammit, Sam. I wasn't there to talk about the weather. What I had to say seemed pretty goddamn irrelevant as I watched the two of you. He went in with you. For the night."

"You're not in in much of a position to feel miffed over that."

He stepped so close to her that not even an inch separated them. A vein pulsed at his left temple. Deep at her core, she quivered with anticipation. She reached for him and tiptoed, bringing her lips closer to his.

"Please stop talking," she said, wrapping her arms around his neck, trying to pull him down to her.

"This isn't how I wanted this to happen," he said, arms lifting and meeting behind her back. His voice was low, an agonized whisper. As though his words were using the last of his willpower. Forehead bent to hers, touching her, warming her, he said, "I want to clear the air first. Please talk to me first. Really talk. About what happened seven years ago. About how we should go forward. I didn't want this to happen when you're practically engaged to someone else. It's wrong."

"Justin and I have an open relationship."

He frowned. "Open? As in you sleep with other people?"

"We have the option of having sex with other people. You do understand the concept, don't you? And we're going to have an open marriage. Discreet, of course. But open."

"Jesus Christ. Why the fuck would you—"

She put her index finger on his lips. "Shhhhh. Not going to talk about it any more than that."

He was breathing heavily, as though he'd just stepped off the treadmill. So was she. He'd showered just a couple of hours earlier, when they'd come in from the trial. The scent of fresh soap mixed with his musky male, woodsy scent. His body, already warm from the run, was getting hotter. Desire had her knees and arms trembling, and deep inside her internal muscles pulsed with need.

He groaned, pulling her closer, pressing her body flat against him.

With the very last of her willpower, in a throaty voice that didn't sound to her own ears anything like herself, she said, "Just so you're clear, nothing is happening here but sex, and it has nothing to do with what happened before. We're not going to have that conversation. Ever."

"Believe what you want to believe," he muttered, as his lips touched hers. "Just so you're clear, I'd prefer to clear the air now. And we will go ther—"

"Forget it."

"Give me a second," he said, separating from her, turning, and walking away. He went into his bedroom, and reappeared before she caught her breath. He had a condom packet in his hand.

"Sex was a foregone conclusion on this job?"

Serious black eyes glanced at her with a complex look swirling with undercurrents that she couldn't decipher. "If this were just a job, I wouldn't be here."

"I'm on the pill," she said, a fact that had been sufficient for him before.

"Learned the hard way that the pill isn't foolproof," he said with a frown. "And I'd still prefer to clear the air first. By talking."

She stepped closer to him, stood on tiptoes, and whispered, before their lips met, "Not sure the air will ever be clear and don't want to waste time talking." Before he could grab her arms, she gripped the waistband of his shorts and yanked them down.

His mouth found hers as she wrapped her hand around him.

Pressing herself against his abdomen, she felt him shudder as she ran her fingers down the taut flesh of his erection.

Now. Please. Persuade me I've been wrong. Prove my memory distorted reality. Show me you're really not the best.

Chapter Fifteen

Sam had been an impatient, to-the-point lover back then.

Nice to see she hasn't changed.

"Not yet." Reaching down, Zeus pulled her hands off of him, clasping them in his and holding them firmly at her sides. She moaned in protest as he leaned into her and deepened their kiss, gliding his tongue over hers, tasting the sweetness of her.

Bending his head, Zeus moved closer, until her soft breasts flattened against the hard plane of his chest. She rose onto tiptoes and nipped at his lower lip with her teeth. His body shook as fresh anticipation surged through him. She licked the same spot with the point of her tongue, applying soothing pressure.

"Kick off your shoes," he murmured, returning to enjoying their kiss, pressing his mouth onto hers while he held her arms down at her sides. He stepped out of his shoes, one at a time, as she did the same.

Sam flexed her fingers in his hold. "Let go of my arms."

As soon as he freed her, her fingers closed around his hard dick. Again. Resisting the urge to lose control, he muttered, "Stop."

She never did listen worth a damn.

Short fingernails scored the sensitive skin where his penis met his balls, lightly scratching as he slipped on the condom. He grit his teeth while sparks of want and need exploded along his spine. He'd gone from semi-erect to straining for release as they'd talked, and her blood-red lacquered fingernails were going to push him over the fucking edge.

Sex with Sam was like navigating through a war zone. Fortunately, he had prior experience—in war zones and in bed with her. He was prepared for her to fight for what she needed, when she wanted it. How hard. How fast. How deep.

For Zeus, it was a turn-on like nothing else. It typically took an orgasm or two to calm her down. He'd never come across anyone else like her. Didn't care if he ever did. She was all he'd ever wanted. Then and now.

Getting Sam naked, fast, became of paramount importance. He lifted her exercise shirt and the snug, built-in bra and yanked it over her head. The action gave his dick a much needed—but not wanted—break, because it forced her hands off of him.

He drank her moan of protest as he peeled her exercise pants down. Sam returned her fingers to his shaft and squeezed as she glided her thumb over the sensitized tip. He shuddered from the base of his spine up to his very teeth. "Dammit, Sam. Next time I'm tying you."

"Promise?" Voice husky, eyes sultry, she moaned as her thumb pressed the very tip of him, then glided around.

"More than a promise." He groaned, as she squeezed harder. "If you keep this up, I'll come in your hand. That what you want?"

Hell. It wasn't what he wanted. Not when he'd been dreaming of this moment for-fucking-ever. Fortunately for him, he was the stronger of the two. Digging deep, he found the willpower to pull her hands off of him, then shackled her wrists tightly in one hand over her head. Walking toward her bedroom, he pushed her backward with each step.

Two agents were positioned on the other side of the door of the living room. There was no need to broadcast their activities to the on-site agents. Experience reminded him that neither himself nor Sam made love in silence. He'd taken off his mic before the run, telling Ragno to alert him through on-site agents if a crisis occurred. One knock at the door and this would be over.

Eyes gleaming, with a sultry, half-smile on her face, she nodded in encouragement, stepping backward with him as he moved forward. He made it two steps into the doorway of her bedroom and kicked it shut. He'd wanted their first time—this time—to be slow and gentle, but evidently that was a fantasy she hadn't shared.

Back then, he'd made love to her for hours at a time, in the process rubbing out her hard edges until she was malleable and softly loveable, with both of them drifting afterwards in a sea of thoroughly-satiated contentment. Now, assessing the depth of come-on tease and hot desire in her eyes, and the rapid rise and fall of her flushed chest, he gave up on the long-slow-savor approach.

Hell. Sometimes—like now—it's just easier to give Sam what she wants. How she wants it.

In two steps he had her against the wall. With her back flat against it, and her hands locked in his left hand, high over her head, he stepped back as far as he could while keeping her imprisoned.

Inhaling deeply, the scent of jasmine, rose, and natural musk drifted into his consciousness as he stared at her. She was slender and fit, yet had curves and angles. She was soft where he wanted her to be—at the mounds of her breasts, at her small, almost-taut belly, and at her thighs and her ass. Her pale, creamy skin looked delicate, and was a stark contradiction to the fiery, determined woman she was. Definitely not the way she was in bed. There was nothing delicate or demure in the way Sam liked to have sex.

Eyes falling below her waist, he moaned. What he had dreamed of, late at night, when subconscious thoughts overpowered his ability to repress his memories of her, was there, waiting for him. Nestled between the creamy flesh of her thighs, a triangle of soft, golden curls covered her sex. Just thinking about how golden blonde she was—there—drove him fucking crazy in a way that had haunted him for years.

"Ready." She flexed her hips forward.

"Not yet."

He stepped in closer, bent his head to her soft breast, opened his mouth to a pink nipple that hardened into a nub, and felt her lift her right leg behind the small of his back, curling it over his ass. Leg in position, she tried to use it to pull him toward her.

"Not yet," he said again, knowing she'd ignore him until it suited her. *Hell.* He'd never get enough of her.

"Now," she answered as she shimmied herself up him, with her back against the wall. Using her arms and his strength for leverage, she lifted her other leg and locked it behind his back.

Dammit. She always found a way.

Supported by the wall at her back, his left hand that imprisoned both of hers, and the death grip she had on his hips with her legs, she flexed her hips forward. Soft, warm flesh opened onto his dick as she pressed and rubbed against him. Moaning, she arched her back into the motion.

Clenching his jaw with the effort to stave off release, he watched her eyes slightly close, her cheeks become flushed, and her breasts bounce as she rubbed herself into a pre-orgasmic, sexy-as-hell state. His right hand shook as he reached between them, fingers threading through her soft spun-gold curls, probing her flesh.

"Hot," he whispered, sliding his fingers through her folds, drawing a deep breath as he found her opening. He pushed two fingers deep into her tight sheath. She shivered with him. "Mmmm. Wet."

"Like I said. Ready." She looked down, to where his hand was working her, where his penis was poised and straining between the two of them. "Really. Now. Would be good." She met his eyes. There was a wicked gleam in hers. With heavy breaths punctuating each word, with her hips meeting the thrust of his hand, she whispered, "Is this how..." She drew a deep breath. "You want me to come?"

Nope. As usual, she has a great point.

Moving his hand away, and dropping her arms, he gripped her hips with both hands. Lifting her so that he was poised for entry, he used his thigh, butt, and calf muscles to upstroke, and his arms and shoulders to slide her down onto him. Pulling out, he groaned, then pumped forward, forcing every inch of his thick, straining shaft into her as hard and fast as possible. As he repeated the action, again and again, he could tell from her moans, the way her eyes glazed, the way her tight channel contracted around him, the way her hips flexed, that what he was doing was working.

God knows it is for me.

She held on around his neck. For a few seconds he could feel her mouth there, open wide. As her groans grew louder, her head fell to his right shoulder.

"Zeus," she moaned, arching her hips into his. "Oh God. Zeus."

Her channel pulsed and tightened around him in orgasmic spasms that felt like blissful torture on his dick and almost pushed him to completion. He shuddered, resisting the urge to come as she bit into his shoulder. It took him a few seconds to regain control, and he held still while he searched for it. He gripped her hips tightly, lifting her up and down. Slowly. In. Out. Each soft moan of hers provided fuel that kept him going.

Long minutes passed, then her breathing quickened.

When he felt his orgasm building with another of hers, he settled in deep, reached between them with one hand, slipped his thumb into her curls, found the tight nub of her clit, and pressed hard. Her breathing escalated while her channel contracted around him. Sweet, delicious moans escaped from her, punctuated with his name. The sounds she made as she came rivaled the best music he'd ever heard, providing the perfect ending to the heartbreak world of wrong decisions in which he'd been living for seven years.

Her cries grew louder, until she said his name with the same exact wild moan he remembered from the last time they made love. He exploded with a violent orgasm that took his breath and kept going. Each mind-bending spasm chipped away at the hard wall of frustration that had surrounded him since walking away from her.

She turned her head to him, and, as his orgasm waned, he bent to meet her lips. Mouths open, they kissed a long, slow, deep kiss. Breathing with her, he didn't even have energy to open his eyes. After a couple of long minutes, when he stopped seeing stars, he realized their position had never been comfortable for her. By now it had to hurt. He broke away from the kiss.

Without a word, she eased her legs from around his hips. He moved his hips, and slipped out of her, as she slid her feet to the floor. When all he wanted to do was hold her, she squeezed away from the space between the wall and his chest, separating herself from him. She turned her face from him, intent on moving away. Not content to read her body language, he needed to see her expression.

Dammit.

He reached for her arm, but when his fingertips grazed her, she pulled away. Grabbing her and tugging her back against him would have been easy, but something in her quick movement away told him now was not the time to be manhandling her. She kept walking in the direction of the bathroom without looking at him.

"You okay?"

Finally, she turned. The look in her eyes sliced through him with the feel of cold steel. He expected coy. Something teasing. Post-coital laughter. Sam had always been good to give an assessment of how they'd been together, interjecting any number of descriptive words into her pronouncement. But now there was no glib quip. Eyes wide, lips red and swollen from their kisses, she looked as though she'd been stunned into silence. Her uncharacteristic expression scared the hell out of him.

"Dammit. Talk to me. Are you okay?"

She gave him a soft, slow smile, one that suggested it took a lot of willpower, and tried to emphasize the message her eyes were attempting to convey with a nod. Her expression did nothing to help him understand what the hell was wrong. "Fine, Zeus. That was wonderful. I just need a minute."

Her eyes glistened with something. *Fuck.* Tears? She never cried after sex. At least not sex with him. "What's wrong?"

"Nothing," she said, with a headshake that was more alarming than persuasive. "I just need to get cleaned up."

And she didn't do that either. She wasn't a prissy type who had to wipe away evidence of love making the minute it was over.

Hell. Hell. Hell.

One giant step forward, he thought, as he watched her walk into the bathroom. The door shut, and the lock clicked.

Twenty steps backward.

What in the fucking world did I do wrong this time?

Chapter Sixteen

Oh, for the love of God, did I really almost cry?

After their run and their after-exercise activity, after she had showered and recomposed herself into a person she recognized, Samantha returned to her bedroom. Exercise clothes that had been stripped off her body were now folded on the stool at her vanity.

Zeus, ever the thoughtful one.

Missing the warmth of the bathroom, she shivered as she changed into a clean pair of leggings, a long-sleeve T-shirt, and a lavender-colored pullover sweater. The house was large and drafty. It was 9:00 p.m., and the damp chill of the cold winter night seemed to have seeped into her bones. Opening the door that separated her bedroom from the living room, she saw that the door to the hallway stood open.

Zeus?

Nowhere in sight, and she didn't expect him to be. She knew from experience that once she gave him a solid cue to get the hell away, the man was a master at moving on, without looking back. She didn't blame him. She'd do the exact same thing. No matter how much it hurt.

Miles and Jenkins stood in the hallway, backs erect, shoulders broad, in a stance that said they took their jobs seriously. She gave them a nod. "I'll be working in the library."

There, it would be easier to get past the sick feeling that came with knowing her imagination hadn't played a trick on her. She hadn't imagined Zeus was the best she ever had. Now, she knew he was the best she'd ever have.

As she followed Jenkins down the stairs, body aches from deep inside of her and from where his hands had locked on her hips, reminded her just how perfect he was. She may as well make her next therapy appointment now, because she couldn't wait to tell the doctor she hadn't romanticized that aspect of her prior time with Zeus.

Doctor Blackmann, I was right! There really is something magical in the way he fucks. Now what the hell do I do? I can't afford to love him. Cannot.

Blackmann would have a heyday with that statement. Hell. The questions that one would elicit would take hours of his time.

And I know sex has nothing to do with love. But dammit, all I want from him is more. More. More. All of him. In every way.

I can't be this weak. Can I?

More hours of therapy would ensue, and the end result would be that she was going to marry Justin and forget about Zeus. She didn't need appointments with Doctor Blackmann to know the course of action she needed to take. As soon as the judges reached a verdict she was going to put on her running shoes and sprint away from Zeus as though her life depended on it. Because the life she wanted did depend on it.

She heard his voice as she crossed the threshold of the library. In a steady, calm tone, Zeus asked, "What's the radiation level in Grid A-5?"

Bracing herself, she entered the room with a calm, collected look on her face, the polar opposite of how undone she felt inside. Wearing black jeans and a gray sweatshirt with a Black Raven logo, Zeus sat at the table with two of his agents. Laptops and iPads were open in front of them. A camera was mounted on a small tripod, and its lens was directed at Zeus. He glanced in her direction as she walked into the room.

Ragno's voice answered his question, broadcasting through a mic system that made her sound as though she was in the room with them. "Manageable. We marked it orange."

The crispness of Ragno's matter-of-fact voice, the absolute nearness of it, all around them, was disconcerting when her face didn't appear on a television monitor. It was like hearing the omniscient voice of a female god, commanding all who could hear to pay careful attention.

Samantha walked further into the room, Zeus's attention no longer on her, but on the four flat-screen television monitors. Her gaze followed his there. Each played a different scene. Only one was an actual television station, with a news show providing a recap of President Cameron's earlier speech. Two monitors displayed three-dimensional maps of a city, with layers of detail being added at dizzying speeds as unseen hands zoomed in and out on different areas.

The fourth screen revealed a man, with wavy hair and green eyes, high cheekbones, and an intensely serious look that was the exact look habitually worn by Zeus. Looking at him was like looking at Zeus—but not. He had the same full head of wavy black hair, the same high cheekbones, square jawline, olive-complexion, and broad shoulders. The left side of his mouth was drawn down in an almost-frown, exactly the expression Zeus wore.

No two men could look so similar and be unrelated. In that

final conversation seven years earlier, when Zeus had mentioned others in his life counting on him to do the right thing, he'd told her that his family was close, that his mother had never remarried after his dad had been murdered in an armed robbery. Zeus was the elder of two boys.

Like the men here in the library, Zeus's doppelganger—they had to be brothers—tapped away at his keyboard, glancing now and then at monitors showing him, she assumed, the same thing she was watching in Paris.

Zeus's double, save for the eyes, glanced into the camera with laser-like focus. "Zeus, Ragno, Grid A-7. Denver is painting it red, but we'll need to explore it. High priority."

"Says who?" Zeus said.

"Bill Goldman, and if he went there, radiation can't be that bad."

Samantha recognized the name. Bill Goldman was a well-respected freelance reporter who travelled to far-flung destinations on high-profile stories. He was now in Paris, covering the ITT proceeding for 24-7, the cable news show that dominated worldwide news.

She walked to the table where Abe and Charles sat. Their laptops were open, and each had papers related to the ITT proceeding in front of them. Neither focused on their own work. Their attention was captured by the monitors and Zeus.

Charles, wearing a red cardigan over a white T-shirt, gave her a hello nod, and moved his computer to make room for her. "Sit here," he whispered, gesturing to the chair on his left, the one remaining chair at the table that had a view of the monitors and the table where Zeus sat.

As she sat in the chair that he indicated, Charles added, "Just received an email. Proceedings are postponed in the morning, but will start at noon."

She nodded, her attention focused on the monitors. "What is going on here?"

"Analysts are building a map of Praptan for the bounty hunt team to use. They're using intelligence collected since the meltdown, with radiation levels as indicators of where the bounty hunt team can go."

"Ragno," Zeus said. "Do we have all the Goldman data?"

"Yes. Goldman has been there three times. He's theorized for years that Maximov hides in Praptan. Goldman did us a favor by sending me his backup data after I called him this afternoon. We owe him. I suspect that as soon as he has a chance to breathe after the coverage he's doing for 24-7 regarding today's bombing, he'll call."

Zeus nodded. "Got it."

The green-eyed man looked into the camera, at Zeus. "Do not agree to a ride along."

Zeus glanced at the television monitor. A pulse beat at his temple as their gazes locked. "Wasn't planning on it, but don't tell me what to do. Just an FYI, baby brother, I'm your superior. Remember?"

"Yes, Jesus. A fact you never let me forget." Gabe used the Americanized, son-of-God pronunciation, instead of the Latin pronunciation of Zeus's full name.

"Grow up, Gabe."

"Angel, Zeus. Just to be clear..." Ragno's voice was soothing and calm, as though she was used to being an intermediary between the two men. "Goldman knew we were proceeding with the bounty hunt before I said a thing. Yet another reminder that word is out. If Maximov is hiding in Praptan, and if we hope to surprise him, we only have a limited time frame with which to work."

Abe leaned towards Samantha, pushing his tortoise-shell glasses up his nose, his blue eyes sparkling with intense interest in the exchange between Zeus and his agent, and what was happening on the monitors. He wore slacks and loafers, but over his shirt he wore a gray sweatshirt with a Black Raven logo. Though the sweatshirt was large for him, he looked comfortable in it, as though he'd given up his Brooks Brothers-style polish and was trying to be one of them.

"Abe," Samantha asked, "how's your arm?"

He shrugged. "Fine." He gestured with his chin to the monitors, and lowered his voice to a whisper. "Gabe is leading the bounty hunt. Zeus—Jesus. Gabe—Michael Gabriel." He arched an eyebrow, and gave her a slight eye roll and a smirk. "As in Archangels? Do you think their mom had high expectations for them when she named them?"

Samantha chuckled as she glanced from the brother on the monitor to the brother in the room, eyeing each man as they projected a powerful aura of confident determination.

"Ragno, give me a map with nothing but the Goldman areas of interest, and keep radiation levels constant," Zeus said.

Gabe looked into the camera. "Why don't we just see what Goldman says, without worrying about radiation for a while? Remember, we'll be carrying radiation detection devices."

"I remember, and no," Zeus said, tone firm. "Keep radiation levels constant on the Goldman map. I want to assess the importance of each grid in light of radiation levels."

One of the monitors that had shown a map went dark. A new map appeared, as a basic grid of streets. As the map pulsed with an overlay of additional three-dimensional detail, Ragno said, "Radiation levels are red and orange. The Goldman priority areas are purple."

Gabe glanced at Zeus. "No matter how we dissect the intel, it looks like I'll need more men. With Goldman's data, and information I've gathered from other search efforts, there are just too many sectors that warrant a search."

Zeus drew a deep breath, his eyes on the monitors. "We need more intel."

Everyone in the room fell silent as the Goldman map was layered with more detail. Keeping an eye on the monitors, Sam turned on her laptop as she thought through whether any of the information she'd come upon as she'd worked on the ITT proceeding could be relevant to a potential search of Praptan.

Before her laptop had powered up, Zeus slid into the empty chair at the table she was sharing with Charles and Abe. He placed his iPad in front of him. One of the agents at the table where Zeus had been sitting turned the camera in their direction. "Gabe?"

His attention remained focused on something other than the camera for a few seconds, then his green eyes seemed to look right at her. "Yeah?"

"Meet the Amicus team. Sam, Abe, Charles, meet Agent Michael Gabriel Hernandez. Gabe. My brother. He's leading the bounty hunt." Gabe's eyes lingered on her, even though his fingers flew over the keyboard at the same time.

Years earlier, she'd learned of Zeus's closeness to his family only after he had started the conversation that led to him leaving her. Before that conversation, she and Zeus hadn't talked much about the personal issues that had mattered so much to him. They'd been too busy with...other things.

Big mistake.

Falling in love with him before knowing anything of the subtlety and complexity that drove each of his decisions in the real world–the world that she was no part of—had been a bad move on her part. The mistake, of course, had started with the falling in love part. It had simply been exacerbated by the reality of his life. And hers.

Now, as Gabe stared at her with an expression that suggested more than casual interest, she wondered whether he knew that she and Zeus had shared history. Gabe glanced at his computer screen, typed a short burst of commands, and glanced back at her. Something in the questioning look in his eyes made her wonder whether he was typing a question about her, instant messaging Ragno or his brother for more information.

Doesn't matter.

With Zeus's left leg pressed solidly against her right, Samantha nodded hello to Gabe, and shifted her eyes to Zeus as she reminded herself not to dwell upon the interwoven tapestry of personal issues that made him the man he was. Even without thinking of the underlying complexity that drove him, the sheer physicality of him sitting close to her was enough of a distraction.

She shifted her leg away from his, but in a few seconds he found hers again, the solid muscles of his thigh rock hard against hers. The table seated six. It was spacious enough for everyone to have private legroom.

Zeus gave her that slight smirk of a smile, indicating he didn't intend to respect her personal space. Being in a professional setting at the same table with a man with whom she'd just had mind-blowing sex, pretending that nothing happened, was a new one for her. Pretending there was nothing between them, however, was not new, and she could accomplish that despite the warm pressure of his leg, which had her insides quivering.

Because there is nothing there. Remember?

While her body reacted to the nearness of him with a yearning that took her breath, she composed her features to match the coolness in his expression.

Focus on the task at hand.

Maximov. Find him. Convict him. End him.

She tore her attention from Zeus and stared at the maps on the monitors. Although the Goldman map had been stripped of most of the colors and detail reflected on the other map, red levels remained constant, and various areas were marked with x's on both maps. The x's had dates.

"What are the x's?" she asked.

"Reported fatalities among prior teams that had the same idea we're executing," Zeus said.

"I wasn't aware of recent searches in Praptan," Samantha said, "or fatalities there."

"Bounty hunter deaths don't usually make it to the national

news." He shrugged. "Or documents that are admitted into ITT proceedings."

"How did Black Raven get the information?"

Zeus was quiet for a second, as though weighing what to tell her. The eyes of his agents were on him. "We keep ourselves aware of what others in our business are doing," he said, "in a variety of ways. One way that is paying off in this job is our standing tradition of treating other private security contractors and military personnel with respect. The world of special operations with high intensity jobs is small. Military personnel and agents from competing private security contractors are often thrown together in volatile situations. Respect promotes camaraderie. Some of the Maximov bounty hunters over the years have been private security contractors, either working for their company or chasing the bounty in their off time."

He turned to the monitor, his eyes on his brother. As he shifted, his leg moved away, but in a few seconds, it returned. "One of Gabe's many strengths is that he has never met a stranger. He called his friends on this one—and that includes bounty hunters and members of the governmental task force looking for Maximov. They've given him answers. Much of the intel we're layering onto the maps comes from them."

"How generous of them to share," she said, unable to keep a slight bit of sarcasm out of her voice.

Zeus chuckled. "Yes, Sam. We've had to pay for some of this information, and your grandfather is paying for this too. But because of men like Gabe, at least we can be reasonably certain they're not selling us bullshit that will get our agents killed. Though that possibility is always considered."

"I have a couple of ideas for intel," Samantha said. "First—Ragno, have you found the 2010 Joint Task Force Study entitled *Praptan: Birthplace of a Terrorist*?"

There was a pause. "Not yet."

"The study is in high level files that aren't a part of the ITT record, at least not that I know of," Samantha said. "It takes information known in 2010 on Maximov and pinpoints areas of interest in Praptan. In 2010 a team of SEALs went in and searched those areas. Needless to say, searches were unproductive. The study may help this effort."

Before she could say anything else, Ragno said. "We'll find it. You don't need to compromise yourself by actually sending me information. As long as I know what to look for, I'm golden."

"The 2010 task force talked to people who taught at the

university. It was a huge effort, and provided no answers," Samantha said. "With Black Raven analysts looking at it, with new information that has been developed since then, maybe something will turn up.

"Second—in 2009 Vladimer Stollen and Maximov's son, Vasily Maximov, were apprehended and convicted of the hijacking on Northern Lights flight 875." The flight, which was routed for LaGuardia, had been hijacked by a team of six Maximovists. Military aircraft on regular patrol in the area intercepted the flight and shot it down before it reached its intended crash site, which was later determined to be the United Nations headquarters in Manhattan. The plane crashed in the East River. All of the one hundred forty-three passengers aboard died, along with the crew and hijackers. The ensuing investigation revealed that one of the hijackers had been a flight attendant. Two of the hijackers were experienced pilots. Their plan had been a suicide mission. Communications with the hijacking team led investigators to apprehend and convict Stollen and Vasily. Their mistake had been they were in the United States when the event occurred. Now they were both in a U.S. prison and were sentenced to death.

"We have their files," Gabe said. "They weren't helpful to our search for Maximov."

"I'm not suggesting you look at the files," Samantha said, as the door to the library opened. Three agents walked in with steaming pans of food, as the red-headed agent she recognized as the chef in charge of the kitchen made his way to the marble-topped table they'd used as a buffet on Tuesday evening. Once there, he lit waiting chafing dishes and directed placement of the pans. The aroma of roasted meats and vegetables filled the room.

"What are you suggesting?" Gabe asked.

"Except for providing swabs and DNA that will enable us to prove that the man who is ultimately apprehended is actually the man the world knows as Andre Maximov, Vasily Maximov has been a dead end ever since he was apprehended," Zeus said.

Samantha nodded. "His appeals are ongoing. So are the appeals of Stollen. More than seven years after their offense. The public's disgust that these appeals take so long is part of the reason the ITT proceedings have no appeals." She glanced at Gabe. "I'm suggesting we interview Stollen."

"Why?"

"Information Stollen provided led investigators to conduct the 2010 Joint Task Force Study entitled *Praptan: Birthplace of a Terrorist* and the resulting search. Something that isn't a matter of public record, something that I learned as I worked on these ITT proceedings, is that he was offered a pretty sweet deal at the time for the information he provided. The death penalty was taken off the table. His sentence became for a fixed, 20-year term, not life. Once the 2010 search of Praptan proved unsuccessful, the deal was taken off the table."

"We know Stollen was Maximov's second-in-command. In fact, aside from Vasily, Stollen is the world's last proven link to the Maximov-In-Exile organization. I say I try to interview him and ask him what the teams missed in 2010. Stollen has had seven years to rot in a cell and think about the looming death penalty. Plenty of time to think about anything he might have omitted in his prior debriefing."

The chef opened a wine bottle, while the agents who were assisting him made another trip to the kitchen.

Zeus leaned forward, eyes gleaming with a light that indicated he saw possibilities in her comment, while Gabe shook his head.

"No one has interviewed Stollen since then?" Zeus asked.

"As far as I know," Samantha said, "no."

"Access to Stollen is an insurmountable problem," Gabe said. "The attorney who represents him in his appeals is actually Robert Brier—U.S. Defense Counsel in the ITT proceeding. Brier has made it clear that Stollen is off limits to anyone, especially bounty hunters looking for Maximov."

"Brier has gotten court orders in this ITT proceeding that restrict access," Abe added, "and he isn't likely to change his mind, roll over, and let us in. Right, Charles?"

"Definitely not the sort of man to change his mind, unless it's to his benefit." Charles tapped at his keyboard, stopped typing, then read for a second, arching his eyebrow. "Stollen is imprisoned at ADX Florence, Colorado. It's a supermax. The Alcatraz of the Rockies. You won't be talking to him without a court order."

"While Brier is defending the individual defendants, we all know his hidden agenda is protecting Stollen, which means he is protecting Maximov and his organization. Just like everyone's agenda is to pursue Maximov and his organization. So"—Samantha gave Gabe a nod—"Stollen has been off limits to the lawyers in the ITT proceeding as well. Stanley Morgan and I were the proponent of the motion to interview Stollen that was made in the ITT proceeding. Which was denied. There've been concerns regarding relevance, and Brier has won those arguments."

"He must have advanced a damn narrow definition of relevance," Zeus said.

"The concept of relevance is complicated." Samantha nodded in agreement with Zeus. "And subject to interpretation. Brier's argument is that a man who was convicted more than seven years ago obviously has nothing to say about the four terrorist acts this ITT is trying. I might not completely agree with Brier, but he is a well-respected attorney in the community of international law, and he has a great track record on human rights issues. He's persuasive. When he argues, he wins."

"So how can you get us in?" Gabe asked.

Samantha locked eyes with Gabe, while Zeus chuckled. Her eyes shifted to Zeus, who was focused on her. He gave her a smile. A real one, with white teeth showing and a sparkle in his eyes. There was a trace of admiration in it, and her insides melted, while her heartbeat quickened. He loved intelligent women and had loved that she was smart. She knew that, because he'd told her so, years earlier. They'd had that conversation in bed. When he'd shown her just how turned on he became by an intelligent woman.

Chapter Seventeen

"Gabe, Sam's not talking about getting Black Raven in to talk to Stollen," Zeus said, proving once again how well he knew her. "This is too good of an opportunity for her to pass up. She wants to get herself in." He shifted his gaze from her to his brother. "And collect intel for the bounty hunt while doing work for the ITT."

Gabe's gaze bounced to her. Leaning back in his chair, he nodded. "Sounds like a plan to me. But how are you going to get in, when ITT rulings have prohibited access?"

"Hold it a second." The admiration that had been in his eyes was replaced with something he didn't often show. Worry. She readied herself to argue with him, because she knew where he was going with it. He shifted in his chair, pressing his leg harder against hers. "You shouldn't be doing this."

"Why not?" Samantha asked.

"It exceeds your job responsibilities as Amicus Curiae counsel," Zeus said. He turned to the chef who stood silently at his side, and nodded. "Thank you. It smells incredible."

As the Black Raven agents, Abe, and Charles made their way to the dinner buffet, Samantha and Zeus remained at the table. She squared her shoulders. Using her courtroom voice that was steady, authoritative, and professional, she said, "My job is to analyze all information that may be relevant to ITT proceedings, and finding Maximov is certainly relevant. The bounty hunt is public. It isn't secret that a task force is looking for Maximov. Plus, if I tie the interview request to ITT proceedings, I'll be underscoring the need to talk to Stollen."

A frown line bisected his eyebrows. "You'll be fighting an uphill battle against Brier and existing orders of the ITT. This has the potential to make you the focal point in a very heated argument."

She shrugged. "I can handle it. I'll do some groundwork and make a motion."

"No."

Anger simmered through her veins. "I'm not asking for permission, and you're out of line."

"You'll be in the middle of a controversy, advocating for a position."

Abe and Charles returned to the table with plates in one hand, wine glasses in the other. One quick glance at them told her they were focused on her interaction with Zeus, like spectators at a tennis match. The other agents in the room, two of whom were at the buffet table and two at their worktable, had eyes on her and Zeus. "That is my job. In a nutshell."

"And my job is to advise you to keep a low profile."

"No. Your job is to make sure I stay safe, while I do my job. No matter what my job entails."

"Sounds like you're fighting a losing battle, bro," Gabe interjected.

"Don't need your advice on this one," Zeus snapped, irritation evident. His gaze returned to Samantha, and he switched his tone to something quieter, yet authoritative. "In any other proceeding or trial, that wouldn't be a problem. In this circus, it isn't wise for you to be center stage with the spotlight shining on you. Stanley Morgan was at center stage—"

"His death hasn't been classified as a murder."

Zeus nodded. "True. But I don't want the bounty hunt to push you to the forefront so that you personally become a lightning rod for the next terrorist strike."

"Do not attempt to tie my hands on this. Your idea of what security means can't stand in the way of my professional judgment." She saw his counter-argument building behind his steady obsidian eyes. Zeus drew a deep breath, providing a pause before he countered with an argument. "You don't get to define my job," she added, "and I won't back down on this."

Abe and Charles were waiting for her to get her plate before starting to eat. She stood and walked over to the buffet table, knowing she should be hungry. Lunch had been hours ago, and she hadn't eaten much of that. The vigorous run had left her feeling empty, but instead of having an appetite, the burning in her stomach reminded her she should've taken an antacid.

Slices of pork roast were in chafing dishes, alongside baked sweet potatoes and roasted vegetables. A bowl contained a large salad of arugula, endive, slivers of apple, and candied walnuts. Whole-grain bread rolls, the dark-brown crust flecked with sesame seeds, nestled in a basket. Thick slices of yellow pound cake lay on a platter, with a large bowl of berries. It all looked appetizing, but what she craved wasn't this healthy fare. A good pizza would be nice. A sandwich, of thinly-shaved ham and barbeque potato chips, on white bread. French fries.

Her stomach twisted, remembering the last time she'd been ready to eat a French fry, right before watching Eric ingest cyanide. Instead of reaching for a plate, she reached for a wine glass and the bottle of Loire Valley white burgundy that the chef had opened.

Rather than lifting it to her lips, she hesitated. It would be the first food item in her mouth untested since the cyanide poisoning. She had to get over her fear, she knew.

Zeus handled the dilemma for her. He was at her side, took the glass from her, took a small sip, and gave her a glimmer of a smile as he handed it back to her. "Nice. Crisp. All good."

"Zeus. She's right." Gabe's gaze drifted to his computer monitor for a second, then he glanced back at the camera as he typed a few keystrokes. "You're an ace at Black Raven issues and pretty damn smart, but you aren't a lawyer. Maybe you've been in management too long. Maybe it has been so long since you were in the field as a bodyguard that you've forgotten the rules." One of the agents in the room drew a harsh breath. "As her bodyguard, your job is to protect her while she does hers. Not tell her how to do it."

"Remember that discussion we had about boundaries?" Zeus, at Samantha's side, glanced directly at the camera and shot his brother a quelling look that was as harsh as his tone. "You just crossed one you shouldn't have. Stop acting like my brother and start acting like an agent who appreciates his job and wants to damn well keep it."

Samantha leaned against the wall, took three small sips of the wine, and stared at the monitor as she waited for the wine to help settle her stomach and nerves. Neither Zeus's harsh words, nor his steely-eyed glance, did anything to wipe away the gleam of interest in his brother's eyes and the play of a smile at his lips.

The younger Hernandez brother was just as gorgeous as his big brother, with high cheekbones, a solid jaw, and thick hair. Like Zeus, Gabe's eyes had a thick fringe of lashes and an intensity that was magnetic. He didn't have the permafrost coolness of his big brother, though. From what Samantha could see, his expressions more often reflected what he was feeling, and right now, rather than being cowed by his brother's threatening tone, he was stifling a laugh. As he held his brother's gaze, while a smirk played at his lips, Gabe seemed to be thoroughly enjoying his big brother's discomfort.

Zeus drew a deep breath, and exhaled as he squared his shoulders. Samantha was used to all sorts of domination tactics, intended and unintended. In the quiet hush of courtrooms, where professional decorum ruled, subtle moves made a big difference. Silence was a tool people used, and Samantha had learned not to fill in awkward silences with words. Her job was not to placate an opponent who was stewing.

Knowing this pot was best left simmering, because she had the winning hand and Zeus was smart enough to see that, she kept silent. She took another sip and walked back to the table.

The man was beautiful when he was perturbed. Quiet, but cheeks flushed. His frown was slight, but there was an unmistakable pull at the left side of his mouth. She placed her glass on the table, sat next to him, and settled into her chair. When his leg found hers, he gave her a brief nod of acquiescence.

As if I need his permission.

Samantha bit her tongue and considered this a win.

"Assuming I agree to this tactic," Zeus said, apparently not done stating his case, "of which I'm still uncertain, why do you think your request to interview Stollen will be successful now, when prior attempts weren't?"

Good question.

Samantha glanced at the television that once again showed highlights from President Cameron's earlier speech. She reminded herself of Morgan's constant worry that the ITT proceeding would be nonproductive, and his concern that a failure of this last ditch, civilized attempt to conquer terrorism would leave the world in a worse position. Morgan's fear was coming to fruition. The direct terrorist attack on the ITT proceedings underscored the fact that the terrorists were winning. "I have a feeling the landscape may have changed after today's events. Prior to now, the judges were focused on expediency. I'll emphasize efficacy and leverage today's events into an argument that our search for information on Maximov's whereabouts needs to be more inclusive."

Zeus frowned, dark eyes studying her. "We have to assume any request to interview Stollen will be made public, correct?"

"Yes. Most of the business of the ITT becomes accessible to the public, and the more important the information is, the more visible it becomes. Media and interested parties are constantly scouring the record, looking for items of interest."

"Do these judges have authority to give you bargaining chips? Without something to offer Stollen," Zeus said, loading his plate with salad and vegetables, a small spoonful of potatoes, and a few slices of meat. "He sure as hell won't talk to you."

"Let me think about it for a second." Samantha considered his question as she assembled her dinner, placing a generous pat of butter on her potatoes.

"No vegetables?" Zeus asked, his voice low, their backs to the camera.

"I don't like that assortment."

"What about salad?"

"Seems like all the exercise I did this evening would earn me the right to eat anything I please. By the way, I beat you in that race. If you recall, that wasn't the performance of someone who is suffering nutritional deficiency. Nor was my performance after the race." She placed another generous pat of butter on her potatoes, and added a third pat when she saw that Zeus was watching her with a slight frown.

Returning to the table, she unrolled her fork and knife from the linen napkin she had picked up at the buffet. Zeus sat down next to her, reached over with his fork to her plate, getting ready to test the food for her, as he'd done with everything she'd eaten since Monday night.

She reached for his arm, holding her hand on his bicep, and gave him a slight headshake. "I'm okay here. I've got to get over this fear. But thank you."

"Good. Progress," he said, as she removed her hand from him. He dove his fork into her plate anyway, scooped up one of the pats of butter she'd put there, and put it on his own potatoes.

"Hey. I wanted all of that butter. Every precious drop of it."

"I know. I just forgot to get some." Chuckling, he slid his fork under some of the salad on his plate, and placed it on hers. "Just try a bit of the salad. You'll like it. The walnuts have sugar on them."

"Well, give me more of them, and less of the green stuff." With her fork, she pushed the greens to the side of her plate, reached into his plate with her fork, and scooped up a few walnuts and apple slices. As she deposited them back on her plate, she realized Abe and Charles were watching them. So were the other agents in the room. Glancing at the monitor, she saw that Gabe was focused on them, as well. His eyes were narrowed. Questioning.

Busted.

Glancing at Zeus, she saw that he wasn't focused on Gabe, or his unasked question. His dark eyes were on her. He gave her a slight shrug, suggesting that he didn't give a damn if the world knew there was more between them than the decorum with which professionals should act.

He needs a reminder about discretion...just as I do.

Eating off his plate could be interpreted as flirtatious

behavior, and openly flirting in public while at a dinner table when she was practically engaged to a U.S. Senator was not wise. Her relationship with Justin—one of the most important things in her life—demanded discretion when she had flirtatious or sexual relationships with other men.

Pretending that their exchange had been nothing but professional, Samantha squared her shoulders, and tried hard to think back to the last topic of conversation that had been relevant to the ITT proceedings. "ITT judges have authority to offer leniency on any sentence previously imposed by a member country, in exchange for information that will assist the ITT in its objectives."

"Would they do that here?" Gabe said. "Stollen is pretty much hated by everyone, universally."

"Maybe." She locked eyes with Zeus. "Let me work on strategy. When I ask for permission, I want to make damn sure I get it. I need to formulate an approach designed to get the answer I want."

"Now that's the kind of attitude I like to see," Gabe said, reaching for a carafe, and pouring a stream of steaming black coffee into his mug.

As her gaze bounced between the brothers, her mind raced through strategy. Since prior decisions of the ITT prohibited access, all the judges must agree to reverse those decisions. Should she approach Brier directly? Should she go through Judge O'Connor? She decided she needed to call Judge O'Connor in the morning, but go through proper channels. While proceedings were in France, protocol required that a motion be filed in the record and Judge Ducaisse, the chief judge from France, would be the decision maker. Calling Judge O'Connor first would enable him to apprise Judge Ducaisse of the motion and the position of the judges from the United States.

"That being said," Samantha continued, her eyes on Gabe, then Zeus. "I may need your help with facts. To underscore the necessity for access to Stollen, I may have to reveal something about the need to go to Praptan."

"No," Zeus said. "Not an option. Word will get out. I don't want to facilitate an ambush."

"What if you fake it?" Gabe asked. "Make up a story about where the bounty hunt is going. Make it plausible based on something in the Stollen files?"

The eyes of everyone in the room focused on her. Abe, as second chair attorney, knew her concerns as a lawyer and specifically as Amicus counsel. Through Abe's tortoise-shell glasses, his blue eyes were lit with a caution warning. She gave Abe a reassuring nod, a signal that she wasn't forgetting her professional and ethical obligations as an attorney.

"The duty of candor that I owe the tribunal requires truthfulness," Samantha said. "However, I'm sure your intel would enable me to come up with a scenario of options." She glanced in the monitor at Gabe, whose open expression and wide smile told her he was persuaded her plan was a good one. Zeus's brooding look told her he wasn't so sure. She focused on Gabe, as she continued. "Options that would support an argument that interviewing Stollen is of paramount importance without revealing where Gabe's team is going."

Gabe gave a low whistle. "Welcome to the team, Sam."

"Samantha," she said, correcting him. Only one living person got away with calling her Sam, and he wasn't the green-eyed Hernandez brother. "Not Sam."

"Sorry," Gabe said. "Zeus calls you Sam. I've connected a few dots on my own, but I didn't realize he had an exclusive on your nickname."

He was obviously going to tease his brother—and anyone connected to him—every step of the way. Just like an adoring, pesky, in-your-face younger brother would.

"Ragno," Zeus said, once again ignoring Gabe, "can you pull up everything we can find on Stollen?"

"We've already got a wealth of information, and we're crawling through databases, looking for more," Ragno responded. "Some of what Stollen said is already factored into our decision to go to Praptan. By the way, I've found the 2010 study—*Praptan: Birthplace of a Terrorist*—that Samantha referred to earlier."

"Great," Zeus said. "That was fast."

"It helps to know what I'm looking for," Ragno answered.

"Ragno sent the report to me while you were stealing Samantha's butter," Gabe said. "Or maybe it was when you were giving her your salad. Check your inbox."

Zeus ate a forkful of salad. Eyes on his brother, he said, "Ragno, look for something that could present a plausible argument requiring Sam to talk to Stollen now."

"Such as the bounty hunt is headed to caves in Afghanistan, or the Mexican desert?" Ragno asked.

Zeus shrugged. "Wherever might make sense. Any area Stollen frequented. Anything that gives us a link to Stollen and a destination. When Sam talks to him, she'll ask him the real questions. Word might get out, but it will be nearer in time to our mission. Less time for ambush prep."

"Understood," Ragno said.

"Gabe," Zeus said, "we're signing off for now."

"Oh, come on," Gabe said. "I'm enjoying the family time."

Zeus glanced at Agent Small, lifted his right hand, and gave a signal with his index finger. Gabe disappeared from the monitor. "Sam. There's more," Zeus said, "and this information might produce something that can underscore the need for you to talk to Stollen. Based upon your request that we share the information we're uncovering in the bounty hunt, we've created a file-sharing database for the three of you. We call it OLIVER."

"Why OLIVER?" To Sam it sounded like a name for a beagle. Maybe a war hero. Not a database.

"It's an acronym that has to do with drives, access codes, encryption, and filters. None of it makes sense to anyone other than the designer and his team. You'll be receiving a memo from R. Barrows in a few seconds. He designed it. It contains information regarding what we've put into OLIVER and directions on how to manipulate the database."

Samantha glanced at Charles and Abe. Charles was finishing his last bite of pork roast. Abe's plate was empty. Earlier in the evening, she'd explained that she'd asked Zeus to share the Black Raven data from the bounty hunt with her. Now, they looked like eager students, ready for any and all knowledge Zeus could provide.

"R. Barrows," Abe said. "As in Richard Barrows?"

Zeus gave a casual nod, as though there was nothing exceptional about the fact that one of the world's leading cyber geniuses now worked with Black Raven and was providing assistance on the bounty hunt. "Most of the information in OLIVER is highly sensitive. OLIVER is a subset of a larger body of Black Raven data. Our sourcing tactics are..." he paused, his words tapering, "cutting edge."

"Meaning you don't have authority to have most of the information that is in OLIVER?" Samantha asked.

He gave no indication he planned to answer her direct question. "Information from OLIVER cannot be shared, distributed, or used in any manner without prior permission."

"From whom?" Charles asked.

Zeus's sweeping glance encompassed the Amicus team. "Me. Also, your actions in OLIVER will be monitored. Any attempt at information sharing or duplication, without my approval, will result in termination of access. Understood?"

Charles cleared his throat. Abe looked at Samantha. As she glanced at her team, their discomfort at Zeus's dose of reality was palpable. In a low voice, Abe said, "So on top of data sourcing problems, by having Black Raven monitor what we do in the database, we're potentially compromising the attorney client privilege."

Which meant that their thought processes, which were typically protected by the attorney-client privilege, were not protected. Abe and Charles cast an uneasy look in her direction. Charles stood and walked to the buffet.

"Sam?" Zeus's right eyebrow arched. "I'm spelling it out so we have a clear understanding. Anything from OLIVER can only be used with my approval."

In the Congressional hearings following the Barrows incident, detractors of Black Raven had alleged that the company used its cyber skills to hack through databases with reckless abandon. Some called it cyber theft. Black Raven called it getting the job done. The hearings had ended in favor of Black Raven. There'd been no reprisals, nor had there been any type of legislation designed to curb the methods employed by Black Raven, or other companies who were attempting to follow suit.

Considering the implications of what Zeus was saying in terms of her career path, she hesitated. She wished she had time to confer with Justin on this one. Whether the end would justify the means in the ITT proceeding was an open issue. What wasn't an open issue, though, was the certainty that by looking at information that had been obtained through questionable means, she was as complicit as the person who hacked into the data. Her integrity could later be questioned.

If things soured, using Black Raven data was potentially a career-limiting move, because anything was fair game for the review committee that would ultimately consider her for a judgeship.

Was the Black Raven data worth the potential negative fallout for her career? She didn't know.

Won't know, until I see what they have.

"Are you in," Zeus asked, "or out?"

Being given access to the database was no different than using the information they'd gathered on the bounty hunt, she reasoned. It was just that having personal access made it seem different, made her feel more complicit in Black Raven's illicit data collection efforts. In the legal world in which she lived, the words accomplice and co-conspirator applied to those who acted in concern in criminal acts, and co-conspirators were prosecuted to the same extent as the ringleader.

Yet she remembered the cracking sound of the bomb, the acrid smells of smoke, blood, and fear, the feel of Zeus's strong body protecting her as they fell. The moans and cries of the wounded, people who didn't have security protecting them. People who were there merely to express an opinion on the proceedings. She'd been safe, but only because of Zeus and Black Raven. Survivor's guilt told her that the world needed to be safe for those who didn't have ace security teams.

Period.

Charles returned to the table with a thick slab of pound cake, piled high with berries. Eyeing the red, blue, and black berries spilling over the yellow cake, Samantha nodded. "I'm in. Let us see what you've found. I'm not sure we'll use any of it. I want to be perfectly clear here—we're not agreeing to your tactics. However, the events of today, from the bombing to the resulting pandemonium, are enough for me to know I'm making the right choice." She glanced at Abe and Charles. "Are you two okay with this?"

They nodded.

To Zeus, she said, "Move forward."

Zeus gave her a nod. "Ragno? Alert Barrows we're ready."

After a second, the monitor with the news show went dark, and a middle-aged man, with gray hair and clear blue eyes appeared on the screen. "Samantha, Abe, and Charles," Barrows said, as their computers dinged with an alert indicating they were receiving a message from R. Barrows. "The email contains download, access, and search instructions to OLIVER. We've made it as user friendly as possible. Because we're integrating information from sources known to the ITT and sources not produced in the ITT proceeding, I'm providing mapping for sourcing details. I've equipped each of you with a search bar that should be easy with plain language techniques. Just type a question, and you'll receive hits in response.

"Responses will be prioritized in terms of frequency and color-coded as to information sensitivity. If your search result is green, you can use it in the ITT proceedings. Green means most everything in the search result is in the ITT record. If the search result is red, you can't use the information at all. If the highlight is yellow, maybe you can use it. You'll need permission from

Zeus."

All roads from OLIVER lead to Zeus. Understood.

Barrows continued, "We have a team of analysts running through scenarios that have taken the searches that the three of you did in the ITT proceeding and research databases—"

"Excuse me?" Abe said.

Barrows's gaze fell to Abe. "We're not underestimating your brainpower, nor are we ignoring the other lawyers in the ITT proceeding. We'd be foolish at this point not to employ the collective brainpower amassed to assist the ITT proceedings. Searches that others employ, you and anyone else, are rerun every few hours as the Black Raven databases—including OLIVER—grow with new information."

"As though our brains are all tied together," Abe said, drawing a deep breath. "That's right, Abe," Zeus interjected. "With OLIVER, Barrows has created a freaking orgy of brainpower for you guys, coupled with the most sophisticated data assimilation methodology on the planet. If I were you, I'd enjoy the hell out of it."

"But don't get too excited," Barrows said. "So far, from OLIVER, nothing particularly interesting is green. Most search results are red. A few are yellow."

"Wait a second," Samantha said. "You indicated that the searches we run in OLIVER will be rerun in another Black Raven database. You're working in a database that's separate from OLIVER?"

Zeus glanced at her. "Some of our sources only share information with strict confidentiality agreements in place. Just because you have access to OLIVER doesn't mean you have access to Black Raven databases. No one is integrated with Black Raven. Ever. OLIVER is separate from the total body of information Black Raven is pulling together on the bounty hunt."

"That is correct," Barrows said. "Any search you're performing in OLIVER will be automatically rerun in the private Black Raven database."

"I thought you'd want to know that," Zeus said.

Damn right.

"Zeus will determine whether to share with you the results that are produced in the Black Raven database," Barrows said.

"Understood." Not that she liked it, but she did understand. "You've also said most data results in OLIVER are red. So you've come up with information that might be relevant to the ITT proceedings, you've shared that information with me and my team through OLIVER," Samantha said, "but it's not from information in the ITT record, and it's from information we can't use?"

Zeus gave her a curt nod, standing with his empty plate, and heading to the buffet table.

"That's exactly what we're saying." Barrows leaned forward and typed commands. The image of him disappeared, replaced with a mostly empty screen that had the Black Raven logo, the word OLIVER, and a blank search bar with a blinking cursor. "This is how you could run a potential search, keeping in mind that your searches will be monitored and facilitated on our end."

The words *assimilation grid of Duvall phone contacts throughout all databases* appeared in the search bar.

Samantha's heart skipped a beat. Her fork, full of potatoes, was almost in her mouth. She returned it to her plate, more interested in the search result to Barrows' query than eating.

"Simple, right?" Barrows asked. "We'll all receive alerts if information relevant to the bounty hunt appears. Next order of priority is information relevant to official ITT proceedings appears. For example, Samantha, you'll be continuing your cross examination of Duvall tomorrow. Correct?"

"Yes," she said. "I want the results of that search query."

The cursor moved to the search button, and clicked there. "Here you go," Barrows said. "I'm sending it to each of you. The first screen is raw data."

A list of documents appeared on her screen. All were red. AT&T. Comcast. Verizon Communications. Deutsche Telekom. Vodafone Group. Orange S.A. Softbank. Telecom Italia.

Zeus returned to the table with a fresh plate loaded with berries.

"Jesus Christ," Abe said, reaching for his glass of wine, and taking a swallow. "How do you have access to all these phone company records?"

"Is this legal?" Charles asked, the worry in his voice indicating the reality of looking at Black Raven data was a bit different than the abstract concept of wanting to see it. "Phone companies don't just produce their customer's records. Court orders are needed, and..." He reached for a glass of water, and gulped it.

As his voice trailed, Samantha felt like she was being offered handfuls of the world's most precious diamonds. Hers for the taking, with the promise of not getting caught.

But it's still wrong.

"We only employ this technique when necessary, and we employ strict controls with the data," Zeus said.

In other words, what I'm looking at is totally illegal. Unless—

Glancing at Zeus, she said, "You've been working on this longer than one week, haven't you?"

He gave her a hard look. No answer.

"Who is your client, and what is the project?"

Again, no answer. She didn't expect one. Yet she wondered what kind of job they were working on, who had hired them for it, and how much of it dovetailed with the ITT trial.

Barrows continued, "When you click on any of the data files, you'll automatically receive only information relevant to your work."

"Wait a second," Samantha said. "How do you decide the parameters of relevance and how is that implemented throughout the databases? What kind of technology are you using?"

No one answered. She locked eyes with Zeus. Her palms tingled as she realized what she was looking at. Output from Shadow Technology, the brainchild of Barrows, originally produced for the United States government. The government had denied that it had implemented the cutting edge data collection and assimilation method.

"In the Senate subcommittee hearings, Black Raven said Shadow Technology was destroyed. Was that true?"

Zeus met her eyes, his expression unreadable. He slid his fork under a mound of blackberries and raspberries, stabbing a chunk of pound cake as he did so. "Barrows created Shadow Technology."

"That isn't an answer. In the Senate hearings you said James Trask destroyed the technology." Samantha watched Zeus eat as her mind raced. Now it made sense to her why Black Raven came out of the hearing unscathed, given the virulence with which the company had been initially attacked. "You claimed the technology was destroyed because that's what the government wanted you to say. That was why Black Raven wasn't reprimanded for its tactics. It was a compromise. You helped the government, which, I'm guessing," she acknowledged her guess, but her gut told her she was correct, "means the government has some version of Shadow Technology in place, something the government still denies. Or maybe the government has hired you to assimilate the data that it's gathering."

Zeus glanced at her before his gaze scanned the quiet room. All eyes were on him, waiting on his response. He shifted in his seat. "Best if we don't go down that road. Barrows and Black Raven are now working together, and his knowledge and work product, whether it's called Shadow Technology or not, makes databases like OLIVER possible."

Enough said. Samantha clicked open the very first document, read for a second, then glanced at Zeus. His focus was on her. She looked at her screen. Her palms tingled as she clicked through the search results.

"Oh." Abe said, leaning forward as he clicked through the same search results. "Good God."

Chapter Eighteen

Samantha pushed her half-empty dinner plate and wine glass to the side, and pulled her laptop closer. After a few minutes, she glanced up at the monitor, into Barrows' blue eyes. "You're identifying a common link as Caller X."

"Correct," Barrows nodded. "A potential common link. We need more information. And even then, the link isn't a direct link with each of the four incidents the ITT is looking at. Yet. We're working on it. These analyses take time. So far, Caller X is only a potential common element in the French metro bombing and the Miami cruise ship bombing. The link is tenuous, and we don't have his identity. Caller X may be more than one person. Among other things, we're analyzing usage of burner phones and attempting to correlate that usage with electronic footprints from other co-existing devices. Historical analysis, though, is problematic."

"Aren't calls from burner phones typically dead ends?" Charles asked as Samantha stood, depositing her dinner plate at the buffet, while an agent removed the trays of food and brought in a silver urn of coffee.

"I assume there are no dead ends," Barrows said, "as long as I'm dealing with humans, who are incapable of operating without error. Burner phones make their calls over existing networks. People carrying burner phones often carry other phones, which constantly communicate with cell towers even when no calls are made. With smart phones and tablets in the mix, there are multiple ways to analyze telecom data and digital footprints these days, even when law enforcement agencies haven't seized the phone. Forensic methodologies are constantly changing to keep up with the technological changes. As I'm sure you're aware, the technical aspects..."

While she listened to Barrows explain the ever-changing world of forensic methodologies in the telecommunication world with mind-numbing complexity, Samantha placed a wedge of pound cake on a dessert plate. When she returned to the table, she watched Zeus finish the last of his berries. He glanced at the wedge of cake she'd placed on her plate, and gave a slight headshake. Below the table, his leg pressed harder against her thigh.

He grumbled, "Not even berries?"

As he watched, she popped a bite of buttery, dense, pound

cake into her mouth. *Grow up*, she told herself, incapable of denying that she'd skipped the healthy berries just to see if he'd notice. The delicious, almond-flavored taste of the cake was only slightly marred by her adult inner voice.

Getting a rise out of Zeus on something as ridiculous as food choices shouldn't make you feel so good.

Task at hand: OLIVER's data.

Caller X—a possible link between two events the ITT is examining.

A potential smoking gun, perhaps pointed at Maximov?

"So, if you're trying to hide your calls, you not only have to use a burner phone; you have to turn off all your other devices?" Charles asked.

"Our precise methodology of analyzing usage of co-existing digital devices is proprietary," Zeus interjected before Barrows could respond. "But you're on the right track, Charles."

"I've been involved in cases where experts are employed to analyze telecommunications and cyber data." Samantha put her fork down on her plate, after cutting one more square of pound cake that she planned to eat. "Isolation of co-existing digital devices while burner phones are used is something I haven't come across before. The technique hasn't been used by experts in the ITT proceeding."

"It's a new technique," Barrows said.

"New techniques spell problems for admissibility." Having experience with dealing with experts and consultants in a variety of fields, the one commonality she found was a tendency towards mind-boggling complication as the experts communicated the results of their analyses. Barrows' reputation as a genius, one of the greatest minds of all times, meant he could take the complications to a new high. Anytime she came across new analytical techniques, warning signals sounded. In litigation, attempts to admit the results of expert analyses were often met with bitter opposition, which attacked not only the results, but also the qualifications of the experts employed to do the studies.

"Complex issues such as this were supposed to have been brought to the court's attention months ago, so any attempt on my part to work with the results of your analysis will have to be carefully crafted. Can you keep this simple for me by focusing on Duvall or his co-defendant Tombeau; how is any of this relevant to them?"

"Caller X is only one line removed from Duvall and Tombeau," Barrows said. "Caller X potentially had direct communication with David Thompson, the alleged perpetrator of the drone attacks on the Miami cruise ship."

"I don't see it," Charles said.

"More details are proprietary," Zeus said, with a stern gaze directed at Barrows. "Barrows can't explain more about his methodology. However, he can explain more about analyzing digital footprints, in general. Basic stuff."

Barrows nodded, and continued. As Samantha listened to him, she watched Zeus stand, stretch his arms over his head, walk to the buffet, and pour a cup of steaming black coffee. Another agent joined him there. Both of them turned to the monitors, leaned against the wall, and focused on Barrows.

"Is there a potential Caller X link with the London trade show bombing and the Colombian court house bombing?" Samantha asked.

"Not yet. Of the four participating countries, the French and the American investigators have done the best job with compiling data. We've taken what they did and expanded it. With the Brits and the Colombians, we have to basically start at ground zero to determine whether there is a link. That will take several days." Barrows frowned as he glanced at her, then glanced down, presumably at an off-camera computer screen. "Perhaps as long as a week. In any event, focusing on what we've figured out since Sunday night, when we accessed the ITT data, once we were able to see the inputs used by the French investigators, we broadened the parameters—"

"Sorry to interrupt you, Mr. Barrows," Samantha said, "but can you focus on Duvall, the witness who is on the stand?"

Blue eyes bounced back to her. "Sure. The intermediate line that links Caller X to Duvall is someone who has been considered and rejected by authorities."

"Wait a second." Abe stood and leaned on the back of his chair with his elbows for support. He glanced at Barrows, who had turned away from the camera for a second, his attention focused on a computer monitor. "Intelligence agencies have had forensic investigators scouring phone records for months. Why haven't they found this?"

Barrows glanced at the camera for a second, his gaze finding Abe. "OLIVER's data pool is larger."

"How can that be?" Charles sat erect, shoulders back. "It takes court orders to accumulate most of the data. Either you're using the existing data, or—"

"Black Raven access isn't limited by the same legal restraints that are controlling the ITT proceeding." Samantha didn't need Barrows or Zeus to answer her team's questions. "The information we have in the ITT proceedings was produced pursuant to court-ordered subpoenas. Those subpoenas typically have court-approved time frames, designed to secure only relevant information while protecting privacy."

"That's correct, Samantha. Plus," Barrows added, his attention now focused on the camera, his gaze on her, "information in the ITT proceedings is only produced after human thought went into determining what was necessary. My technology assumes that very small judgment modifications on data sets produce enormous variations in the end result, so I use technology to assist me in the variables. For example, if someone determines the time period relevant to the Paris metro bombing is only sixty days, that will limit the responsive data produced by the telecommunication companies."

Abe moved from behind the chair to sitting in it, his arms folded. "That assumption was made by French investigators, in subpoena requests that are in the ITT record."

"Correct. I didn't limit the time frame. Additionally, while the scope of the data search used by the French investigators was broad with respect to Duvall's known phones, it was not as broad with respect to the people with whom he was in contact. I broadened the scope to include usage patterns of Duvall's contacts and their contacts, with extended time periods."

Samantha looked at the data, her eyes not finding what she was looking for. "Who is the intermediate person between Duvall, Tombeau, and Mr. X?"

"As simple as it gets. Duvall's mother."

Zeus returned to the chair next to her.

Abe said, "But authorities talked to her."

Once Zeus slid into his chair, under the table, his leg found hers again. Enjoying the feel of his muscular leg, she realized she had missed having him there, while her mind sent a stern warning. *It was only a leg. Should mean nothing. Focus. Distractions come in all shapes and sizes. He might be the mother of all exams, but he won't be your last test. He's just a practice run. Get over it.*

"Authorities did talk to her, without knowing about Caller X," Barrows said. "And without seeing what we see regarding a link to Caller X and the other Miami cruise ship bombing, the French investigators didn't realize her potential importance."

"I'd need to follow procedure before I can talk to her, if I want the interview to become part of the ITT record," Samantha said. "At a minimum, I need to contact the French authorities who interviewed her."

"You might need to jump through the hoops of decorum and political correctness to talk to her—"

"You call it hoops. I call it the procedural rules of the ITT, and the rules are meant to be followed."

His shrug gave an indication of how much he planned on following the procedural rules. "She isn't in prison. Not even a person of interest, from what we can tell. Problem is, since Barrows found this information this afternoon, we've been trying to find her. So far we haven't."

"I need to use this. Tomorrow. When I'm examining Duvall."

"I knew you'd say that," Eyes serious, he shook his head. "But so far, I can't think of a way you can. You can't just walk into court with phone records, which aren't in the ITT record and which we won't acknowledge we have, and wave them in the air."

Elation turned to a sinking feeling, because the fact that Duvall talked to his mother looked perfectly innocent, and without establishing the link between his mother and Caller X, she was going to miss an opportunity to get evidence of Caller X into the record, assuming that the evidence needed to be in the ITT record.

"There has to be a way," Samantha said. "Something simple. Something already in the ITT record that I can use. Something that ties in Duvall's mother and brings in Caller X."

"I'm not a lawyer," Barrows said, "but Black Raven has lawyers who are data analysts. We haven't come up with an answer of how you can use this information."

"I'll find a way," Samantha said, eyes on her laptop as her mind raced with options, some producing dead ends, some producing possibilities.

"I'm here if you need me," Barrows said. "Spend a while familiarizing yourself with OLIVER. Run a few more searches. If you look here"—the clicking cursor moved to the top right corner of the search screen, on an image of a book that she hadn't noticed before—"this icon will permit you to analyze historical searches in light of current information." The mouse shifted to the Black Raven logo. "This will provide instant messaging access to me and my team. Or you can just call. We're here to provide support, twenty-four seven. At times, we'll send you an instant message and offer suggestions. Agent Small and his team can provide you with on-site tech support as well."

Sam looked across the room to the agent manning the camera. Agent Small nodded. She'd met him the first night. Brown hair. Nice eyes, but serious. He was muscular, but smaller than Zeus. He was quiet and seemed to be constantly with Zeus or nearby, anticipating Zeus's needs with barely a word exchanged between them.

"Mr. Barrows," she said, glancing at the monitor, which had gone dark, then at Zeus, who was looking at her with a slight smile at the corner of his mouth. "I had another question."

"Ask me," Zeus answered.

"What else, exactly, is needed to put an identity on Caller X?"

Zeus shook his head. "Answer to that is proprietary. Rest assured, though, you'll know his identity when we know it."

Her stomach twisted. The intense look in his eyes was exactly the look that had always been there. The expression she'd always thought was preternaturally distanced. Only now she realized that the expression was really just the opposite.

Earlier that evening, she'd asked, *"Sex was a foregone conclusion on this job?"*

He'd answered, *"If this were just a job, I wouldn't be here."*

His statement hadn't clicked, because all she'd wanted at the moment was good, hard sex. With him. Deep inside her. Thank God, he'd obliged, because if he hadn't, by now she'd be clinging to him and begging for it.

In retrospect, she recognized that his statement indicated he had no problem with his feelings for her.

He wasn't conflicted on that issue.

She was. She had enormous problems with her feelings for him.

Yet they were stuck with each other, and, clearly—given his performance earlier—neither one of them felt like depriving themselves of sex.

Sex was just sex, and this was just a job.

I have to do a better job of reminding him—and myself—of that fact. It is just a job. For both of us.

"Zeus," Ragno's voice commanded his attention.

Samantha glanced up as well, expecting to see Ragno in a monitor. But there was no image of a woman. Instead, the monitors each had iterations of the maps. Hearing her voice, without knowing what she looked like, was disconcerting.

"Can you take a look at the latest iteration of the Praptan map?" Ragno asked.

Zeus stood and walked over to the table where his agents worked, his eyes on the television monitor that showed Ragno's creation. "Get Gabe back on the line."

As Zeus and the agents worked on the map, Samantha, Abe, and Charles ran a variety of searches through OLIVER. They kept reaching dead ends, because every search result was highlighted in red, meaning the information wasn't in the ITT record and was likely too sensitive for them to put into the record.

After a while, Abe pushed his chair back, pulling off his glasses, and rubbing his eyes. "We can't force something into the ITT record that isn't there. And if the French knew what they were overlooking, they'd be stumbling all over themselves to expand the record."

Samantha stared at him for a second, her heartbeat racing. She suddenly felt as though the spirit of Stanley Morgan was giving her an answer. "Oh my God, Abe." She pushed her chair back, and stood. "That's brilliant."

He shook his head, eyes heavy with frustration and skepticism. "What? In my mind, I hit a dead end."

"We'll back door it. The French want there to be a link between these four terrorist acts as badly as we do, and their subpoena requests—the ones that were drafted too narrowly—are in the record. I'll get them to expand the requests. I don't have to tell anyone what's in OLIVER. I can go to the French prosecutors and persuade them to expand the record. I can do that off the record. If I phrase it correctly, they'll file the subpoena requests."

"And why would they take your word for it?" Zeus's question, from across the room, proved the man's multitasking skills, and his hearing, were sharp.

"Because I'm going to tell them I'll file the expanded subpoena requests if they don't," she said. "No one wants to be caught overlooking something. I'm giving them an opportunity to fix a potential problem that no one's spotted until now. I'll call it a hunch. They'll know there's more. This is record manipulation, Stanley Morgan style. I learned some tricks from the best. I may as well put them to use now."

Zeus's eyes narrowed. Skepticism? Worry? "You can't reveal anything about our data gathering techniques."

"How could I? You haven't revealed anything to us. All you've said when we've asked questions is it's proprietary." Confident her plan would work, she sat down, and talked with Abe and Charles as she compiled her thoughts on how to proceed with the French, and also about securing an interview with

Vladimer Stollen.

When she next glanced at her watch, it was 1 a.m. Charles and Abe were bleary-eyed, while she felt energized with the possibilities of expanding the record and interviewing Stollen. "Let's call it quits for the night. With tomorrow's proceeding starting at noon we'll have time to regroup in the morning." She paused as they nodded. "As early as you feel like getting up. I'd like to develop a plan for Stollen and getting the French to expand the telecommunications records and, assuming there will be motions to file, I'd like to get them filed as early as possible."

Lifting her laptop, planning to work more upstairs, she left Zeus in the library where he continued to work with Ragno and his agents. Back on the third floor, brushing her teeth, she considered two options.

Option A–climb into her own bed, work, and fall asleep wondering whether Zeus would come to her room when he finally came upstairs.

Option B–go to his bed, work there, and hope he'd be happy to see her. Happy enough to give her a replay of his evening performance.

Ridiculous to even consider Option A.

She wanted sex. He wanted sex. They were together, at least for a while. He was a freaking Maserati of a man. May as well enjoy the ride. She'd keep it distant. Impersonal.

Win. Win.

She slipped on a black lace camisole and matching panties and went to his bed, laptop in hand. She climbed under the covers, worked till her eyes crossed, then shut the computer and pushed it to the side.

Chapter Nineteen

"Best invitation I've ever gotten." Zeus's low voice pulled her out of her dreams.

Lying on her side, with her head nestled in his pillows, her body buried in the warmth of his king-size bed's linens and goose-down duvet, she'd been able to smell his rich masculine scent as she drifted off to sleep. She focused on him, and not the dream of him she'd been having. "Accepting it?"

He shut the door behind him, then placed his iPad and laptop on the credenza on the far side of the room. Eyes locked with hers, he pulled off his earpiece and watch, pressed a button on his watch, and placed the items next to his iPad. Not breaking eye connection, Zeus crossed over to the bed with purposeful strides that told her the answer. Yanking the covers off of her, his eyes traced from her head to her toes. With dark eyes clouding with lust, he knelt on the side of the bed, gently pushed her shoulder so she was flat on her back. Lips on hers, his fast, hard, open-mouthed kiss took her breath.

Breaking away, his eyes held hers. "In the library, I couldn't stop thinking about," he paused, the corners of his lips lifting in a slight smile, "being inside you."

"Mmmm." She shivered, but not from the drafty, cool air in the bedroom. Heat came off of him in waves that warmed the chilly air and her. "Show me."

He lifted her laptop off the bed, put it on the bedside table, and bent his head to her breasts. Gentle fingers pushed aside the delicate fabric of her camisole, and he opened his mouth on her left nipple. He tongued her as he lifted his hand to her right breast. Sparks ignited down her spine, and she ran fingers through his thick hair, pulling his head tighter to her with her right hand, while her left hand slipped inside the waistband of his jeans. He grabbed her hands, broke his mouth away from her with a groan, then stood. She sat up, reaching for his hand, and tried to yank him down.

Shaking his hand free, he said, "Thanks for the reminder."

He walked into the closet, leaving her to sit on the bed, legs dangling on the side, wondering what he was doing. A few seconds later, he returned, an assortment of neckties in his hand.

Red, green, gray, paisley—the vibrant colors went well with the dark business suits that he wore to the ITT proceedings. The steady, focused look in his eyes as he approached the bed told her that the ties wouldn't be used for their intended purpose.

"Told you I'd tie you the next time," he said, his tone low, almost a growl.

"I thought you were kidding," she whispered, sitting up, unsure. She hadn't yet ventured into the world of bondage. No one had ever suggested it, including Zeus when she'd been with him before. She'd certainly never volunteered for it. Sex was sport, and like running, she liked being a pacesetter, with her hands, legs, and every inch of her body.

Being restrained? Fun for a moment. Maybe. Not for any length of time and certainly not for the duration of the act.

He dropped the ties on the bed, next to her, the silks softly brushing against her bare thigh as the ties settled into a pile. "I'm not much of a kidder. Ready?"

"Really?"

An arched eyebrow told her he was dead serious.

"I thought you liked my hands on you."

His gaze, travelling along her body with the force of a hot touch, flicked up to hers. "Love it. But not this time."

Standing, fully dressed, about a foot away from the bed, his eyes were on her body. In response to his visual touch, her nipples formed hard peaks that showed through the silk camisole. Warmth at her core emanated through her. She was wet. Ready. She had been ever since she'd climbed in his bed. What was happening between her legs was a wonder of pheromones and hormones, mixed with certain knowledge of how damn good he'd feel inside of her once again.

"Ready for me to tie you?"

Her body didn't care whether she was tied to the bed, whether he did her against a wall, or if he did her any damn way he could think of. Nerves and muscles tingled with the possibilities, but her mind was the problem. "Maybe not."

He lifted the left corner of his lip in an almost smile. "But maybe yes?"

"Problem is, I like to be in control. And so do you. I'm not saying I don't trust you, but—"

"You don't, do you?" Eyes serious, he added, "Not one bit. And given what happened seven years ago, I can't say that I blame you."

The elephant in the room reared up on its hind legs and

demanded attention. She was determined not to go there. "Keep this focused on the problem with the ties in your hand, and why you're not using them on me."

"You're worried I'll make you take it slow." His voice was husky. "And you don't like to say please in bed, do you?"

He had her number and she couldn't deny it. "Bondage isn't something you just spring on a person. There needs to be a contract."

"We can do a verbal." He lifted the sweatshirt over his head, revealing a white T-shirt underneath. He pitched the sweatshirt to a chair. "Name your terms."

"No terms needed. I'm not going there."

"Should we have our lawyers negotiate it?" He untucked the T-shirt from his jeans, and stopped before pulling it off. *Damn.* Her mouth watered for the eye candy that was his chest and he took his time with his strip tease, a slight, puzzled expression on his face, more teasing than serious. "Are there lawyers who do that sort of thing? You would know better than me."

"Not funny. It's late, and you're wasting time, Hernandez. I'm not in your room for sparkling repartee and chit-chat."

"How is this for terms? I promise I'll never hurt you. I did that once. At least I think what I did hurt you. Not that you ever acted hurt." He arched an eyebrow and waited.

No, Hernandez. I'm not going there.

Apparently giving up on his fishing expedition for comments from her about their past, he continued, "And I'll never do it again. I promise. Come on, Sam. Talk about what happened so we can move on from there. Really talk abou—"

"Careful, Hernandez. We're talking about sex. Either you want it now, or you don't. You're going off topic. Don't be a buzz kill."

His eyes flashed with anger. He nodded, jaw set. After a second, he shrugged, the annoyance hidden behind that stoic emotional shield. "Sex. Got it. Just a fuck or two, or many, while the job's taking place, right?"

Yes. Please. She nodded.

"Fine. Understood. How's this," he continued, his tone matter of fact, though she could tell from the pulse that was throbbing at his temple that he was still irritated. "Let me tie you. Choose a safe word. I'll untie you when you say it."

He pulled off his T-shirt and threw it to the chair with the sweatshirt. Ahhh. *Hell yes.* Lamplight illuminated tawny skin stretched taught over well-defined abs that led down to the waistline of his jeans. "Good enough?"

"Fantastic. Yes. Wait." *What was the pending question?* Oh. *Hell!* He was talking about bondage. Tying her to the bed, and she'd just said yes. "No. Why don't you be the submissive one? Let me tie you."

He chuckled. "Seriously?"

"Sure. With the tables turned you're suddenly not so sure? Scared of relinquishing control?"

"Hell, no." He gave her rare a full smile, the grin of a man who was about to have a fond wish granted. The offer seemed to dispel his irritation, and now a different emotion heated his gaze. *Oh hell.*

"Ever engaged in bondage before?"

He arched an eyebrow. "Truth?"

"Assume this—anytime you're talking to me, I want the truth. Even about your sexual exploits. We're just having sex, without an emotional commitment. In my book, the more experience a man has, the better. I don't have a lot of time for sex and I don't want to waste time with someone who fumbles. I don't care if you've done it with three lingerie models at the same time—"

"Really? Well, that's a relief, because—"

"I'd say hoorah to you. Take your pants off while you tell me about it."

"Answer's yes." He unzipped his jeans, rolled them down, and kicked them to the side. His smoky-gray trunks went to mid-thigh and fit like a second skin, cupping his butt, his balls, and his penis. If he modeled them, the company would sell out in mere minutes. With the hard-on he sported, the image wouldn't be an advertisement at all. It would be called porn.

"Tell me more," she said as he reached for his nightstand and pulled out a condom.

She grabbed the condom out of his hand. "Don't put that on yet."

"I don't have sex without one."

"And I'm not planning on having sex for a few minutes," she whispered, eyeing his erection and fighting for willpower. She wanted to forget the ties and just climb on top of him. "Tell me about your experience with bondage."

"Those days were a while ago. Before marriage. Before you."

He still hadn't taken the damn grin off his face. He did a slow strip down of his boxers. What was fully erect, and pointing to heaven, was a sight to behold. Her fingertips tingled with the need to touch the smooth skin that stretched around the girth and length of his hard, straining penis.

"Don't just stare." His voice was gruff. "You've got work to do." He gestured with his chin to the pile of ties. "Pick a color. I'll help you with my ankles."

She handed him a tie as he sat on the bed and spread his legs. As she eyed his erection, she said, "I'm not sure I really get the point. Seems like a waste of time, when I could just climb on top of you right now. You certainly look ready for me."

"Just get me tied me up and you'll see. This is about anticipation, something not high on your list of accomplishments." He got to work on his right ankle. "Tying the restraints properly is an art, and"—as she tugged on his left ankle, he glanced at her work and frowned—"you're doing a piss-poor job."

She didn't bother checking his knot, nor was she too careful with hers. At this point, she didn't care if the damn thing held. "Tell me about your most memorable bondage experience."

"Twins. I was the bottom, which means I was the one who was tied. The three of us came at the same time." Studying her expression, he threw back his head and laughed as what he said registered.

"How did that even happen? Oh my gosh, one of them was sitting on—"

"I'm pulling your leg. I won't give you details about my sex life. Not now. Not ever."

"Spoilsport." She mumbled, kneeling on the bed, at his side, eyes on his penis as she snapped the red tie, extending it to its full length between her spread hands. "Give me your wrists."

"Gimme me that condom back."

"No. I'll put it on you."

"Dammit, Sam," he said, running his fingers through his hair. "I'm warning you. I've had a hard-on for the last five hours. I'll last longer with a condom."

"Awwww. You're adorable. Worried about performance?"

His frown, real and marked, told her he didn't like her ribbing. "You'll pay for that."

She laughed. "God, I hope so. Hey, I might not have tied up a guy before, but I know my way around a good hard on. And this..." She glanced at his penis, licked her lips, and met his eyes. "Is a great one. Don't worry. I won't waste it."

He extended his arms to her, one wrist over another. She wound the tie around them, pulled them over his head and bound his hands to the headboard. "If you—"

"Shhhh." Pressing her fingers to his lips, she said, "Now that you're all tied up, you have to listen to me, don't you?"

His eyelids were half-closed, his chest flushed. He still smiled, as though he enjoyed every single second of what she was doing. "That is part of the fun of it."

"Don't say another word until I untie you. If you do," she whispered into his ear, "I won't do a thing."

She watched his chest rise and fall with each deep breath as she removed her camisole and panties in a slow strip tease. Until he was fully restrained, she had planned on mounting him and using his penis as the great Creator had intended when designing it with well-honed perfection as a tool to give a woman pleasure.

Something happened, though, between thought and execution when she stepped back and got an eyeful of his glorious body, all muscle and sinew, immobile, an offering for her. It was the same thing that had happened earlier in the evening, when he had tried to hold her after he had fucked her so hard she'd seen stars.

She became someone else, transported to a time when sex hadn't just been sex. There had been a time when she hadn't been such a hard ass, a time when she'd believed in the gifts of happiness and love and that her life could—and would—have both.

That time had been with him, seven years earlier, and it had ended abruptly when he'd told her he was going to Miami to marry his pregnant ex-girlfriend.

There was a huge problem with having sex with Zeus.

His goddamn penis—glorious as it was—was a divining rod straight back to that time, to a person who no longer existed.

Being with him again was too tangible a reminder of who and what she no longer allowed herself to be. She was no longer the naïve woman who'd believed that upon falling in love with him, with every unquestioning molecule in her twenty-six year old brain, that he was going to be a part of her life forever. That he'd light the shadows of her darkest days, that he'd be there to walk with her on every ambition-fueled journey through which she travelled. That he could be a facilitator of her dreams.

He made her miss the naïve, hopeful person he'd inspired her to be.

The person who had never existed with anyone but him.

In the soft lamplight, as she stood at his bedside, his obsidian eyes were on her. Still lustful, but now tinged with concern.

Dammit. He could always read her, and now he saw that she was hesitating, as though this was more than sex-play, as though this was a momentous occasion.

Which it isn't.

Her hand shaking, she reached for one of the leftover neckties.

The days of showing vulnerability are long in the past.

Bending over him, she kissed the frown in the middle of his eyebrows. "Close your eyes."

When he did, she slipped the red necktie around his head and blindfolded him. Better that he not see, because she didn't trust herself.

Knowing at her very core that what was about to happen was ephemeral, she lay on top of him, her chest pressed to his, her hands holding onto either side of his head. Drawing in a deep breath, her eyes clouded with tears.

The first one can't fall.

It did. Another one dropped, on his chest.

She shut her eyes tightly, tried to stop the flow, tried to keep her hands from shaking as she touched him. She gave up and allowed her tears to fall freely. Shimmying up his chest, she pressed her lips to his. Lingering touches. Gentle touches. As though each soft, slow connection mattered. Lingering at his lips, she memorized the soft texture, kissing the corners that throughout each day reflected just a trace of his emotions. Would she ever tell him that she watched for each slight smile, smirk, frown?

No. Never.

He was still, his entire body rigid. As though he was holding his breath, waiting for her next move. Applying pressure, parting his lips, she slipped her tongue into his mouth, moaning with him as he groaned. As he kissed her back, lifting his head from the pillow and joining his mouth with hers with all the force he always used when kissing her, as though he knew he'd never get enough, more tears fell.

She broke away for a second. *Stop crying. Stop crying. Oh God, what is wrong with me?*

She kissed the hard ridge of his jawline, feeling the sharp hair of his evening shadow, and moved her lips to his neck and chest. With each kiss producing a yearning for something that could never be, she stopped caring about the fat tears that slipped from her eyes.

He couldn't see. He had no idea.

She allowed herself to kiss him like she loved him, as though each touch of her lips on him mattered. The woodsy-clean taste of his skin blended with the salty taste of her tears and still she kept kissing, her hands shaking as she held onto him at his shoulders and his chest.

Kneeling at his shoulders, she placed her right breast in his mouth, aching for his touch there. He lifted his head, using his teeth and tongue with the desperation of a man having his last drink of water. Her insides clenched with the force of it, leaving her breathless. She shifted and offered the other breast to him, seeing stars when he closed his mouth around her, sucking hard as he tongued her nipple.

Her tears fell in earnest as she traveled lower, while his groans intensified. When she finally put her mouth on his hard, straining penis, he thrust his hips up and down as much as the restraints would allow. She gripped the shaft as she slid her tongue around the smooth head. Glancing up, vision filmy with moisture, she saw that he was shaking his head from side to side, drawing in deep breaths. His jaw clenched. His chest covered in a sheen of perspiration. He was close. So close.

She glanced at the condom packet. Not going to happen. She wanted to feel him.

She positioned herself above him and held onto his shaft, pausing for a few minutes to give him time to recover. She slid her hips down, inch by delicious taking him into her.

"Hey. Put that cond—"

Eyes closed, focused on the feel of him filling and spreading her, she said, "No talking."

He took a few harsh breaths. "I give up. Feels fucking fabulous."

With her walls clenching around him, electrical shocks blew her mind, prompting her to forgive his breaching her rule that he not speak. When she absorbed the full length of him, she tried to stay still. Involuntary twitches, from her and him, happened where they were joined, as her internal muscles magically clamped around his length and girth, adjusting to him and accommodating him.

She had no control over what was happening deep inside of her, but the feeling of her body slowly welcoming him was more powerful than anything she'd ever done. The only other movement was the rise and fall of their chests that came with their deep, heavy breathing.

Samantha held the back of her hand against her mouth, choking back a loud sob, believing with every fiber of her being that this was as close as she'd ever come to making love to him. To anyone. Her need for release built, edging out the raw emotion that had overcome her.

Panting, she braced her palms at the bottom of his ribcage, and her knees at his waist. She rode him, lifting up and down in smooth moves designed to let him slide in, and almost all the way out. Her thrusts became more urgent, while her inner walls clenched around his girth. Within seconds, she was moaning with him, grinding down onto him and rocking her entire body with the effort.

"Oh. Zeus. Oh."

He answered her with a loud, low groan and a slight shift up in his hips, as much movement as the ties would allow. As she felt him explode into her, she leaned forward, onto his chest, and held on.

After some time, she realized she'd drifted off. Her face felt like it was glued to his chest, with her hair tangled in between. His soft inhalations and exhalations told her he had no problem that she'd fallen asleep on top of him without untying him, because he'd managed to fall asleep as well.

His penis had slipped out of her. What a shame, because she could feel it against her thigh. He was now semi-erect, even in sleep. The man was insatiable when it came to sex.

Thank God.

She slid off of him, ran her fingers through her hair to get it out of her eyes, and sat at his side. His steady, even breathing didn't change. Planning to untie him and go catch a few hours of sleep in her own bedroom, she undid the ankle ties. He didn't move. When she reached for the tie that bound his wrists to the headboard, she gasped. Although the tie remained wrapped around his wrists, it was loose. The end of it was no longer attached to the headboard.

In a quick move, Zeus shifted from his supine position to tackling her, gently pushing her onto her back, chuckling as he laid her head on his pillow. He shook the red necktie off his eyes as he covered her with his body.

"Bastard! You were faking. When did that come untied?"

"Somewhere between your right breast and your left. I deserve an award for pretending I couldn't touch you."

He drank her next words of protest with a deep kiss. Travelling down her body, marking his progress with a trail of kisses, she realized that having sex with Zeus would always be a double-edge sword. One deep cut was sensual bliss. The other cut was a deep gash that would make her long for someone she'd never be again, while making her want something she'd never admit to wanting.

Wasn't much to be done about that when the man had his face just inches away from her mound, when he was using his thumbs to part her folds, and when she felt his warm tongue slip into her. As she moaned, he shifted his mouth upwards and closed his lips around her clitoris, sucking and tonguing the hard nub. Suddenly, his fingers were thrusting in and out of her, hard, as though he owned a claim to her vagina and could use it any way he desired. Exactly how she liked it—plunging in and out of her with so much force it almost hurt, but not quite. As he manhandled her in a manner that no one else had ever mastered, all she could do was moan his name, lift herself up on her elbows, and enjoy the show.

Each time she was on the precipice of a mind-blowing orgasm, his touches became gentle and soft, prolonging her agony as his gaze swept up to meet hers. It was torture and, as he met her gaze, he gave her a look that said he knew it and was damn well enjoying it.

Hell.

It was, really, nothing but a pure heaven that made her forget anything else but the two of them. He finally let her peak, and as she did, he applied steady, sucking pressure on her clitoris, tonguing the hard nub while holding it steady with his teeth and lips. As her hips bucked into his mouth, he thrust his fingers deeper inside of her, anchoring her to his mouth. She screamed her release, loud, at first, then remembering they were in a house with others, she grabbed the pillow and muffled her cries.

He covered her body with his, pressing flat against her. Along her right thigh, she felt his erection. He was hard, hot, and straining, when she was flat on her back, almost too spent from her orgasm to do anything but spread her legs.

"Sorry. I. Don't. Think. I. Can. Move."

He kneed her legs further apart, giving her a concerned glance. "Should I stop?"

"No. Please. Don't know if I can help. Or make this good for you. I've lost every ounce of strength."

Gripping her hips, he lifted her up while sliding down her body. He hooked her knees at his shoulders, positioning himself for entry. "I've got enough for both of us. All you have to do is..."

He thrust into her, burying himself to the hilt, filling her.

"Be. You," he whispered, "God, you're heaven."

Their eyes held as their bodies melted together more with each thrust. Her hips started flexing to accommodate his thrusts. His chest became flushed as he buried himself in her and brought her to the peak again. As her muscles clenched tightly around him, she whimpered while she came, riding higher with each of his hard thrusts. When she cried out his name, he responded by throwing his head back, groaning, and arching into her. His body trembled from head to toe. She felt his release, deep inside of her. When he was through, he fell to her side, half on her, half off.

She'd have given a year of her life—or more—to have curled up in his arms and fallen asleep there. Problem was, if she did, she'd wake up a different person, and she'd be giving up far more than time off her life. She'd be losing everything that mattered. When his ragged breathing eased, when her own body stopped trembling from the intensity of her orgasm, she shifted away from him and eased herself off the bed.

"Stay."

"No." She stood, glancing at him as she bent to snag her panties and camisole.

He was on his side, head resting on his hand, eyes narrowed as he studied her. "Dammit, we have to talk. Really talk." He moved fast, sitting up, then standing, and walking to her side. "This is insane."

With her other hand, she grabbed her laptop, and continued walking towards the door. "There isn't anything to talk about. We had sex. End of story."

"Why were you crying?" His voice was low as he stepped closer to her, concern etched in his dark eyes.

Oh hell. Could the man see through a silk blindfold? "You're imagining things."

When he lifted his arms to reach for her, she stepped away from him. "I felt your tears. I tasted them on my lips. Your hands were shaking when you touched me. Dammit, Sam. Talk to me."

She opened the door.

"Coward."

Ouch.

She turned to him as a blast of uncontrollable anger simmered up through her veins. "You have no right to call me names. No right to pass judgment on me on any matter. As a matter of fact, if you weren't so good at sex, I wouldn't be wasting my time with you. Do you understand that if you weren't such a good fuck, we wouldn't even be having this much of a conversation?"

Ah. There. His anger was back. Cheeks flushed red, he drew a deep breath, shook his head, and ran his fingers through his hair. "Don't act like what we just did means nothing. I know what a meaningless fuck feels like and I'm willing to bet, at this stage in your life, you do too. It doesn't feel like what we just did. I know it, and you know it. As a matter of fact, I'm pretty damn certain that when you masturbate you don't goddamn cry and your hands don't shake."

Only when I remember you.

Which is something you will never know.

Never.

As she slipped out of the bedroom door, she glanced back at him and said, "Wouldn't you love to watch and find out?"

Chapter Twenty

Five degrees Celsius. Not freezing, but the light breeze made the damp air cold on H.L.'s face. The sky was gray. Glancing over his shoulder as he walked on the Ile St. Louis, he made sure no one followed him.

He should be enjoying the walk to the apartment on the Ile de la Cite, relishing the cold air as he mentally relived the highlights of the day before. The bomb blast of Wednesday afternoon and its aftermath had been stunning, even viewed from his safe place. The moment of eerie silence afterwards had been electrifying. The screams thrilling.

Of course, at first, he had reacted to the event not as H.L. but as his public persona. He'd behaved appropriately post-explosion, yet dignified and calm. He'd been articulate and tried to make others feel safe, all the while rejoicing on the inside.

For the rest of the evening he'd celebrated a job well done. Returning to his hotel room, he was just in time to catch the first news report. They had it on every channel, and he flipped between stations as he settled in for a working evening. It was gratifying to see how much coverage the event garnered. He was damned proud of what they'd achieved today. Damned proud.

Later, a nightcap of bourbon had been followed by one of life's great pleasures—a blow job from a beautiful, young woman, who knew precisely what to do with her hands, mouth, and teeth. Watching the television news as she sucked him dry, he was as excited by the graphic images of death and chaos as he was by her mouth.

Afterwards, alone, he'd slept his deepest sleep of the New Year, in his dreams reliving each moment of the day. He'd woken up feeling wonderfully alive. Economic analysts opined about a possible yearlong slow-down in the economy, due to the blatant attack on the ITT. They stated it was now apparent the ITT would be ineffective at stopping the current wave of terror.

He'd been ecstatic.

Like a meteor crashing to earth, at precisely 9:15 in the morning, his feeling of self-satisfaction had ebbed when he logged into the ITT database and read pleadings that had been filed that morning. Two motions had been filed, both consisting of requests to expand the ITT record and both as unique as they were unexpected.

The court had responded promptly to the filings. They were

set for a hearing at noon, before the continuation of Duvall's examination.

Now, stepping into their working apartment for his mid-morning meeting with J.R. and M.C., H.L. did so with an awareness of bright yellow caution flags fluttering in his thoughts. They weren't foremost on his mind. They were there, at half-mast, a constant reminder they were now navigating a delicate operation.

H.L. reminded himself he was up for the challenge. If what they were doing wasn't tricky and complex, it was boring.

The heat was turned up in the small apartment. The living room felt stuffy, all the more so due to J.R.'s incessant smoking. Drapes were drawn. The three large screen televisions played news coverage, much of which showed the bombing from the prior day. Volume was muted.

M.C., sitting at a table with his laptop open, sipped tea from a delicate cup. J.R., on the couch, basked with pride at success of the bombing and the murder of Judge Devlin's wife.

"The press reported that Judge Calante died during the night," M.C. explained, as H.L. poured piping hot coffee into a mug. "The alternate judge from Colombia will take his place. The Colombian prosecution team, already in shambles from the Boulevard Saint-Germain bombing, has tendered two resignations. That leaves only the lead prosecutor in place for the proceedings next week. Judge Devlin, of course, has returned to the United States to make plans for his wife's funeral. Alternate Judge Amanda Whitsell will take his place. Among bystanders there were twenty-two fatalities and numerous other injuries."

"All well and good. We may have injected fear into the proceedings and the world," H.L. said, standing as he sipped his coffee, facing the two of them. "But today is a new day, my friends. The landscape for us is changing, and not for the better."

J.R. lit a cigarette off one that was almost burned to the filter, casting H.L. a questioning glance. "How so?"

"Two electronic filings caught my attention this morning. Both are motions to expand the record. The first is from the French prosecution team, expanding subpoena requests for telephone records. They are seeking to enlarge the time frame and reach more telecommunication companies."

M.C. frowned. He took off his glasses, then pulled a cloth out of his pocket and started cleaning the lenses. He looked up myopically, as his hands were busy with the task. "But the discovery period has been closed for weeks now. Hasn't it?"

H.L. nodded, then shrugged. Well-steeped in the world of trials and court rulings, he knew judges often changed their minds. "Doesn't matter. If the French provide a good enough reason, the ITT judges will grant the request. Given the urgency of the proceedings, and the power of the ITT, the phone records could be produced within twenty-four hours. Give analysts a few more days to look at the information, and clues could be developed."

"After today there is only one more day of proceedings in Paris," J.R. said. "Why would the French have the right to expand the record now?"

"While we're almost through in France, this ITT trial has three more weeks," H.L. explained. "With the permission of the court, the parties can introduce documentary evidence into the record at any time, as long as it is appropriately authenticated."

"I don't think we have anything to fear from phone records," M.C. said. Tortoise-shell glasses freshly wiped and clean, he placed them on his face, adjusting them as he glanced again at his laptop screen.

"You don't think?" H.L. asked. His imaginary yellow caution flags were hoisted higher as he heard the uncertainty in the voice of the man who was in charge with managing the details of their business. "I want absolutes, dammit. I want you to tell me we have absolutely nothing to fear, on any level."

M.C. gave him a cool look. "You can lose that imperious tone with me. I can't give absolutes and I won't say something just to make you feel good. We're operating in a world where sometimes a phone needs to be used. That is the harsh reality of dealing with terrorists." He gave an eye roll, as though the people they used as tools weren't worthy of the name. "More often than not, they are in their twenties and their phones are as much an extension of them as their hands. Give a twenty-eight year old a task and he can't resolve it without using an electronic device."

Silence fell heavily among the three men as J.R. drew a deep drag on his cigarette. He ground the butt of it into an ashtray and didn't light another. He stood, folded his arms, and glanced at M.C., then H.L. "While I have made every effort to minimize our risk, the truth is everyone has something to fear in phone and data records."

"We should not," H.L. said. "We've taken every precaution. Believe me, if I could always communicate with you via telephone, I would. The stink of your cigarettes is something I'd rather not experience."

J.R. shrugged, lighting another cigarette. "I believe the motion by the French prosecutors to expand the record has the potential to be a problematic development."

"Yes." H.L. nodded. "It depends on the depth of the search, the data that's produced, and how experienced the forensic experts are who are looking at the data. It also depends on who might be questioned about the phone records."

"Yes, to all of that," J.R. said. "But would you please stop and think like a human being for a goddamn second? Keep it simple, stupid. This motion represents a change to the status quo. The real question is why now? What are they really looking for, and what provoked it? And for this commonsense approach, you should be calling me Mr. Brilliance."

H.L. fought the urge to wrap his hands around the man's neck and throttle him.

"I'll have to talk to our contact," M.C. said, somehow remaining calm. "We need more details."

"In due time," H.L. said. "We have to assume that telecommunications and cyber exchanges are now subject to being intercepted by Black Raven."

M.C. nodded in agreement. "Will the court grant the subpoena request?"

"We have to assume yes and do damage control from there," H.L. said. "Assume the worst. Assume there is some link somewhere in phone records to someone who might reveal who we are. Where we are. What should we do about that?"

"Send out a strong message so that no one talks," M.C. said. "Scare the crap out of them so they keep their mouths shut."

J.R. smiled. "I have that covered. Plans are in place here. Remember, we have access to the prisoners in France and London. By the time we get to Columbia, we should have access there, if we need it. So far, we do not have access to prisoners in the United States."

"Duvall?" H.L. asked.

"Of course. He is our weakest link. But we have to decide quickly." J.R. glanced at his watch. "The transfer to the proceeding will take place at 11:00 a.m."

"Do it," H.L. said.

J.R. returned to the couch, a humorless smile playing at his lips. "I have to use a phone."

"Is it a burner?" H.L. asked.

"Yes. Untraceable," J.R. said. "And after I use it once, I'll destroy it. There is no way this phone call can be linked to us."

H.L. nodded, and J.R. made the call. When someone answered, he said, "Duvall. Stat. Kill him with whatever option I've given you that is most expedient. Be sure to cut out his tongue."

When the call was over, J.R. disconnected the call, tore the battery out of the casing, and stepped on the phone with the hard heel of his shoes. Gentle eyes looked as though he'd just had a conversation about something as benign as flowers. He reached into his pocket, pulled out a pack of cigarettes, and tapped one out. Lighting it, he glanced at H.L., and took a deep drag. "You said two electronic filings caught your attention. What was the second?"

"Samantha Fairfax made a request of the ITT Judges to interview Vladimer Stollen."

J.R. sat up straighter. "Well, holy hell. I predicted she'd pick up where Stanley Morgan left off. But you two ignored me."

"Past time to stop her." M.C.'s matter of fact statement was made without tearing his attention from his laptop screen.

H.L.'s discomfort grew. Control seemed to be slipping through his grasp. A feeling he wouldn't tolerate. "No. We didn't ignore you. If you recall, our attempt at damage control with the cyanide poisoning didn't work as planned. Rather than focus on the Amicus team, or her, we must continue with our efforts at targeted randomness. Those efforts are working. Duvall's murder this morning, and continued pressure on the families of participants in the proceedings, as we planned."

"I disagree with your suggestion that we can't target individuals," H.L. said. "Our acts of terror may as well be productive. If we were worried the judges were going to listen to Morgan, we should be equally concerned that Fairfax knows everything that Morgan knew, and we should be concerned that the judges will listen to her. As Amicus counsel, she is the impartial voice of the United States."

"Her reason for talking to Stollen now?" M.C. asked, his tone reflecting growing concern.

"Her motion didn't contain details. I'll learn more during the argument today and we'll learn more if our contact manages to give us a communication. Given the climate we created with yesterday's bombing," H.L. answered, "I'm concerned this motion might have some headway."

"And if you're simply considering Fairfax's role as limited to Amicus counsel, with only the tools that participants in the ITT proceeding have at their disposal," M.C. clicked at the keyboard of his laptop as he spoke, then turned the screen to H.L. and J.R., "you are sorely underestimating her capabilities."

Trepidation burned H.L.'s insides as he looked at the photo on the computer screen. On the monitor, M.C. had pulled up images of Zeus Hernandez of Black Raven carrying Samantha Fairfax away from the explosion. There were multiple images. One was a video. M.C. played it.

Hernandez's jaw was set, his serious eyes grim. He looked like a man who was physically strong enough to conquer anyone, and the intensity in his dark, fathomless eyes suggested he could be damn creative as to how he did it. As he ran with the woman in his arms, there was tenderness in the way he cradled Fairfax to his chest. H.L. stepped closer, staring at the screen. His stomach churned. He hadn't seen it last night. Oh, he'd looked at the footage and the images of Hernandez with the beautiful blonde in his arms. The images had been hard to miss. But he hadn't focused on them. Hadn't stared at them in isolation. He'd been so damn thrilled at how the explosion had been successful he hadn't realized the depth of what he was looking at, the image of a powerful man who so obviously was carrying something that mattered to him.

"Hell." H.L. didn't want to admit that he hadn't thought of the possibility that Jesus Hernandez and Samantha Fairfax could be working as a team the very instant he'd seen her motion to interview Stollen.

"We have to assume Black Raven is the impetus for the motion to interview Stollen. Yesterday I said I was worried that having Hernandez on the scene, with Black Raven working the bounty hunt and with access to ITT data, was going to be problematic. Rather than relaxing last night"—M.C. shot them both a hard glance, as if the man knew how they'd both spent their evening, and disapproved—"I did some research on Black Raven, including analyzing the records of last year's Senate hearings examining the tactics employed by the company to rescue Barrows."

With growing unease, H.L. listened as M.C. provided information about the strength of Black Raven, the growth of its cyber-capabilities after the company rescued and hired Barrows, and his well-founded suspicion that the government now used Black Raven as a resource. After what seemed like an eternity, M.C. fell silent.

"So you're saying we should assume that Black Raven is integrated with data from U.S. Intelligence agencies?" H.L.

asked.

"I'm saying that my most trusted sources indicate that the government has contracts with Black Raven that are classified. We have to assume that DHS, NSA, and other agencies now outsource collection and assimilation of cyber data, and the most likely outfit that is getting the contracts is Black Raven. Because of Richard Barrows."

"It was a yes or no question." H.L. waved away some of J.R.'s smoke.

"No one I know seems to know the agencies that have outsourced or the scope of the contracts." M.C. leaned forward, his gaze bouncing from H.L. to J.R. "So we should assume the worst. Assume yes. And for now, the problem isn't simply Black Raven's access to God knows what kind of data. The problem is that Fairfax, Hernandez, and Barrows are very likely working as a unit. Fairfax has access to the Black Raven body of knowledge, and she can use the ITT proceeding to gather data for Black Raven. Her motion to interview Stollen is, no doubt, a joint effort. She, Hernandez, and Barrows are likely the impetus behind the French motion for expansion of the record. It is only a matter of time before the ITT, Barrows, and Black Raven are all breathing down our necks."

M.C. shifted in his chair. "Stopping the ITT proceedings was and is a great goal for our continuing enterprise. However, stopping anyone who might start looking at us, with the capability of finding us, is a fundamental prerequisite to our self-preservation," M.C. said. "We must stop Fairfax, Hernandez, and Black Raven."

"Agreed." H.L.'s earlier hesitation at targeting individuals who threatened them, rather than simply targeting the proceedings, dwindled away to nothing. He glanced at M.C., then focused on J.R. "Come up with a plan, Mr. Brilliance."

J.R. lit another cigarette, leaned back on the couch, and gave H.L. a slow smile as smoke oozed out of his lips. "Knew you'd come around."

"And Stollen?" M.C. said. "Nothing he'll say will help our cause. As a matter of fact, he can damn well hurt us."

"We'll know this afternoon if the court is granting Fairfax's request," H.L. said.

"Just to be clear here." M.C., normally cool and controlled, was toying with his glasses and fidgeting with his laptop. His nervousness was infectious. The yellow caution flags that had been hoisted in H.L.'s mind became red flags of danger as M.C.

continued. "I'm as worried about Hernandez as I am about Fairfax. Hernandez's company is on the bounty hunt for Maximov. If Hernandez lifts his nose and starts sniffing in our direction, with the resources he has at his fingertips, he and his company will quickly escalate to the biggest threat we've encountered to date."

"Understood." J.R. settled into quiet contemplation by taking a deep drag on his cigarette, relaxing his shoulders, and crossing his right ankle to his left knee. His gentle dark eyes were focused on M.C.'s laptop screen, with its news footage of the video feed of Zeus Hernandez holding Samantha Fairfax.

"What do we know about the Black Raven safe house where the Amicus team is staying?" H.L. asked.

"Heavily armed agents guard the perimeter and roof. At least fifteen are inside constantly," M.C. said. "An assault there would be too risky."

J.R., eyes still on the video, said, "Yesterday they exited Ile de la Cite on the Pont au Change."

"What are you proposing?" H.L. asked.

"Assuming they take that route again, we could meet them on the Quais des Grand Augustins. Attack while they're in transport," J.R. said.

"Won't work. The Black Raven vehicles are bulletproof," M.C. said, turning his laptop screen, bending forward as he typed.

"Tires aren't," J.R. answered with a shrug and a deep drag of his cigarette. "Bulletproof only goes so far. I can work around it."

"Using four cars, we could isolate the vehicle with Hernandez and Fairfax, and go in for the kill," H.L. said.

"A possibility. However, that kind of attack would require ground power by serious talent. We'd need at least," J.R. paused, narrowing his eyes for a moment, "ten men. We've got the capability. However, I'm thinking no. Hernandez has teams all around him. We'd be quickly outnumbered. Our men would be captured, if not killed. Too risky. Not that I give a damn about men getting killed, but I do care if they can be traced back to us. If men get captured, there is always the risk they'll start talking."

"Absolutely," M.C. answered.

"Sniper?" H.L. asked. "That blonde-haired American princess would make a great dramatic exit from the world."

J.R. nodded. "That could work. I'll assess. Options may develop."

"Meanwhile," H.L. said with a smile that was meant to

reassure M.C., "let's not forget that in my public life, Fairfax knows me. She trusts me. I'll see what I can learn from her."

"I'll continue to explore ways to exploit their weaknesses. Remember the family angle we're pursuing among participants in the ITT proceeding?" With a smile, M.C. turned his computer screen to them.

Three images appeared on the screen. H.L. recognized two of the three by sight. The first, Samuel Dixon—the eccentric, brash billionaire who was Samantha Fairfax's grandfather. The second, U.S. Senator Justin McDougall—Fairfax's boyfriend. The third photo was an image of a man's back, broad shoulders, and dark hair. The man's head was slightly turned to his left. The photographer had captured a partial profile of his strong jaw, solid, straight nose, and high cheekbones.

Hernandez. He was holding a young girl.

"Daughter?" J.R. asked, the uncharacteristic joy in his voice unmistakable.

M.C. nodded. "She's six now. In this image she was five. Name's Ana."

The child had her chin resting comfortably on Hernandez's right shoulder, while her arms dangled over his back. She clutched a teddy bear in her left hand. In the safety of Hernandez's protective arms, she stared absently behind him, in the direction of the camera. Eyes slightly heavy with fatigue, she looked like a sweet young girl, too young to know to avert her face from a photographer who had no business taking her photo.

"I know which target I'm choosing first," H.L. said, his eyes riveted on Hernandez and his daughter. "That's an Achilles' heel if ever there was one."

Blowing out a plume of smoke, J.R. leaned forward, eyes narrowed as he stared at the image of the little girl and her father. "Give me a few moments to think about how we can maximize impact. We need to hit that one hard. So hard it cripples Fairfax, Hernandez, and Black Raven's bounty hunt."

Chapter Twenty-One

The blustering shitstorm that was Zeus's Thursday had started the minute he called Sam a coward, made the asinine comment about what she might feel when she masturbated, and drizzled darkness down from there.

After the ominously quiet slam of his bedroom door 0445, he turned off the lamp, but couldn't sleep. That was a problem, because he damn well needed sleep. At least three or four hours when on a high stress job, and every few nights he needed more.

She's only having sex with me because I'm good at it?

Could be both a compliment and an insult, but given the tone and words she'd used, he knew her intent, and it pissed him off to no end. Hence his ill-advised masturbation comment.

At 0545, he turned over one last time, face down in a too soft pillow that still held faint traces of her sweet perfume, and gave up. A quick shower, and he was walking into the library at 0610.

Sam was already there.

Good.

He was perversely grateful she hadn't slept either. He hoped she was as unsettled as he by the parting after-sex fire volleys they'd thrown at each other.

He studied her face. *Nope. Ice queen doesn't seem fazed at all.*

She was in the library for work and focused on it. Hair pulled into a sleek ponytail, glasses on, and wearing socks, exercise leggings, and an oversized sweatshirt, she sat at a table with Abe and Charles, immersed in an early morning meeting. She barely acknowledged that he'd walked into the library.

A fire crackled in the fireplace. Agents glanced up briefly to acknowledge his presence, then went back to working quietly on their laptops.

Zeus opened his own laptop and started clicking through email, answering those he could and forwarding some to Sebastian for his attention. For the next couple of hours, he and Sam acted as professionals, as though nothing but the Amicus Team/Black Raven job existed between them. Everyone worked in complete silence. Only the sound of padded footsteps crossing the plush carpet to pour more coffee, the *click click click* of fingers at keyboards, and the occasional rustle of papers broke the snap, crackle, and pop of the fire.

When he was on his third cup of black coffee, Zeus couldn't

resist sending her a private instant message. *We should talk at some point this morning. Without verbal cheap shots.*

Her reply came quick, without even a glance in his direction, as she worked at the other table. *No.*

He zinged another message to her. *Won't stop asking.*

Answer won't change.

If he were the type to get irritated, he'd be pissed off. Officially. And, truth be told, he was getting pissed off. Irrationally, he was pissed off at her, at the world, at Maximov. At Samuel Dixon for hiring him to do the job. At whichever politician—even President Cameron—had dreamed up the idea of this clusterfuck of ITT proceedings in the first place. Most of all, and not irrationally, he was pissed off at himself, for being in this situation.

Should have said no to the hiring call.

Yet he was used to repressing his feelings, and with a subtle roll of his shoulders and a deep inhalation, Zeus was able, for a moment, to send his emotions into the stratosphere, refocusing on his laptop and not the way her blood-red lacquered fingernails sounded as she clicked on her laptop keyboard. Type, type, type. Pause. Read. Type, type, type. Pause. Read. Type. Read.

Parking his emotions elsewhere was a technique he'd learned young, when self-preservation had depended on it. When Zeus was sixteen, the highest crime days had supposedly come and gone from Miami Beach. Tourists flocked there for the glistening water and newly refurbished art deco hotels, but despite the illusion of safety, a man who made a habit of carrying cash was still a lightning rod for crime.

Pressing his hands on the gaping, sucking hole in his father's chest as he tried to stop the river of blood, Zeus watched the thugs who had shot his father run away. With his mother's crippling anguish, there was no room for Zeus's own grief and profound fear of living life without the father he adored.

His mother needed a crutch. Zeus became it. Gabe had been only ten years old. He needed a strong big brother and a father figure. Zeus, already one, became both. As Zeus made the burial arrangements for his father, as he made all the decisions that came with death, and the harder decisions that came with being the man of the family at the age of sixteen, he learned to work methodically through personal turmoil.

He became adept at ignoring his own feelings, because emotion got in the way of obligation, duties, and life. Pushing emotions to the side, parking them far away, was a technique that had served him well. The universe was now full of his unsaid words, feelings that weren't allowed, emotions that were repressed. All mentally parked elsewhere, never to be retrieved. He'd been fine with that.

Until Sam.

Meeting Sam seven years earlier had taught him he wasn't immune to strong emotion after all. From the first moment Sam's clear green eyes glanced in his direction, he'd felt more emotion than he'd allowed himself to experience since his father's murder. Any bliss that came with finding head-over-heels love came to a crashing halt when Theresa's call yanked him back into his reality—a world full of personal duty and obligation. He'd thought that marrying Theresa was the right thing to do. His mother, who had died shortly after Ana's fourth birthday, never would have understood how Zeus could consider not marrying the mother of his child.

Now, the woman who was inspiring his mental gymnastics seemed oblivious to his torment, and that pissed him off to hell and back. When he was around her, he felt too damn much.

Hell.

Feelings. And the point to them was—what?

Nothing he was aware of.

Sitting in the library, clicking through endless emails related to the Black Raven insurance project he'd been neglecting while on this job, he hated that he was so aware each time Sam flicked back her long blonde hair, leaned towards her computer, pushed her dark-framed glasses up her nose, and stared intently at the screen.

As if he had a goddamn lifetime of cool repression to make up for, the devil was giving him his due by forcing him to contend with Sam, who inspired a clash of feelings inside of him with just a blink of her long-lashed eyes. Losing his cool over a woman was a high price, one that told him that payback for years of repression was a fucking bitch.

Embrace the suck, because this suck-ass job isn't going to get better, and your feelings for this woman aren't going to go away.

For now, he could only pray that when Sam looked at him, he wouldn't feel a goddamn thing. That his racing heart wouldn't steal his breath, that he'd feel as cool as he acted, and that his fucking acting was damn good.

By 0730, when he had a million Black Raven issues that

needed his attention, he was wondering what the fuck was his problem.

Hell if I know.

If he could just turn back time...but he couldn't. Not an hour. Not a minute. And certainly not seven years. And now that he'd gotten a major load of the present-day Sam, he was pretty damn certain that turning back the clock wasn't the problem.

Fuck. The niggling thought that perhaps he'd made the right move by walking away from her all those years ago was now more than a glimmer, more than a trace thought shimmering through his brain.

Fuckfuckfuck.

If only my heart had gotten the message when I put on my walking shoes and left her.

At 0745, she glanced at him. "We figured out what to do with the telecommunication data in OLIVER. I've drafted a motion for the French to use on that. We need to talk about Stollen before I file the motion for an interview with him that I've drafted."

Her cool, calm tone reminded him, thank God, that first and foremost, Sam was a client, and his feelings—things he shouldn't be having, anyway—shouldn't interfere with work. Not only a client, the woman he had accused of being a coward was a damn smart client, with an important job to do.

For the next hour, he and Sam worked together, with input from Ragno and Abe, strategizing what argument to present to the court regarding the need to interview Stollen. The motions had been filed at 0900.

At 1100, he was in his closet, choosing a necktie, getting ready for the short drive to the ITT proceeding. He picked an emerald green and gray striped silk.

He and Ragno were talking bounty-hunting issues. The ITT task force search in Turkey the night before hadn't resulted in the capture of Maximov, just as Gabe had predicted. "Angel persuaded the team heading to Syria tonight that they need Black Raven assistance," Ragno continued. "So your brother is on his way to them, with six of our agents."

"Yeah. I saw those emails from Gabe." He was damned if he'd call his devilish younger brother Angel. As he pulled the ends of the tie down, and tightened the knot at his collar, his eye caught the pile of silk ties on the floor of his closet. The ties that she'd used on him were wrinkled and destined for a trip to either the dry cleaners or a trashcan.

Muscle memory of the feel of her wet, hot slide onto his fully engorged dick, the intense feel of her flesh, her walls pulsing and gently coaxing the life out of him, had him instantly hard and on his way to throbbing. "Dammit. Fuck me to hell and—"

"Anytime you want to talk through this foul mood of yours," Ragno said, "just let me know."

"Thanks, Ragno. Sorry. Don't want to make you a dumping ground for my frustration."

"Reality check, Hernandez. Your tension is off the charts. Angel figured out most of it, you know—"

"How the hell?"

"He knew you were shot on the Dixon job. Said all he had to do was take one look at you carrying her through Paris in that news clip. He saw the way you looked at her in last night's conference call. He knew the client you're body guarding now is Dixon's granddaughter. He did the math with the first Dixon job and the timing of Theresa's pregnancy. Angel isn't stupid. Your brother knows you better than you know yourself. I swear I gave him nothing but the barest details. He was instant messaging me last night the minute he laid eyes on the two of you. Now he's worried that you've lost your heart for a female velociraptor."

"A what?" Done with the tie, he smoothed his hair. He shifted his rock hard penis to the side where it belonged rather than dead center, aiming upwards on a hope and a prayer, neither of which were going to be answered anytime soon.

Fuck.

"Velociraptor. A carnivorous dinosaur that hunted—"

"I know that," he muttered, "but Sam isn't that."

"I'm just reporting Angel's take. Says she's gorgeous. Compelling. Riveting. But wondering whether she has a heart. He's worried you've fallen for a female version of you."

"Beautiful. Fucking beautiful. Glad to hear that's what Gabe thinks of me as well. And he knows all of this from seeing her in one video chat?"

Ragno was quiet for a second. "He got into the files we have on her. You know the type of information I'm compiling for you. Oh, and he had more than a few words when he learned that she's almost engaged to Senator McDougall."

"Son of a bitch, Ragno. Back up. You allowed Gabe to access your file on her? What the hell!"

"I've never been able to control your brother. No one has. That is partly why he's so good."

"Well, do me a favor and remind him about boundaries. Professional and goddamn personal ones. Seems like he isn't getting the message from me, and I swear, I'll hand him his ass on a platter, or better, fire him, if he doesn't—"

"Angel is one of our best field agents, Zeus," Ragno interrupted, her tone soothing. "Clients request him by name. He commands triple the normal fee in places most agents don't want to go. You love your brother and respect him. You will not fire him, nor will you hand him his ass on a platter. Your partners would pitch a fit. Myself and Sebastian included. I will, however, discuss with Angel boundaries and decorum."

He didn't break the connection with Ragno; they'd be live the rest of the day. At 1115, Sam stepped into the living room as Zeus came out of his bedroom, ready for their 1125 departure.

It was their first private moment of the morning. Wearing a slim fitting winter-white suit with black leather piping accents, two-inch high, relatively practical pumps, with a light touch of blue eyeliner and dark mascara accenting her clear green eyes, and her lips matching her red nails, she could have been the star of the show in any fine Parisian restaurant. In the ITT courtroom, composed mostly of men wearing navy blue and gray suits, she'd be a knockout.

An ivory suit had never looked so good on anyone. Her apparel wasn't just fitted, it seemed tailor-made for her body. A woman who loved beautiful clothes, she had enough money to afford the best. Chanel. Dior. Prada. Whatever.

I don't give a rat's ass what she wears. She's so goddamn pretty she steals my breath every time I look at her. Always has. Always will.

"Are you wearing your vest?" It was custom fitted, but still. He couldn't tell by looking whether she had it on.

"Yes," she said, her tone cool, her one-word answer clipped.

Unfortunately, their private moment came just a couple of minutes after he'd tied his necktie. His erection wasn't going away anytime soon, even though the look she was now giving him, with eyes that were both tired and irritated, didn't suggest a happy ending.

Not now, not ever.

She'd removed her glasses and put in contacts. She drew a deep breath, focusing on him with a look that told him their first private moment of the day wasn't going to end well.

None of this is going to end well, dumb fuck. Read the tea leaves. You're so fucking upside down over her you'll be crapping out of your eye sockets before this job's over.

"Sam, I'm sorry last night ended the way it did."

"Just to be clear, I'd prefer not to talk about masturbation with you."

"And I'd prefer not to be called the equivalent of a human dildo."

She flinched, but nodded. "Fair."

"I just wanted to talk about why you were crying."

"I wasn't crying." Eyes nonplussed, expression cool, her tone was quiet and subdued.

"Come on, Sam. As a lawyer, I know you're trained in the art of a damn good poker face."

"Are you saying I'm good at lying?"

"No. I'm saying I know you were crying." Detecting a glimmer of hurt in her eyes, he continued in a softer tone. "But what I don't know is why and I sure as hell don't know why you'd deny it with me."

She glanced into her purse, mumbled that she'd forgotten something, turned and strode into her bedroom. As he waited, he reminded himself that he'd taken the job with the healthy expectation that things wouldn't work out between them. He also reminded himself that the baseline goal for him was to walk away from her this time with the capability to expunge her from his brain, body, and soul. Right now, he had little hope of meeting even the baseline objective.

He hated having a need that he couldn't fill, but hated more that she had a need that he had no goddamn clue how to fill.

Her tears the night before proved something was wrong.

But what?

Glancing around the beige, well-appointed living room, his eyes rested on the treadmills. Dammit. More blood flowed to his dick as he remembered doing her against the wall after their run. Instead of taking the edge off of his desire once she'd opened up and decided sex was a good idea, the last twenty-four hours had only managed to whet his appetite for more.

He wasn't wrong about the tears. The drops that had fallen on his chest, along his cheeks, his lips, and his chin, as she surprised him by kissing him gently and slowly—when he'd fully expected her simply to mount him and ride until she came— they'd been tears. He'd held his goddamn breath, not knowing what to do. He'd been so fucking shocked he felt like he'd been transported to another world. He'd have sworn another woman had entered the room and Sam was gone. That moisture was tears, no matter how much she denied it. He'd bet his left testicle that she'd been crying and he was pretty goddamn fond of both his right and left.

How could he help her, when he didn't know what the fuck was wrong?

She reentered the living room. Evidently the break had given her time to regain her composure. She threw him a cool gaze, and his heart responded with a beat that was a steady metronome of time ticking away. At that moment, sharp slivers of certainty shot through his veins.

Face facts, buddy. Instead of walking away from this job with her expunged from your mind, you're only going to have her more deeply embedded there. Backfire is going to be a fucking bitch on this one.

He folded his arms, gave her a cool stare, and waited for her to say something. She wouldn't. She imitated his posture, squared her shoulders, and jut out her chin, proving she could beat him even at a silent staring match, when he was a master at it. And the most pathetic goddamn thing was that he was pissed because she didn't want to sleep with him after sex. Sleep. Really sleep. Most women he'd been with loved to hold on afterwards. No. Not Sam. At least not the Sam she was now.

The Sam she was now didn't want him to hold her. Didn't lean into him in all her warm and naked and sweetly exhausted glory and hold on as she fell asleep. Didn't want him to kiss her and tell her how much he loved her.

She had to fucking know he wouldn't be here if he didn't love her. Right?

Nope. She doesn't give a rat's ass about any of that. She's just having sex with you because you're good at it.

As she stared at him and remained perfectly silent, his thoughts continued to race. Not holding her after having sex was like having icing without the cake. Great while he was feasting, but just weirdly empty after. Would've been fine with any woman he didn't give a damn about. Rolling over and going to sleep—or better, leaving—was just fine with any other woman.

But not her.

Just how irritated he was by Sam's seeming inability to touch him after sex brought up a mountain of emotional issues, none of which he wanted to think about as the silent match continued.

Please God, it's Jesus here. You know I don't bother you for much. But I'm at a loss. Can't seem to think this one through. Please do something to take my dick out of the equation. Because it's getting in the way. Is this TMI, God? Of course not, you know what's going on down here. She's the one for me. The one. The only. And I'm blowing my chance with her. I royally fucked up in the first go round and I'm fucking up again. I'm smart enough to figure this out. To figure her out. I think. If I could just fucking think instead of constantly think about fucking.

When I'm with her my body takes over. All my body wants is to make love, cuddle, repeat, when I need to figure out how to persuade her that she loves me back. Making love to her obviously isn't doing the trick, and she's certainly giving no indication she wants to hear the words. Help me figure this out. That's what I'm praying for. Please.

In a voice as moderate and cool as he'd ever heard her use, she said, "I've done some thinking. It would be best if we keep our contact on a professional level from here on out. What happened last night was..." her voice trailed, "unnecessary and distracting."

"Distracting?" Suddenly seething at her, instead of wallowing in the slow-bubbling-simmer he'd been feeling all morning, he tried not to show just how pissed off he was. *I'm cool. Dammit. I'm the one who doesn't fucking show emotions.* "Unnecessary? That's what you call it?"

She gave him a nod. "And tiring. I'd have been better off with a few hours of sleep," she said, her voice as clear and calm and unemotional as any he'd ever heard.

"Understood," he said, allowing the word to drip with sarcasm. Though he didn't. Dammit. They had to talk. Or do something. He had to find a way to icepick through her cool resolve, because the slow-easy-melt method wasn't producing anything but misery on his end.

She arched an eyebrow. "You disagree?"

He stepped closer to her and bent his face to hers. With their lips almost touching, he said, "Totally. Given the slightest bit of encouragement from you I'll be back at it. With great enthusiasm. And by the way, I know only one of us is being honest here."

He gripped her hips, pulled her closer, and cupped her ass. With one butt-cheek firmly in the palm of each of his hands, he pulled her to him, rubbing her soft belly with the hard ridge of his erection, using his body to give her his message without words. *I want you. I need you. I can't stop thinking about being inside of you. This is what you do to me and I know you want me too. We have something rare. It isn't just sex. It's real,*

dammit. That's why it's so good. Don't you understand that?
Why can't you enjoy it? Be thrilled by it. At least excited.

Bending his face close to hers, he drew willpower up from
his toes and stopped before letting his lips graze the perfectly
applied red lipstick on her goddamn perfect lips. "I'm willing to
bet you won't hold out either. If you recall, you made the first
move after our run, and I didn't go looking for you last night. I
found you in my bed. Asking for sex. With me. And your
goddamn tears were fucking real." He released her, almost
groaning with the effort of letting go when all he wanted to do
was hold on.

She turned on a heel and strode out of the room, her butt-
cheeks, perfectly cupped by the slim fitting skirt, flexing with a
fuck-you message as she walked with each purposeful, solid
stride.

The woman had mastered the art of the pissed-off exit. What
he needed her to do was to turn around and confront him, deal
with their past, and tell him exactly what the fuck was wrong, so
that he could fix it.

Obviously, his simple reappearance wasn't doing the trick.

In the ensuing silence as he followed Sam down the stairs,
Ragno said, into his earpiece, "Sorry, big man, but your day's
about to take a turn, and not for the good. Though with that
bomb Samantha just dropped," she said, concern filtering into
her tone, "I suspect things are already pretty dim in the City of
Light. By the way, I'm pretty sure she could've done without the
last couple of asinine statements from you. Sweet Jesus, Zeus.
No woman needs that kind of reminder. Even when she is being
a bitch."

"Sorry. I should've muted the mic." On every job he'd ever
been on until now, even the first job he'd worked for Samuel
Dixon, when he'd first met Sam, he'd managed to keep personal
drama out of it. Back then, his connection with Sam had been
instant and real, but they'd only become intimate after the three-
week job was over. Which explained why, for the first four days
after he showed up on her doorstep, all they'd done was have sex.
They'd kept at it, until the phone call that had changed his life
came through.

"Not a problem on my end and frankly, this is one area
where I'd love to meddle, cause it sure sounds like you're royally
screwing up on your own. Knew you were headed into the world
of complications the minute Samuel Dixon made the hiring call,"
she said, her tone low and concerned. More friendly than the

clipped business tone she typically used. "I'm here if you want to talk. Don't know if I'm really qualified to give relationship advice, but I'm a woman and, last I checked, I'm still one of your closest friends. You're in deep—"

"Don't worry about me."

"Okay, tough guy. I've got a list of things demanding your attention. Theresa needs to talk to you. ASAP, she says."

"What's wrong?" His ex-wife wasn't the type to do an ASAP call while he was working. His heartbeat ratcheted up as he stopped on the first floor and helped Sam into her coat. Then again, Theresa had tried calling him the day before, and he'd had Ragno keep her updated. He'd told Ragno to tell Theresa he'd call her later, and he hadn't gotten around to it. His mind had been on work and Sam and he'd only concentrated on those two things.

Dammit. He'd forgotten to call his ex back.

Sam cast him an odd glance, as though she was wondering whether he really expected an answer at all, much less with agents and her team all in the foyer, putting on overcoats. He pointed to his ear, and whispered, "Ragno."

Ragno responded with, "Not sure. But she sounds unhappy. As in tell him to damn well call me now. Also, Dixon wants to talk to you. ASAP."

"Wait. Is Ana okay?"

"As far as I know, yes. Agent Martel has reported no problems, and you and I would be the first to know if she had."

"Tell me about the other things," he said. "The car ride'll give me about fifteen minutes to talk. Doubt I'll get to all the items, so I need to prioritize."

"Aside from Theresa, and Dixon, I've finally managed to get Blaze to agree to a phone call. I've talked to his scheduler. He is available for the next ten minutes. After that, they say two days from now. Can you believe that? This motorcycle gang leader has a scheduler, like he's the CEO of a Fortune 500 company. I've got a host of other issues, including bounty hunt issues and management issues."

"Blaze, Theresa, Dixon, in that order. After that, I'll tackle the rest of the items. If I run out of time, I'll communicate mostly via text and email when I'm in the courtroom, but talk when I have to." Zeus could speak in the mic with barely a twitch of his lips, quietly enough that no one in the room would hear him. Yet Ragno would be able to hear him, loud and clear. It was a practiced skill.

"Sam," Zeus said, scanning the sidewalk as they stepped into the gray, chilly morning. "Second car."

She turned to follow his direction, a poised, statuesque woman in a black cashmere overcoat, tied close at her narrow waist. Without making eye contact, she hesitated at the rear door of the car. He opened it for her and slid in next to her. Jenkins got in and sat on the other side of her. Zeus gave the driver a nod, wishing like hell he didn't have to smell the sweet rose and jasmine of her perfume while attempting to suppress the foul mood she had caused.

Chapter Twenty-Two

As the cars moved forward, Ragno said, "Zeus. Power up your iPad. I'm sending a link for a video chat with Blaze. Beginning in thirty seconds."

"Where is he?"

"His people won't say."

He opened his iPad and waited for her link. "You can't figure it out?"

"Not yet. They've got serious encryption protocols in place, and they originated the call. I may be able to figure it out later. Here's the link."

When Zeus clicked, a guy with long brownish-blonde hair that fell across his broad shoulders appeared on his iPad. He wore a black T-shirt, a white leather vest, and a cluster of silver and gold chains around his thick neck. A tattoo of red, orange, and blue-black flames crept down his right arm and up his neck. He wore a tough-guy look in his blue eyes that indicated he could deliver bad shit—anytime, anywhere. Zeus knew enough about the guy to know that he did.

Sam glanced at his iPad, and Zeus turned it just enough so Blaze wouldn't see her. Best if Blaze thought his conversation private. The audio would be transmitted through the feed in his ear.

"So," Blaze said, "you're Jesus Hernandez."

"That's right. Thanks for the call."

Cool eyes assessed Zeus. "Would prefer an in-person chat. I've got some bullets saved for you, and your agents. Hollow tip. Wondering why you'd want to talk to me."

"I hear you have information on TRCR."

Blaze gave Zeus a slight frown, but other than that, there wasn't even a flinch that showed surprise. "You heard wrong."

"Don't think so. My sources are damn good."

Hard blue eyes stared directly into his. "If I did have information, what would you do with it?"

"Depends on what the information is." Zeus scanned the road as the car turned a corner. Light traffic. Pedestrians talking on cell phones. Nothing abnormal.

"Tell me who said I talked about TRCR." His harsh tone indicated he considered it a transgression of the highest order.

"Can't do that." Zeus absorbed a bit of the menace that crept through the iPad screen, conveyed by Blaze's eyes and the red flush that had crept across his cheeks. "I can tell you that the whole world is looking for Maximov. Me included. And if you have information that leads to him, I'll damn well pay for it."

"Don't know if my information will lead you to Maximov. What I can tell you, is the TRCR consists of some evil motherfuckers. The sooner they're shut down, the better."

"For who? You?"

Blue eyes burning with an intense look of hatred, he spat out, "For the whole fucking world."

"Tell me what you know."

A cool headshake greeted him. "Not unless you agree to end them. Or promise an assist so I can."

"Didn't think you were the sort of guy who asks for help."

Blaze's frown reappeared. "You're damn straight. That should tell you how big they are."

"Can't promise I'll come in to fight your fight for you without knowing what you've got to say."

"That's fair." He gave Zeus a shrug. "Have your people call me if you ever get serious. In the meantime, when TRCR makes a bang by blowing up good Americans who are doing nothing but living their lives in the grand old U.S. of A., home of the formerly-free and now-scared-shitless, whether it's the Vegas strip—"

"Whoa. Do you have information indicating they were involved in the New Year's Eve bombing?"

"No." He shrugged his shoulders. "What I'm telling you is they're capable."

"Shitloads of people are capable. Including you."

"Understood." He arched an eyebrow. "And so are you. Fuck it, and fuck you. Call back when you're serious, cause I'm tired of this bullshit call. In the meantime, I'm giving you a big heads up so I can say I told you so. There I was, being a fucking stellar American citizen by making a call that could get my ass, and my people, in some serious trouble, and this is the thanks I get? Should've known not to call those pussies. They've pawned me off to a private security contractor, who runs a firm that consists of murderers-for-hire?" He narrowed his eyes. "I should lock you in a room with the widows of my men your agents have killed. Go fuck yourself."

The screen went dark. The car took a right, and a delivery van pulled up on the side of them. The dark-haired driver looked down, into the car. Right when Zeus was about to tell the driver to accelerate past the van, he did. Zeus breathed easier.

"Ragno?"

"Yep."

"Now he knows I'm interested."

Ragno chuckled. "It went better than I expected. He's in Texas, by the way. South of Sierra Blanca. Hudspeth County. Near the border. Barrows managed to break the encryption while you guys chatted. Which happens to be in the general vicinity of where he told the Department of Homeland Security TRCR was based. Now...Theresa's holding for you."

"Put her through."

"How can you do this to her?" Irate, Theresa's voice was far from the usual amicable-yet-slightly-perpetually-pissed tone that she used with him. This morning she was irritated, with great gusto, and wasn't trying to conceal it. "Come on, Zeus. Every after-school activity on hiatus for the next three and a half weeks? That's insane. Ana is hysterical over it. And by the way, I should be hearing about your parenting decisions from you. Not from Agent Martel. And we should be having discussions about them. You don't get to issue orders like a—"

"Not a parenting decision. A security decision. One of the judge's wives was killed yesterday."

"I'm not an idiot, Zeus. Ragno told me about it, and it was blasted all over the news. I was expecting a call from you." Zeus hadn't touched base with Theresa after communicating with Agent Martell about the additional security measures to be employed for Ana and Theresa, in light of the heightened threat directed at the ITT proceedings.

"I've upped security for you and Ana and assessed how to proceed."

"No shit. I feel like we're living in a combat bunker. Agent Martell, plus her team, now make six."

"So what are you not understanding? You go to work. Ana goes to school. After, you both go home. Period. Just three weeks, Theresa. Everything will return to normal when this trial is over."

"Three weeks is an eternity to a six-year-old. How can you not comprehend or consider that? I fully understand the need to curtail activities. Art? We'll make do at home. Piano? She's probably thrilled. She hates to practice anyway, and without practice, it is all a waste of your money. But dance? No way. There are three mandatory practices three times a week, Monday, Wednesday, and Thursday, from 5 to 7:30 p.m. Mandatory, Zeus. Understand? She has to go."

"No."

"Then you can be the one to tell her she won't be in the recital."

A red light couldn't be avoided. Zeus glanced around as their car stopped. A yellow Peugeot. Two women inside talking, their heads turned to each other. A black Fiat, with a gray haired man, two hands gripping the top of the steering wheel, staring dead ahead. Nothing particularly interesting. Or threatening.

Sam, sitting next to him, was scrolling through filings on her iPad, giving no indication that she was paying attention to the conversation he was having with his ex.

"What do you mean? Recital's in March." He knew, because being invited to do a solo dance seemed to be the most exciting thing that had ever happened in his daughter's life.

"Yes, and if any student misses four classes in the first quarter of the year they can't be in the recital. Period. It's a Las Munequitas school rule."

"Oh come on." He stretched his legs, accidentally rubbing against Sam as he did. She shifted away from him. "That's ridiculous."

"To you, maybe, but in the world of dance schools and recitals, it's pretty standard. Las Munequitas is the best, Zeus, and Ana is lucky to be in it. She is really, really good, and to be invited to do a solo at her age is almost unheard of. When I told her you wouldn't allow her to go to rehearsals, she cried all night."

Fuck, fuck, fuck. If anything ever happened to Ana, especially anything I could've prevented, I'd die. I'd place the bullet in my goddamn fucking brain myself.

"Do what you do best, Zeus. Make it safe for her. It is simply a dance school for young girls in Coconut Grove, for God's sake. If Black Raven can't protect Ana when she goes there, you tell me what, exactly, are people paying your company a fortune for?"

"It isn't a necessary risk."

"Damn you, Zeus," Theresa answered. "How can you be so cold?"

He shut his eyes for a second, thought of his little girl crying all night, thought of her absolute joy when she talked about her costumes for the dance recital, and bent. As they crossed the bridge leading to the Ile de la Cite, he said, "I'll talk to Agent Martel and see if we can work it out."

"Hurry. There's a class this evening. I'd like to tell Ana your answer before she goes to school, so she isn't miserable throughout the whole day." Something in her tone told him she wasn't done.

"That it?"

"Samantha Fairfax is the one, isn't she?"

Fuckitall. "Excuse me?"

"The reason why your heart was never in our marriage. I saw you on every news show yesterday, holding her." *Carrying* her, he mentally corrected his ex-wife. "I put two and two together when her name was familiar. Seven years ago, you went on a job for a few weeks. The Dixon job. We were having issues."

Issues? *Even before the job, I told you we needed to see other people. My way of saying I didn't want to move our relationship forward.* It was a damn hard statement to make to someone he'd been seeing for three years, someone who'd been a lifelong family friend, who his mother adored.

As he sank further into the seat, she continued. "I'd figured out I was pregnant, I didn't tell you right away, and you got shot while on the Dixon job. The job for the billionaire. Her grandfather. I wrestled with the decision whether and when to tell you. I had no idea where you were when I made that phone call. You came back and proposed, looking like a man who was doing the honorable thing."

Her voice was quiet and controlled, the tone of a woman who had the confidence that came with being undeniably correct. The French government buildings loomed in the distance. As he let his ex have her say, Zeus scanned the streets for signs of trouble, trying not to be distracted by the raw pain in her voice. "But you weren't a man who was excited to be proposing to the one great love of his life. You always referred to the job where you got shot as the Samuel Dixon job. Odd, that you never mentioned Samantha Dixon Fairfax, even though you were different after that job, and the differences had nothing to do with getting shot. After seeing the look on your face as you ran through the streets with her, I know. She's the reason why you could never be happy with me. Isn't she?"

Zeus didn't know what to say. *Yeah. You're right* seemed damn callous, especially when he'd always denied that there was anyone else. Which had been the truth. Once he committed to the idea of the marriage, he never would've gone back to Sam.

Not that Sam would have taken him back, a fact that was now perfectly clear. The problem was that once the excitement of their new marriage wore off, once Ana was born, and they settled into routine life, Theresa sensed something was missing.

Yeah, dumb shit. Like your heart.

Four or five years into it, Theresa got worn down by what she called their spark-less marriage. His distraction-by-design. His half-hearted presence, even when he wasn't working. The way he was distant with her, especially during sex, and afterwards. Finally, she'd been the one to file for divorce, citing irreconcilable differences in the pleadings. In person, she'd told him she was tired of being lonely.

He got it. He understood. Totally.

Next to him, Sam shut the cover to her iPad and bit the side of her lip as she looked out the front window of the car. One of the many new security measures in place was that no pedestrians without proper clearance were allowed within a mile of the building that housed the trial. In comparison to the crowds that had lined the streets the last couple of days, the empty sidewalks on the Ile de la Cite seemed eerie. Sam glanced at him, a worry line bisecting her brows.

He mouthed, silently, to Sam, "We're fine."

"Answer enough," Theresa whispered, tired of the extended silence with which he'd greeted her question, the exact silence he always gave when he chose not to go down an emotional road. "I only wish that you'd been honest from the start. With me. With yourself. We didn't have to play the charade. I didn't, at least. Don't know what you were trying to prove to yourself. Yes, I needed you, but not that badly. Let me know your decision as soon as you can about dance school. Goodbye."

The phone clicked, and Theresa was gone.

"Ragno," he said, "You heard that?"

"Want me to say no?"

As the car pulled up to the side door of the courthouse, the one he'd decided the Amicus team would enter, he said, "Nope. Need you to act on it. Ask Vick to draft a plan for team coverage while Ana's at Las Munequitas. Also, send me the plan for school coverage and transfers. I want to reevaluate logistics and coverage for both Ana and Theresa. Monitor their GPS trackers from here on out."

"Will do."

Zeus had a ground team in place, headed by Agent Small. ITT participants, judges and lawyers alike, were to use the same entrance. It was different from the entrance where the bombing had taken place the day before, which remained a crime scene. The new entrance was on the north side of the building, and media was there to showcase the arrivals. The rationale was that they were going to show the world that the ITT participants weren't scared. That the terrorists weren't winning.

Bullshit on that.

The Amicus team was no longer part of the dog and pony show. They were going to enter through a side door. Their path and the entrance had been cleared in advance by a ground team of Black Raven agents. An exterior security team, consisting of French military officers, awaited them.

As the car pulled to a stop, Zeus said, "Small. Are we clear?"

"Yes."

He opened the door, and turned to help Samantha out the car. In a few seconds, they were in the building, without incident. "Ragno. Ready for Samuel."

"Okay. I'll find him. Give me a sec."

After clearing interior security, he ushered Sam into the courtroom, took her coat, handed it to Agent Jenkins, and waited at her side while she opened her briefcase. Lawyers were filtering into the cavernous courtroom. Abe and Charles took their seats. The gallery was filling with press and onlookers.

He pulled her chair out for her. As she settled into it, he leaned down, inhaling the scent of jasmine as he bent to whisper in her ear, "Need to go to the bathroom before the proceedings start?"

It was a question that didn't need asking, because Sam sure as hell knew how to let him know she needed to go to the bathroom. The beauty of being her bodyguard, though, was that no matter how cool she was towards him, she couldn't get rid of him. Even to pee.

When the month ended and the verdict was reached, he'd lick his wounds and shake her out of his system. For now, though, he watched her back stiffen as she absorbed his tone and question. He was going to enjoy the hell out of being near her. Even if all he did was manage to irritate her and get blue balls for his trouble.

She gave him a cool glance, shook her head no, and powered up her iPad.

Turning to find a seat in the gallery, he walked past the American defense team, led by Brier, as they entered the courtroom. Brier's sharp brownish-green eyes held Zeus's for a second. The charismatic attorney gave Zeus a nod, then his second-chair attorney, a long-haired brunette with large blue eyes, said something that captured Brier's attention. She wasn't as striking as Sam, but, like Sam, the brunette managed to exude feminine grace while looking professional and intelligent.

After finding a seat in the front, Zeus shrugged out of his overcoat and handed it to Agent Jenkins, who took it and proceeded up the crowded aisle. His gaze was on the table of lawyers for the United States. Brier and his team of three attorneys were now sitting across from Samantha. His pretty brunette associate was seated to Brier's right. Not much space separated the two of them as they bent their heads and talked. Brier's hand lingered between her shoulder blades. In reply to something Brier said, she moved even closer.

A fling? Maybe. Or two business associates trying not to be overheard? Probably.

Zeus guessed that Brier's associate was at least fifteen years younger than him. Even if they were having a fling, was it relevant to anything? Doubtful. Interesting, though. His eyes slid to the prosecution team, made up of four men with grim faces and look-alike dark suits, sitting at the end of the table, heads together in conversation. Sam, facing Zeus's direction, was talking to Charles.

Samuel's voice boomed through Zeus's earpiece. "Zeus, this call isn't about business. It's personal."

"Okay."

"Got a call from Samantha's boyfriend last night. Senator McDougall. Fine man. Says he'll see her this Sunday in London."

"I'm aware."

"It's an interesting turn of events."

Ragno had informed Zeus of the dinner plans the night before, based on a conversation that had taken place between Sam and McDougall. Zeus sank into the aisle seat. When Ragno had broken the news to him, he hadn't focused much on the full implications of what it meant that McDougall was showing up for a dinner date with Sam. Eyes on the American flag behind the now-empty dais and the black leather, tall-backed chairs, where the judges would sit when proceedings commenced, he now wondered what he'd done wrong to deserve having to bodyguard Sam while she was on a dinner date with McDougall.

Don't have to wonder for long.

He fully deserved this express shipment of reciprocal, suckass payback. After all, he'd delivered an abrupt message that he was marrying someone else within hours of spending days in bed with Sam, making love to her as though he meant the words behind the deed. He shrugged, rotated his neck a bit as he shifted in his chair, and let someone slip past him to a seat down the row.

Embrace the suck. Dinner with her boyfriend is nothing compared to what you did to her.

Awww. Fuck. Whether they planned an open marriage or not, McDougall flying across the Atlantic for a dinner date sure as hell meant McDougall expected to sleep with her. And guess who the fuck is going to be standing on the wrong side of that bedroom door?

Raging jealousy—the likes of which he'd never felt before—burned a hole in his gut.

Fuck. Fuck. Fuck.

Embrace the fucking suck.

He exhaled, when he didn't even realize he'd been holding his breath. "We'll work it out. She told us they were having dinner. We're coordinating the logistics with the Senator's security detail. Don't worry, she'll be safe."

"For the moment, it isn't her security I'm worried about."

Refocusing across the courtroom to Sam, who now had both Charles and Abe leaning into her for a discussion, he said, "Okay?"

"Do you remember the conversation you and I had the evening before you took that bullet for me?"

As Jenkins reappeared and slipped into the seat on Zeus's left, Samuel's question transported him for a moment to the night before the Dixon protective detail had gone to shit, when Dixon had confronted Zeus in the library and told him to stay away from Sam. It had shocked the crap out of Zeus that the man had even been aware that something was developing. The man was eagle-eyed when it came to his granddaughter, and clearly the many long evenings of hushed conversations in the library between his bodyguard and his granddaughter hadn't been lost on him. "Glued in my memory."

"You were the first, and so far, the only person who told me to fuck off."

His heart did a stutter beat. "Did you ever tell her about our conversation?"

"No. Not that conversation, nor the same conversation I had with three other men with whom she became involved. In case you're wondering, two before you. One after. Seemed to me she fell the hardest for you, though."

Zeus felt blood coursing through his veins as his blood pressure ratcheted up. "Have you had that conversation with Senator McDougall?"

"Saw no need. I approve of him."

The meddling son of a bitch.

"Good to know," he spoke through a clenched jaw. "But why is any of this relevant to my job now?"

"Because the way I see it, my granddaughter has a choice coming up. She can either choose McDougall and enter into an important marriage that will clearly facilitate the career for which I've groomed her all her life." He paused. "Or she can follow her heart, and choose you. That is, if as I'm assuming, there's at least a possibility that you two have picked up where you left off seven years ago, before you decided you needed to marry your pregnant girlfr—"

"Sam told you what happened between us?"

"Of course she did, though I could have figured most of it out on my own. But that was years ago. Somewhere in the intervening seven years, our relationship has become less open. More strained. Now, I don't always know what she's thinking, like I once did. And this week, I'm sure as hell out of the loop. We usually talk every morning, when she's on her second cup of coffee. As you damn well know, she hasn't spoken to me since our argument, when she refused to resign."

"Something tells me the argument started before her refusal to resign."

"Yes, and I bet you damn well know you're the reason for it."

Zeus drew another deep breath, trying to tamp down the anger that roiled up from his gut. "Samuel, you hired me. Understand? I'm not the one who set the wheels in motion on this. And by the way, don't even bother asking me to name my price to stay away from her. Answer would still be to go fuck yourself." Glancing at Jenkins, he realized he was talking loud enough for the man to overhear. His agent was doing a damn good job of looking straight ahead and pretending that he hadn't gotten an earful of personal shit he had no business hearing. "Just like it was the night before I took a bullet for you."

Samuel chuckled. "I know that. Don't you understand? I approve of you as well. I wouldn't stand in your way. As a matter of fact, by the way the charges are adding up for the protective detail and the bounty hunt, seems to me I'm doing just the opposite of paying you to stay away. I'm paying you to be in her face and make her realize she's at a fork in her personal road and for this she's giving me the silent treatment. She's that pissed off that I hired you. You're a different matter entirely. If there is anything between you and my granddaughter, I want her to give it some thoughtful consideration."

"Dammit, Samuel," he muttered, "You can't play people like this. People's lives aren't a game. Hers especially."

He watched Sam lean back in her chair, pause for a moment with her eyes resting on Brier, whose head was still bent to his second chair attorney. He'd seen that look in her green eyes before. She was thinking. Weighing options. Assessing the situation, trying to gain control. She pushed her chair back, walked around the counsel table, and leaned down at Brier's chair, interrupting the head-to-head conversation between him and his associate.

Brier rose to his feet. His associate rose to her feet as well. Brier was about Sam's height. Maybe, at most, five eight. He seemed larger, though, due to his considerable brawn. And his loud voice.

One of the prosecutors from the United States joined Samantha, and the four lawyers, heads shaking and fingers pointing as they talked, looked like they were engaged in a verbal schoolyard brawl.

The teams of lawyers from France—prosecutors, defense attorneys, and Amicus counsel—were at the counsel table next to the United States counsel table. They turned to watch the argument among the American lawyers. Zeus couldn't make out Sam's words, but over the other voices he heard her low voice, and could tell from the way all the lawyers were looking at her that she was holding her ground. Zeus assumed she was trying to persuade the lawyers, including Brier, of the need to interview Stollen. She wasn't backing down, even though from Zeus's vantage point he read skepticism on their faces.

That's my girl. Give 'em hell. Win.

"There is real danger," Samuel continued, "and that's why you're there. You're the only person I trust with her life. Circumstances and timing beyond my control have put these personal matters into play now. I'm good." He chuckled. "But not this damn good."

Samuel fell silent. Zeus, irritated, dumbfounded, and generally wishing he could wrap his hands around Samuel's neck and throttle the smug cockiness out of the man, decided not to say anything.

"Call it a game if you want," Samuel continued. "Doesn't much matter to me how you view it. Just wanted to give you a bit of perspective about McDougall. If what I've done is create a game where the three of you are players, I think you're the kind of man who damn well plays to win. Thank me later. Or not. Act on it. Or not. Up to you. Goodbye."

"What the hell was that about?" Ragno asked in the split second after Samuel ended the call.

"You heard it, just like I did." Across the courtroom, Sam and the other lawyers were still talking and arguing. A couple of lawyers from the counsel table of the Colombians had joined the argument. Out of respect for the courtroom, their tones were hushed, but Brier's face was flushed. Samantha looked as cool as ever. Over the inaudible hum he heard Brier say, "I will oppose," "Stollen," and, "fishing expedition disguised as expansion of record."

At Brier's last comment about a fishing expedition, the French Amicus counsel, Sam's counterpart for France, stood, his head shaking. Another lawyer from the French table joined in the argument, standing firmly at Sam's side.

"Sorry," Ragno said. "I'm just a bit lost on the part of the conversation where you and Samuel talked about his offering money as a bribe for you to stay away from her. Jesus H. Christ. Really?"

"Yep."

"Holy hell, Zeus. That kind of behind-the-scenes manipulation is what isn't showing up in the information on her that I'm pulling together."

"What do you mean?"

Ragno provided details on Sam's life and in particular, the relationship she had with her mother and father, before they died in the car accident. She summed it up with, "Her father, handsome charmer that he was, was a loser, with a capital L. An alcoholic, and arguer. Prior to marrying Elizabeth Dixon, he had serious financial problems. He was ultimately considered a liability by the review committee that considered Elizabeth for a federal judgeship, and that is why her mother was denied the position. The tragedy that ended Elizabeth Dixon's life started the minute she met him and fell in love."

"I know Sam's ambitions are her mother's ambitions." He didn't need Ragno for that bit of information. Sam had shared her ambitions with Zeus, and the root of them, when they'd been together all those years ago. As someone who also carried a torch for a deceased parent, every day, every step of the way, he fully understood the burning drive to succeed. It was part of why he loved her, part of why he wanted her to realize every dream.

"That's right, but did you know it was Elizabeth's love for her husband that kept her from attaining her goals? Samuel raised Samantha after her parents died. He raised her to realize her ambitions. From the very moment her parents died in that car crash when she was thirteen, Samuel took over—the best schools, the highest opportunities, and pulling strings behind the scenes to remove every obstacle that might lead to failure. Now that I know about that conversation—the bribe he offered you and others—the puzzle pieces that make up her life are all falling into place.

"Geez, Zeus. Imagine if you believed romantic love led to failure, because your parents were the role models for that truism. And then, everyone you ever loved suddenly disappeared, and some of them did it for no apparent reason? I'd be one tough cookie, too."

And you'd run like hell from real love. Because the only glimpse of it you ever saw resulted in the destruction of a parent who you loved.

"If that's so, why is she a hair's breath from marrying McDougall?"

"Jesus H.! *Bingo!* You are brilliant, Zeus. Remember, I've listened to their phone calls. I said it sounded like they're talking shorthand. They're friends. They talk to each other like they're besties. She has even talked about you to him."

I could only hope they were just friends.

"Zeus, aside from this bucket load of bad news, you also have a really big problem looming with Samantha."

"Really? Gee. How astute." A door beyond the dais opened, signifying that the judges were ready to enter the proceedings. The conversation among the lawyers stopped. Zeus rose to his feet with everyone else in the courtroom.

"Not any of the obvious ones that you've already thought of, Mr. Smartass-Irritated-Bodyguard," Ragno said. "Call me lucky, call me correct. Hell, just call me a woman whose brain isn't operating on oversexed testosterone deficits. Don't even think about shooting the messenger on this one. Gonna hurt, but I'm calling you out on a mistake you made. When you and Sam were last together, when the job was over, and you two became intimate, you didn't tell Sam that her grandfather offered you money to stay away from her, did you?"

Instead of the judges, two clerks, one Zeus recognized had been at the side of Judge Ducaisse on prior days, and another who was constantly at Judge O'Connor's side, entered the courtroom. The French clerk walked to the center of the dais, while the American clerk walked with a purposeful stride off the center stage.

"No," he muttered, tone low, as the others in the courtroom ended their conversations to focus on the clerks. Sam returned to her chair, and stood beside it. Her gaze remained on Brier. "My mind was on...other things, and then I got the call from Theresa. My conversation with her grandfather seemed irrelevant."

Beyond lame, but an excuse that made sense.

"The fact that you didn't give her this pertinent info is going to royally piss her off, when she finds out."

Ragno's words placed a shiny red-candied cherry smack dab in the center scoop of the hot-fuck, sticky mess of a sundae his life had suddenly become. To further embellish the dripping concoction, he had only a few days before the world's modern-day version of Prince Charming, U.S. Senator Justin McDougall, had a dinner date with the woman he loved and did God knows what else afterwards.

Gazing across the now-crowded courtroom, he fixed his eyes on Sam as her gridlock focus was on Brier. His blood ran cold, because no strategy for dealing with her seemed apparent, obvious, or destined for success. With the host of personal issues Sam presented, there wasn't a goddamn thing he could do about any of it except let it play out as he kept her safe, because that was the only legitimate part of this job.

Embrace the fucking suck, buddy.

Chapter Twenty-Three

"Proceedings will commence at 12:45," Judge Ducaisse's clerk announced to the courtroom from the center of the dais, then stepped back without an explanation for the delay.

Good. She needed more time to work on Brier, who had just informed her, with belligerent, in-your-face bravado, that he was planning to oppose both the French-sponsored motion for expansion of the record with additional telecom data and her request to interview Stollen.

Thinking through counter-arguments to the points Brier had raised, she watched Timothy Adams, Judge O'Connor's law clerk, as he navigated around briefcases in the aisle that fronted the tables for lawyers. His gaze rested on her as he headed in her direction.

Now what?

"Judge O'Connor wants to speak to you before the proceedings start," Timothy said. "In private."

Samantha glanced at Zeus, who stood as she stepped forward. Jenkins also stood. On the courtroom side of the private door behind the dais, the space was crowded with lawyers, clerks, and reporters. Immediately on the other side of the door, there was silence in the long corridor that led to the chambers of the ITT judges and their staff members.

"That was quite a scrum," Zeus said, catching up and falling into step as they followed Timothy through the narrow hallway, the walls adorned with photographs of French judges and dignitaries. Jenkins trailed behind them. A U.S. marshal walked past with a German shepherd. Ears alert, the K9 turned and sniffed in their direction, then the pair continued down the hallway in the opposite direction. "Motions aren't going over very well, are they?"

Their eyes held for a second. A bit of a smile played at the corner of his lips, enough of one to erode some of the self-protective wall she'd erected around her feelings since her early morning departure from his bedroom.

"Understatement," she acknowledged. "Though we knew Brier would oppose. He's just doing his job, and he' good at it."

"Looked to me like you were holding your own."

With Zeus, being cool and indifferent was an effort. He was not only a damn vigilant protector, with his eyes on her at all times, she liked that he took an interest in what she was doing.

She liked even more that he didn't stay perturbed with her for too long—because that slight smirk of a smile told her he wasn't angry any longer about her telling him she'd prefer sleep over sex. She thought it funny that he equated her comment about being good in bed to a human dildo insult.

She hadn't intended it that way. Not at all. Well. Maybe. God, he drove her...crazy.

The problem was, she liked everything about him, even the way, despite his tall stature and super-sized physique, his footsteps were light and barely audible beside her as her heels clacked on the marble floor. Not to mention the way the hard muscles of his arm brushed against her as they walked together, or the way the soapy smell of his morning shower faded to just a lingering wisp, or the way an afternoon shadow was beginning to play on his jawline and hollow cheeks, despite it being barely past noon.

Cool. Indifferent. Remember? He isn't the man for you. He makes you feel too much. He drives you crazy. Remember? Not good.

Judge Amanda Whitsell, the alternate who would be taking Judge Kent Devlin's place while he attended his wife's funeral, walked past them with U.S. Judge Mark Kennedy. Marshals and clerks were at their side.

A middle-aged redhead, petite with a pixie haircut that perfectly complimented her heart-shaped face and large brown eyes, Judge Whitsell looked smart, serious, and naturally pretty. Judge Kennedy had dark hair, dark eyes, and a serious look on his face.

"Hello, your Honors."

The judges nodded at Zeus, Sam, and the clerk, then continued down the hallway.

As Zeus's eyes scanned the doorways lining the hallway, he said, "Looked to me like you went over to Brier to pick a fight."

"Hmm. That obvious, huh? I was trying to learn his argument before the judges take the bench."

"Can't believe he fell for it." Eyes dead ahead, he asked, "Any idea why proceedings are late?"

"No," she said, "but it happens, even in regular court proceedings. Any intel on timing from your sources?"

"Ragno? Any news pointing to a delay in proceedings?"

Zeus was quiet for a moment as he listened. Dark eyes flickering to her as they turned a corner, he shook his head. "No idea."

Timothy paused at the shut door that led to Judge O'Connor's office. Marshals flanked either side of it. Timothy glanced at Zeus. "Sir, the judge requested a private meeting with Ms. Fairfax."

Samantha glanced at Zeus. "I'll be safe. He is a judge of the United States Second Circuit."

A stony gaze held hers. "I know who he is."

"President Cameron's best friend and confidante—"

"Know that too."

"If you notice, his security is outside the office. Not inside."

Zeus's hard look, and the slight turn down at the corner of his mouth, told her he assumed she was safe with no one. "Not necessarily the judge I'm worried about. I'll do a walk through, then exit." He entered the office at her side, with Jenkins, Timothy, and a marshal on his heels.

Judge O'Connor, pen in hand as he sat behind his large desk, stood as they entered. He hadn't yet put on his judicial robe. A dark business suit, white shirt, and red tie, revealed broad shoulders and the beginning of a paunch. Close-cropped curly hair, black and sprinkled with gray, gave the aging jurist a distinguished look. His warm, dark-eyed gaze, serious but welcoming, encompassed both of them. "Samantha. Zeus."

"Hello," Zeus said. "It's good to see you, Ted. How are you?"

Samantha stopped as Zeus stepped forward, leaned across the desk, and gave the judge a firm, friendly handshake. She shook off her surprise, reminding herself that Black Raven was a player in Washington's elite circles. Zeus, an owner of the company, no doubt made it his business to know those in power, yet he wasn't the type to name drop or flaunt his connections. For all she knew, he and President Cameron were on a first-name basis as well.

"Just trying to herd this proceeding to a resolution that satisfies the powers that be." Strain in his dark brown eyes revealed more tension than his words. "And you?"

"Never better," Zeus said, his eyes scanning the room.

Judge O'Connor folded his arms and stared at Zeus, just the way he stared at lawyers in court as they presented cases. Analytical. Assessing. Thinking. "I receive task force reports on the hunt for Maximov. I understand Black Raven has joined the bounty hunt."

"You're correct."

"Black Raven intel will be a welcome addition." A smile that matched the gaze in the judge's eyes momentarily softened his features. "And here you are, pulling guard duty. Samuel Dixon is a hard man to say no to, isn't he?"

Zeus chuckled. "You're correct on that." He glanced at Samantha, a sea of unsaid words underneath his cool, calm exterior. To the judge, he said, "I'll be out of your hair in a second. Just doing my job as bodyguard." To the U.S. marshal, Zeus said, "You have personnel on the other side of that door?"

Two doors led to the office. They'd entered through one. Another was closed. As the marshal nodded, Zeus said, "Jenkins," barely flicking his head in the direction of the second door. Jenkins crossed the office, opened the door, stepped outside, and shut it behind him.

Zeus gave the judge a nod and stepped towards the door. As the marshal exited the office ahead of him, the judge said. "Zeus. Stay." Zeus turned back to the judge, who unfolded his arms and gestured with a raised hand and open palm for them to sit in two armchairs facing his desk.

When Timothy hesitated at the open door, the judge shook his head. "Timothy, thank you, but you may step out."

Eyes returning to Zeus and Samantha as they sat, he sank heavily to his chair and drew a deep breath. "What Samantha and I will discuss will soon be a matter of public record. Before that, though, I wanted to acknowledge to both of you that the timing of three occurrences isn't lost upon me. First, the French motion for expansion of the record. I've spoken to the French judges, who have ferreted out the root of the French prosecution team's motion for sudden, and dramatic, expansion of the record with telecommunications data."

His sharp glance at Samantha indicated he'd figured out she was the force behind the French motion. "Second, Samantha's motion to interview Vladimer Stollen. It is destined to be an uphill battle. Third, the appearance of Black Raven in this proceeding coupled with your hunt for Maximov. As I said, the timing isn't lost upon me."

Heart pounding, Samantha mentally formulated an argument designed for damage control, knowing the judge would disapprove of her seeking guidance in the ITT proceeding from the unconventional tools Black Raven used. While it was the judge's job to enforce the rules, her job was to play by them. The rules said that the ITT proceeding was to be the product of a carefully composed record. Not a record influenced by Black Raven's questionable data-assimilation and gathering tactics.

"Your Honor—"

He lifted his hand and gave her a sharp look, effectively silencing her. "To be perfectly blunt here, I'm less interested in the guidance behind your thought processes, Samantha, than the results. President Cameron and I trust that you'll carefully and astutely navigate through the minefield presented by using data that is outside of the ITT record to influence this proceeding—data secured by means that I cannot begin to understand."

Stunned, Samantha kept her mouth shut. Desperation underscored the judge's words, and the statement was as close to blanket permission to use Black Raven's ill-gotten data as she was going to receive.

Reading between the lines, the statement was also a solid don't-get-caught warning.

Instead of being thrilled, her palms turned clammy and her stomach twisted. Still, she managed, "Yes, Your Honor."

With the weight of the world on his shoulders, his look—both solemn and worried—encompassed both her and Zeus, who had shifted slightly in his seat and was leaning forward, his gridlock focus on the judge.

"Then Godspeed." The judge's deep breath was loud and heavy in the silent office. After a pause, he said, "There have been additional developments this morning that may make the conversation we've had thus far moot. Duvall was murdered this morning. Strangled. Tongue cut out."

Samantha drew in a deep breath.

The judge's eyes were grim. "Intimidation message to other witnesses clear."

Her chest felt hollow. "Duvall was in the custody of French officials, under the protection of armed officials. Who got through? And how?"

"We only know enough to know we likely won't know either, except for the claim of *I Am Maximov* found in his cell."

"But Maximov was never an organization that killed its own," Samantha said.

"Obviously, the historical objectives of Maximov have devolved into general anarchy." The judge shrugged his shoulders. "Another problematic development is that the lead prosecutor from Colombia will move for a mistrial when the proceedings begin this afternoon."

Samantha's stomach churned. "But a mistrial will end the proceedings prematurely. No verdict will be reached, not even one that reaches the defendants who have been apprehended thus far. Each of the four crimes at issue have someone like

Duvall, and others. If the proceeding ends in a mistrial, all the defendants will go free. It will all have been a waste of time. No headway will be made in the war on terrorism. A mistrial is," she paused, "something that shouldn't even be discussed at this point."

"You're preaching to the choir." Lines creased at the corners of the judge's eyes, and his lips were drawn in a marked frown. For the moment, he looked worried, older, and defeated. "But I can't say that I blame the Colombians. They lost lawyers due to the Boulevard Saint-Germain bombing, and Judge Calante's death from the explosion yesterday is an overwhelming loss. He was well-liked. Popular in his country. A great jurist. Especially with Duvall's death, the motion for a mistrial will have legs. Once the media catches wind of it, we're not going to get one more word from witnesses in this proceeding, so what is the point of the trial? Tombeau, Duvall's friend, was more talkative than Duvall, correct?"

"Yes," Samantha said.

Judge O'Connor's marked frown reappeared. "He won't be any more. Tombeau found Duvall's tongue. In his cell."

Stomach churning, Samantha held the back of her hand to her mouth.

The judge continued, "Not that the live witnesses were giving us much of anything. Still, Duvall's death gives the Colombians fodder for their mistrial motion, which they were planning on making even before they knew of it."

"President Cameron's feelings about the mistrial?" she asked, though she knew the answer. This sitting of the ITT was the president's brainchild, something he had conceived and for which he'd fought long and hard.

"He's gravely concerned. He strenuously opposes the early termination of this ITT proceeding through a mistrial."

Samantha nodded as her mind raced through scenarios of how the argument would proceed. "Defense counsel will argue in favor, and I hope prosecutors—except those for Colombia—will oppose. A mistrial requires a vote of nine judges. Any idea of how the judges will vote?"

"American judges are inclined to vote no. But that leaves nine others, and from what I understand, the judges from the other three countries are wavering. As Amicus counsel"—his eyes held hers—"President Cameron and I need you to present solid arguments in opposition to the motion for mistrial." His words hung heavy in the room.

"Your honor, Amicus counsel is supposed to be an adviser to the court." Samantha leaned forward, keeping her tone even. "Even in the hybrid world of ITT proceedings, the judges aren't supposed to tell Amicus counsel what their arguments should be."

The judge folded his arms, the mask of congeniality gone in an instant. A deep frown matched the intense look of frustration in his eyes. "Counselor—"

"But in this instance," Samantha tried to make her tone placating, but firm, "your directive coincides exactly with what I know my role should be. I will do my best to defeat the mistrial motion and the arguments presented in its favor."

The judge gave her a curt nod. "Prior to his death, Stanley Morgan believed this proceeding was doomed, and he was vocal about his belief. He believed the underlying goal of using the proceedings to draw out Maximov was never going to come to fruition. He believed the evidence wasn't adding up for a conviction of Maximov."

"Your honor, with all due respect," Samantha said. "Stanley Morgan believed the proceedings could draw out Maximov, but not within the existing parameters. And given the state of affairs and the pending threat of a mistrial, I'd say his fears were well founded and are coming to fruition. The record must be expanded to make this trial as productive as it should be."

He gave a slight headshake. Shrewd brown eyes locked on Samantha. "Yesterday your questions to Duvall highlighted the weaknesses in the case against Maximov. When we talked on the phone yesterday evening, I was more than displeased. Your desire for an interview with Stollen is something that Stanley Morgan also attempted. Before I became a judge, I was a litigator. I recognize the value of a second-chair attorney who is both brilliant and hard working. Now, I'm wondering—did you agree with Morgan's opinions?"

Samantha gave Judge O'Connor a slow nod. "Yes."

He frowned. "Based on what?"

She swallowed. "Hunches from cold, hard facts. It's been my job for the last year to analyze, with a bird's eye view, every investigative report that's been admitted into the ITT record and even information that isn't in the record."

In the chair next to her, Zeus shifted and turned to her. The judge asked, with laser-like focus in his dark eyes, "Elaborate. Please."

"I believe Vladimer Stollen will have information that is

fundamental for finding Maximov. Information we don't currently have. Once we find Maximov, we can determine whether he is calling the shots. It he isn't, we can find the people he is using to breathe life into the low-level cells that are doing the street work. We can locate the revenue streams they use and cut them off. Maximov—the man—has to be terminated, because he has become a myth to every young anarchist around the world."

"Your belief that Stollen has information. Based on more than a wing and a prayer?"

"Stollen and Vasily Maximov were the last two known cohorts of Andre Maximov to have been captured. Stollen was always believed to be second-in-command to Andre Maximov, and therefore one of the forces behind the group—Maximov-in-Exile. Vasily Maximov, Andre's son, was right behind Stollen. In the intervening years after Stollen was arrested, law enforcement agencies have only managed to capture people like Duvall. No one who has a direct link to Maximov or even, in reality, the Maximov-in-Exile organization. They're simply young anarchists who've seized upon a convenient cause and claim a link. Interviewing Stollen is worth a try, though I can tell you that Brier will strenuously oppose the motion."

The judge arched an eyebrow, glancing at Zeus. "And if Stollen gives us anything, it will be helpful to task force and bounty hunters?"

"Yes," Samantha said.

"Your motion refers to Stollen's familiarity with known Maximov hideouts in Turkey, Syria, and even Greece."

"Yes," Samantha said.

He gave both her and Zeus a knowing look. "These are areas that the task force has combed through—and will continue to do so. My understanding is there is another mission in Syria tonight—of which I'm sure Black Raven is aware." He paused. "Am I correct in assuming that you intend to ask Stollen questions about areas that have nothing to do with Turkey and Syria?"

"Yes." *Please don't ask me where.* She trusted the judge, but she didn't want to have to reveal the true locale to him. Not now, not when Zeus and Gabe believed advance knowledge that Black Raven was headed into Praptan would be detrimental to the search. "And that is why we want the interview to be conducted under seal, with as few participants as possible. Black Raven is planning an operation, based upon the expectation that Stollen will provide helpful information."

The judge leaned forward, his elbows on his desk, the fingers of both hands pressed together, with his chin resting on his thumbs. "Why do you think Stollen will tell you anything helpful now?

"If there is an offer of years off his sentence—"

The judge shook his head. "That was offered before."

"I propose we sweeten the deal," Samantha said.

"How?"

"Immediate release from prison to house arrest upon his information leading to the capture of Maximov. Also, given the reach of the terrorists who are attacking this proceeding, I suspect that Stollen feels more secure in a super-max prison than out in the world. Provide him with security that will enable him to live in relative freedom. Offer Black Raven protection. For life. If he gives information that leads to the capture or apprehension of Maximov."

The judge nodded. "Not a bad idea."

"Judge, Samantha and I have conferred on this." Zeus shot Samantha a sideways glance, as unreadable as any he typically threw her way. "But before Black Raven protection is officially part of the inducement package, I need an official sign-off. I'd like you to have an understanding of the cost to taxpayers. We're coming up with an estimate now. As with all of our estimates, I can assure you the number will go up."

Judge O'Connor gave Zeus a nod. "Fine. Assuming the tribunal grants the motion, when my aide is putting together the package of bargaining chips, I'll have him consult you. He'll communicate directly with me on this, and I'll officially sign off."

The judge frowned as his phone rang. "Excuse me." Listening, he shut his eyes. "Good God." He put the receiver down and pressed a button on the intercom. "Bring Brier to me." To Samantha and Zeus, he said, "His wife and her security detail were murdered this morning at Brier's home in D.C. The usual '*I am Maximov*' note was written in blood in the bathroom mirror."

Stunned, Sam rose to her feet. Zeus rose alongside her.

As the judge listened to the caller, he gave her a nod, whispered, "Don't leave," and resumed the call by saying, "Do we know who?"

There was a sharp tap at the door, then the judge's security put his head in the office and announced Brier.

When Brier entered the office, the judge stepped around

from his desk, directed the attorney to sit, and delivered the harsh news. His tone and words, concerned but firm, conveyed immeasurable sympathy.

In the silence that followed, the charismatic lawyer who boldly and deftly overpowered judicial proceedings and presented arguments with the force of a freight train, devolved into a beaten-down, stunned man. His shoulders slumped forward. With his elbows on his knees, Brier dropped his face into the palm of his hands. Long seconds passed with his silver-gray haired head down, where his harsh sobs were rattling gasps for air.

While the judge and Zeus both stood in firm-jawed, stoic silence, Samantha knelt to the floor in front of Brier and placed a hand on his shoulder. "Robert, I'm so sorry. So very sorry."

When he looked up, tears filled his eyes. He opened his mouth, as if to speak, but no words came out. He slowly sat up straight, reaching for her hand with his left hand and holding on to her as he did. With his right hand, he reached into his jacket pocket for a handkerchief, then dabbed the tears from his cheeks and the corners of his eyes.

"We'll assist you with arrangements to get home as quickly as possible."

Brier nodded. "Thank you. I'll leave when proceedings conclude today."

The judge, thoughtful eyes on Brier, shook his head. "Are you sure you wouldn't prefer to leave sooner?"

Brier dabbed moisture from his eyes. "My wife. Madeline. You know she is a lawyer." He drew in a deep, shaky breath and shook his head. "Was. She was a lawyer. We worked together for the last thirty years. She had a very firm understanding of the importance of my work as a defender of civil rights and those who are falsely accused. She knows how important this proceeding is. Knows how important it is that the International Terrorist Tribunal does not become a result-oriented court."

Samantha admired the man's ability to provide a compelling speech in the face of such abject grief, while tears streamed from his eyes and down his cheeks. Zeus, standing a few feet from Brier, had gridlock attention focused on the lawyer, who seemed to be drawing strength from his profound grief.

"I've been a defender of the rights of the criminal accused for my entire career. Can't the terrorists see that? Why would they come after me?"

"They're not choosing sides," the judge said. "They're not

being selective. They are anarchists, and they want the ITT to stop. It is now clear that they're going after the loved ones of anyone involved."

"The Colombians have informed me they will be moving for a mistrial when proceedings commence," Brier continued. "Madeline, God rest her soul, would want me to remain here to argue in favor of the motion." In a tone that became both bitter and grief-stricken, he stood as he added, "I will draw upon her indomitable spirit and present an argument to the tribunal that will result in the termination of this ITT proceeding."

Chapter Twenty-Four

Once the judges took the podium, the first order of business for the tribunal was the Colombian motion for a mistrial. Second was the French motion for expansion of the record. Third was her own motion to interview Stollen. For the next three hours, Samantha was on her feet.

Throughout the arguments, she stayed at the podium, facing the twelve judges and paying close attention to Judge Ducaisse, who was dictating the order of the proceeding. She also paid close attention to Judge O'Connor, who with a nod or shake of his head informed her whether he thought her arguments were hitting their intended mark. She made snap-fire decisions, carefully crafted her words, addressed each argument presented by counsel—while making sure she sounded authoritative and calm.

Stanley Morgan had taught her to sound calm, decisive, and cool—a balm for proceedings that were in disarray. Confident that she could be the glue that held the proceedings together, she forged ahead. As the other lawyers argued, Abe instant messaged counterpoints to her. She'd scan through his messages. If she deemed the points important enough, she'd incorporate them into her argument.

Each move she made, she was mindful of the need to be delicate when she responded to Brier, whose grief was palpable with each word, giving him an air of solemnity and persuasiveness that seemed to overpower the entire proceeding.

A fifteen-minute recess came midway through the afternoon. She turned and glanced into the gallery the second the judges exited the dais. Zeus was already walking in her direction. Thank God. She'd been sipping water at the podium for three hours, and now there was only one place she needed to be.

As she washed her hands in the bathroom, he stood with his back to the door, arms at his side. "You're doing a great job."

In the mirror, she glanced in his direction as she reapplied her lipstick. His eyes were on her hand, the black lipstick tube, the bright red paste of the season's newest red, and her lips. "Thanks. I can't tell whether I'm scoring with the judges."

Reaching for a napkin, she blotted some of the red lipstick from her lips, before reaching in her purse for a tube of gloss. As she slid the applicator along her bottom lip, her eyes caught a flicker of his frown.

"Well, that's hell." His tone was low, his voice gruff.

"What?"

"Not knowing whether you're scoring."

"Oh." Through the mirror, she watched his slight frown deepen. "So red lipstick turns you on?"

"On your lips, apparently yes."

Dropping the gloss into her purse, she pulled out a roll of antacids. "We're not going there, Hernandez."

"Couldn't agree more. For the moment. About the proceedings, every time you speak, the Colombian judges look down, at their tablets. Or notes. They're working hard on ignoring you. News reports in Colombia are grim. Public opinion there is Colombia should never have joined forces with the U.S., the U.K. and France."

Slipping her thumbnail between the foil-lined packaging, she separated one chalky tablet from the others as she turned away from the mirror and faced him. "I've given up on securing the votes of the Colombian judges."

"Wise move. If body language is an indicator, the French are more receptive to you. Americans are nodding in agreement. The judges who are most undecided are the judges from the U.K."

"I'm watching. I agree." She chewed on an antacid, and peeled another from the roll.

His slight frown reappeared. "Your breakfast was hours ago—"

"I ate a power bar while I was getting dressed. At eleven."

"You should eat another. What you're doing is strenuous. Food would be—"

"I don't eat much during proceedings."

"Figured that out. But why not?"

"Stomach's usually in a knot when I'm arguing," she said, dropping the roll of antacids into her purse, and walking in his direction, to the door. "Just like my neck."

He frowned. "I'll arrange a masseuse for you this evening."

Message received.

His eyes? Unreadable, yet she knew he wasn't considering doing a neck rub. And why? Because she'd been damn effective at giving him the don't-touch-me-again message that morning. And who the hell could blame her? Sex with him was a distraction.

Don't think about how his warm strength seeped from his fingers into the coiled-up tendons and muscles of your too-tight neck. Don't think about that.

You were right when you told him you needed sleep. Bitchy

as it sounded— Yes. At this point in the day, a bit more sleep last night would've been good.

With a steady, coolly unbothered and very professional look, he pushed the bathroom door open for her. "There are two male judges from the U.K. One female. The male judge who is the furthest to your right. Allen Normand. You know him?"

"Not personally."

"Make eye contact with him," Zeus said, walking down the hall with her, in step with her security team. "As much as you can."

Samantha thought through everything she knew about Judge Normand. Nothing told her he'd be more amenable to her arguments than the other two U.K. judges. "Why?"

"Ragno's intel tells me he is quite a ladies man." He glanced at her when they reached the wide double-doorway of the courtroom. "And my eyes tell me he thinks you're hot. Play up the beautiful-and-smart woman card."

"Ridiculous."

He arched his left eyebrow as he glanced down at her. Lowering his voice slightly, he said, "Why aren't you wearing a dark, navy-blue, boxy suit, instead of that form-fitting, attention-grabbing ivory with black leather piping get up? And some neutral-colored lipstick, instead of Sex-and-Blowjobs-Red?"

On her immediate right, she saw Jenkins shoot his boss a surprised look, then recover quickly and stare straight ahead. "Because I'm confident enough in my capabilities to look like a female who appreciates nice clothes, and I believe the judges don't focus on gender or appearance when they're assessing the merits of an argument." She lowered her voice to almost a hiss. "And the name of the lipstick is Remember the Classics. Not Sex-and-Blowjobs-Red."

He nodded as they reentered the courtroom. Conversations hummed as the lawyers and attendees stood, taking advantage of the break by conversing with each other. "Cosmetic companies are making a fortune off of bullshitting you women, cause the only classic that shade has to do with is sex, in all its glorious forms." He lowered his voice, leaning in, and whispering, "I'm in the gallery, watching each judge as they watch you. Underneath that black robe, Judge Normand is just a man, and he damn well is noticing that you're a super-intelligent woman, who happens to look damn good while she argues. He might be your swing vote."

He bent to her ear as she sat at counsel table for a quick

discussion with Abe and Charles before arguments would resume. "You've got it, Sam," he whispered, in that low, gravelly voice he used that sliced straight through to her heart and made her insides quiver. "Whether it's the merits of your argument or your looks, you're catching his attention. Just like you steal my breath every single goddamn time I look at you, no matter what shade of lipstick you're wearing." She couldn't help but shift closer to him, feeling his warm breath in her ear with each of his words. "Even when you tell me you'd prefer sleep over sex. If you want to win this argument, use the tools God gave you. All of them."

At 6:45 p.m., after three more hours of argument, the proceedings ended with a firm bang of the gavel. Samantha held her breath for rulings, but Judge Ducaisse announced that all matters would be taken under advisement.

Although she'd have preferred an immediate ruling, relief coursed through her as the judges exited the courtroom. She felt good about the points and counterpoints she'd been able to make, but she didn't dare predict the outcome. Predicting a ruling so soon after an argument was bad luck.

Fatigue came on the heels of the relief. Feeling the effects of the night with little sleep and the strain that came with six hours of extreme focus and on-her-feet argument, she had the presence of mind to walk to where Brier was sitting, place a hand on his arm, and give him a nod of sympathy before exiting the courtroom. Mindlessly following Zeus's instructions as he directed their exit from the building, she melted into the middle of the rear seat of the car. He slid in next to her, thigh to her thigh, shoulder to her shoulder.

She resisted the urge to rest her head on his shoulder and drift off to sleep. Irritated that she was too damned tired for rational thought, she snuggled deeper into her overcoat. She stared blankly ahead into the dark night as the driver exited the Ile de la Cite via the Pont Neuf, a different bridge than the one they had used that morning. Her mind registered they were taking an alternate route to the safe house. Her mind also registered Zeus's low voice as he communicated short commands with the members of the security teams.

The details weren't her concern. She just needed to get to the safe house, ease her shoes off her feet, take a hot shower, and fall into bed.

Traffic caused the car to stop. Staring blankly ahead, the brake lights of the cars in front of her flashed red at the same time a harsh *pop-pop-pop* rattled through the night. Cars screeched to a halt, their tires skidding on wet pavement. Next to her, Zeus stiffened.

Jenkins, on the right side of her, said, "Shooter. Two o'clock."

Adrenaline charged nerves jangled the fatigue from her brain. Samantha gasped, sat up, and looked out of the front window. She saw only a misty night. Streetlights. Cars, with red brake lights. Ahead, about four cars up, a car turned onto the pedestrian walkway that lined the Pont Neuf—and stopped, as more gunfire filled the air.

***

"See him." Zeus pushed her shoulders down as he pulled his Glock up. "Sam. To the floor. Now!"

A staccato *pop, pop, pop* blasted through the air. The gunfire was more persuasive than his order or his push. Sam turned sideways and slid to her knees on the floor, hands over her head.

As if her hands could fucking deflect a bullet. "Stay down." Zeus shrugged out of his overcoat and spread it over her head and shoulders. "Your hair will be the first thing he'll see if he passes the car."

"No need to point that out Hernandez." Her voice was acerbic and muffled. "I get it."

He was too fucking scared on her behalf to smile. He considered removing his own flak vest and putting it over her head. But it was his only defense when he went out there. "Jenkins. Cover her."

Her vest, coupled with Jenkins's vest and body mass, would work to protect her. It had to work, until he figured out a way to stop the shooter.

"The car is armored," he reminded Sam. "Windows bulletproof. You'll be ok, just keep your head down and stay out of sight."

"Not arguing, Hernandez."

His heart filled with emotion. She was damn brave. Sam was a lot of things, all of which he admired, even though stubbornness wasn't exactly a positive character trait. He'd never fucking forgive himself if she died on his watch. There were things that had to be said, things he wanted to do. And none of them included both of them being dead.

The shooter was weighed down with explosives. Take him out prematurely, and the whole bridge, along with everyone on it, would blow.

When Zeus wanted to go in like a bull in a china shop, he had to bide his time. Tackle this with kid gloves and a plan. A damn good plan.

"Ragno, you have a visual?" The Black Raven cars had telematics, with cams. Because there were three Black Raven cars on the bridge, Ragno had multiple views.

"Yes."

"I want your best guesstimate on what he's carrying, and what the kill zone will be if it blows."

"Working on it."

"He's shooting tires." Jenkins adjusted his position on top of Sam. Zeus heard her groan as the agent settled his weight over her. But that was her only response. She neither complained of suffocation, nor the uncomfortable position. Not that Zeus gave a damn about her discomfort, only that she had something— someone—between her and a potential explosion.

But the reality was, bulletproof glass or not, an explosion would take out the whole car and everyone in it.

"Amicus team is on the Pont Neuf. Facing a shooter. Potential suicide bomber. Manage traffic, if you can," he instructed his men as he crouched low. "No vehicles are moving. Agents. Go live with Ragno. Ragno, Small is at the safe house. Alert him."

The bulky silhouette of the man walked toward the vehicle carrying Sam, holding a flashlight in one hand, his assault rifle in another. He went from silhouette to spotlight as he moved between the cars.

"Five-eight, five-ten. Explosives secured to his body. Chest, shoulders, legs... Anything, Ragno?" She'd be able to tell them what they were dealing with faster than just their eyesight.

"Working."

"Eighty yards, and closing." With no room for his legs, he crouched on the back seat waiting for the moment to spring into action. His entire body felt coiled. Ready.

Bullets went wild while the gunman fired as he zig-zagged between the cars. His powerful flashlight strafed the occupants of the cars as he wove between them.

Seventy yards.

Screams and shouts mingled with honking horns and shattering glass.

Misty rain on the windows made visibility crappy. Headlights turned night to day, red brake lights gleamed in the darkness. Interior lights went on as drivers opened their doors.

Shit. Everyone wanted to see what was happening and the people Zeus could see seemed to have no real clue. In normal lives, gunshots sounded like backfires. Too many movies and television shows depicted violence as entertainment, leaving the viewers untouched physically. They were in for a rude awakening if this clusterfuck progressed, as Zeus knew it would.

Pop. Pop. Pop. Glass shattered, metal screeched. More screams. Doors slammed as some people scurried back to the relative safety of their vehicles. Others scattered, presumably abandoning their cars and running off the bridge.

Great. Fucking cars weren't moving anytime soon.

The gunman was sixty-five yards away. Reloading and moving with purpose, but in no hurry, Zeus considered exiting the vehicle and dodging between the cars up ahead to circle behind him. But the lights, coupled with milling public, guaranteed a high percentage of collateral damage, and the very real probability that the perp would detonate sooner than later.

He waited.

Agent Mike Prantz—the driver of Sam's car—had the windshield wipers going. *Swish, swish, swish.* Momentarily clear field of vision, then sparkling diamonds of raindrops obscuring the scene.

"Gridlock ahead," Zeus told those without a ringside seat. "Pedestrian walkway on our right not an option. Blocked with vehicles and pedestrians. Perp on approach. Now sixty yards from my position. Weaving. Doing a slow zigzag through traffic, going over to the pedestrian walkway, and stepping back into traffic. Looking inside cars."

For what? For who?

There were at least ten cars boxed in on the bridge from the ITT proceeding. Marshals, and other security.

Zeus's blood went cold.

Sam?

Pop. Pop. Pop. Hisssssss.

Their car shifted slightly, to the right.

"There go our tires," Agent Prantz said.

Through the front window, Zeus observed the shooter's progress. The closer he came, the more detail Zeus was able to see. Head to toe black garb. Car headlights and the lights of the Pont Neuf illuminated enough of the dark, misty night for him to observe the man's head was covered by a bulky ski mask. He wore a belt of rectangular, plastic-wrapped explosives. He also wore a flak vest, with plastic-wrapped squares. Packets of explosives were also strapped to his legs.

"Don't shoot until I give the signal! Shooting will risk detonation. Axel. Lambert. I need your eyes on him. Tell me, from your vantage point, every place you see explosives positioned on his body."

"Sir. Everywhere. Even on his head, strapped to his ski mask. Belt. Vest. Packets of explosives are also strapped to his thighs and calves."

Zeus knew the likely explosives. TNT. Plastics. Triacetone triperoxide. All were in current use by anarchists worldwide. All were damn effective.

"Axel?" Zeus turned to look out the rear window. "You're three behind us. Between us is Judge O'Connor. A damn likely target."

Which meant that the minute the shooter saw the judge, immediately recognizable as his face was plastered on every news show, every night, the shooter would detonate.

Which meant they had about two more minutes, at the rate the shooter was edging along the traffic. It felt as though hours had passed since they'd stopped, but a quick glance at his watch showed Zeus that it had been mere minutes. His rapid heartbeat counted off the seconds as the man approached.

"Zeus, best guess is TATP," Ragno said.

The current favorite explosive of anarchists. TATP—aka Mother of Satan, due to ease of detonation. Typically enhanced with bolts and nails, the bombs were lethal for anyone within reach of the shrapnel, and even the bones of the bomber became shrapnel in an attack.

"Understood."

"With the quantity I see on him, I'm estimating kill zone is fifty yards. Easily. More depending on the quantity of hardware he's packed for shrapnel."

Car windows were no match for shrapnel and there were a hell of a lot of innocent people on the bridge, both from the ITT and innocent John Q. Public. He glanced down, saw Sam looking up at him, her eyes wide with fear. For good fucking reason. "Head down. On the goddamn floor. Jenkins. Cover every inch of her."

"With traffic stopped like this," the driver said, "God knows how many people he'll kill when he blows himself up.

Zeus eyed the pedestrian sidewalk to their right. The bridge's railing stood about hip-high to him. Below, in the distance, the Seine looked choppy and dark.

An idea formed. *Fuck*. It was a long shot, but it was the only idea that made sense. The idea became a plan.

"Why hasn't he blown himself up yet?" Axel asked.

"Great question," Zeus muttered. "Nerves? Having too much fun with his gun? Looking for a specific target."

Yeah. The latter.

Another staccato *pop, pop, pop* blasted through the night. Too close to them. "Axel. Lambert. He's about twenty paces away from my car. Anyone see a handler?"

"Negative," Axel said.

"Negative. Looks like a one-man op," Lambert said.

That was good news. Handlers often remotely used a cell phone or other wireless device to trigger the explosion. Given Zeus's plan, the handler would trigger the explosion the minute Zeus acted. The problem was, Zeus's action involved his hands on the shooter, which could very well trigger the explosion. Even prior to detonation, explosives were sensitive to heat, shock, and friction. TATP, the likely explosive strapped to the shooter, was especially sensitive.

I've faced worse fucking odds.

"Agents, secure your charges. Hunker down. I'm stepping out. My plan is to get my arms around him and throw him over the fucking side of this bridge."

"Sir." Jenkins glanced up. "I'm good for this."

"No." Zeus's curt, one-word answer ended the discussion.

"Prantz, disable the interior lights. Going to do this as quietly as possible. Don't want to surprise him with lights when the door opens."

Sam was gripping his calf as he crawled across the back seat. He glanced down at her, hesitating before he pushed the door open.

"Don't." Her voice, strong and pleading, was infused with panic. "Don't go out there."

Removing her hand from his leg with a solid grasp of his larger, stronger hand, he said, "Stay down."

Glancing at Jenkins, he said, "Cover her, dammit."

Zeus eased the car door open as the shooter stepped, one more time, onto the pedestrian walkway. The man didn't see him. Zeus hunched low, and quickly ran, closing the fifteen-foot gap between them.

When Zeus was ten feet away, the gunman saw him. Weapon in hand Zeus lunged to the side, but continued moving forward.

Pop. Pop. Pop.

A bullet hit his vest, throwing him backwards. As he went down another bullet grazed his left arm, slicing through his suit jacket, shirt, and skin. Neither hurt in the moment. But later...

Gunfire will soon be the least of my problems if this suicide bomber decides to detonate. Or if my touch triggers an explosion.

Staggering to his feet, Zeus drew a deep breath, and lunged forward in a fast run as the shooter ejected his clip, then reached for his waist. He was either reaching for more ammunition, or—worse—a detonation cord. Given that the guy kept the weapon firmly in his hand, Zeus assumed the reach was for another clip.

Zeus took a flying leap, landing squarely on two feet, and turned and kicked the weapon out of the shooter's hand. As the gun hit the ground and slid along the pavement, Zeus closed his hands on the man's forearms—the only place where he didn't see explosives. When it came to muscles and brawn, Zeus clearly had the upper hand.

Yanking back the shooter's arms as hard as he could, Zeus held them steady. The man grunted in pain, but tried to work his hands free as he shouted garbled, incomprehensible French. A hand on the guy's wrists, Zeus yanked, twisted them up and away from his body. He screamed, not with fear, but with harsh fury that he'd been stopped.

The man swore, face contorted and used his feet as brakes. Zeus felt the snap and break of tendons and bones as he pushed the man across the sidewalk to the bridge railing. Six feet to go.

Zeus kick-pushed him forward. Three feet.

The shooter managed to wrench an arm free.

Fuck!

He was reaching across his body, presumably for a detonation cord. Twelve inches to the railing. Zeus wrapped his arms around the man, picked him up, and threw him over.

Not waiting to hear or see the splash, Zeus turned and ran like hell towards the line of stopped cars. One step. Two step. Three. When he heard the explosion start, he dropped and rolled, covering his head as he wedged himself between the rise of the pedestrian sidewalk and the nearest car.

Chapter Twenty-Five

Pausing in mid-stride as he walked through the small corporate airport to the waiting Gulfstream, H.L. focused on the television monitor showing flashing news. The live news show had a banner on the bottom of the screen indicating breaking news from Paris. A suicide bomber had attempted an attack on traffic on the Pont Neuf. Included in the snarl of stopped cars were participants in the ITT proceeding.

The media had secured cell-phone video footage taken by an eyewitness. The videographer's hand had shaken, and the dark night made the footage seem grainy. Nonetheless, the camera had captured enough spectacular footage of Hernandez's struggle with the suicide bomber.

Using a one-time phone, H.L. punched in digits for J.R. "Are you watching the news?"

"Yes."

Stepping into the drizzly Paris night, H.L. said, "I thought we agreed any attack on the vehicles this evening would be futile."

"We did. Fortunately"—J.R. drew in a deep intake of breath and exhaled—"we're not the only anarchists in town."

"Given the trouble Fairfax and Hernandez created today, I say end them. At the first possible moment."

"Proceeding forward with that plan," J.R. said.

"Are you mindful of the warning I received earlier?"

Earlier in the afternoon, their deep, undercover contact had a few seconds to give H.L. a hurried, almost breathless communication of what was transpiring with the Amicus team and their ability to access Black Raven data. The hurried communication had been for them to be careful with the use of burner phones, to make sure other phones were disabled, and to turn off other devices.

"We're mindful of it. Yes. He isn't telling us anything M.C. didn't already figure out. Black Raven has to be stopped, if we're going to continue. And we will continue."

"Be more than mindful." H.L. climbed the steps of the jet.

"We're two steps ahead of you. We're not only going to put an end to Jesus Hernandez and his meddling with the Amicus team, we're going to put a serious end to Black Raven's cyber-data collecting capabilities."

"How?"

"The details of the plan M.C. and I have developed will

fucking amaze you." J.R. chuckled. "This is what we set into play."

As J.R. explained the plan, H.L. listened. J.R. was right. He was amazed, because the plan was goddamn brilliant.

Chapter Twenty-Six

Zeus stepped into the suite that he shared with Sam. Touching his watchband, he muted his microphone on the connection he had with Gabe. As he listened to his brother recount the facts of the fruitless search for Maximov in Syria, he said to Sam, "You waited up for me?"

"Answer is obvious," she whispered.

She'd been on the couch and rose to her feet as Zeus entered their private living room. A pillow nestled against the armrest had an indent where her head had been. Glasses on, hair hanging loose and straight, her laptop was on. It rested on the cushion, next to a rumpled blanket. She wore form-fitting leggings and a black sweatshirt unzipped enough to show the ridges of black lace on her camisole.

He hadn't bothered with a shirt after the doctor had bandaged his arm. With her eyes on the now fist-sized, round, blackish-purple mark on his chest that showed where the bullet had hit his flak-vest, he asked, "You okay with looking at a bruise?"

She went pale, but nodded. "That must hurt."

"Not if I don't think about it."

In his earpiece, Gabe was winding down his narrative. "Face facts, bro. Maximov is a ghost. It's either Praptan, or nowhere. As far as I can tell, the government-sanctioned task force has no other leads."

To Sam, Zeus said, "The search in Syria for Maximov didn't pan out."

He pressed his watch, making the connection on his line live again. "Gabe, Ragno, I'm with Sam now. She had strong opposition to her motion to interview Stollen. The judges took the matter under advisement."

"We're in position to go in now. The ruling could be days away. The interview could take even longer to set up," Gabe said.

"You're waiting till we have a ruling and if it's favorable, you're waiting until after Sam interviews Stollen."

"I propose that we go in now, then if Stollen adds any additional intel leading to ground we haven't covered, I'll go in on a more targeted search," Gabe offered.

"I know you don't like waiting, but that's part of the job right now. Stop arguing. Sam, when should we expect a ruling on the motions? And what is the earliest the interview could take place, assuming the ruling is favorable?"

Some of the color had returned to her cheeks. She kept her eyes on his, steady, as though she couldn't bear to see the wounds. He didn't blame her. After-effects of what had almost happened still jolted him, and he usually didn't feel aftershocks from putting himself in harm's way.

"Tomorrow, or Monday for a ruling," she answered. "Given that Stollen is Robert Brier's client, even if we get a favorable ruling, I think the court will defer to his request to delay the interview until he can be present. So, perhaps Tuesday for the interview."

"Ragno. Gabe. Hear that?"

"Yes," Ragno said. "So Tuesday at the earliest for Gabe to go into Praptan."

"Fuck me," Gabe said. "We're supposed to cool our heels till then?"

"No. Strategize. Think," Zeus said, walking closer to Sam, "Gather more intel."

"Maybe I should come work with you," Gabe said. "From the looks of what happened tonight, it sure looks like you need an extra hand. I just watched the cell-phone video. Here's the count. One. Two. Three. That's all the time you had before becoming ash."

"Thanks, Gabe," he said, his stomach churning with the reality of almost dying before he had a chance to see Ana's dance recital, watch her graduate from high school, or walk her down the aisle. Ana was only six, for God's sake. She needed a father. Even a mostly absent father was better than a dead father. He wasn't afraid of dying. He was afraid, however, of permanently checking out of her life before she was old enough to handle it. "Didn't need that reminder."

"It was a brilliant move on your part," Gabe said. "I love the hell out of you. Live my life for the day that I do one thing as powerful as what you did tonight. You're my hero. I know you know that, but if I was with you, I'd be wrapping you in the biggest hug of your life."

And that was why people loved his brother, Zeus thought, because the guy had a way of infusing cocoon-like warmth into a chilling, dark night. "Thanks, Gabe."

Ragno said, "Zeus, get some good rest." Lowering her voice, she said, "Or whatever is coming your way. You deserve it."

He yanked the earpiece out of his ear, breaking the connection as he heard Gabe chuckling over Ragno's whatever comment. In the intervening five hours since he'd thrown the suicide bomber over the railing of the bridge, he'd seen Sam once, between an interview with the French military officers in charge of ITT security and the hour it had taken the Black Raven doctor to examine him and repair the long slice along his left bicep, where a bullet grazed him. He'd taken a bullet to the chest, on the right side, a few inches below his shoulder, but the vest had done it's work. He was bruised and sore, but intact.

Sam had the television on the news show that had picked up the cell phone video. The grainy footage of his struggle with the bomber was chilling, given the mere three seconds that elapsed after he hoisted the man over the railing and the fireball explosion that lit the night sky as the man blew himself up.

"Funny how people who are scared shitless still manage to take damn good cell phone videos," Zeus muttered as he watched the video footage near its conclusion. He'd seen it, downstairs, while the doctor had been cleaning and stapling his arm.

When she didn't say anything, he glanced at her. She visibly paled as the screen turned orange, the light from the television glinting in her wide, frightened eyes. He walked over to the coffee table, picked up the remote, and turned the television off. "Stop looking at it."

She nodded, glancing in his direction, but not quite seeing him. Instead, he could see from the way her eyes were focused inwards that her mind was replaying the scene. Over and over again. She held her hand against the back of her mouth, her shoulders trembling.

"Sam, you're safe. It's over."

She shook her head. "Not me I was worried about." Squaring her shoulders, she said, "I was, oh, God. Zeus, I was so afraid."

All the color faded from her face. Without heels, without makeup, without any of the sophisticated-shine and impenetrable style that she wore during the day, she seemed frightened and vulnerable. He had no choice but to step closer to her.

"So afraid for you," she whispered, as he closed his arms around her, pulling her into the warmth of his bare chest.

"Breathe," he said. "Slowly. One—Two—Three —Now hold it."

She was trembling more, and not listening to him as he smoothed her hair down and drowned in the fresh, sweet scent of jasmine.

"Come on, Sam. Give me a deep breath in. Fight past the

fear."

He felt her inhale.

"Good girl. Hold it. One—Two—Three—Hold it. Now exhale. Slowly."

Her face was turned into his chest, at his heart. A warm puff of air hit his bare skin as she exhaled.

"Breathe in. One—Two—Three—Hold it, hold—"

"Not me. I was scared for—"

"Don't talk. Hold your breath. Now inhale again. As deep as you can. Hold it." Long minutes passed where she did nothing but breathe in sync with him, following his instructions.

"The breathing thing—"

"Don't talk. Inhale."

She did.

"Hold it." More time passed.

"That really works," she whispered.

"It's the one—two—three—hold it that does it. Go on. Breathe. One—two— three—hold it."

Her shoulders stopped trembling and holding her became about something more than helping her breathe. She exhaled. "God. Why am I such a wimp?"

"Not a wimp. What happened tonight was pretty damn horrific. Even experienced agents have some creative techniques to talk themselves back from the ledge." Arms holding her tight, he inhaled deep, the scent of jasmine and rose and everything that was Sam. "In our case, the phrase 'We'll always have Paris' means something different than the norm, doesn't it?"

With her face buried against his chest, her arms around his waist, she sighed. "Gosh. I'd love to have the cliché right now. Long strolls on grand avenues, roaming through museums, champagne in a sidewalk café, the romance of it all, and the shopping. Oh. And French macarons. Fresh, small, delicious bites of heaven."

He chuckled. "Macarons?"

"My favorite cookies."

"That, I can deliver. Even this week. We are in Paris, after all."

Glancing up at him, she looked uncertain. "You'll have to eat a bite out of each one."

"Not a problem. As long as your favorite flavor isn't pistachio."

"Nope. Almond. Or coconut. Or strawberry. Even chocolate will do." She drew a deep breath. "I was so scared for you. And so relieved"—she pushed slightly back from him—"when I knew you were fine. Jesus, Zeus. How can you put yourself in that much danger?"

"Just my job, Sam. It's what I do."

God, he thought, grinding his teeth together as his body responded to being pressed against hers. Wanting to be nowhere else in the entire world at the moment, his only thought was simple and demanding. *This fucking day needs to end.*

"You should try to get some sleep."

She walked with him, hand in hand, to her bedroom. There, she turned to him. "Would you like to stay with me?"

More than I want my next breath. Or any of my tomorrows.

He pulled down the thick comforter of her bed. "Climb in."

Standing beside him, a slender hand on his right arm, she shook her head. "Not without you."

He turned to see her eyes searching his. Using his index finger, Zeus pushed wayward blonde strands behind her ear. "Given how we started the day, how you made it clear you'd prefer to sleep than have sex, I'm not sure I should be taking advantage of the situation—"

"You said you would, though. I think you said you'd be back at it, if given any opportunity."

"Not now, Sam. You're exhausted. Scared. Probably suffering from shock, and I'd feel like I was taking advantage of you. Aside from my threat to do so this morning, I don't do that kind of shit. Don't need sex that bad."

She tiptoed fast, catching him by surprise as she threw her arms around his neck. "Don't always take the high road, Hernandez. I'm asking you to stay and I'm not so exhausted that I don't know what I'm doing. Please. Just stay." Face pressed upwards to him, her beautiful lips bare and naturally moist, inviting his—regardless of whether she intended an invitation. "This isn't about sex. I'd be surprised if you even had the inclination, given what you just went through. I want you to hold me. Please."

Hell. Hold her? Yeah—that was what he'd thought he wanted earlier in the day—like at five a.m. when he'd been satiated. But not now. Did she really expect him to get in bed with her and not have sex?

Fuckitall.

Even though it was now technically Friday, his craptastic Thursday was never going to end. He unbuttoned his jeans and stepped out of them. Keeping his boxers on, he watched her strip off her sweatshirt and unpeel her leggings. She dropped them on the floor and climbed into bed wearing a black thong and camisole. Sliding in next to her, he reached for her and pulled her close, not bothering to hide the fact that he was now almost fully erect.

Her warm lips were in the hollow of his neck. "Didn't think you'd have the energy for that."

"He didn't shoot my dick."

"Mmmmm," she said. "Thank God for that."

"I'm taking that as an invitation." From her, he'd never refuse it.

"We don't have to," she said, shimmying herself up so that her head was next to his on the pillow, his lips were almost touching his. "You've got to be exhausted."

Yes. I am. Sure as hell doesn't matter, though.

He bent his lips to hers, groaning as she opened her mouth to his. Sinking his tongue into her moist mouth, sliding it along her silken tongue, he reached between her legs, and pulled the silk panties to the side. Sliding his fingers through the soft folds that that led to her core, he dipped one into her moist heat, swallowing her moan with a deep kiss.

Wet and hot, she was ready for him. Energy at a premium, he removed his hand, pushed his boxers to mid-thigh as she pulled her panties down to her knees. Opening her legs just enough for him to enter her, he thrust up and deep, until he was buried to the hilt, his dick rejoicing with the power of the first good thing that had happened that day. As her walls welcomed him with pulsing, tight contractions, she folded her arms around his neck. They rocked together, both working their hips, so that their movements were minimal, but effective. They came together, fast and hard.

"I was so scared," she whispered, when she could breathe.

"Don't think about it."

"And then so relieved."

I love you.

Not anything she wanted to hear. Besides, she had to already know it. Knowing the words would not only be wasted, they would be a sure mood killer on a day when they had both had enough, he kept silent. Drawing in deep breaths, fatigue now coming over him in waves, he didn't give her the opportunity to exhibit the after-sex remorse that had come immediately after their two prior times together. He kissed her on her cheek, shifted to the side of the bed, and pulled his boxers up. Standing, he said, "Get some sleep."

"Stay with me."

He glanced at her. Surprised. Uncertain, but reading her eyes and seeing that she meant it. "You sure?"

She nodded.

He reached over to the night table, turned off the lamp, rolled back into the bed, and scooped her into his arms. As she nestled onto the non-bruised side of his chest, her arms fell around him. "Tell me about those sunsets at your Keys house, again."

Warmth flooded through him. "What do you want to know?"

"If your daughter watches them with you. If you've told her to look for the emerald flash."

He chuckled. "Ana is still young and sweet enough to indulge me. This past October she swore she saw the green flash. The evening was spectacular—with wisps of clouds on the horizon that blew up with pink, rose, and golden bursts of light." Within minutes they were both asleep, limbs pretzelled together, his arms around her, his leg over hers. A couple of hours later, she moaned, gasped for air, and cried out, into his chest. "Sam. Wake up. You're having a nightmare."

Her entire body was shaking. "You didn't survive in that one."

"But I did." He reached over to the lamp and turned it on. "See. I'm here." Reaching for her hand, he took it and placed it on something he hoped would distract her.

Fingers wrapping around his hard dick, she shook her head. "Sex isn't a remedy for nightmares, Hernandez."

"Fatigue is."

Chapter Twenty-Seven

Paris, France
Friday, February 4

Soft morning light peeked along the border of the closed drapes, enough so that Zeus could see Sam's eyes were open and on him. "It's six," she said. "My alarm is going off in fifteen minutes."

Sitting up, with his lower back resting against pillows, and his upper back resting against the headboard, he drew her to his chest. "Feel okay?"

"Fine. You?"

"Hmm." He shifted his legs a bit, pulling her hips closer to his with a hint as to his favorite way to say good morning. His body certainly knew what rise and shine meant and was almost ready for a demonstration.

"Not that, Hernandez. Your chest. Arm."

"Sore, but fine." Rubbing her hair so that it was smooth, he tried to resist the urge to talk about their past. *Fuck.* He might not get another opportunity, because another man was proposing to her—soon—and anything he told her after the proposal was destined to be a sorry, forgotten footnote in the story of her life.

He had to tell her the end result of what he had figured out. It was her choice whether to do anything about it. Her choice whether to change things.

Now or never, asshole.

"You were relieved."

"Of course I was." Silken hair brushing against his chest as she lifted her head so their eyes met, she nodded. "I thought you were going to die a pretty horrific death."

"Not talking about last night. Talking about seven years ago."

As though he'd delivered a physical hit, her body stiffened, but, thank God, she didn't pull away from him or do anything else to shut him out.

"When I told you that Theresa had called and said she was pregnant, when I told you what I thought I needed to do, I read shock in your reaction. I read hurt. Hell—I read heartbreak, and I still don't think I was wrong on that. I read all kinds of things in those few minutes. Time stayed still long enough for those awful minutes to be buried in my brain for the rest of my life." He paused. "What I didn't figure out until now was that underneath all of your surprise, anger, and cool recovery, that you were relieved that I wasn't sticking around. You might have loved me, but you were happy to see me go."

Palms flat on his chest, she pushed away from him. He let his arms fall to his side as he let go of her. He exhaled, waiting for her to end the conversation prematurely. To stand up and charge to the bathroom. Instead, as more light filtered into the room, she sat up in the bed within touching distance. The sheets covered from her hips down. The slope of her breasts inspired an erection, but he managed to focus on her face, with her unreadable eyes.

Her chin up, and dry-eyed glance told him she wasn't feeling regret, hurt, or denial.

It was more like, *"Bingo, buddy'. You caught me. Now what?"*

Fuckitall.

Here's confirmation. She might have loved you, but she was relieved you walked away, dumb shit.

Why the hell had he not realized it? Answer to that was simple enough. He'd been so goddamn miserable, he'd barely managed to find his way back to Miami.

Bigger question—would realizing then that she was relieved to see him go have changed anything in his life?

Maybe. But speculation's a waste of time on this one. Make it change your life now.

Clearing his throat past the crash and swirl of lost opportunities, he said, "This is what I've figured out. You'd prefer not to have the kind of commitment I'd offer."

Do not tell her she's scared. You'll only piss her off. It will end this conversation.

Mind desperately searching for words that would keep her listening, knowing with every fiber in his soul that he needed to get out the words that he'd never managed to say before, he continued, "One-hundred percent commitment. That is what I'd give you. Heart, body, and soul. It's what I'd offer, and it's what I want. Until death do us part. Being a couple. Meaning we live for each other. The kind of commitment your parents—"

"Don't talk about my parents," she whispered. Honest eyes glanced at him. With a shake of her head, she whispered, "I don't like to focus on them."

And that was the crux of the problem, because she didn't realize what their relationship had done to her. He barely understood it himself, and that was with the bird's eye view Ragno had given him—which his gut told him was one-hundred percent accurate. It was the only thing that made any sense.

"We don't need to go there," he said, his voice low, allowing her to be in denial, though he knew she'd never cross the hurdle that would lead her to him if she didn't own it. "But I want you to tell me why you were relieved that someone who loved you with all his heart, someone who you loved back, would walk away. I have all kinds of ideas. This time around, I'm learning everything I can about you, because if I don't understand what makes you tick, this time...when I walk away from you I'm going to wonder about it. Wondering about you leads to wanting you. Hoping for you. And I can't do that again. Won't do it again. The answer as to why you're relieved will have to come from you. You've got to own it, Sam. Got to understand it. Overpower it." Glancing at her, it seemed like she was listening. Understanding what he meant. She wasn't stupid, after all. "Or not."

"You never said you loved me."

Well, she has you on that one.

"But you knew it, didn't you?"

She nodded, eyes on him.

"Know it now, don't you?"

Her nod was barely perceptible, as though acknowledging his love for her came with a high price that she wasn't ready to pay.

"With all of my heart," he added. "Body. Soul."

In the perfect world, she'd be able to tell me she loved me in return.

Silence in the room told him he was light years away from hearing those words from her. Even if she loved him with every fiber in her body, she was incapable of saying it. Acknowledging it. Admitting it. And if she couldn't admit it to herself, he was royally screwed.

Glancing at him with a look that told him she was waging a deep, inner battle, one that he couldn't fault her for, because he now thought he understood the source of it, she drew a deep breath. "Why?"

"Hell. I've done a lot of thinking on that one. You reached into my chest and stole my heart the first time I laid eyes on you. I can't honestly tell you all the reasons why. It's more than just my physical attraction to you, though that's unlike anything I've ever experienced before. More than the fact that you're the one and only woman I've ever met who I'd never need to apologize to for my endless dedication to work. More than the fact that I'm mesmerized by your brain. More than admiration for your ambition. More than the fact that I hang on every word you say. I think one of the things that hooked me early on was that you didn't need me for a goddamn thing. Since my father died, I've lived every day of my life fulfilling needs."

"I understood that," she said, her voice soft. "Theresa was pregnant. She needed you. I understood you were doing something because of someone else's need. I got it, Zeus."

He nodded. "One reason I could walk away from you is a reason why I loved you." He reached for her chin, ran his fingers along the soft skin. "You didn't need me for anything. But you wanted me. It was unlike anything I'd ever felt in my life. I felt...important. You made me feel like I had the world in my hands. I felt like I'd finally found a part of myself that went missing when I watched my father die. A part of me that I didn't even know was missing. The fact that you wanted me made me feel better than whole. I was virtually levitating from it. I felt...things. Feelings. I feel things when I'm with you, Sam. I don't feel things with most other people. I've trained myself not to."

He traced his fingertip along her neck, arm, shoulder, and went back to her chin and lifted it, because she was now studying the sheets, as though looking at him had become painful.

When her eyes once again rested on his, he said, "If I don't make you feel that way, if you don't want me enough to overcome your fear of committing to me—"

"I'm not afraid of commitment."

"You're afraid of me."

Her alarm rang. She reached for her phone on the bedside table, turned off the alarm, and took the opportunity to stand on the other side of the bed. "As I was saying—if you don't want me as badly as I want you, if that want doesn't have you ready to fight your demons, then I don't know if there's anything I can do about that. It's got to be reciprocal. You have to know that I want you more than my next breath. Really want you. Like want you with me every step of the way. Forever."

"I don't know what to say."

As his gaze took in her nude body in the dim morning light, he knew there'd never be a time when he'd forget her curves and angles, how pretty and honestly vulnerable she looked at that moment. Nor would he forget the way her eyes were glistening with unshed tears, or the way her lack of an appropriate response was the equivalent of an icepick jab into his heart.

The inescapable truth that he now faced was that when the job was over, when they parted ways, she was going to be one of the biggest regrets of his life. His heart stung with the rejection, but his mind told him it was inevitable. "That's answer enough."

She stayed silent as he stood, each second she didn't say anything shooting slivers of ice into his heart. "Ball's in your court. Game's over when the job is done. Not an ultimatum. Just a fact. I'm not angry. I want you to use every ounce of strength you have in your body to conquer whatever it is that has you scared of my brand of love. I understand people and their demons, Sam. I get it." He drew a deep breath. "Not that I'll resist you while we're stuck with each other."

He scooped his jeans off the floor, found his boxers underneath the sheets, and threw one last glance at her. It was enough of a glance to change his mind about exiting her bedroom, because she was walking in his direction, a look of tortured misery in her eyes as she drew near to him.

"You know it isn't just our past that's in the way now, don't you? Justin and I will eventually get married, Zeus. Nothing that's happening between us will change that."

"Don't marry him."

"I will. I just thought you should know." Eyes tortured, voice low, she looked like the least happy bride-to-be he could ever imagine. Stepping closer to him, she reached for his left shoulder with her right hand, and slipped her left arm around his back.

"Do you love him? With all of your heart?"

Her hesitation was an answer. *Wasn't it?*

"That part in the marriage vows about until death do us part." His voice was throaty now, and low, as he opened his arms around her and gave her the comfort she was seeking. "It's just words. Until reality hits and you're spending the rest of your fucking life with someone who you like enough to sleep with—"

"But I do love him. Justin is my best friend, and really, you don't exactly have the right to talk about my relationship with him."

"I don't buy it. If you loved him, you wouldn't be making love to me."

"This is sex," she whispered. "Just sex."

"Yeah. That was why your hands were shaking and you were crying the other night when you thought I wouldn't know." Her eyes flashed with something—anger, hurt, embarrassment—hell if he knew. She shifted her gaze away from his, and he didn't get the chance to figure it out.

"When that person is a great friend, when you sort of love them, the reality that you're going to spend the rest of your life with them makes every day seem like an eternity. Months seem endless. Years are unfathomable." He bent his face close and lifted her chin in the crook of his finger until she looked at him. "When that person isn't someone who makes you feel that when you leave them you'd rather die than keep going, further and further away, marrying them...just isn't worth it."

"Marriages shouldn't be based on emotion. Look at what happened to yours."

"I'm talking about you, dammit. That's how I feel about you. My marriage to Theresa fell apart because I didn't feel that way about her."

Her breasts were smashed into his chest. Her nipples had become hard nubs. He wished like hell he could walk away from her, but he couldn't. The fact that he couldn't festered for a second as she lingered in his arms. His blood, simmering since the job had started, became a slow boil of frustration. He pushed her away. She held onto his arms, gripping them tightly at his elbows.

"I still want you," she whispered. "I'll always want you. You had me heart, body, and soul seven years ago. I was relieved when you left, because that kind of love was never in the cards for me. Now, I can only offer my body."

She tiptoed, raising her lips to his, softly moaning as his hands moved to her breasts. When she gave in, for those moments when they were joined, blissful sensations assuaged the rawness that accompanied the swirling emotions, feelings, and disappointment she inspired. He placed his hands on her shoulders and eased her against the wall. Not so gently, he turned her to face the wall, intending to show her exactly what plain old, meaningless sex could feel like with him.

Everything I ever do with her backfires.

Instead of taking her fast and hard, and pounding into her until he was spent, as he planned, she turned her beautiful face to the side and sighed his name. He couldn't just gaze at her profile while he pumped into her. When he bent to kiss her ear, her mouth found his. She reached behind her back and his, holding him to her with his forearm. He changed the pace of his body to give him time to savor the taste of her mouth.

Next thing he knew he was holding her tightly across her chest with one arm, his fingers kneading her breasts, while his other hand reached around and he was softly fingering her where they were joined. The hard fuck he had planned became an extended caress of the joining of two bodies that perfectly fit together, the kind of caress that spelled love even more than words. As her moans grew louder, he used the pads of his index finger and thumb to work her clitoris, gently thrusting up and flexing into her, until she lifted her hands, palms flat on the wall, and arched her hips back as she climaxed, meeting his thrusts with a backwards hip motion. "Zeus. Oh. Zeus."

Upon hearing his name, the tight, pulsing feel of her walls drew an extended climax from him, every moment of it making the heartache she caused him worthwhile. As he arched into her and peaked, he knew that he could handle any amount of pain she caused, as long as it came with such exquisite, mind-numbing release.

After, he held her as they both leaned against the wall. "Why is sex always so good with you?" Eyes closed, she whispered her question as though she wasn't expecting an answer.

"Not sex. Don't you understand?" Planting kisses along her hairline, he wasn't afraid to admit the truth to himself, or to her. "Whenever I touch you, I'm making love."

Chapter Twenty-Eight

Annoying as hell rhythmic beats of low background music resonated throughout *Tapas de los Dioses*. A bottle of Dom Perignon produced a soft pop as the cork came out. Zeus had positioned himself so he could see Sam and McDougall in his peripheral vision. Stationed fifteen paces away from her in the intimate Soho restaurant, Zeus was both too far, and too close

Eye aversion was a learned skill. He'd done enough time in his early career as a bodyguard to know how not to look directly at the package. And he couldn't forget that Sam was the package. Not the woman he loved, but the person he was tasked to protect.

He knew how to observe everything they did, everything that needed to be seen in the narrow, rectangular restaurant, without staring. His direct gaze was on the door leading to the street, and his back was to the right of the door that led to the kitchen.

Sam would stand out wherever she was, and in whatever she wore. Tonight, seated in one of ten, six-top crescent-shaped booths in the stark black and cream restaurant, she was breathtakingly beautiful. She wore a sea-foam green, softly touchable-looking sweater dress that exposed her collarbones and conformed to every luscious curve. Close up, the color made her eyes look like light, exquisite jade. Tonight, but for the drive over, he wasn't the one getting to enjoy the color of her eyes. McDougall was so fucking close to her he was almost occupying the same space.

Backup, asshole, she isn't on the menu tonight.

But she is.

And the fact that Zeus had to stand here, stoic and invisible while it all happened, ate at his gut.

Soft light from chandeliers in a variety of styles and sizes hung over crescent-shaped booths. Candles on the table where Sam and McDougall sat added to golden light that reflected off her creamy skin. A white marble bar top extending the full length of the south wall, was backed by illuminated glass shelves that made bottles of liquor look like an art installation.

Her smile—directed at McDougall—was radiant. It hurt his fucking heart to see her look at another man that way. Fingernails scraping along a chalkboard would have grated on his nerves less.

McDougall had orchestrated a relaxed meal. Chef Diego, a rising star in the world of celebrity chefs, had closed his newest restaurant for the private dinner. Private as in: Sam, McDougall, and eight bodyguards. Four agents from EDGE, and four Black Raven agents, including Zeus. The remainder of the restaurant, with its white tablecloths and fresh flowers on each table, was dim. The warm light on the happy couple made their table for two the focus of the room, and the focus of Zeus's attention, whether he liked it or not.

Not.

According to Ragno, before becoming a chef with a flair for creating restaurants that became instant hits, Daniel Diego had gone to Harvard for his undergraduate degree in marketing. He'd met McDougall there, and they'd become friends. The good-looking chef, of medium build and stature, with slick-backed, jet-black hair, had popped the cork for the couple himself and was pouring the golden liquid into two crystal flutes.

"Please, stay and dine with us," Sam said to Diego, her voice carrying across the empty space, to where Zeus stood like a fifth wheel, his dick in his hand.

"Samantha, I'm the chef. I'm actually cooking tonight. Your security teams insisted on minimal personnel." Diego chuckled. "Which means I have to actually work."

"At least have a glass of champagne with us," she insisted, "then cook."

"Don't even try to resist her, Diego. Pour yourself a glass of champagne and sit for a few minutes." McDougall's voice was deep. Authoritative. Steady. Confident.

Fuck.

Of course his voice would be perfect.

"My guiding principle with Samantha is to give her what she wants. She doesn't ask for much, but what she wants, she will get. One way, or another."

Amen.

Did he know that just a few hours ago Sam had melted in his arms? Did McDougall give a damn that when she came, it was Zeus's name she called? Over and fucking over again?

Diego lifted his hand. At his signal, a waiter brought him a crystal flute. He poured himself a glass, and sat in the booth next to Sam.

Hell. This night will last forever.

Since Zeus had thrown the suicide bomber over the bridge

on Thursday evening, he and Sam hadn't been able to get enough of each other when the doors were closed and when both could take a break from their never-ending work. They hadn't talked more about personal issues, which was fine with him, because in the early hours of Friday morning he'd said what he needed to say.

On Friday afternoon, the last day of the trial in Paris, the judges ruled on the motions they considered on Thursday. The judges denied the Colombian motion for a mistrial, granted the French motion to enlarge the record, and granted Sam's motion to interview Vladimer Stollen.

Later that evening, in bed, between other activities, they'd worked their way through a box of almond, strawberry, coconut, and chocolate macarons to celebrate Sam's victories on the motions. Zeus had enjoyed pointing out that U.K. Judge Normand, the male judge who couldn't tear his eyes from her as she argued, voted in Sam's favor on each of the arguments she'd made.

With proceedings beginning in London on Monday morning, the Amicus team had transitioned to London on Saturday morning. Sam's suite of rooms had a set up similar to her rooms in Paris—which meant there was plenty of private space for him and Sam to go at it upon their arrival in London the day before.

She hadn't given any indication she was interested in further conversation. She was damn well smart enough to understand what he meant when he told her the ball was in her court. And he damn well knew her continued silence regarding personal issues with him, and now her glittering eyes and light, happy, positively-fucking-floating demeanor with Prince Charming, was a response.

Her body.

It was all she had offered, and it was what he hadn't been too proud to take. Until now, as her soft laughter drifted to him, he swore to himself he was done.

D-O-N-E.

Under other circumstances, Zeus would've liked McDougall. Would've liked that intel painted him as a smart, hard-worker who honestly cared about his constituents. Would have liked that so far McDougall was navigating the murky D.C. waters with integrity, which wasn't always the norm. Would have liked the fact that though the guy came from a rarified world of privilege and money, he seemed like a normal guy. The kind of guy who was happy that his brother had become a star NFL quarterback, the kind who went to sporting events and cheered, wearing a jersey and baseball cap, with popcorn in hand.

The kind who truly loved his golden retriever, Tricks, who photographers captured as they walked the D.C. streets. The kind of guy who was smart enough not to be photographed with every good-looking woman who had to be lining up to be with him. The kind of guy who tried hard to keep his personal life under wraps, though being with Sam at every charity and political event in D.C. had lifted some of the wrapping.

Hell. He would've liked that so far, in person, the guy seemed a bit quiet and subdued, as though he was a steady, well-grounded thinker. Zeus would've even liked the guy's easy smile—which reminded Zeus of his brother Gabe's smile—and the dimples that made McDougall look not only handsome, but approachable.

Would've liked him but for the fact that Sam had made it perfectly clear she wasn't breaking up with the guy and planned to eventually marry him.

Hell, but the guy even has a dimple on his chin.

Zeus guessed women melted when they saw it. To Zeus, the dimple made the man look like his chin was a butt.

In addition to the sea-foam green sweater dress that Justin was going to watch slip from her body, Sam wore the red lipstick that drove Zeus crazy. The color he'd dubbed Sex-and-Blowjobs-Red.

Had she done that on purpose? She goddamn knew the lipstick lit him up, because she'd teased him with it the night before, applying a layer of dewy gloss over her red-kissed lips, before easing her beautiful, moist, mouth onto his hard, strain—

"Zeus?" Ragno's timing was perfect. Flashbacking, with crystal-clear hindsight, about the best blowjob he'd ever received in his life was pretty goddamn stupid under these circumstances.

"Yep."

"Your ears only. Where are you positioned?"

"Raven's view." Meaning *my eyes are on my client,* who was sitting between Diego and McDougall, both of whom were focused on her as she laughed at something Diego said.

Ragno's sigh of exasperation filtered over the airwaves. "Why are you doing this to yourself?"

"Doing my job." He shifted on his feet, nodding to an EDGE agent as he stepped through the swinging door that led to the kitchen.

"Jenkins could've taken the lead tonight."

"Best if I see this."

It will help me get over her, so I'm standing up, like a man, taking the punch on my solid, square chin, which doesn't have a fucking ridiculous butt-looking dimple. And which is only made of glass with her.

"So how can I help you get through it?" Tone low, voice worried, Ragno sounded like she wasn't going away.

Glancing at Sam, he watched Diego lean closer to her. The dark-eyed man bent to kiss her on the cheek, but instead of Diego's eyes lingering on Sam, they were focused on McDougall, whose blue eyes held Diego's gaze. It was a long enough moment for something to click for Zeus. He shrugged it off.

Sam giggled at something they said.

Giggling?

Holy shit. Sam didn't giggle.

Not with you, dumbshit.

"Zeus?"

"Don't worry about me."

Diego walked towards Zeus, to the kitchen door. Before pushing the door open, Diego leaned into Zeus, patted him on the arm, and with a welcoming grin, said, "I'm preparing enough food for all of the security. Hope you're hungry."

"Appreciate it. But we don't eat on duty." As Diego slipped through the swinging door, Zeus said, "Ragno. I'm fine. Don't worry."

"Zeus, you're my Polaris."

He dropped his voice to a whisper. "Sweet of you."

"Hell—you're Polaris for everyone at Black Raven. Our North Star. Our guiding light. Steady. Always there, giving comfort in your absolute pragmatic brilliance, bravery, stoicism, and wisdom."

"Hell, you really are worried about me."

"Yes. This is the first time I've ever known you to be shaken. So, whether you like it or not, I'm not going anywhere until Senator McDougall is on his jet and headed back to the States. Flight pattern says his wheels will be up at 8 a.m. Sam plans to depart his hotel at 6:30 a.m. Means you have ten and a half more hours to deal with them together."

"Not just the next ten and a half hours. A lifetime." Self-pity bubbled up from his feet and spilled from his mouth before he could stop it. "Never should've taken this fucking job."

"You'll shake her off. She's got issues, Zeus. Issues that she's got to want to overcome. For some reason, you bring out every single one of her insecurities. She feels safer with him. That's all you're seeing tonight."

"I know." He drew a deep breath and squared his shoulders. "Payback's a bitch. I made a mess of things years ago. This is what karma is handing me. I'm really only getting what I deserve. You don't have to babysit me."

"Not babysitting you. Just taking this little walk through your personal hell with you. Friends do such things."

He exhaled, watching as McDougall and Sam finished their champagne and a waiter stepped forward to pour more. She was laughing at something McDougall said, and her laughter faded to a giggle.

Jesus. Fucking. H. Christ.

Next to the night his father had died, this was going to be the longest night of his entire freaking life.

The. Longest.

He needed to think about something other than the way Sam looked so comfortable and happy with McDougall. The way their eyes held when they talked. The way she laughed with him, the absolute ease they seemed to have with each other, the way they appeared as though they were the best of friends. The way her eyes shone with happiness with McDougall, but how with him, the shine came from unshed tears.

He makes her happy, dumb fuck, while you make her come and you make her cry. What kind of life could that possibly add up to?

Dammit, he wasn't going to make it through the night if all he did was think of how damn good they looked together and how she looked more effervescent than the goddamn champagne. Diego's lingering look on McDougall hadn't been all that odd. Diego was world-famous, and didn't hide the fact that he was gay. What was odd about that lingering glance was the way McDougall returned the glance.

And there were other facts—*holy fuck*!

Turning and walking to the far corner of the bar, Zeus found a vantage point on Sam's table that was as far away as he could be. They were out of earshot, and so was he. No EDGE agents were within earshot, and the Black Raven agents were all stationed elsewhere. He lowered his voice to a whisper that only Ragno would be able to detect through the mic. "Could McDougall be gay?"

A harsh intake of breath was all Ragno gave him.

"Well?"

"I've seen no indication of that, but we haven't done a Black Raven profile on him. Still, that would have come out in the election."

"If he ever came out of the closet, yes. But not if he hasn't."

"Who doesn't these days? Besides, he could have used that fact to his advantage with the electorate in his district."

Turning, glancing at the two of them, deep in avid conversation, he added, "Some people value privacy. Maybe he's one. Plus, who knows how his family would have reacted? You said that McDougall and Sam talk to each other like best friends. They look like friends. Best buddies. He hasn't kissed her yet. I mean really kissed her. Lips to cheek don't count. And, according to her, they're planning on having an open marriage. Discreet, but open."

"So? Some couples look like friends. And some people do have open marriages. Doesn't mean he's gay."

"What kind of man chooses a tapas restaurant?"

"Oh, come on, Zeus. Really? Plenty of men who aren't gay."

"I fucking hate tapas."

"Men who are college friends with chefs who open tapas restaurants."

"Chef Diego, his good friend, is gay."

"So? You have gay friends. We have a Black Raven partner and agents who are gay."

"McDougall met her at the restaurant."

"Your point?"

"He hasn't seen her in at least a week. If I flew across the ocean to see Sam and hadn't seen her for a week, we might be doing dinner together, but it would be in bed."

"Jesus, Zeus. You really do have the mentality of a horny sixteen-year-old—"

"Only with her."

"I know that. Which is why I don't think you should be there tonight. About him meeting her at the restaurant, not everyone has your testosterone-driven view of the world." She paused. "But, okay, I'll run with it for a moment. Let me do some digging."

"Careful. He's a senator. One day we'll need his vote on a damn big hiring contract. Or something."

"If he were trying to hide something, or even just not make something public, it would have come out. His race was hotly contested."

"Maybe he's never acted on it. There could be all kinds of

reasons why he'd enter into a beard marriage. The marriage could be a mask for being gay."

"Which means you'll never have a sure answer. Unless one of them admits it to you. Pretty damn doubtful she'll tell you, since she hasn't told you yet...and I doubt he'll be confiding in you."

Glancing directly at Sam, he saw that her eyes were glittering with unshed tears. The full smile on her face as she held Justin's gaze told him it wasn't the kind of tears she shed with him.

These are happy tears, asshole. The kind you don't see from her.

McDougall slid closer to her, lifted her chin in the crook of his finger, and Zeus didn't need to be able to hear the words the man said. The words *I love you* only looked one way on a man's lips, and the first real kiss that McDougall gave her was a solid, on-the-lips—*aw fuck*—steady kiss.

Not the kind of get-a-room kiss Zeus liked to give her, but then again, Zeus wasn't doing that kind of stuff in public with her either. At least not now. Not on the job, not when she was the girlfriend of a public figure. Not when she admitted to no one—not even herself—that anything was going on with Zeus.

"Never mind," he muttered.

"Wishful thinking ran away with you?"

"Guess so."

"Even if their marriage is a beard. Even if they have no sexual relationship at all. Where does that get you?"

McDougall placed a black velvet box in her hand. Ragno's words went to background noise, as his heart lifted into his throat. Sam's gaze slid to Zeus. She shifted her body, turning her shoulders to McDougall, facing him.

"She's still planning on marrying him one day," Ragno was saying, when he could focus. "If you haven't managed to make her change her mind yet, I'm not sure you'll be able to. You'll have to shake her off, Zeus."

"Hard to do when my eyes are on her. And fuck—I've now got a front row seat to his goddamn proposal."

"What?"

"She's opening a ring box."

"Oh hell. And?" Ragno fell silent.

"And fucking what?"

With a slight nod of her head, he knew the woman of his dreams was lost to him forever. The part of his heart that had feelings died a sudden death.

"Is she saying yes?"

"Of course she is. Told me she would the other morning, when we woke up together." His sarcastic words tasted bitter. She might be having a goddamn open marriage, but he wasn't going to be a part of it. He wasn't going to beg for fucking leftovers like a starving dog.

Done. D-O-N-E.

"Oh, Zeus. I'm sorry. Call Jenkins. Give him the Raven's view."

"Nope," he muttered. In his peripheral vision he watched McDougall lean in for another goddamn kiss.

Jesus H. Christ. Just go get a fucking room.

"I'll stick it out. I'm embracing the suck, and there's a hell of a lot of it."

"I'll be with you every step of the way."

He squared his shoulders, leaned his upper back against the wall, and lifted his right leg so that the bottom of his foot was pressed into it. Resting his body almost comfortably, while his chest felt like someone had reached in with a meat hook and was tearing at his heart, he said, "Well, since you're with me for the long haul, let's work."

"Awesome. Bounty hunt, security detail, or do you want to work on email?"

"Insurance. But first, return to the live mic." Zeus glanced to the front door. "Jenkins? Anything?"

"Clear. Normal busy sidewalk. Beautiful people everywhere. I'm turning away diners who were hoping for tapas tonight."

"Deal? What are you seeing?"

"Nothing to worry about. Diego's cooking. Otherwise, kitchen's clear."

"Good. I'm talking with Ragno about insurance. Break in with three-minute updates. More frequently if needed. Ragno— I've narrowed down the insurance contenders to Sullivans of New York and International Underwriters." The Black Raven insurance project he'd been working on was tedious and time-consuming. He wanted to formulate an answer for his partners by the end of the week. Options were self-insurance, Sullivans of New York, or International Underwriters.

"I thought Sullivans was out because they refused to negotiate coverage without including their clause for business interruption due to terrorism in the overall contract?"

"They're giving me a pretty good overall quote, though, so I want to analyze the advantages of their liability coverage over the liability coverage provided by International Underwriters. On another note, though, I'm wondering how Sullivans gets away with forcing people to buy the terrorism coverage."

"They're making a hell of a lot of money off the terrorism clause," Ragno answered. "Given the fact that every country in the civilized world is operating at the highest threat level right now, most businesses are asking for terrorism coverage. Our business is thriving, but, for example—the cruise ship industry. Ever since the Miami cruise ship bombing last year, the one the ITT is examining, that industry is in the toilet. Those companies are probably happy to pay Sullivan's top-dollar rates for the terrorism clause."

"I've studied the clause, though. Backwards and forwards and I've gotten our lawyers to look at it. That would be one hard claim to make them pay on. The way the clause is written, Sullivans isn't going to have to do many payouts." Zeus was quiet for a second. Thinking, as he stared straight ahead, at the front door. He'd seen enough to know that his ability to see details through his peripheral vision shouldn't be used to see Sam and McDougall. "Ragno, when you next have a few spare minutes—"

"Like that ever happens."

"Then delegate, preferably to someone with clearance for Jigsaw."

"Well, that means me, you, Barrows, and Sebastian. Most of the analysts who are working on the project only know pieces and parts. Few know the totality. Gabe has slivers of it. Enough to know that it is highly sensitive information and for once, he's not pushing me for details."

"Keep it that way. You decide who gets the project. I want to figure out if we can learn the names of the secret partners in Sullivans, and stakeholders in the insurance companies that offer this coverage against terrorist threats. Mostly because I want to know who we're dealing with. I don't believe in silent partner bullshit."

"Why give this to someone with clearance for Jigsaw?"

"Because the clause spells terrorism, and when terrorism is involved there is an off-chance it may produce puzzle pieces to throw into the mix."

"Understood, but finding their identities will be near to impossible. In Sullivan's case, they've been in business for over 200 years, and the secret partners are always secret. It's part of their charter. These old companies are all like that. A few partners are public faces. Others operate in the background. Identities are closely guarded secrets. More is known about the identities of the Masons than the secret partners in these international insurance conglomerates.

"Well, when you have time, start trying to figure out who they are. For now, for my insurance project for Black Raven, just do a comparison of terms of coverage. Focus on liability. Incorporate what our lawyers have done." Dammit, but the rock McDougall put on Sam's finger sparkled as much as the chandeliers, and as much as he willed himself not to see it, he couldn't fight the glare. "While you're working, I want to hear the words, sentence by sentence, in plain English."

"I'll do a flow chart." He could hear her fingers clacking on her keyboard, attacking the new project with gusto. "With a line by line comparison. I'll have it ready by the time you're standing outside Senator McDougall's hotel room. You'll at least have a project to sink your mind into."

"Great, but while you're working on that, read to me what you're doing."

Her pause was long and extended.

"Ragno?"

"You want me to read insurance provisions to you? Really?"

"Absolutely," he said, eyes on the door.

"I love you, but I've got things to do. I'll have Sally read to you. Good enough?"

"Fine." He welcomed, for the next three hours, the mind-numbing exercise of focusing on insurance provisions and clauses. With each word, he tried to block the fucking kaleidoscope of sparkling, colorful happiness presented by McDougall and Sam as they shared tapas, one small, exquisite plateful at a time.

Chapter Twenty-Nine

Chef Diego softly kissed her cheek before stepping away from the table. Samantha drew a deep breath, sipped a bit more champagne, and tried to look anywhere but at Zeus.

"Damn. I haven't eaten anything yet, but the champagne isn't making my stomach happy. I've already got heartburn. Did you bring antacids?"

"Yeah. Knew you'd need them tonight."

He slipped a roll from his pocket and passed it under the tablecloth into her lap. He was so good this way. Always prepared.

"Samantha." Justin's voice was low. "Look at me."

The concern in his dark blue eyes almost made her choke. His face wavered as her eyes filled with unwanted tears. She plastered a smile on her face. Without a funny thought in her head, she made herself laugh. At nothing. Absolutely nothing.

Justin arched an eyebrow and frowned. "You're scaring me."

"I'm fine," she said.

"Why are you going through with this?"

"Because we agreed we would do this. Our plan makes sense, for both of us. He's just a speed bump and I'm damn well not going to let him become a detour that ends badly." She made herself giggle again as she forced herself to focus on Justin's beautiful eyes. Reaching for his hand, she held on for dear life.

"All right, I might be able to handle your fake smile, but not that fake laugh, and definitely not that giggle. You don't giggle. I can't take it. Stop it, and tell me why you're insisting on this preemptive strike now?"

Reaching for the champagne flute, she took a sip, and whispered. "I don't want to talk about the reasons. Let's just do this, and move on."

He narrowed his eyes. "Will you even be able to eat at all? Diego will send us a taste of everything, and I can't eat it all by myself. We could leave. Say one of us has come down with a sudden something."

Yes, like Zeus disease. I believe it's fatal.

"I'll make myself eat." Without allowing her gaze to rest on Zeus, who was either talking to himself or had Ragno in her ear, she took another sip of champagne. "I'd hate to disappoint Diego."

Justin studied her for a long second. "You look like you've

lost five pounds in the last week."

"I haven't had much of an appetite."

She watched Justin's eyes slide over to Zeus, who'd walked further away from their table. "Jesus. Oh shit—that is his full name, isn't it? Anyway, he's built better than the guys on my brother's offensive line. I certainly wouldn't pick a fight with him."

"Don't talk about him."

"Seriously? Although you two are doing a damn good job of not looking at each other, he is the overpowering Greek God in the room, commanding more attention than any elephant I've ever come across. How could I not talk about him? Why are you doing this?"

"Do you love me?"

"Of course."

"Then don't ask why. You know why our arrangement is better for both of us. Just give me the ring and kiss me."

"No." With concern flooding his eyes, he shifted closer to her. "I couldn't imagine a woman less happy about receiving four carats of brilliant, emerald-cut diamond perfection. You're not acting like yourself. Not at all. Tell me why you're going through with this."

"I'm sorry, Justin." He was right. She didn't really care what the ring looked like, and she was mortified that she didn't really want to see it on her finger. They'd planned the details of their bands, and had selected the stone for the engagement ring months earlier. One option could have been for her to wear her mother's diamond. She'd rejected that idea the minute it came to her, because there was no need to remember that tragic marriage. "Let's do it. We've been through this."

"Not this week. Not in detail. Not in person since you and"— he glanced at Zeus, lowered his voice—"tall, dark, brooding and handsome have had your reunion."

"Not a reunion," she whispered, careful to keep her smile on her face. "Just recreational sex."

Which she and Justin both expected the other to have. They'd use utmost discretion, of course. It was the only way their marriage would work.

Justin gave her a slow, knowing headshake. As he studied her, she knew she really couldn't act as though the sex hadn't been anything special. As though Zeus didn't make her feel better than anyone had ever made her feel. As though he didn't make her feel positively treasured and cherished each time his hands touched her. As though he didn't fit inside of her with a feeling of fulfillment that didn't come with anyone else. Sensations with him were so unique, each time he stroked into her, the last few nights had convinced her that her body had been built for him, and him alone.

"Recreational sex," she repeated. "It means nothing."

Justin's full frown was deep. "You're only fooling one of us, and it isn't me."

Eyes filling with more tears that she would not spill, because Zeus had given her that same line only a few days ago, she threw her head back and laughed. If she started crying now she was going to dissolve into a miserable heap, and Zeus, the man she wanted to pick her up off the floor, was not Justin, the only man who she'd allow to pick her up.

After a few deep breaths, she found some composure. "I love you," she whispered, wondering why those words flowed so easily with Justin, when what she felt for him wasn't anything like what she felt for Zeus. "I can't thank you enough for putting up with this."

"We'll have to put up with a lot more over the next fifty or so years, assuming we still do this. I'm not sure we should. Seeing you now, I don't think you can handle what we're setting ourselves up for, and I'm not sure you should—"

"This is only hard for me because of the past I have with him. It makes him the perfect storm, because I was weaker when I first fell in love with him."

"When you first fell in love with him." Justin arched an eyebrow and gave her a slow headshake. "Do you realize what you just said? Meaning you're in love with him now."

"No. I'm not."

"Lie to yourself, Samantha. Not to me."

"What I feel for him emotionally doesn't matter. Reason and logic will rule my life. Not my heart. He'll be my biggest test. There won't be others like him. I won't put you through this kind of drama again. I promise."

Because no one else will make me so aware that I'm turning my back on my last hope for a normal, full life. No one else will make me miss that woman I once was. The naïve woman who allowed herself to think a man like him could make her a better person.

"Honey, it isn't me I'm worried about, and you know I'd walk over coals for you."

Sipping more of the champagne, she found courage in the

bubbles. At least it made her voice stronger. "I'm going to be fine. Really. Give me the box and a kiss. A real kiss. Like you mean it."

Justin shook his head. "You deserve more."

"And so do you."

"Which means we're both settling for something less than ideal."

"And we've been through this a million times. We're both going to come out ahead."

"Once I get past that fake smile of yours, you're looking so heartbroken I'm dying for you. Those aren't tears of happiness in your eyes, and I'm sitting close enough to you to know it. He isn't though, and he looks like—"

"He always looks like that."

"Seriously?" Justin took a sip of champagne as he let his gaze sweep the restaurant, then rest on Zeus. "That impenetrable-looking barrier he throws out to the world isn't fake? He walks around like that, without a trace of emotion?"

"You just have to watch him. Closely. Sometimes there's the faintest hint of a smile, or a frown, but mostly, he's intense. Always calm. Strong. Stoic. He is a rock, when underneath—"

"Come on, Samantha, listen to yourself describe him."

"How?"

"You love him. Really love him. Old-fashioned, life mate kind of love. You two should be together. For better or worse, regardless of what it does to your career path or your ambitions. Can't you just face that fact?"

"I've faced it. The other night, when I thought he was going to die, fear and abject misery hit me with a certainty that I'll never forget. It's the exact kind of love my mother felt for my father. The all-consuming, horrific kind of love that would eat away at me, bit by bit, and destroy me." She drew a deep breath. "Like my mother's love for my father destroyed her."

"But you can't just will it away."

"Oh, yes, I can. I sure as hell don't know why I feel like I need to tell him I'm sorry. To tell him all the reasons why I can't go there."

Justin shook his head. "The fact that you feel like you need to apologize—"

"I didn't say I was going to."

"You really should have that discussion with him."

She shook her head. "Too painful. I'm not going there, Justin. If you're truly my dearest friend, give me the ring, kiss me, let's eat, and we'll go to your hotel room. Each step will take me further away from weakness. I need to do this."

Justin lifted her chin with his finger, drawing her gaze and holding it. "You sure?"

She nodded, "I need to get my equilibrium back. Please. This is the most important thing I've ever asked of you. Let's do this, and let's make it look good. Like there's more to us than a friendship."

"I love you, Samantha Dixon Fairfax." He bent his head to hers. Their lips touched and lingered together, long enough for Samantha to confirm that kissing her best friend was nothing like kissing Zeus.

Justin reached into the pocket of his sports coat, and pulled out a black velvet box. Her glance accidentally went to Zeus. Their eyes met for a split second. His hard gaze sent shivers down her spine. She turned her shoulders, focused on Justin, and tried to look happy.

"My best friend, my future wife, my partner and architect of the beautiful life we'll have, full of ambitions and goals we'll meet, will you marry me?"

She drew a deep breath, opening the black velvet box, as the right words, from the wrong man, and the fiery diamond engagement ring, from the wrong hands, sliced through the heart that beat normally for others, but erratically and hopelessly for Zeus. As Justin again closed his lips on hers, she mentally put the first shovelful of dirt on the coffin of the woman who was in love with Zeus Hernandez.

Chapter Thirty

London, England
Monday, February 7

Hell. An arm's length away for the duration of a transatlantic flight? *Fuck.* Too close. He'd smell sweet, soft jasmine for hours. He'd had enough of that fragrance for a lifetime and certainly since that morning, when he'd resumed the lead position on Sam's detail.

She'd stepped ahead of him onto Raven One, the Black Raven Gulfstream 650 ER taking them from London to ADX Florence, Colorado, the federal supermax prison that housed Stollen. He'd stopped on the tarmac to talk to the captain and co-pilot, who he hadn't seen in a while. Deal, Jenkins, and Miles filtered into the back of the jet. She was settling into the seat across the aisle from the A seat, the reclining chair he usually rode in, unless he opted for the private berth in the back of the plane.

As he decided whether to take the A seat, he said to her, "You could go in the back. Shut the door. Get some sleep on the couch."

"I prefer the front."

Dammit to hell. So did he. The A seat. It was the closest to the door and the closest to the cockpit. It was the seat he and other partners in the company vied for if they were flying together, and they weren't afraid to act pretty damn juvenile to get to it. He wasn't going to fly across the goddamn Atlantic in another seat just because sitting in the A seat meant sitting on the opposite side of the aisle from her.

Besides, his agents expected him to take the A seat. They'd think it odd if he didn't, and he was willing to bet they'd know exactly why he opted out. The whole job had been a clusterfuck from the start, because it hadn't just been a job for him. He'd hand-chosen the agents on Sam's team and personally given them a discussion about discretion before they'd started the job.

He made it a practice to deal with adversity head-on.

Why change now?

Settling into his preferred seat, he turned on his reading light, opened his laptop on the slide-out table, and stretched his legs out in front of him. Miles, Jenkins, and Deal were far enough out of earshot to not hear any conversation that transpired between him and Sam, assuming they kept their voices low.

Doesn't matter. As they stood on the other side of the door, they probably heard God-knows-what over those nights as you and Sam went at it like there was no tomorrow.

Hell.

Joke's on you, buddy, cause now there is no tomorrow. To top it off, last night they probably heard her screaming McDougall's name just like she screams—no, screamed—your name when she comes.

He didn't anticipate talking about anything with Sam his agents couldn't hear and even if the conversation went there, it would just be an accompaniment that went with the other aspects of this fucked-up job.

Sure as shit, as he tried to focus on his work, he felt her green eyes sliding over his face, burning the path they crossed. For the hundredth time that day, or maybe the two hundredth time, he felt that she was waiting for him to say something about her engagement to McDougall.

The fact that she thought he'd have something to say about it irritated the goddamn living shit out of him. What the hell was he supposed to say? *Congratulations? Best wishes?* Worse, at some point during the first day of proceedings in London, when he'd caught her watching him from across the courtroom, he'd decided she was looking at him with a slightly concerned, perturbed look that spelled *P-I-T-Y* and said *I'm sorry*, even though the words hadn't crossed her mouth.

Sorry? Pity? Flying fuck to both ideas.

He didn't want to hear her say, "I'm sorry" and certainly didn't want her pity. Throughout the day, upon getting the feeling some variation of those words were coming from her, he'd braced himself for the moment she articulated the thought.

He wasn't so desperate that he needed an apology. Never would be. Just pissed. And feeling raw, and the last thing he wanted to do was anything that would reveal to her how his heart felt like it had been macerated to shreds.

With a signal from the cockpit, he fastened his seatbelt. He opened his laptop, and scrolled to the folder of insurance information downloads. He turned to the flow sheet of insurance provisions that Ragno had prepared. It would be a sure cure for insomnia borne of irritation, but only if he didn't start thinking about the serious liability that accrued on Black Raven jobs that went south. As the Raven in charge of operations, until the current job, and as a cleaner of some of the company's trickier messes, like the fall-out that happened over the Barrows incident, he understood the considerable dollars that were wasted when the company was sued.

Instead of analyzing the flow sheet, he glanced out the window. It was a cold, cloudy Monday night in London. As the jet lifted off the runway, swirling gray mist concealed the lights of the city. Now that they were on their way to interview Vladimer Stollen, Sam had left her second chair lawyer—Abe—to handle the witnesses in London on Tuesday, which were government investigators setting forth the evidence on the trade show bombing. Charles would provide assistance to Abe.

Stollen's interview was scheduled for 10:00 a.m., Mountain Time, on Tuesday. A team of Black Raven agents was meeting them upon landing, and they'd assist with transfers. Robert Brier—already stateside for his wife's memorial service—was meeting Sam at the prison for the interview of his client. The lead prosecutor for the U.S. in the ITT proceeding, Benjamin McGavin, had flown home over the weekend and would meet her at the prison as well. Other necessary parties would participate via videoconference. Judge O'Connor would monitor the conference and make necessary rulings to facilitate information gathering. By 1500 on Tuesday, Zeus would have Sam back on Raven One for the return trip to London.

He'd been man enough to observe the Sunday evening proposal, until Sam was safely in the hotel room with her fiancé. He'd even walked into the suite, made sure it was secure, glanced at the king size bed they were going to sleep in, lost his breath for a second when he thought about her with McDougall, and told them both goodnight. McDougall had given him a slow nod, his blue eyes revealing bucket-loads of unease. Sam, arm in arm with McDougall, had nodded as she looked past him, her cheeks flushed pink from champagne and happiness.

Closing the door to McDougall's hotel room had been the final straw. Zeus relinquished control to Jenkins and the other members of the team. By midnight, he was in exercise clothes, running through the streets of London, weaving on and off the route they would take in the morning to bring the Amicus team to the proceedings.

In the drizzly, almost freezing night, he'd run along the Thames River, crossed it via the Waterloo Bridge. He sprinted along the wide sidewalk of the Strand to the Royal Courts of Justice, where the ITT proceedings would be held over the next week. The Gothic building looked more like a cathedral than a courthouse.

Once at the barricades that blocked the entrance to the courthouse, he'd stretched, and returned calls to both Sebastian and Gabe. Given the genuine concern he heard in their voices in the messages they'd left for him, Ragno had obviously been working behind the scenes and let both men know what had transpired between Samantha and McDougall. He kept the conversations with both his friend and his brother short. Two sentences with each were adequate to end the discussion on his personal issue. *Thanks for the concern*, and *I'm fine*. He focused on work issues with each of them, and ended the conversations.

He ran back to One River Thames, a high-rise building that was partly exclusive private suite hotel and mostly private residences, where Black Raven would guard the Amicus team while the London phase of the proceedings were ongoing. Residence One attracted wealthy, international business clientele, who paid big bucks for discretion, safety, and anonymity. The sleek building boasted two floors of conference rooms that were equipped to handle business functions, and panoramic views of the London skyline and the Thames. Black Raven had consulted on the security of One River Thames and had, from time to time, provided on-site protection for various clients there.

At 0630 on Monday morning, Jenkins, Miles, and Deal, had escorted Sam from McDougall's hotel to One River Thames. Zeus hadn't reappeared at her side until 0830, when it was time for her to leave for proceedings. The day had been full of necessary communication between him and Sam. There were directional instructions, mostly related to transit to and from the first day of proceedings in London, such as *"second car," "wait a second, we need clearance," "ready?," "there's a bathroom down the hall for you"* and *"here's the flight plan."* He'd kept those communications as generic as possible.

Zeus also had to communicate with her on the security detail Black Raven was putting together for Stollen. The post-interview security detail, assuming the terrorist produced helpful information, was part of the package Sam would be offering the terrorist in return for credible information that led to apprehending Maximov.

Planning the details of keeping the terrorist safe and protected, free yet isolated, for the rest of his life, in a manner approved by the Federal Bureau of Prisons and the trial court judge who was overseeing implementation of Stollen's sentence, required a task force of agents at Black Raven headquarters to develop the project parameters and estimate. Once the site was selected, Zeus had directed the agents to provide Sam pictures. She'd need them in the interview.

Now, with the darkness of the cold night outside, the jet window had become a mirror. She was watching him, waiting for his attention. Her blonde hair spilled over her shoulders, her black turtleneck a perfect backdrop for the lightness of the silken strands. Her eyes were stark with seriousness. Her lips, neither a smile nor a frown, were perfect. She wasn't wearing makeup. At least he didn't think so. Her white-gold, creamy-complexion beckoned his fingers, looking soft and touchable.

Bracing himself for a dose of bad-tasting medicine, he turned from the window to face her, because he didn't think he could get away with ignoring her for the entire journey across the Atlantic. "Now that we've leveled off, there's food in the galley. You should eat."

"Thank you. I will. Later." Glancing towards the rear of the jet, she dropped her voice to a whisper and leaned his way, closing some of the distance between them that the aisle provided. "Zeus, I'm sor—"

"Don't."

Her brow furrowed and her eyebrows drew together. "But we need to talk about it. I'm trying to tell you how sor—"

"Anything you have to say that starts with an apology, and ends with *'but I'm going to marry him anyway,'* is a discussion we don't need to have." He had lowered his voice to a whisper, but the words were so painful he felt like he was shouting.

Her cheeks became flushed. Good—his message was hitting home. "Save your breath. Marry McDougall. Gear your life for your career. Work hard, exercise hard, live a steady life with him. Sit in front of a fireplace together on winter nights as you both work. Watch your sunsets together. Share your ambitions. Help each other realize them. Talk about your days. Have your active vacations, get your two Golden Labs."

She flinched, as though he'd deliver a blow, and he immediately ground his teeth in frustration. Why, exactly, did he give a rat's ass that he was hurting her feelings?

"What'd you think? That I forgot any of the things we talked about seven years ago? I remember everything about you, Sam. Even the inconsequential crap. Why do you think the caterer provided ham sandwiches on white bread and barbeque potato chips in the galley of this goddamn jet? Because I know that's your favorite late-night snack. There are even macarons in the galley, for God's sake. I know you don't sleep well on an empty stomach, and you skipped all the healthy stuff we had at dinner earlier. Tomorrow's a big day for you." He frowned, trying, but failing, to keep bitter petulance out of his voice. "And I'm willing to bet you didn't get much sleep last night."

Now she didn't look like she was going to apologize. She just looked damn miserable, and the reading light directly over her seat bounced off her diamond engagement ring and shot a fucking prism of brilliance into his eyes. "Come on, Sam. Did you think we'd resume where we left off on Sunday, before you accepted his proposal? Sharing a bed? Me making love while you tell yourself all we're doing is having sex? Well—"

"Understood." Her one-word interruption came with a cool nod. "You don't have to say more. I've heard enough."

"Don't think you have." He was on a roll, and seething. Furious at her for fucking up both of their lives, he wanted to make damn sure that she understood his position. Glancing back at Jenkins, who was closest to him, and at Miles and Deal, who were further back, he saw that they weren't paying attention. Or they were doing a damn good job of looking like they weren't paying attention. Didn't fucking matter. He was going to say what he needed to say, and after that he was going to damn well forget about it. And her.

"Now I understand why you didn't want to talk to me about what I did seven years ago." He inhaled, almost laughing at the puzzled look and surprise that crossed her features, then realizing he was looking at both heartache and relief. "Yeah. I get it. You're just doing to me what you think I did to you. Well, the reason why we don't need to talk about it—what I did to you or what you're doing to me—is that it hurts too fucking bad to talk about heartache with the person who is causing it. I get it now. Loud and fucking clear."

He had to believe heartache came for her before the relief. Heartache because he knew she had fallen in love. Relief because she never wanted to feel that much for anyone. Not that she was going to confirm it, or deny it.

"Great," she said, a punch of sarcasm delivered with the word. "You needed the insight. Glad I provided it to you."

"Thank you for that gift. Now, I also goddamn-well understand why we personally have nowhere to go from here."

"Your choice," she said, her cheeks flushed red.

"Not really a choice. I'm damn happy for the symbolism on your ring finger, because that big rock is a pretty constant reminder of things gone wrong. That goddamn diamond is my kryptonite. If you're going to marry him, I'm done. Do your open marriage thing. I won't pretend to understand that and trust me, I'm not lining up to be a part of it. Got it?"

She shot him a fulminating look. "I *am* marrying him."

"Fine. Done." He shifted in his seat, pressed the arrow down button on his laptop, pretended to stare at words that could just as well have been Mandarin, a language he did not understand, and glanced back at her. "Stop acting like marrying him isn't a choice. It is a decision that you're willingly making."

"I fully realize I'm making a choice. Even you had a choice," she said, her low whisper sounding more like a hiss than fully articulated words. She unfastened her seat belt, and stood. "You made a choice seven years ago."

"No. I had no choice. I had to marry her," he said. "Especially since you weren't asking me to stay. And especially when I was giving you an out, gift-wrapped with a fucking bow on it, so you didn't have to claim responsibility for being relieved. Have you even admitted that to yourself? That you were relieved? Which means you have no right to feel wronged by what happened."

Standing in the aisle, Sam folded her arms, and glanced down at him. "Fine. I admit it. I was relieved when you left me. I'll also be relieved when this damn trial is over so we can both get on with our lives. And..." She drew a deep breath, her eyes glistened with moisture that he knew she was going to will away before the first tear fell, and said, "I'm sorry that it has to be this way."

"Save your apology. Don't need it. What you're not understanding is I've given up. Get it? I'm going cold turkey. I fold. Understand? I'm done. Giving up on you, on us, on what we could be."

She had the fucking nerve to look surprised, cheeks flushed red, before she turned away from him. But for the gut-wrenching feeling of regret that came with things that had gone wrong, he almost laughed as she strode down the aisle to the small galley. *Dammit*, but she'd gotten her apology in, and she didn't seem to care whether he accepted it.

He closed his laptop, stood, found a pillow and a blanket in an overhead compartment, and reclined in his chair. He needed sleep and he was damn well going to get it.

Before shutting his eyes, in his peripheral vision he watched as Sam returned to her chair, nibbling on finger sandwiches and barbequed potato chips as she opened her laptop, and settled in for work.

Gabe is right. She's a goddamn velociraptor. The twenty-first century version of the man-eating monster, giving new meaning to the war cry of 'I am woman, hear me fucking roar.' In control of everything, even her emotions, and determined to thrive in a world where old-fashioned notions of love were meaningless.

He shut his eyes tight, blocking out the vision of her, and pushed his head deep into the pillow.

She might love me with every fiber of her being, but she isn't going to admit it. Not to herself, not to me. The reasons why? Goddamn irrelevant, because the rule of survival of the fittest created this highly evolved, modern-day version of a female with a cast-iron will that will allow her to fight anything she feels.

I fully understand—because, damn Gabe, correct again— I'm just like her. Except with her. Thanks for the reminder, Gabe, because I'm cured.

I'm fine.

I'm over her.

He promised himself that the beautiful monster sitting across the aisle from him had taken the last bite he'd give her of his bloody, ripped-to-shreds heart.

Chapter Thirty-One

Aboard Raven One, over the Atlantic Ocean
Tuesday, February 8

A not-so-gentle shake on his shoulder roused Zeus. "Sir."

The captain was in the aisle next to his chair, crouched down to eye level. Most of the lights in the cabin were off. Floor lights were on. A reading light had been left on midway down the aisle. It made the entire cabin dim, not dark. Sam was in her fully-reclined chair, head on a pillow and nestled under a blanket, turned towards the wall. Only her sleek ponytail was visible.

Sitting up, he glanced at his watch as he stretched his arms over his head. He'd been asleep for two and a half hours. The jet was steady. No turbulence. The low hum of jet engines sounded normal. It was climbing, though, and banking left. There was no need for a mid-Atlantic course change, or for the captain to be waking him, unless something was wrong. "Mechanical problems?"

"No." The captain—Agent Phillip Canwell, five years in Black Raven—had a look of concern in his eyes that was serious enough to tell Zeus there was big trouble.

"But we're altering course?"

"Yes. Miami."

No!

"Ragno's on the satellite phone." Canwell placed the satellite phone receiver in Zeus's hand, then continued down the aisle, rousing Jenkins, Miles, and Deal.

"Ragno?"

"Zeus, brace yourself." The concern in her voice pinged off of his spine, sending shock waves that reverberated in his brain.

He watched his team go from dead sleep to instant attention as Canwell's words registered. Jenkins stood, and walked up the aisle with the captain, to Zeus. They flanked him in the aisle, one on either side, a show of support for the bad news that had yet to be delivered.

Zeus knew.

Maximov's organization was cherry picking. Going after families of those involved in the ITT proceedings, and twice over the last week, Zeus had been the star of the goddamn show—first, when cameras had caught him running through the streets of Paris with Sam in his arms and then when he'd thrown the suicide bomber off the bridge.

From the back of the plane, Miles and Deal, both standing, cast him glances that were full of unmasked concern. Sam stirred, turned over, and rested her eyes on him. She sat up, immediately, without a trace of sleepiness.

"Goddammit. Tell me."

"Ana's been kidnapped."

"GPS?" He choked out the question. He'd chipped his daughter with the same type of chip he'd put in Sam.

"Not detectable."

He gasped for air. Whoever had her knew what the fuck they were doing.

"Are you with me?"

"Yes," he managed the outright lie. Being able to utter an automatic response wasn't the same as being ready to handle the news with his usual equanimity, his unparalleled ability to park his emotions and feelings on a back burner.

"At 1955 Eastern time—"

As though self-control hadn't ruled every single fucking day of his life after his father's death—except those days involving Sam—as Ragno spoke, Zeus's world became a chilling blur of horror. His vision narrowed until all he could see was a pinhole, which gave him nothing on which he could focus. Mentally, he was alone and in darkness, lurching and tumbling in the ice-cold, ink-black night that covered the Atlantic. A place where Ragno's words had no meaning. Where nothing had meaning.

He didn't know when he stood, but knew when his knuckles punched into the hard wood that lined the cabin of Raven One, a sleek and beautiful landing for the fury that came with his fist. Again. And again. He tried hard to feel the pain that each hit caused, because it gave him something to focus on that was different from the horror that was playing out in his head.

"Sir." Jenkins's plea wasn't enough to stop him, because when he looked into the man's eyes, and the eyes of his other agents, they mirrored his own abject fear.

His agents knew how much could go wrong. They, like him, had seen too much evil in the world and knew that a six-year-old girl was no match for it. Thinking of the countless jobs where things went wrong, no matter how perfectly Black Raven performed, he punched harder at the wall, throwing his body into the effort.

Captain Canwell, Jenkins, and the other agents spoke words designed to calm him, but the words had no meaning, because he was lost, free-floating in space to a time where he was holding his baby girl in the palm of his hand, minutes after her birth, wondering how he could've been involved in creating such a tiny miracle. Knowing, that if he only did one more thing in his life that amounted to anything, it was to make sure that his girl grew into an adult who could stand on her own two feet and handle whatever life threw her way.

He'd failed.

Oh God.

Is she already dead?

Bile rose up from his gut and choked him. If not dead, she had to be terrified. His baby. He had to get to her. Had to. But he was hours away from landing and he didn't have the capability of sitting on the jet, waiting to land, powerless to take action.

Strong arms tried to restrain him. They couldn't. He threw them off of him. Hammer fisting into glistening wood, he pushed Jenkins away from him. Howling with fury, his mind snapped to his last sight of her. She wore a party dress with a red ribbon in her inky-dark hair. They were at Sebastian and Skye's wedding in New Orleans. He'd left from there on Raven One and gone directly to Paris, leaving Agent Martel to get Ana safely home. When he'd finished the hiring call from Ragno for Sam's job, he'd gone back into the reception hall.

Ana had been sitting at a table, waiting on him, so she could give him the piece of chocolate cake she'd gotten for him. She'd gotten a slice for herself and had waited to eat with him. As his fist connected, once again, with shiny wood, he could taste the lush sweetness of the dark cake.

He remembered telling her not to eat too much icing, but gave up when he tasted the creamy, smooth richness of it. After all, good chocolate didn't give his baby girl a stomachache. He could see the light in her eyes when he'd played dueling forks with her for the last bite of her piece. He'd let her have it, along with the final forkful of his. Her skinny arms had wrapped around his neck for their goodbye hug, her soft lips had kissed his cheek, and she'd promised in her best good-girl voice to do her homework, right before she'd said, *"I love you, Daddy."*

Ana. *Gone.* Ana. *Taken.*

Darkness swirled around him, with octopus-like tendrils of fire becoming rope that grabbed hold of reason and logic. Someone placed a light, but firm hand on his shoulder. It felt different than the hands of his agents.

He turned, and glanced into clear, calm green eyes that

imparted the thought that if he didn't fight the sticky, burning tendrils that were pulling him further and further into hell, they'd yank him to a depth from which there'd be no escape.

It was a place he wouldn't be able to help Ana.

"Zeus," she said. "Breathe. Slowly. One. Two. Three. Now hold it."

He knew she was trying to help him, but he couldn't focus. So much fear infected his brain that there was no room for Sam's urgent words, or any action to take from them.

"Come on, Zeus. Just like you taught me to do. Give me a deep breath in." She was kneeling on the floor, her hands on a portable oxygen mask that she was trying to put in his hand. He had no memory of sitting, but he was on his ass, between the A seat and the door that led to the cockpit. His back was against the door of the jet.

Staring into her eyes, he inhaled.

"Good. Hold it. One—Two—Three—Hold it. Now exhale. Slowly."

His left hand felt like mush, as though he'd pounded it against a steel wall.

"You're going to find her. But first you have to think. Take this, put it on, and breathe. Inhale. Make it deep."

He focused on the strength in Sam's eyes. Unlike his agents, Sam gave him a solid, steady gaze that told him she had faith he was someone who could right this horrific wrong. He took the oxygen mask, placed it over his nose and mouth, drew a breath, and tried to make it deep.

She nodded. "Good. One—Two—Three—Hold it. Now exhale. Slowly."

Her gaze locked on his. Her hands squeezed his forearms.

"Stay with me, Zeus. We'll be in Miami in three hours. Or we'll go wherever there are leads. You need to be able to think. You've got an entire company scrambling to find her right now, along with law enforcement. Black Raven is the best, and you're the best of the best." Her eyes told him she believed what she was saying. "Breathe. Okay?"

Ana. *Unimaginable. Gone.* Ana. *Taken.*

"Breathe. Come on. Inhale with me. Purse your lips, breathe in deep. One—Two—Three—Hold it."

She was using the calming technique he'd used with her in Paris. It fucking scared the crap out of him to realize how badly he'd lost it, how badly he needed to get a grip, how badly he needed help so that he could...think. Rationally. He breathed with Sam, letting the oxygen fill his lungs.

"You're smarter than whoever took her. By a long shot. You're the smartest person I know, and I know a hell of a lot of smart people. Do you understand that?"

Firm conviction in her eyes told him she believed what she was saying. For that, he'd always love her. No matter who she married.

"One—Two—Three—Hold it. When you put your mind on a task, you achieve it. You need to focus, get the facts, and you will think of a way to rescue her. Now exhale."

With each breath of oxygen-infused air, he was able to wrap the logic of his mind around the horror that had become his life. That he found solace in the strength of the woman who had broken his heart was just part of how off-kilter things were in his life.

"Okay, now breathe in again," Sam said. "Long. Slow. One. Two. Hold it."

He nodded, slowly finding his equilibrium, and glancing at Jenkins and Captain Canwell, who were standing right behind Sam. The captain held a full syringe in his right hand, needle exposed, his thumb on the business end of the plunger. Lorazepam. A serious dose that would've done the trick to calm down a wild stallion, or anyone in the throes of a full-fledged anxiety-induced rage. It was standard issue in Black Raven in-flight first aid kits, because Black Raven business came with serious fall-out. Usually, though, it wasn't the agents who needed the tranquilizer.

Moving the mask to the side for a second, he nodded to Canwell. "You can pack that up. I'm past the detour into oblivion. Won't be beating the walls of the jet any longer."

"We weren't worried about the walls, sir," Jenkins gestured with his chin to the door handle. "You were close to the door handle. Didn't know if you were going to try to open the door and Superman it."

As that sunk in, Zeus shut his eyes for a second, making a mental note that Black Raven had to better train agents—and himself—for this exact situation. The evil that was now pervasive in the world guaranteed that this type of situation would happen, again, to someone, somewhere, in relation to some job that had turned to shit.

"Can't say any of us would have acted differently," Jenkins added.

"Put the satellite phone feed on the intercom." Mentally

distancing himself from the feelings that came with being the father of a daughter in peril and forcing himself to think calmly about the situation, he took a few more oxygen-assisted breaths as he waited.

With Canwell's nod, he put the mask to the side and let go of Sam's hand, which he'd been holding, without realizing it, in a steely death grip. He stood, gave her his hand, and pulled her up, mouthing a 'thank you' to her as he did. "Ragno?"

"Here."

"Zeus. Sebastian here. I'm en route. Was working remotely near New Orleans. Wheels were up five minutes ago. One hour forty minutes away from landing in Miami. I'll take the lead." He drew a deep breath. "Won't let you take the helm so don't argue. Until I get there, Agent Blackwell is lead agent on the ground. He's on the call."

"Hello, sir. Standing by."

Blackwell was second in command on the Ana/Theresa security detail. Zeus himself had approved the parameters of the detail, once they'd adjusted on Thursday to include Ana's three-times a week, including Monday evening, dance classes.

On this Monday evening, at 1940 Eastern time, Zeus knew that Blackwell had been scheduled to be with Theresa, who'd had an evening of parent-teacher conferences planned at the school where she taught. The school where Ana went was also in Coconut Grove, just five blocks from Las Munequitas Dance Academy. Dance school was supposed to end at 1930, and from the dance school the team was supposed to take Ana to Theresa. From Theresa's school the two vehicles were to convoy for the drive to Fisher Island, where Theresa and Ana lived. Their condo was in the same building as his. That way, when he was in town, Ana was free to pop in at any time, even on days that technically weren't his days with her pursuant to the custody decree.

I'll die without her.

Can't think like that.

Agent Martel—Nanny Vick to Ana, so much like family she'd become simply Vick to Zeus—was first in command. Her absence from the call became deafening. "Vick?"

"Taken with Ana," Sebastian responded in the matter-of-fact, calm tone that he used when on a high-stakes job.

"Theresa?"

"Safe," Blackwell responded, tone low. "I've delivered the news, sir."

"Where is she?" No one had to tell him how Theresa was

reacting.

"Still at her job, where I am. She's with friends, in the teacher's lounge. My eyes are on her. MPD has patrols outside."

"I'll talk to her in a minute."

"Hey, bro," Gabe broke into the call. "I'm on the call from the airbase in Germany. Making strategic calls to local law enforcement at home." Home being Miami, the place where Gabe and Zeus grew up, the place they knew like the back of their hands. The place where his daughter was supposed to be safe. "Putting out a Black Raven version of a fucking Amber alert. Should I head to Miami?"

"No. Assume you're still heading into Praptan on Tuesday night. Whether or not Stollen gives us anything. If you find Maximov, I'm giving you the green light to torture the fucker until he tells you where we can find Ana."

Because his gut was screaming that all of this—the ITT trial, Maximov, the abduction—was related.

"You'll have her before then," Gabe said.

Zeus drew a deep breath, hoping like hell Gabe was right. "What happened to the rest of Ana's transport team?"

"From the team of four, two of them—Riggs and Looms—are dead," Sebastian responded. "One—Sanchez—is critical. Bullet to the head. Alive, but unconscious."

Fuck.

"Did we get any of them?"

"No. We're thirty minutes out now."

Zeus adjusted his watch to 2025. Current Miami time. He split-screened it to a stopwatch. "1955 was zero?"

"Yes. That was the time the distress call came out from the Range Rover transporting Ana, and the time Martel and Ana's GPS went off grid."

Drawing a deep breath, he managed to choke out, "Fucking GPS has been gone this entire time?"

"Yes," Sebastian answered. "We're dealing with pros, or damn smart amateurs who anticipated that Ana and her agents would be chipped and they knew how to effectively work jammers."

Or they cut the chip out of them.

Don't go there.

"Any leads at all?"

"Not yet. From what we can tell, it was an ambush at a stop sign. Narrow residential side streets of the Grove worked against us. No crime cameras on site." Sebastian gave him the intersection.

It was three blocks out from the dance school, which itself was located in a small strip mall. Zeus knew the area well.

"I'm collecting crime camera footage from the area," Ragno said. "However, other than the camera on our vehicle, there are no cameras within three blocks of the abduction site. Our cameras captured partials. Nothing solid."

"Who is on scene?"

"MPD. Forensics and investigators. Area's now shut down," Sebastian answered. "Police Chief Manuello is there, communicating directly with Ragno and Denver through Gabe." Manuello was an acquaintance of Zeus and a close friend of Gabe. "We had three teams working in the Miami area on other jobs. Three of our agents from those teams are now on scene. We've mobilized everyone at Last Resort. Twenty agents are on their way with combat choppers. Twenty-five more are on standby, ready to depart for parts unknown."

"C130J?" As with other operations that went to hell, the Black Raven cargo plane that they kept stationed in Colorado, and the assortment of weapons and manpower provided reaction capabilities for whatever was thrown their way. He wanted every bit of firepower the plane was capable of carrying, because he was going to unleash it on the fuckers who dared to touch his daughter.

"Mobilizing. They'll be in the air in ten minutes."

Zeus drew a deep breath. "Blackwell, put Theresa on the line."

He shut his eyes, bracing for her anguish. It came, with chokes and sobs and gasps for air. "Zeus, I'm sorry. You tried to tell me no. It was just dance school. She didn't need to go. You were right. I'm sor—"

"Listen to me. Not your fault. Do you understand that? Theresa, we'll find her," he said, wishing he believed in a good outcome that went with those words. "She'll be fine."

He didn't know that, either. What he believed was he was going to ultimately find whoever was responsible. When he did, he was going to kill them.

Chapter Thirty-Two

Miami, Florida
Tuesday, February 8

"I have a read from Martell's chip," Ragno said, her audio feed automatically going to Zeus, Sebastian, and team leaders in a Black Raven staging hangar, at a private airport in Miami, Florida.

Zeus marked the time. It was 0730, Eastern time. A day, so far, that had been sent straight from hell. The balmy, but cool, air in the hangar became electrified, as everyone who heard Ragno stopped mid-sentence, mid-stride, mid-whatever-the-fuck they were doing.

He and Sebastian had been looking at a large-screen monitor showing a map of South Florida and talking to MPD Chief Manuello, and Lieutenant Colonel Simeon from the Florida Highway Patrol. With each hour that passed without a lead, the geographic area of concern expanded. They were eleven hours, five minutes post abduction.

Law enforcement officials in the entire state of Florida, and points beyond, were on alert. Without even knowing what the needle looked like, they were sifting through a haystack for it, and more hay was being piled upon the stack with every passing minute.

"The chip is off the coast of Boca Raton. One mile off. Perhaps two." Ragno read the longitude and latitude. "Agent Martel only. Not Ana. I repeat. I have a solid feed on Martel's chip. Not Ana. Agents Michaels and Getty? Copy?"

Zeus knew Michaels and Getty were lead agents on teams positioned in the water. Given that Miami and the rest of South Florida was surrounded by water, and they had no leads pointing to an exit on any roadways, they'd anticipated the need for a maritime rescue.

"Michaels. Copy that. Sir? Awaiting instruction."

"Getty. Ditto."

"Standby," Sebastian said. "Ragno, give me a map and nautical chart." Working from Denver, Ragno switched the large screen monitor to a map highlighting the coastline. "Red x is the chip. Appears stationary. If she's moving, she's going no faster than the current."

Shit! Stationary?

In the fucking water? As far north as Boca?

Hell, by now, the kidnappers could have gotten as far as the Bahamas. Easily.

"Swimming?" Zeus asked, his eyes fixated on the x. He tried hard not to humanize the x, at the same time he wondered where the hell Ana was.

"Perhaps."

"Ragno," Sebastian asked, "what are seas right now?"

"Three to fives. Larger swells coming from the North."

In other words, high.

"Our teams in the water are here." A Black Raven logo lit up on the map as Ragno worked from Denver. "That's Agent Michaels. He's off of Miami, near the Government Cut inlet." Another Black Raven logo appeared on the map just south of Fort Lauderdale. "That's Getty."

"Getty and Michaels. Proceed to Martell's position." Sebastian glanced at Zeus, who stood at Sebastian's right. "Getty's closest. Maybe an hour out."

"Coast Guard is already on alert," Zeus said.

Sebastian nodded, his eyes on the map. "Ragno, contact Lake Worth Inlet Coast Guard station. Request an assist. Marks. Brachs?"

"Yes, sir," the voices of two helicopter team leaders answered.

"Mobilize. Stat. Take divers."

Zeus was torn. Vick was there. Not Ana. Hell. Maybe not Ana. And if the kidnappers had cut the chip out of Vick, maybe she wasn't even there. But maybe they were both there. His people wouldn't know, until they reached the area and searched it.

Kidnapping—rather than outright murder—implied that they'd use Ana for barter, but the terrorists could be doing just that—terrorizing. Distracting. If that was their end, they were doing a damn good job of both. Whether they wanted to use Ana for barter was a moot point, until they actually made a demand.

Zeus hoped like hell they'd try barter.

Damn straight he'd bargain with them.

Yet if the abductors were related, in any way, to the people who'd murdered Patricia Devlin, the wife of Judge Kent Devlin, or Madeline Brier, the wife of Robert Brier, he was fucked. Because they hadn't used Patricia Devlin or Madeline Brier for barter. Neither of the others was abducted. They were ambushed and killed. Murder had been sufficient to get their point out to the world that Maximov was an insidious force, capable of wreaking havoc on a court that was supposed to be stopping cells that claimed to operate on his behalf. What they were doing with his daughter was different. For now, he had to cling to that difference, as though it had meaning.

"Sebastian." Zeus had to stop the swirling thoughts that were expanding in his head. To do that, he needed to move. "I'm going with the choppers."

If I stay still for one more fucking minute I'll go crazy.

"Agree." Sebastian said, reading his mind with a glacial cool, seemingly unruffled, once over. Sebastian, mic'd to Ragno and all the team leaders, would be able to orchestrate the operation while on the go. "We'll take the Sikorsky. Marks and Brachs will have full teams in the Bell 525s," Sebastian said. "If we're in the Sikorsky, we can go elsewhere. Fast. If needed."

As Sebastian directed the Sikorsky pilot to mobilize, Zeus turned to the large, open doors of the hangar. His eyes immediately found Sam. Several long tables with electrical outlets had been set up in the middle of the room. Agents with duties that required laptops and tablets were sitting there, working. Upon their arrival at the hangar, Sam had established a workstation for herself at one of the tables, and whenever he turned in her direction, her blond ponytail caught his eye. As Zeus paced around the hangar, he'd stopped by her workstation several times.

The horror he was going through over Ana enabled him to park his feelings about Sam's rejection elsewhere. Perhaps never to be retrieved. Nothing he was going to worry about until he had his baby girl safely in his arms.

Sam was a professional, and so was he. They were both able to work in times of crisis. She'd been communicating with Abe and Charles, who were now midway through the Tuesday ITT proceedings in London. She'd also been preparing for Stollen's interview, and, because Zeus was focused on Ana, she was now communicating directly with Gabe on all issues related to Stollen.

She stood, closing her laptop, with Jenkins was at her side. Raven One was preparing to depart to Colorado.

"Jenkins," Zeus said, stepping between his agent and Sam. "Keep me on audio, along with Ragno and Gabe. You're lead for Sam's detail, as of now. Gabe has overall responsibility for the Amicus team detail, but you're his second if and when he goes to Praptan. Feel free to bounce issues off of me. If I'm not responding, due to my preoccupation with killing the fuckers who have my daughter, use Gabe and Ragno."

He nodded. "Understood, sir."

Sam zipped her briefcase. Jenkins took it from her. She turned to Zeus, reached for his forearm, and gripped it. Her eyes, full of concern, matched the earnest worry in her soft tone. "I hope and pray, with every fiber of my being, that you find her."

He nodded. Couldn't do much else, because the compassion she conveyed made him want to reach out and hold onto the woman he loved, until he found strength to move forward.

Do not falter.

No emotion. Remember? Send your feelings to the fucking stratosphere, into a galaxy far, far away.

Her eyes hardened. As though she knew him well enough to know that he couldn't handle any outpouring of empathy. Taking her hand off his arm, she lifted her chin. "I've got a question regarding the Black Raven data gathering and assimilation system that produced OLIVER. Or the job that produced OLIVER."

Jigsaw. "Which I haven't acknowledged?"

Sebastian, on his audio feed, said, "Zeus. Three minutes. Wheels up."

To Sam, Zeus said, "Walk with me."

Jenkins flanked her right side.

She fell into step with Zeus as he walked to the door of the hangar. "The one that produced Caller X. I know Barrows has to be using it to search the Miami telecommunication grid right now. Right?"

He nodded.

"Are you finding some commonality? Some clue?"

"Not yet. Unfortunately." As they exited the hangar, a blast of balmy wind whipped them. He had to yell to be heard over the *chop-chop-chop* of the helicopter rotors. "This kind of data collection and assimilation takes time. We're only now receiving results from the searches Barrows did in connection with the murder of Patricia Devlin. If the fuckers had left a phone behind, though, all bets would be off."

"Why?"

"It gives us a concrete base of known contacts. I'm not saying our program won't eventually get to the same answer, but it operates faster when we start with known contacts." When they were twenty yards away from the helicopter, Sebastian passed him, going at a jog. Zeus pointed in the direction of Raven One.

"You'll be safe with Jenkins. We're also beefing up your detail once you arrive in Colorado. Intention could be to make Black Raven's guard go down."

He paused as a flash of worry crossed her face. "They will fail in that objective." This was a goodbye, and he was too numb to care. That was the beauty of parking emotions in a different galaxy. He didn't feel a goddamn thing. "You'll be just as safe now as you were before. Jenkins has a direct line to me, and Gabe. Gabe will be your go-to if I'm unavailable."

Before he turned to the Sikorsky, and she turned for Raven One, she gripped his hand. Looking down, her engagement ring caught his gaze, carrying him back to the evening before when his broken heart had seemed like a problem. Now, a mere broken heart—of the romantic kind—seemed so inconsequential it was laughable. "If there is anything at all I can do, I'll do it."

He nodded. A world of people were offering assistance. He'd gladly take it all, if it would help. Even if finding Ana required calling in every goodwill chip—and there were plenty—that he'd laid out on behalf of Black Raven, he'd do so.

She gripped his hand tighter. "You'll find her."

"Yes," he said, his voice as cold as his insides had become. "I will."

Because I will never stop looking. I'll find her, even if I'm only finding a memory in the minds of the monsters who've taken her. No matter how I find her, I'll make them pay.

One hour later, they had what the bastards had left of Agent Victoria Martell. Ana's beloved Nanny Vick. She'd been decapitated, her naked torso strapped onto an open-air life raft. The words *I am Maximov* had been carved into her abdomen with a knife. With her torso, there was a handwritten note in a watertight box that had directions on how Zeus was to secure Ana. The kidnappers would release her, to her mother—and only her mother—unharmed, under two conditions.

One, Zeus would take Ana's place.

No problem.

Two, Richard Barrows would accompany Zeus.

Big problem.

Chapter Thirty-Three

"Tell me, Ms. Fairfax. Why should I agree to answer your questions?" Vladimer Stollen, who'd been born in Chalinda and lived in Praptan until the 1986 nuclear disaster, spoke English with a heavy accent that indicated Russian—the native language of Chalinda—was his first and primary language. His thinning, close-cropped black hair was peppered with gray. His orange jumpsuit, the standard uniform of inmates at ADX Florence, Colorado, cast a yellowish pall on his pale complexion. He was middle-aged, thin, pale, and clean-shaven. He was unremarkable looking, but for the intensity in his ice-cold-killer blue eyes. All of that intensity was focused directly across the table, at Samantha.

Impeccably dressed in a navy blue suit, Brier sat to the right of Stollen. Deep creases and dark circles around Brier's gray-green eyes indicated that his life, now marred by the murder of his wife, had become hell. Now, he was doing his job, letting his client have his say, and giving Samantha a steady, wary look that told her she was on her own. He had, after all, opposed her request for the interview. The ITT lead prosecutor from the United States, Benjamin McGavin, sat to Samantha's left, not at her side but in a chair at the head of the table.

Samantha focused on Stollen. *Please. Please God. Make this monster of a human being say something helpful. Please.*

And help me focus, because whenever I blink, I see Ana.

Photographs of Ana, some alone, some with Zeus and Theresa, others with Zeus alone, had been continuously streamed onto a monitor in the Black Raven hangar for hours overnight. The memory of her sweet voice, overjoyed at telling her daddy hello, in the video conference that Zeus had with her just a few days earlier made the photos all the more poignant.

And I see Zeus.

Jenkins had given her the grim news about Agent Martel, sharing with her the demand of the terrorists. He didn't know, or wouldn't tell her, whether Black Raven—whether Zeus—would comply. If it was just a case of trading himself for his daughter, Samantha knew unequivocally that of course he would comply. But handing Barrows over to terrorists—that was the sticking point. Her heart torqued tighter in her chest, while her stomach twisted with fear.

Stop. Focus.

The interrogation room had a dingy white tile floor, walls that were painted an even dingier white, no windows, and one stainless steel, rectangular table. Six matching aluminum chairs were bolted to the ground. Cameras and recording devices watched them, unblinking, in one corner of the ceiling. A television monitor in the opposite corner showed Judge O'Connor, wearing a black robe, reading through a stack of papers as he waited for this interview to proceed. There was one door.

Two prison guards, along with security—including Agents Jenkins, Miles, and Deal—were in the hallway outside the door. Four other Black Raven agents—new members of her protective detail—were strategically placed throughout the prison. Samantha wore a wire, and had an almost-invisible Black Raven audio feed in her right ear, concealed by her hair. Gabe was listening. He'd break in with questions for her to ask Stollen, if and when anything Stollen said became relevant to the Black Raven planned mission into Praptan.

"Yesterday evening Mr. Brier presented the terms of the deal I'm offering you. You informed him you would talk."

She glanced at Brier. He was a formidable opponent, but he didn't deserve what had happened. He'd long been a defender of people such as Stollen. Brier's advocacy had ensured that even the worst of the worst received trials that were fair and that the justice system operated in a manner that actually did justice. For all of his hard work, due to his spotlighted presence at the busy intersection of justice and terrorism, terrorists had murdered his wife. Presumably the same terrorists who had murdered Patricia Devlin and who had now kidnapped Ana.

Whether those terrorists were related, in any way, to Stollen, the client who Brier was now defending, was anybody's guess. It was a crapshoot of horrors, and the dice were rolling as unpredictably as ever.

Samantha was guessing yes.

Praying for yes.

Brier obviously didn't think so, because he wouldn't be there, facilitating an interview that would earn Stollen a measure of freedom. At every chance he got, Brier argued that Stollen—who'd been imprisoned seven years earlier—could have no bearing on any crime after he was imprisoned.

The burial of Madeline Brier, who had been murdered five

days earlier, on Thursday, had been early Monday morning. Memorial services for Patricia Devlin, who had been murdered six days earlier, on Wednesday, had been on Saturday evening. As of Tuesday morning, both men had returned to work. Judge Devlin was now in London, and Brier was in Colorado.

Please God, let this monster tell me something that gives us a real break. Something that helps us find Maximov. Helps us find Ana.

McGavin sighed and shifted in his chair. He gave her a glance that indicated he was worried they were all wasting their time. It was the argument that he'd made in opposition to the motion to interview Stollen, and Sam had responded by arguing that covering every known base should not be considered a waste of time. Not when the stakes were this high. Her argument had persuaded the judges.

Dragging her eyes back to Stollen, she said, "I flew halfway across the world because you agreed to talk."

"And I am talking to you." Stollen leaned forward, as though enjoying their not-quite conversation. So far, Samantha had asked questions, and Stollen had not provided answers.

Chains looped through manacles at his ankles and wrists met in a lock at his waist. His hands, clasped together due to the tightness of the chain at his wrists, were on the stainless steel table that separated her from him. As he leaned forward, the chain slid along the edge of the table with a grinding, metal-on-metal sound that resonated through the small interrogation room.

"So I'm fulfilling my end of the bargain. I'm here. My mouth is moving. Give me a good reason why I should answer anything, baby doll?" His gaze travelled slowly from her eyes to her mouth, to her neck, and down her chest, where they lingered as he spoke. "Start again, slowly, and do your best to persuade me. Tell me the details of the leniency package."

Clear, cold, and calculating, his eyes provided a direct route to 2009. On a beautiful spring day, he and Vasily Maximov—Andre Maximov's son—had terrorized the world by almost succeeding in orchestrating a hijacking of Northern Lights flight 875. News shows had played endless footage of American fighter pilots shooting missiles into the civilian aircraft, an act that had stunned the world. One hundred forty-three souls—the number of innocent people aboard the aircraft—were sacrificed that day to avoid the civilian aircraft suicide crash into the United Nations headquarters, which would have killed far more. The footage from that day rubbed raw wounds from September 11, 2001, and reignited the ball of emotion-driven fury and fear that had been hoisted upon Americans with Osama bin Laden's attack on the twin towers.

Acutely aware that she was negotiating with the devil, Samantha allowed herself to return his gaze, forcing herself to focus only on the flesh, bones, and brain that made up the man. Not on anything he stood for. Not on any act he'd done. Not on her own memories of that day that were forever etched in United States history, where the military had been forced to kill one hundred forty-three innocents, because of this monster.

Focus.

If he knows something that will enable us to find Andre Maximov, you damn well need to know it.

Now.

But her mind and her thoughts were scattered across time zones. While it was 10:15 a.m. in Florence, Colorado, where she was conducting the interview of Stollen, in London, where Judge O'Connor and others from the ITT proceeding were listening to the interview, it was 4:15 p.m. ITT proceedings for Tuesday, February 8, had ended. It was 12:15 p.m. in Miami. Sixteen hours and twenty minutes post-kidnapping.

Don't think about it. Focus on the task at hand. Focus.

Calmly, as though she had all the time in the world, and wanted nothing more than to be sitting in the sterile white room with a convicted mass murderer, Samantha gave him a stony look, preparing, once again, to play his game and present the deal she was offering in the best light possible.

Be persuasive.

Persuasion took skills, from word choice to tone inflection to body language, and she was damn good at persuasion. God knew she had persuaded herself of enough in her own lifetime, just as right now she was persuading herself that she didn't love Zeus, that she needed to live her life without him, that her mind and heart weren't locked in a silent scream of anguish for the nightmare he was suffering.

Don't think about Zeus.

Don't think about how not having him at your side has created a void that you never imagined possible.

Don't think about the hell he is going through.

Task at hand.

She delicately cleared her throat and pushed some of her hair behind her left ear. She'd used a curling iron in the bathroom of Raven One, to make her hair a soft distraction for the monster who'd seen precious few women in the last seven years. Other than that, she'd dressed conservatively in a burgundy suit with a cream colored turtleneck. She'd put on makeup, but not much. Now, she was glad her suit was conservative, because Stollen's roaming, lingering eyes gave her chills.

"Listen closely, because I'm not repeating this. Upon your information producing the apprehension of Andre Maximov, you will immediately be released from ADX Florence to a private residence in the United States. You will be under house incarceration for life, but the premises of your incarceration include an extensive property and access to the outdoors."

"The house is on a small island. You will be its only inhabitant. You will be able to walk along the coastline. You will have freedom to manage your days as you see fit. You can sleep outdoors in a hammock, at night, under the moon and stars, or on long lazy afternoons." When he met her eyes, she gave him a soft smile as she ignored her churning insides. "Can you visualize that, Mr. Stollen?"

He drew a deep breath and nodded, matching her smile with a slight softening of his lips.

"On top of that, you will have Black Raven security protection for life."

She paused to let that thought sink into his murderous skull.

"Take it or leave it, Mr. Stollen. For a man who has spent most of his days in solitary confinement in this prison"—she gave him an arched eyebrow look of soft, feminine wonder—"I'm surprised you're even hesitating."

"Will I have access to news?"

"Yes." Samantha leaned forward on the table, putting herself a few inches closer to him. "You will have access to news via television, three newspapers of your choosing, and five magazines of your choosing. No access to computers, internet, or telephones. But still...imagine holding the remote control in your hand. For hours."

On her left, McGavin cleared his throat as he swallowed a chuckle.

Stollen gave her a full smile, revealing white teeth kept healthy, Samantha knew, compliments of U.S. taxpayers and prison dentistry. She wondered, for a moment, if yanking teeth—without novacaine—out of convicted of mass murderers would be a deterrent to crime.

Focus.

"Access to books?"

"Yes. Ten a month. More if wanted. Subject matter of your choosing."

"Access to women?"

"No," she said.

"I need pictures."

She paused. "Of?"

"My new home."

She shook her head. "I have them, but right now they're just photographs of a house and scenery. It isn't yours yet."

"It will be. Pictures, Ms. Fairfax."

Reaching into her briefcase for her laptop, she gripped it, pulled it out, stood, and moved to his side of the table. She opened the laptop next to him, sat in the chair next to him, and flicked her hair back behind her shoulders. Resting her hands on the keyboard, she opened his file, and started clicking. Images appeared on her screen—a quaint, wood-framed house, with a porch overlooking a deserted beach. A fireplace on the interior, with large windows in the living room and kitchen. A wooded path. Foamy waves crashing against rocks.

"Where is it?" Stollen asked. He'd asked the question before, and she'd told him she couldn't provide an answer. Geographic details that were too particular to any given region had been deleted through photo-shop. The location could have been anywhere.

"Precise location is a need-to-know basis. I don't know," she answered honestly. "And you also will never know. For now, all you need to know is that the self-contained island has a house on it, and you'll be able to walk along this beach"—she clicked to the photo of the beach, and the wooded path—"and through the interior area at any time you choose."

He sat back in his chair, with chains rattling as he placed his hands on his lap. "Ask your questions, Ms. Fairfax."

She opened the file of recent drone footage of Praptan, the haunting footage that Black Raven had acquired and shown to her, and played it. "This is what Praptan looks like today. If Maximov were hiding in Praptan, Chalinda, where would we—"

"Counselor," Brier said, "you're addressing an area that was not mentioned in your motion."

She gave Brier an arched eyebrow. "I know."

"I object. You're wasting time. Everything Mr. Stollen has to say about Praptan was covered extensively when he was interviewed in 2009. As you know, the information Mr. Stollen provided led to a search of Praptan in 2010."

"I know that, counselor. Which proved unsuccessful. Today I want to revisit that area with him."

"But—"

"Stop interrupting her, Brier." McGavin rose to his feet and used every bit of his prosecutorial imperiousness in his tone. "We're here. The court has sanctioned this interview, even if it is a waste of time. The court should let Ms. Fairfax explore any avenue she thinks worthwhile. I plan to do the same thing myself."

Brier also rose to his feet, glancing at the television monitor and drawing in a deep breath as he prepared to argue his case to the judge. "Your Honor, Ms. Fairfax is bringing up issues she didn't mention in her motion to interview Stollen. Her motion was simply a sham. If Ms. Fairfax is merely going to rehash the same material that was covered extensively in 2009, in Mr. Stollen's post-arrest debriefing, I request termination of the interview. Now. This must end. We all have more important things to do."

"Not all of us," Stollen said.

Samantha locked eyes with Stollen. Eyes pregnant with unsaid words, he was studying her. Throughout the argument among the lawyers, the killer's gaze—resting on her—had become less leering and lewd, than a look of cool, thoughtful, assessment.

As Brier paced a short path, back and forth, and gathered steam in his argument to Judge O'Connor, Stollen, lowering his voice, whispered to Sam, "I need to talk to you."

Samantha bolted upright, standing, and blocking Brier. "Your Honor, Mr. Brier is grandstanding. Yes, Praptan was covered years earlier, but the record of that proceeding is incomplete. Any information that Mr. Stollen—"

The judge raised his hand. "No need to continue with argument, Ms. Fairfax. Mr. Brier, your objection is noted, but overruled. Proceed with your questions, Ms. Fairfax."

"Wait," Stollen said, his eyes riveted on her laptop screen, which was playing the drone footage. "Stop it there."

She clicked on pause, and downtown Praptan, which now looked like buildings were growing out of a forest, froze on the screen. After a few seconds, he tore his eyes from the screen. "Replay it from the beginning."

As Samantha pressed rewind, then play, she gave Stollen a few minutes to see the footage of the now-derelict, overgrown city that had once been his home. "Mr. Stollen, I have the reports that were prepared from your debriefing interviews in 2009. What I'd like to do is go over a few of the statements that you made."

He nodded, his attention still focused on the video, which was now showing the University area. "I'd like to see the transcripts."

"I don't have those documents with me," Samantha bluffed. She didn't plan on telling Stollen she hadn't seen the transcript. Nor would she tell him one didn't exist.

Truth was, there was no transcript of the debriefing interviews in the record of the proceeding against Stollen. Samantha's knowledge of what Stollen said in those interviews came from a summary that was in the record of presentence proceedings, and the summary had few helpful details.

Gabe, his voice deep and quiet, said through the audio-feed in her ear, "I've read everything that Stollen ever said. There is no transcript of the debriefing interview anywhere. Only a summary report of what was said in the interview."

Her heart twisted, because there was no denying genetics. Gabe's rich voice sounded...like Zeus.

God, please let him be all right. Let him find his little girl.

Focus.

Task at hand.

The summary report on Stollen's debriefing that Samantha saw was compiled by the prosecutor who had conducted the 2009 interview. Brier and Stollen had both signed off on it. The lack of a transcript wasn't unusual in a file that was seven years old, compiled before electronic records were the norm in the federal judicial system.

"Mr. Stollen, transcripts aren't necessary. You either know places where Maximov might be, or you don't." She gestured with her chin to her laptop screen, which now showed the rusted and overgrown amusement park. "What you said in 2009 isn't necessarily relevant to information you provide today."

There was silence in the room as the video footage ended. Ice-blue eyes shifted back to her. "I didn't know they didn't find him."

"Holy shit," Gabe whispered.

Stunned, Samantha glanced at the television monitor. Judge O'Connor was leaning forward, his eyes intent on Stollen.

She managed, "You didn't know?"

"All I know, Ms. Fairfax, is that I was offered a deal, I gave information, and I've never heard back. My term of imprisonment remains fixed at life. I never actually expected the government to keep their end of the bargain. After all, the United States was instrumental in destroying my country."

"Mr. Brier—your lawyer—didn't inform you that Maximov wasn't found?" Judge O'Connor asked, with a frown.

"Over the last seven years, my lawyer," Stollen glanced at Brier, his tone bitter, "has had one-sided phone conversations with me and has mailed me pleadings that have been filed in my appeals. Today is the first day I've seen him since that interview in 2009."

"Then let me inform you." Samantha leaned forward. "Andre Maximov was not apprehended when authorities searched Praptan in 2009."

Tearing his glance from Brier, Stollen shook his head. "Did you say apprehended?"

"Yes. I said he was not apprehended. He remains at large. He, and the Maximov organization, are perpetrating criminal acts worldwide every day."

"Forgive me, Ms. Fairfax, for my lack of knowledge about current events. You see, I've been subject to seven years of solitary confinement. My only reading has been from the prison law library, which is out of date and deficient. With my prisoner designation, I haven't had access to news of any kind for seven years. My lawyer"—he glanced sideways at Brier—"told me yesterday that this interview is being conducted in connection with a trial. Is that correct?"

She nodded. "Yes."

"What are the issues that are being tried?"

She explained, quickly summarizing the four terrorist acts the ITT was examining and explaining that an issue the trial was considering was whether the terrorist cells were linked to Maximov and the Maximov-in-Exile organization.

When she was through, Stollen was silent. From the end of the table, McGavin's breathing was heavy. Brier remained standing, his back against the wall, facing them.

"Crimes conducted in the name of Andre Maximov and his organization occur daily," Samantha repeated. "It is an organization that has to be stopped, and to do that, we need Andre Maximov."

Stollen shifted in his seat. His chains rattled in protest as he leaned forward on the table with all of his attention focused on Brier. "You're fired."

"Excuse me?" Brier asked.

"You heard me." Turning to the monitor that showed Judge O'Connor, Stollen said, "And I do not want the prosecutor in this interview room, either. Just me and Ms. Fairfax. I want no one else to hear what I have to say."

"Your Honor—"

"Don't waste your breath, Mr. Brier. You will have an opportunity to explain yourself later, if needed."

"No explanation needed, your Honor. My client..." He caught himself with a headshake. "Former client, if he really intends to fire me, is a pathological liar and an extremely convincing one. That fact is well established in the record. He is now manipulating—"

"Mr. Brier, exit the room." Judge O'Connor was leaning forward, his eyes on Stollen. "Mr. Stollen, for this interview, you have the ability to fire your lawyer. You also do not need to have the prosecutor in the room. But my tolerance is stretched as far as it will be stretched, and unfortunately for you, this interview will not take place without my presence. Make this damn productive, or else this interview is terminated, and you can go back to your dark cell and live out the remainder of your days there. Brier and McGavin, leave the room. Now. The other parties who are in the courtroom with me are now exiting. Ms. Fairfax, would you bring a member of your security team into the room?"

After the requisite people movement occurred, Samantha nodded at Stollen. "Where can we find Andre Maximov?"

"Ms. Fairfax, take me to my island. Once I'm there, I will tell you where to find him. I'm not giving you any information while I'm in this prison."

"The person you have to persuade is Judge O'Connor." Samantha gestured with her chin to the television monitor.

Stollen turned to focus his attention on the monitor. "Once I have reached the island, once I walk on the beach and smell the fresh salt air, I will tell you and Ms. Fairfax precisely where to find Andre Maximov. Pardon my lack of trust, but this isn't the first time I've tried to tell authorities where to find him. The real question is this: Why didn't the authorities find him before? I certainly gave them a roadmap."

"It could be that Maximov simply wasn't using the hiding places with which you're familiar, Mr. Stollen," Samantha said.

"Impossible."

Judge O'Connor leaned forward, getting closer to the

monitor, giving the impression of eagerness to have a frank discussion. "Before we take you to the island, you must give us something to go on."

Stollen glanced at Samantha, then focused on the judge. "If you actually look for him this time around, you will know that I'm telling the truth. You will find him precisely where I say he is, because I am not a pathological liar, and I know with certainty where he is."

It was what she'd been hoping for when she'd requested the interview. Stollen's cold certainty, though, begged a question to which there could only be one answer, and the answer meant the world had been duped. "How do you know with such certainty where he is?"

"It's very simple." Stollen's smile sickened her. "Andre Maximov is dead."

Chapter Thirty-Four

Maximov's name sliced into Agent Martel's torso sealed the deal on any speculation whether the kidnaping was related to the ITT trial.

Undeniably yes.

The instructions accompanying her body were explicit. At precisely 1915, Zeus, Barrows, and Theresa were to skydive to a remote location in the desert in the State of Chihuahua, Mexico. No firearms, no GPS trackers, no backup, no law enforcement.

The perps claimed to have surveillance for a fifty-mile radius. No telecommunication devices were to be carried. No GPS transmitters of any kind—internal or external—were allowed. Every move they made would be under surveillance.

Upon arriving at the drop zone, Theresa would be reunited with Ana. No Black Raven vehicle or plane was to approach the drop zone to pick up mother and daughter until 2015. Ana's life depended upon strict adherence to instructions.

Zeus didn't have to be told twice. Strict adherence, though, was a matter of interpretation. How much he could deviate, without causing his daughter's death, was a judgment call.

Intel told them the drop zone, DZ for short, was in a valley in a desolate, isolated area of the Chihuahuan desert. Miles away from any known road. Hills to the East. A canyon to the West. Caves, both natural and manmade from now-abandoned mining activities, peppered the area. In the near vicinity, there were tunnels to facilitate transporting illegal aliens, drugs, and weapons across the border. Ragno and her team were collecting intel on the tunnel system.

The manner of transmitting the message was foolproof. Not one clue came from Martel's body or the life raft, which had been saturated with salty ocean water from rough seas where the raft had been dumped. Non-negotiability was firmly established by mode of transmission, because the perps sure as hell didn't leave a return number.

Once they received the instructions, he and Sebastian, with assistance from an army of agents and analysts, had planned for any contingency. They scrambled and shifted their primary base of operations—manned by Sebastian—to an airport outside of

Odessa, Texas. From there, they ran parallel scenarios. One—the perps kept the action in desolate areas of Mexico, or nearby. Another—the entire Mexican stop was a smokescreen.

They prepared for the eventuality that they'd have to move in another direction, fast.

Each scenario twisted with every variable Zeus, Sebastian, Ragno and their team leaders could devise. Given the operational experience of the agents, the variables were plentiful. Black Raven's C-130J cargo plane was circling a route from El Paso, Texas, over the city of Ciudad, Juarez, and on to Chihuahua City, the capital of the State of Chihuahua, at 27,000 feet. The minute intel provided a clue as to where-the-fuck it should go, airborne hell would descend, mobilize, and unleash its fury. More agents assembled in Ciudad, Juarez, the Mexican city closest to the DZ.

"Zeus," Sebastian said, "you're watching the time?"

Zeus glanced at his watch. 1830. One hour and forty-five minutes before jump time. "Yeah. Each passing second."

Twenty-three hours, twenty-five minutes post kidnapping.

It was fucking impossible to stay focused when he knew stats that came at him, randomly. Seventy-five percent of abducted children are murdered are dead within three hours of their abduction. Estimates were that at least twenty percent of children involved in nonfamily abductions were not found alive. Those facts, taken together, painted a bleak picture.

The perps knew a father would come. That was a given. But they must know he was coming anyway, because he'd gladly hand them his own life if there was any chance to save hers. But there was absolutely no reason to keep a child alive, when dead would be easier.

Fuck.

Zeus, his ex, Barrows, and fifty Black Raven agents had assembled at a small corporate airport outside of El Paso, Texas. The jump would take place from a Black Raven Cessna. He and Agent Sylvia Leon—a Black Raven agent impersonating Theresa, would tandem jump. In real life Theresa had no clue how to skydive. He had no clue whether the perps knew that fact, but they decided Agent Leon would stay in character from the beginning. In character meant tandem jumping. Agent Dennis Cox—the agent impersonating Barrows—would solo jump.

The remaining Black Raven agents who were operating out of the El Paso airport, and agents on standby at an airstrip in Ciudad, Juarez, would be ready to deploy. The agents had Cessnas, choppers, Range Rovers, all-terrain jeeps and motorcycles. They'd deploy when it was deemed safe, determined by when Ana was in the arms of Agent Leon—as Leon imitated Theresa—and on her way away from the perps. Away. In any fucking direction Agent Leon deemed safe.

Not necessarily on the timeline set by the perps.

Sebastian, Ragno, and Zeus had thought hard about implanting a comm device in Zeus's ear and the agents who were going to accompany him. Black Raven was testing devices that were no larger than a grain of rice. The problem? Even their most sophisticated comm devices were detectable by state-of-the-art scanners. Given how the perps had managed to detect and use Martel's GPS chip to their advantage, they'd deemed it too risky to implant comm devices. Following the instructions they'd been given, GPS chips had been removed from Zeus, Leon, and Cox.

Every now and then a team leader stepped into the small conference room where he, Theresa, Agent Leon, Barrows, and Agent Cox were prepping. The utilitarian room, with out-of-date magazines and a basket of bagged snacks that no one felt like eating, carried the weight of each minute.

Sebastian was commanding operations from the Odessa hangar, where more agents were awaiting instructions. He was live on a video monitor that hung in the conference room. Sebastian kept everyone in the loop, his voice low, quiet, and constant. Ragno, from home base in Denver, was ever present on the audio-feed in Zeus's ear.

Tearing his attention from a map of Eastern Mexico and West Texas he'd been studying on his laptop, and the stream of intel that Ragno was layering on the map, Zeus glanced at his ex. Theresa, in a chair next to him, had her knees drawn up. Her forehead rested on them and she was hugging them close. Her dark hair had mostly slipped out of a clip and fallen around her face. In the hours post-kidnaping, she'd gone through crying jags and anxious pacing. When she stopped blaming herself, she'd started blaming him.

He let his ex have her say. No need to stop her tirade, because he also blamed himself. For a million reasons. Most started with taking the Amicus team job for the wrong fucking reason—to be near a woman who made it clear he was best viewed in hindsight. Maybe if he'd spent more time thinking while on the job, rather than fucking, his daughter's life wouldn't be in jeopardy.

If it hasn't already ended.

Thankfully, by midafternoon, Theresa had slipped into a

quiet state, her ability to get through each long minute seemingly hanging on nothing but blind faith in Zeus's assurances that their daughter would soon be in her arms.

Dear God, make it happen.

"Zeus." Sebastian focused on him from the monitor, his expression no less intent than if he was standing next to him. "You did that thing Gabe and I suggested?"

"Not yet."

Sebastian gave him an intense *what the fuck are you waiting for* look. "Think how much something like this would've mattered to you. I'm going to be real honest here." His friend and partner lowered his voice, as though that would keep half of Black Raven from listening to him. "Tonight carries a great bit of risk. FUBAR is a possibility. You know that."

Understatement. Fucked up beyond all repair—FUBAR. Reality was, the priority order for this rescue mission meant Zeus probably wouldn't make it out alive.

Zeus understood why the bad guys wanted Barrows, because everyone did. Even if they didn't have a need for Barrows' cyber genius, the man was worth a fortune at a black-market auction, merely for what the man carried in his head. Though there was one niggling thought that Sebastian, Ragno, and Zeus had all voiced—why Barrows and why now?

It was a question to which they'd find an answer. Eventually.

He was willing to die to save his daughter. Yet he sure as fuck didn't want to subject the agents who had volunteered to impersonate Theresa and Barrows to the same fate. Hence the priority order for the rescue:

Priority One: Ana.

Priority Two: Agent Leon—as she impersonated Theresa and rescued Ana.

Priority Three: Agent Cox—as he impersonated Barrows, Black Raven's most valuable asset.

Priority Four: Zeus—Only after Ana, Leon, and Cox were safely returned to the Black Raven fold.

The priority was consistent with how they'd operate if they weren't using doubles. A major flaw with using impersonators was that the perps could figure out the fakes. Zeus doubted it would happen with Leon—she'd transformed herself into a virtual double of dark-haired Theresa. Cox, an agent whose impersonation skills were part of his unique skill set, had, throughout the day, transformed himself into a man who bore an uncanny resemblance to Barrows. Yet there was no telling how much the perps knew about Barrows, who until his incarceration had been a public figure, making routine appearances on news shows.

Zeus had to assume they'd eventually figure out Cox wasn't Barrows—because only Barrows had his unique capability for data analysis and computer programming. Uncovering the fake could take hours or days. When they did, they'd kill Cox. Which made it necessary for them to extract Cox as soon as Ana and Leon were safe. By then, Zeus would likely be dead—because if the goal was to kill him, there was no reason to keep him alive. Zeus had insisted that no one attempt to rescue him until Cox was safe. Hence the thing that Gabe and Sebastian had suggested—which Zeus had put off for as long as possible.

Time's almost up.

"Cox, Leon—we're fifteen minutes from departure." Zeus drew a deep breath. "Last chance to head for the hills." He managed a forced, strained smile. *Never let them see you sweat.* "I'd understand if you changed your minds."

Leon glanced at him. Five years in Black Raven and on her way to being one of the elite agents called in for high-risk jobs. She'd excelled in her work, aced every test ever given to her, and had recently completed a harrowing survivalist course with eleven male agents. She gave him a slow shake of her head, in character as Theresa. Speaking with the forthright, but frightened tone that Theresa, a high school teacher used, said, "No, sir. Won't happen. I'm honored to be a part of the team that rescues your little girl. Thank you for the opportunity."

Cox, looking like an uncanny resemblance of Barrows—from the blue eyes to the salt-and-pepper hair, to the absentminded glance he gave Zeus, said, "Sir. I echo Leon. Besides," he lowered his voice to the tone used by Barrows, with a slight Northeastern accent, "I absolutely live for operations like this."

"Thank you. Both of you."

"You're welcome, sir," Leon said. Cox gave a nod of agreement. They resumed their tasks—Cox, stepping into the jumpsuit he'd wear for the jump, and Leon, pinning her shoulder-length black hair, cut to look like Theresa's, back before putting on her helmet.

Theresa still had her head buried on her knees. Barrows, pecking at his laptop, gave Zeus an absent-minded nod and continued typing, his narrow-eyed focus directed solely at his laptop screen. The seeming absentmindedness of the genius was something Zeus had gotten used to in the last year. Blue-eyed, with salt-and-pepper, thinning hair, Barrows had mostly recovered from the torture he suffered at the hands of James Trask. He still walked with a limp in his left leg, though—compliments of the sick, sadistic Trask. Even though he hadn't been in the public eye after the kidnaping, and it was unlikely the perps knew about the limp, Cox had perfected an imitation of the man's gait.

Upon arriving at the airstrip, Barrows divided his time between his laptop, the wall-mounted monitor that showed his son-in-law, Sebastian, and Cox. Agent Cox had been Barrows' shadow, giving himself a crash course on mimicking the eccentric genius.

When Barrows had heard the terms of the demand, he insisted on accompanying Zeus to the DZ. Everyone else in Black Raven who had a voice—Zeus, Sebastian, and every partner in the company—had insisted that he not. Barrows' work was too important, they'd reasoned. Jigsaw, and a host of other projects that now relied on the genius's cyber-capabilities, would be crippled without him.

Barrows glanced at Zeus and said without preamble, "Jigsaw gives the probability of the death of Maximov as early as 2007, as Vladimer Stollen claimed in his interview today, a high probability of eighty-two percent. However...it matters not."

Matters not? Zeus knew where Barrows was going, but the leap of logic was a big one. That Maximov could be dead, as Stollen had claimed in the interview, was earth-shattering.

Ragno and Gabe had given Zeus the details of the interview. After telling Sam and Judge O'Connor that Maximov had died in 2007, Stollen had explained that he took up the reigns of the Maximov-In-Exile organization from 2007 to 2009. Stollen claimed to know where Maximov's body was buried in Praptan, because Stollen had buried him. Sam had pressed Stollen for more details. She'd explained that authorities weren't likely to believe his claim that Maximov was dead, since Stollen had not told authorities of Maximov's death in 2009. Stollen had insisted to Judge O'Connor and Sam that he did previously tell authorities of Maximov's death.

He'd also told them where they could find Maximov's body. With Stollen's information, there was only one thing to do. Gabe was now mobilizing for the trip into Praptan to see if Stollen was telling the truth.

Barrows continued, "Even if we recover Maximov's remains, we still need to figure out who is, and who has been, pulling the strings of the cells claiming to operate on behalf of Maximov. Jigsaw is now assessing the parameters of the kidnaping. The dropping of a body on a life raft in the Atlantic Ocean, the logistical difficulty of transporting a child from Coconut Grove, Florida, to the desert of Chihuahua, and constructing tunnels of the scale that Ragno is now placing on the map, and..."

Zeus nodded as though he was listening, but tuned Barrows out. Black Raven's most valuable asset tended to ramble things to the Denver-based analysts that made no sense to people who didn't have innate knowledge of cyber-jargon, algorithms, and statistics. Even when not addressing intricate details of Jigsaw, Barrows's thought processes were often a distraction, when—like now—every second mattered.

In the final fifteen minutes, Zeus would prefer to focus on agent deployment, strategic use of assets, firepower, and whether to trust any goddamn thing that Blaze—with Protectors of Peace—told them.

Zeus and Sebastian had struck a deal with the devil.

West Texas was the birthplace of the Protectors, after all, and the bordering land of Mexico was also part of their claimed gangland territory. It was the reason why Zeus had searched out Blaze within a minute of reading the instructions left with Agent Martel.

"Sebastian, Zeus, I've managed to integrate Protectors of Peace intel," Ragno said. "It isn't particularly encouraging in terms of pinpointing likely geographic locations where Zeus and Cox will end up. Whether Blaze's information will lead to rescuing Zeus and Cox—"

"Wrong order, Ragno," Zeus interrupted. "Cox first. Before me."

"Understood. Well, whether the intel from the Protectors will lead to us finding you after Ana and Agent Leon are in the fold, or whether it is yet another distraction, is anyone's guess."

Zeus stared at the twisted, worm-like maze that was now appearing in 3-D on the map of West Texas and Eastern Mexico. Subterranean tunnels? Cutting through West Texas, snaking under the border, and into the Chihuahuan desert?

Ragno was using the map to highlight the intel that Blaze had provided in terms of a likelihood that the subterranean routes would be used and coordinating that intel with information obtained through Jigsaw.

If the TRCR were the ones who had Ana.

If they planned to utilize the tunnel system.

If Blaze's information was accurate.

If Blaze could be trusted.

For fuck's sake. There are way too many goddamn fucking ifs and the first if is if my daughter is still alive, because there was no goddamned contact info on Martel's body, there was no way to demand proof of life for Ana.

The father in him felt growing fear and wrenching heartache that his baby girl might very well be dead, and this was all an elaborate trap to capture Barrows and take Zeus out of the picture. A win-win for whomever had snatched Ana. To them, a child would be an inconvenience.

There is just no reason to keep her alive. Unless they know what Black Raven stands for. Unless they knew they'll be hunted to the ends of the earth and their bodies chopped with a dull knife to chum-sized pieces if they dared to cross the line and kill a child of a Black Raven agent.

Oh God. My baby girl.

The Black Raven agent in him ignored the terror and dread, and focused laser-like on all the information, and variables from the information, as the data rolled in. If Ana was dead or alive didn't change what had to be done in the next few hours, because someone had picked a really big fight, and Black Raven would rise to the occasion. This bully needed to be stopped. There was no going back. No second-guessing the decision to follow the kidnappers' instructions.

Zeus forced himself to listen to Ragno.

"We've known of tunnels along the U.S./Mexico border for years, but what Blaze is telling us about far exceeds any intel we have. And he claims they're all utilized by the TRCR. Safe to say, if we don't succeed in rescuing you quickly, it could be days before we find you."

"Ragno. Sebastian," Zeus said. "Keep in mind that for all we know, Blaze and his Protectors of Peace are the perps."

"Understood," Sebastian said.

"I'm not so sure," Ragno said. "If so, this would be the first time the Protectors have shown an affiliation with Maximov or the ITT. Also, I've looked a little more into Blaze and the Protectors since your phone call with him. Kidnapping a young girl would be inconsistent with their code of conduct, as indicated by their activities of record."

"Good to know. Theresa." Zeus placed a gentle hand on his ex's shoulder. With his other hand, he reached into his briefcase, found his iPhone, and held it in his hand for a moment, without taking it out. The device weighed heavy in his hands, for reasons that had nothing to do with how much it weighed.

His ex lifted her head and stared blankly at him. He caught a tear on his fingertip, a gesture he hadn't done with her in a long, long time—even though there'd been plenty of tears. He held her chin up so her gaze remained on his. "I'm sorry that you're going through this. She'll be there. She'll be fine. Trust me on this. Okay?"

"Send her back to me." More tears started falling. "And be safe."

Nice of his ex to include the afterthought. He patted her on the head as she put it back down on her knees, her shoulders shaking with her sobs. Standing, he turned and walked to the corner of the conference room and entered the bathroom. There were two stalls. Both empty. Zeus locked the outer door and turned his back to the mirror. He drew a deep breath, lifted the phone, and couldn't start.

"Ragno," he said through his audio feed, dropping his hand with the iPhone to thigh level, "what's going on with Gabe and Sam?"

"Sam landed. She's aboard Raven One, stationed a half-hour from the island. Stollen will reach the island in one hour. Gabe's ready to depart from the base in Germany. The window for reaching Maximov's body is five to seven hours."

"Why so long?"

"Radiation concerns. Circuitous route necessary."

"Once we have remains, we'll do DNA testing. At most, six hours after acquiring remains we'll know whether the body is Andre Maximov by doing a paternity test from Vasily Maximov's DNA."

"How is Sam doing?"

A pause. "You could talk to her. You have a few minutes."

"Asking you."

"Stressed. Anxious, but still cool and professional. She keeps asking Gabe and Jenkins about you and Ana. They've given her the standard answer." *Operation in progress. No details can be provided.* "Which I'm suspecting isn't helping her stress level."

"Let her know when they've secured Ana."

"Will do. Geez, Zeus, if Maximov is really dead, this throws a monkey wrench in the ITT trial. Samantha has been on the phone with President Cameron and Judge O'Connor, trying to reason through the implications."

"Ten minutes out, Zeus," Sebastian cut into the audio feed.

"Ragno. Sebastian. I'm going silent for a few minutes."

Zeus pressed his watch, muting their connection. He raised his phone to his face, switched the camera view, drew a deep breath, looked into the lens, and hit video. "Hey, my sweet angel. Just thought I'd tell you how much I... He swallowed hard. "Love you. You know I don't talk about feelings much." He visualized his daughter, her sweet, velvety brown eyes, and almost stopped recording. Clearing his throat, keeping his eyes steady, he imagined what his own father would have said, if given a chance for one last heart to heart talk, and continued. "Uncle Gabe and Sebastian are going to decide when you're old enough to see this, so...you may have figured out some of these things on your own."

He ticked off the laundry list of items he felt the need to remind her about. *Homework's important. Listen to your mom. Tell her you love her. What happened between your mom and me wasn't her fault. Try hard to find something you love to do, and do it every day. Don't worry about things you can't control. Be considerate of others. Go out of your way to be nice. Don't be judgmental—ask your mom about that one—it is one of her strengths. Be strong. Be independent. Ask Sebastian and Uncle Gabe for guidance on those points. But also, ask them both for any help you need.*

They love you, unconditionally.

Those were the easy points.

"Most of all honey—I'm sorry. Sorry this night happened, sorry I won't get to be there with you when you do all the wonderful things you're going to do in your life. I sure would've loved to cheer you on. I never wanted to leave you when you were so young. My dad died when I was sixteen, and I didn't handle it well. His death took all my happiness from me. You were one of the people in my life who brought it back. You taught me the importance of happiness, so strive for it. Make it happen. Insist upon it. And ask Uncle Gabe how to make sure your life is full of it, because he's mastered it. Follow his lead. Be your sweet, silly, funny self, even when you're thirty, fifty, and ninety."

He drew a deep breath, wondering if there was anything he hadn't covered. "Oh. Men—don't fall into the trap of thinking you need one." Zeus paused, thought about Sam in the tapas restaurant—kudos to her, for picking the man who made her smile, laugh, and glow with happiness. He only hoped his daughter would have Sam's toughness and resilience. "When it comes down to choosing a man, make sure Gabe and Sebastian approve of him, and after that, pick one who makes you happy.

They all come with their own drama. If he doesn't make you happy, drop him. You don't need him. If he doesn't make you feel special—and I mean as though his world won't turn without you—don't waste your time on him. I love you, my sweet angel, with all of my heart."

He pressed stop on the video, and forwarded it to both Gabe and Sebastian's private email addresses, with the message—*For Ana, when she's old enough. Sebastian—If the worst happens, please help Gabe take care of my baby girl. She needs solid father figures. Two isn't too many.*

He typed a quick email to his brother. *Gabe—I know you're going to look at Ana's video, even if I ask you not to. So I'm not wasting my time asking. I've never told you this, but thanks for being that awesome little kid who actually looked up to me after dad died. In those dark years, the fact that you depended on me for so much gave me a reason to get out of bed. Many days, it was the only reason. You're one of our best agents, but more than that, you grew into a goddamn magnificent human being. I know I was always hard on you. Just want to say I'm proud of you. You didn't get to know him as well as I did, but I know Dad would've been proud of you too. Keep smiling. Love you, brother.*

He thought about the other person in his life who might like to know that at this moment, she was on his mind. He lifted the phone, pressed video, and said what needed to be said to her. Next issue—who should safeguard the video. There was no way in hell he was sending this one to his brother. He typed Ragno's email address, gave a quick instruction and pressed send.

Chapter Thirty-Five

The Chihuahuan Desert
Tuesday, February 8

"Sir." Agent Stone glanced at Zeus as they made their first pass over the DZ. "We're picking up body heat and warm engines from vehicles."

Stone knelt on the floor of the Cessna, directly in front of Zeus, Leon, and Cox, focusing on his laptop. He was analyzing intel produced from thermographic cameras that were affixed to the body of the aircraft, which was 14,000 feet above the Chihuahan Desert. It was 1905. Ten minutes before their scheduled jump. Heat signatures produced from the forward-looking and sideways-tracking cameras were providing real-time life onto a map of the uninhabited, desert area of the DZ.

"Turn your screen. You're blocking my view." Zeus slipped on his helmet. He was no longer in communication with Ragno and Sebastian. Without his mic, and without Ragno and Sebastian's voices streaming into his thoughts, the whir of the Cessna's engines throbbed against his eardrums.

The utilitarian plane had two pilots in the cockpit. Behind the pilots, along either side, there was bench seating. Leon, Cox, and Zeus sat together, near the door. So they'd have full night vision upon exiting the aircraft, most lights in the cabin were off, with only a dim red glow provided by floor lights.

Stone shifted sideways in the narrow aisle, and turned his laptop screen toward Zeus as he pointed at pulsing red, orange, white, and green blobs on a map. "Here. Light blue X marks the DZ. Three vehicles, one further back from the other two. As many as twelve people."

Forcing himself to remain in analytical agent mode, rather than desperate father mode, Zeus scanned the screen. The intel didn't give the one answer he wanted.

"Eight adults outside of the vehicles. Too large for a child." Stone's matter-of-fact words hammered home what Zeus had already figured out. "However," shifting his finger up, to a large orange and red blob that was the furthest from the blue x, "the heat signature of this vehicle is obscuring human heat." He pointed to two of the men who were furthest from the vehicles, and pressed a button that gave them a close-up. "Given the intensity of the reading, these men appear to be carrying weapons that have been fired recently."

At what? Or whom?

With ice slivers chilling his veins, Zeus calmly nodded. He slipped on his goggles as the aircraft banked left. Turning to Leon, he lifted a tether that extended from his parachute pack. "Ready?"

Agent Stone shimmied down the aisle to get out of their way. Leon crouched, her back to him. Zeus knelt behind her, pressed his chest and hips against the small and compact woman's back and butt, and tethered her to him with the hooks of the tandem harness—two at her shoulders, two at her waist, and two at her legs. The close, almost intimate contact that came with body positioning for tandem jumping usually prompted a joke or some other tension-relieving comment by the jumpers.

Not tonight.

After finishing with the hooks, Zeus slipped on his gloves as Leon did the same.

"Fifteen more vehicles within a five-mile radius." Stone, who now faced them, turned his laptop screen to provide a full view to Leon, who was tasked with getting his daughter the hell out of there. "They're primarily using a ridge along the canyon to the Southeast, though four vehicles seem to be working a two mile perimeter. Not an exact circle, given the topography."

The DZ was in an area of hills, canyons, sand, and brush. Caves, natural and manmade from now abandoned mining activities, riddled the area. Intel from Blaze, and other sources, indicated the possibility of tunnels to the East, closer to the U.S. border.

Leon asked, "Motorcycles?"

"Possibly. All terrain cycles. Larger vehicles appear to be some variation of a jeep."

Stone and his thermography measurements should let Black Raven know—*hope against all fucking hope*—when Agent Leon exfiltrated with Ana. It would also provide intel on when and how his agents could intercept them. Zeus had little confidence that thermography would aid Black Raven's ability to find Cox or himself, because caves and tunnels could impede the imagery.

The cameras could see through fog, clouds, and brush, but there were limitations. Yards and yards of dense-packed earth blocked heat signatures. If their captors slipped into a cave, or travelled through a deep tunnel, he and Cox would be lost to Black Raven.

From the front of the plane, the co-pilot said, "We're turning into the second pass now."

He and Leon would jump at the second pass. Cox would follow only after getting a signal from Zeus once he was on the ground.

Having Barrows' impersonator jump separately was a major deviation from the instructions. It had been Zeus's idea, and Sebastian had agreed with the call, because it gave Zeus—once on the ground—a small measure of power with which he could negotiate for Ana's safety. Another consideration for the change of plan was that to get Barrows, the perps would have to allow Zeus to communicate and give an all clear. In that communication, Zeus would divulge a multitude of information to Black Raven, something that was SOP in the Black Raven handbook.

When the Cessna straightened and slowed, Zeus glanced back at Cox. "Thank you. Again."

"You're welcome. Again." Cox gave a thumbs up. "Good luck, sir."

Zeus and Leon stood at the door, waiting for the pilot to signal before opening it. "Leon—"

"No thanks needed, sir." She gave him an over-shoulder glance. Through her goggles, her eyes were calm. Her expression revealed no emotion—the serious look of a Black Raven agent on a mission. "I'm looking forward to returning Ana to you. Thank me then, if you feel the need."

Her calm expression changed. Worry filtered into her eyes, lines creased her forehead, and an anxious, yet pissed-off frown, appeared at her lips. She looked like a woman fighting valiantly through her fear—yet fear was winning. With a wink, Leon said, "From here on out, I'm no longer an agent. I'm an ex-wife and mother who is frightened to within an inch of her life for her daughter."

And she damn well looked the part. "Great job," Zeus said.

On the pilot's thumbs-up signal, Zeus opened the door. Cold wind whooshed into the plane as he stared out onto an inky black, cloudless sky speckled with stars. In the distance, a thin crescent moon provided a bit of light. Not enough to illuminate the ground below.

"One," Zeus's count to Leon was guided by the pilot's hand signals. "Two. Three."

Zeus and Leon rolled out, free falling through chilly, dry air. He'd done enough skydiving, including night jumps, that the steps came automatically. With Leon back-bending into him from the force of the drop, Zeus glanced upwards to check that their drogue chute had deployed, then focused on the bright, glow-in-the-dark altimeter on his wrist. At 3,000 feet, he deployed the main chute. Once fully under canopy, he handed Leon the toggles and made a few harness adjustments. Taking the toggles back, he estimated four minutes before landing. The pilots had told him all forecasts indicated negligible winds, and they were correct.

In the far distance, to the west, Zeus saw the lights of Ciudad Juarez. To the northeast, a faint blur on the horizon was El Paso. Below, there was only an inky black sea and above, an eternity of a cloudless night sky, that looked like an artist's rendering of stars on blue-black paint. Only one thought played in his head as he alternated his glance between the darkness and the bright altimeter reading on his wrist.

Please God, let Ana be alive.

At 1,200 feet, Leon pointed to their right. "Lights. DZ."

"Got it." Pushing down on the toggles with his right arm, and lifting his left, he steered them so they had a better view. Vehicles were lighting the DZ, just as the thermographic images had displayed on Stone's laptop.

As they dropped, more details came into view. Black jeeps had a row of lights on their roofs. Bright light illuminated sandy ground. Scrub brush and cactus, green, gray, and brown when illuminated, looked black as the light faded into shadows.

No sign of Ana.

Eight men stood in front of two vehicles, dressed in black, with ski-masks obscuring their features. They held AKs. Four of them had those weapons trained on their descent.

Hello, fuckers.

"Show time." Zeus whispered to Leon at fifty feet. "Go for it."

"Where's my baby?" Leon shouted, voice just this side of hysterical. "You bastards. Where is she?"

His feet found the ground. Carried by momentum for a few steps, Zeus started stripping off the harness and chute as he moved forward, unhooking Leon first. "Getting hysterical isn't going to make them bring Ana to us, Theresa." Zeus shot her a furious look as he pulled off his helmet and goggles and dropped them to the ground. "Shut the fuck up and let me handle this."

They'd landed in an area where machismo was everything. Zeus was selling it for all he was worth.

After slipping off her helmet and goggles, she threw them in the direction of the men, but missed any one of them by a few feet. Then she shoved both hands against Zeus's chest. "If it wasn't for you, Ana wouldn't have been taken, so don't you dare tell me what to do!" Zeus grabbed her, pulling her into him. Spinning on her heels, but still in Zeus's arms, Leon faced the men. "Show me my daughter, you monsters. Now. Where is she?"

One vehicle hung a bit further back, idling. Zeus couldn't see whether Ana was in it. "Don't see her. Maybe jeep. Farthest away," he said, not moving his lips.

Leon gave a small nod before breaking free of his hold. When she lunged towards the men, Zeus pulled her back, closer to him, as though protecting her. Focusing on the eight men who were approaching them, Zeus yelled, "Stop playing games. Give us our daughter."

Because the men were backlit by the glare from the vehicle lights, it was hard to see too many details.

"I don't see Barrows, Hernandez. You know the deal."

"My daughter first." Zeus demanded, nominally struggling as two men grabbed him by his upper arms. Under normal circumstances they'd be flat on their backs, bleeding profusely. But these weren't normal circumstances. "Don't you fucking lay a hand on—"

A rifle butt on the temple cut him off, and Leon was grabbed. Like a wild-cat, she fought and kicked at the two men who had her, screaming her head off loud enough to be heard aboard the circling plane.

The man ended her screams with a solid punch to her jaw. "Shut up, bitch."

Leon, the agent, would never have let him land that punch. As Theresa, Leon did a great job of dodging most of the blow, and a better job of shaking her head in wide-eyed, hurt surprise. She held her hand to her jaw, tears replacing her screams as one man immobilized her with a thick arm around her chest. Another frisked her.

The men were well trained and moved with precision. Their shiny, custom-rigged jeeps looked expensive. They gave the impression of having hefty backing.

With his arms locked down in a vice-like grip by two huge men, a third guy, unarmed, stepped closer. He signaled to a behemoth with a finger directed at Zeus. "Julio. Frisk them. Scan them."

"It doesn't take much of a man to best someone when his opponent is being held," Zeus said, tone mocking. Big and burly, the dickhead who'd gestured for Julio seemed to be the guy in charge. "Don't trust me?"

"Shut him the hell up." To Zeus, the dickhead who was issuing orders—a solid, six foot-tall square of a man—became DIC. Dick In Charge. The other men all wore black hiking boots. DIC, who'd spoken in an authoritative, confident tone, wore cowboy boots with shiny, metal tipped toes. "Knock out that smart-ass attitude."

Taller than Zeus, with shoulders that looked like he could carry a boulder, and wide legs that indicated he had, a behemoth of a man—presumably Julio—stepped forward. He used the grip of his rifle like a club against Zeus's head. The hard blow to his temple made Zeus stagger and see stars. He'd have fallen, but for the grip of the two goons holding him upright. The behemoth frisked him, landing punches as he travelled down Zeus's body. Another man came by with a scanner, ran it up and down his body, and also scanned Theresa.

When the stars in his vision cleared, Zeus focused his attention on DIC. Obviously, their leader. The father in him broke through the cool agent veneer he was struggling to maintain. "You slimy fucking coward. Who's bankrolling you? You can't really believe the Maximov line of bullshit? Either way, it doesn't fucking matter, because—"

"Zeus!" Leon shouted, her voice high pitched as she thrashed and struggled in the hold of the two men restraining her. "Tell them, for God's sake! Tell them we'll pay whatever they ask. We'll meet your demands. Anything. Just please let her go. She has nothing to do with you. And she certainly shouldn't be used to get to..." Struggling against the man who had a firm hold of her arms, Leon glanced at Zeus with disdain-laced fury that only an ex-wife could muster, as though believing whatever bad shit happened was somehow his fault. "...him. Please. Just give her to me."

DIC stepped forward, "I won't ask again, Jesus." Without a trace of a Hispanic accent, he used the Anglo pronunciation of Zeus's name. "Where the fuck is Barrows?"

"He'll jump on signal from me. After you produce my daughter to her mother and give them safe passage."

"Now that I see you in person, Jesus." DIC looked Zeus up and down, his pale pink lips a thin, pensive slash, visible in the mouth hole of his ski mask. White skin. Light eyes. "What do you think, Julio? Is that cross you built big enough for the crucifixion of Jesus?" Saying it with sarcasm and scorn, as though he was a man who had never believed in a higher power and thought less of those who did, DIC repeated the Anglo pronunciation of Zeus's name. "Jesus, Son of God, aka Jesus Hernandez, Mr. Big Bad Black Raven Agent?"

Two of DIC's sidekicks chuckled. Julio—the behemoth—coughed, then laughed.

Zeus failed to see the humor. "We can do this dance all day. Produce my daughter, and let her leave with her mother. Once you do that, I'll bring in Barrows and we'll be fucking done."

"You're in no fucking position to bargain."

"Here is why you're wrong," Zeus kept his voice measured. "You can kill me—and you'll get some mileage out of it. You can even kill Barrows, though I know he's too valuable for you to do that. But you kill a woman and a child? The wrath of God will fall on your fucking head so fucking fast you won't know what hit you. We know where your families live, asshole. There'll be no corner in which anyone you know and love can hide that Black Raven won't find and destroy them."

For the moment, it was a lie, of course. They had no idea who these fuckers were—and no clue how to find their families. But he was going to go down bluffing to his last breath.

"Your threats mean nothing, Jesus." Zeus ground his teeth as he listened to the way the man said his name. The disdain managed to be an effective insult to both Zeus and Jesus.

"What means everything is that I agreed to trade your daughter for you and Barrows," DIC continued, "and I'm a man who lives up to my word." DIC lifted his right hand over his head and beckoned someone forward.

Zeus trained his eyes on the third vehicle, though the lights that streamed from it were blinding. Car doors opened with a click, and closed with a soft thud. The sounds resonated in the arid air. A small, Ana-sized shadow ran in his direction.

"Ana," Leon screamed.

Knees buckling with relief, the goons who held his arms tight let him kneel on the sandy ground as Ana beelined straight for him. Yanking himself out of their grasp, he wrapped his arms around his daughter as she threw herself into his chest without slowing. Zeus let his body absorb the energy of her run. The man who was holding Leon let her go, and the three of them huddled together.

"Daddy! Mommy!"

Shaking with the force of her skinny-armed embrace, a touch that he'd thought had been lost to him forever, Zeus held on tight. He buried his face in her loose hair, inhaled the sweet, sweaty smell of her, touched her forehead with his lips, and looked into her velvety dark eyes. "Baby. Oh God," he whispered. "My sweet angel. Did they hurt you?"

"Nooooo. Daddy. Da—daddy." Face against his shoulder, she started shaking with sobs. "Da—"

"Honey," he kept his voice low. "Listen to me. I need you to go with your mom."

"No. No. I'll stay with you." Ana pulled back and glanced at Agent Leon. Now that she had a close-up view, she wasn't fooled. She glanced at Zeus with a confused look. "She isn't mom—"

Fuck!

"Shhhhhh. Honey, pretend. Make believe," Zeus whispered. "Go with her. She'll take you to mom."

"Well, this is about as sweet as the taste of a virgin's honey pot," DIC said. "But as we all know, the sweetness, eventually, comes to an end. Just like this reunion. Get Jesus away from her."

Immediately, his two captors returned to grab his biceps and, with force that rippled down his spine, jerked him away from Ana. She screamed and tried to hold onto his belt. "Nooooo! Daddy!"

Two men pulled Ana and Leon further away. Zeus stood, as his arms were yanked behind his back.

"Don't hurt my Daddy," Ana, looking back, screamed. "Daddy! Daddy! Don't hurt—"

"Shut the fuck up, kid!" DIC yelled. "Make it happen, Pablo."

One of the men—presumably Pablo—prodded Ana with the butt of his AK, which only caused her to scream louder.

"You bastard—" Zeus howled, the sight of the assault weapon touching his daughter making him momentarily lose his cool. He yanked one arm free, and would have yanked the other one free as well, except Leon leaned over, glancing at him as she shielded the little girl with her own body, and whispering to Ana as they walked. Caution signs flaring in Leon's eyes made him calm-the-fuck down.

He and Leon against assault weapons? A fight he'd take on if his daughter wasn't in the crossfire.

"Cuff him," DIC said.

As Ana's cries reached a manic state, Zeus didn't dare fight. Leon was a professional. Lifting Ana in her arms, she let his baby sob against her neck, comforting her, and keeping her close. Leon was here because Zeus trusted her with his daughter's life.

He had to let her go and get Ana far, far away to safety. That was her job. Ana was his everything, but this was much, much bigger than a loving father and his baby girl.

Tonight I have another agenda. I am Black Raven.

What these men were doing would ultimately provide a roadmap to Maximov—or, if Maximov was dead, as Stollen claimed—whoever was goddamn playing the Maximov card and terrorizing the world.

With Ana's wailing drifting back to him, he narrowed his eyes as one of the goons wrenched his arms up behind his back. Metal cuffs snapped on his wrists, clicking as they closed tight.

"On your knees." One of the three goons who had surrounded him issued the order.

A solid kick in his lower back encouraged him to move faster. The business end of an AK was jabbed into his forehead, providing a close-up of the fully-hooded sight, and answering the question as to which AK variant the men were using. AK-56, a Chinese copy of the Russian AK-47. Blaze had told them the TRCR were known to smuggle Chinese AKs into the U.S.

He felt a glimmer of hope. If these men were the TRCR, maybe some of Blaze's intel would prove useful to Ragno and Sebastian and the search and rescue effort. DIC reached into his pocket, then held a phone aloft. "Go hold it for Jesus."

One of his men grabbed the phone and walked over to Zeus.

"Give him the number. And don't screw around. There are AKs trained on your baby's head. It'd be a real shame to give you a close-up view of her brains. You have three words. If Barrows isn't here in ten minutes you're all dead. Including your daughter."

Zeus shook his head. "I'm not giving the signal until Theresa and Ana have driven away."

DIC chuckled. "Well, that's nice, Jesus, but I'm not letting them drive away until Barrows is in my hands."

"Let them get in a vehicle, then I'll give the number. As he lands, let them drive away."

"I expected a little more trust from a man named Jesus."

Zeus promised himself that if he lived through this ordeal, he'd personally find this fucker, fire a bullet into the man's cocksure mouth, and watch him bleed out. He'd do that, after seeing that the bastard was tortured into giving up the people who had funded this operation. Keeping his voice calm, he said, "You want Barrows, or not?"

DIC gestured to the man who stood on his immediate left.

"Put the woman and child in the far vehicle. Keep your weapon trained on them. I'll tell you when they can go."

Agent Leon and Ana, now walking hand in hand, were guided to the same all-terrain jeep in which Ana had been brought to the DZ. Eyes straining to see through the bright car lights, Zeus watched Leon hug Ana before they both stepped into the driver's side of the car. The man who was guarding them stayed at the driver's side door, aiming his weapon at Leon through the open window. He listened intently—and in vain—for the sound of the engine turning over.

Come on Leon. Go!

"The number," DIC said.

"Theresa," Zeus called. "Start the jeep."

He breathed easier when he heard the engine turn over.

"The number."

Zeus gave Sebastian's number to the man next to him. Fat fingers placed the phone against his cheek. "Barrows can jump." The words and word order were code; *Ana is alive—remains in jeopardy.*

The man pulled the phone away from his face. In the dry air of the desert, sounds carried. The jeep's engine had a soft hum. One man was a heavy breather. Another was a cougher. From far above, he heard the faint sound of the Cessna.

The men were all looking into the sky. If Ana hadn't been just fifty yards away, even with the cuffs on, Zeus would have used their distraction to take them down. He maintained his position, but knew to an inch where each man stood. By the manner in which they held their weapons, he had a good gauge of their skill level.

One pointed at the dark, star-scattered sky. "Chute."

A white chute floated down in the darkness.

"Let my daughter go."

Come on Leon! Goddammit. Go!

DIC glanced at the man on Zeus's right. "Sedate him."

No!

The man held a large syringe filled with milky liquid. As the needle jabbed into his neck, three things happened. One, as planned, Cox landed approximately one hundred yards from where Zeus was kneeling and where the men were waiting for him. Two, on DIC's order, four men jumped into a jeep to pick up Cox. Three, the man guarding Leon and Ana lowered his weapon as he watched Cox land. Leon drove away with a burst of speed and a plume of dust.

She'll be safe. Thank you, God.

Ice-cooled blood pulsed from Zeus's neck into his head and chest. Foggy darkness overcame him as the sedative took effect.

Chapter Thirty-Six

Aboard Raven One, Undisclosed Location
Wednesday, February 9

As Samantha sat in the rear cabin of Raven One, while Jenkins and her security team worked in the front cabin, knots in the muscles and tendons of her neck and upper back screamed for relief. The jet sat in a well-lit hangar, approximately a half hour from Stollen's island.

The door that separated the two cabins was open. As the agents talked, yawned, coughed, or typed, their quiet noises and subdued voices were welcome. Their presence provided a break to the silent scream of agony for Zeus and Ana that, as the day had progressed, had become a spider-web in her mind, present with every thought.

Calm down.

Jenkins stepped into the rear cabin and handed her a convenience store bag. Antacids and aspirin. Throughout the course of Tuesday, she'd chewed her way through a full roll of antacids. It was now 12:05 a.m., Eastern Time, and Samantha figured it would be best if she didn't count the number of antacids she chewed and swallowed. Pulling out a fresh roll, she said, "Thank you. Any news about Zeus?"

He shook his head. "Operation is ongoing. Nothing to report."

Using her thumbnail to separate a tablet, she picked up her Black Raven flip phone and asked the agent who answered to connect her to Judge O'Connor. Ever since Stollen had told them that Maximov was dead, Samantha's job had been to keep Judge O'Connor updated on the Black Raven operation to go into Praptan and determine whether Stollen had told them to the truth. The judge had authority to get the information from Ragno directly. He preferred for the information to be filtered through Samantha, who had more knowledge of the ITT proceeding.

Scanning Ragno's latest instant message, she waited for the judge to answer the phone. Throughout the course of the day and evening he'd been on the lookout for her calls. He answered on the first ring. She stood, careful to keep her voice steady and professional, without revealing that she was caught up in personal turmoil that she couldn't shake. "Your Honor, the latest Black Raven information indicates that the agents are now entering Praptan."

"How far are the agents from the location Stollen provided?"

Although her nerves were stretched taut, Samantha somehow managed to match Judge O'Connor's business-like tone. "We estimate an hour."

"Then we'll at least know whether Stollen is toying with us."

"With all due respect, Judge O'Connor." she turned and walked the seven steps of the narrow aisle that bisected the rear cabin, turned, and walked it again. "We won't be sure of that until we receive DNA confirmation that the remains actually are Andre Maximov."

"We should know that within six hours of finding the body?"

"That is correct. Black Raven has sophisticated testing capabilities that will begin immediately." A long seat lined one side of the small, sleek sleeping berth. Two side-by-side seats, capable of reclining, were in front of a bathroom. "Once we confirm that the remains are Andre Maximov, I'll return to Stollen. I'll continue the interrogation and see what else he has to say."

Samantha, Judge O'Connor, and President Cameron had all agreed that experienced interrogators would have been better for the job of interviewing the terrorist. As a lawyer, Samantha was trained in the art of securing information from witnesses. She didn't, however, have the psychological training to handle someone like Stollen. Yet Stollen had made it clear that he'd only talk to her, which made her lack of experience as a trained criminal interrogator moot.

If Gabe recovered Maximov's body, Samantha would return to Stollen and she'd get more information from him. Assuming he had any to give, and was willing to give it.

"What is the latest on Zeus's child?"

"No news. Operation is ongoing." She repeated the Black Raven phrase she'd heard throughout the day. Their way of providing an answer without giving any information. *A phrase I've become damn tired of hearing.* "That's all I know."

"Keep me informed. I'm awaiting your calls. Good job, Ms. Fairfax."

Judge O'Connor clicked off. As the night progressed, Jenkins and the other agents had grown increasingly somber. Now, she heard Jenkins, from the front cabin, say, "Thank God."

She stepped into the doorway, glanced at the agents who were all talking at once, as her phone rang. Ragno's number. Breath caught in her throat, she answered, "Tell me."

"Ana is safe."

Heart pulsing fast with profound relief, Samantha couldn't say anything.

"She's reunited with her mother," Ragno added. "Scared, but appears unharmed."

When she could breathe, Samantha asked, "Zeus?"

Ragno was silent for a beat that lasted far too long. "Operation is still underway—"

"No! Tell me, Ragno, goddammit." Samantha gave up on poised, professional coolness. Nothing but stretched-to-popping, out-of-control, frantic worry infected her voice. "Is he safe? Is he hurt? Alive? Dead? I can't handle this. I need to know!"

Whatever cool she'd ever possessed had disappeared, and the agents in the front of the plane were all giving her a sympathetic look. Jenkins stood, as though ready to console her, but also hung back, as though he had no idea how to do that.

"Samantha, I can't give more informa—"

"But I need to know. Something, Ragno. Please. Anything. Dammit. I just need to know."

"He traded himself for his daughter. We lost contact approximately three hours ago," Ragno said.

"Three hours—lost contact? And you didn't tell me? What does that mean?"

"Exactly that. We're going to find him, Samantha."

Find him? "You don't know where he is? How can that be?"

"I can't give details. I can only assure you—we will find him."

The last words failed to carry the force of conviction. Ragno sounded like a woman who was persuading herself as much as she was trying to persuade Samantha. In her life, Samantha had been scared, and she knew how to recognize fear in the spoken voice—the careful pronunciation of each word in an effort to hide an underlying tremble. Ragno, with her bird's eye view of Black Raven's ongoing operation, was scared too, and that, in turn, scared the hell out of Samantha.

Leaning hard against the polished-wood wall, staring blankly into the eyes of Jenkins and the other agents, she wondered how she was going to get through however long it would take to know Zeus's fate.

Or the rest of my life, assuming the worst happens.

Her fear that the unimaginable was happening—that Zeus was irrevocably gone—skyrocketed her emotions into outright heart-pounding panic. Shutting her eyes, she realized she'd just found something that mattered more to her than her professional goals, aspirations, and dreams. More than her own life. More than anything.

It boiled down to two simple words—

Zeus.

Alive.

Please God. Zeus. Alive.

Okay. More than just two simple words—my selfish request: I want another chance. That's all I want. I want the chance he was offering from the moment he showed up in Paris. I want it so badly I'm yearning for it. If not that, if that's not in the cards for me, that's...okay. I won't be selfish. Please just let him be alive. Please.

Feeling lost and unraveled, she turned and went back to her seat in the rear cabin of the jet. She settled for semi-privacy by keeping the door of the cabin open, wanting to know the minute the mood of the agents in the front cabin changed. She reached for the flip phone and requested that the Black Raven operator get Samuel on the line. He answered on the third ring. "Well, I've been waiting for this call for far too long."

Her silent treatment of her grandfather had lasted since Zeus's arrival in Paris. Over a week. The longest she'd ever gone without talking to Samuel. "I'm still furious with you."

"I know. Wish I could tell you it's the last time I'll make you so angry...but I can't make that promise."

Rolling her eyes in exasperation, she focused on the jet's sleek woodwork, tracing a fine dark grain that ran along the opposite wall, above the windows. "Can you at least say you're sorry?"

"Of course I'm sorry. I should have listened to you when you asked me not to send him. But can't you admit now that part of the reason you were so mad at me for hiring him is because you love him so much?"

"That doesn't make what you did acceptable."

"Honey, he hurt you when he left you. Hurt you more than anyone ever did. It's okay to admit that, and you're afraid of opening yourself to the same kind of pain."

She choked back a sob.

"Back then I tried to bribe him to stay away from you."

Sobbing forgotten, she gasped. "You didn't!"

"He wouldn't take my money. Yet another indication of how fine of a man he is, which I'm betting you knew from the very beginning."

Under different circumstances, she'd have been furious with

her grandfather for the manipulation, and with Zeus for not telling her about it. Now, in the middle of this long night from hell, knowing of her grandfather's bribe attempt made her wish she'd been more receptive to Zeus upon his arrival in Paris, instead of rubbing his face in her plan to marry Justin.

Dropping her voice to a whisper, she got to the point of her call, knowing her grandfather would help her, just like he always had in her darkest moments. "I'm scared, Samuel. I can barely breathe. It looks really bad."

"I know. Ragno's kept me informed, both with the bounty hunt and with the mission to rescue Ana. Hell. Right now everyone is operating at high anxiety. But you have to believe that Zeus will be okay. I believe it."

"But he's missing, and—"

"Listen to me." Samuel's voice was unwavering and firm. "Black Raven is the best. That's why I hired them and trusted your life to them. Those two-bit thugs who have Zeus don't stand a chance. Not one chance in hell. Now," his voice became gentle, "don't you want to talk about what you're going to do when Zeus reappears? You've made a bit of a mess, and I'm afraid this one is partly my fault, because I've done a hell of a job reinforcing your belief that your father was responsible for your mother's failures. He was. I'm not going to soft-pedal that at this late date. Your mother would've been better off had she never fallen in love with him. But that doesn't mean that you can't find love that will enhance your life. Not every man is like your father. Zeus certainly isn't. Not all love is destructive, and I'm pretty goddamn certain I've misled you into believing that falling in love will inevitably lead to self-destruction."

"I've blown it," she whispered. "And it isn't your fault. I knew what I was doing. I was scared of my feelings for Zeus since the moment I met him. Seven years ago I was so hurt when he left, that I only allowed myself to feel relief. You see, I always thought he was too good to be true, and when he told me he was leaving me, he was proving it. So this time around, I was as cold as I possibly could be. I've lost him again, and this time it hurts worse than before."

"The only time you've actually lost a fight," he paused, and she shut her eyes, knowing what he was going to say next, because she'd heard it from him her whole life, "is when you quit." Her grandfather was a firm believer in fighting till the bitter end for what he believed in. "So let's just reason through what your next move might be. Because Zeus will make it through this night, and you will have a chance to make things right, okay?"

Chapter Thirty-Seven

The Chihuahuan Desert
Wednesday, February 9

Zeus became aware of men talking. Pushing aside the need for sleep, his breath caught. *Ana?* He was able to breathe. Yes—he remembered seeing Agent Leon drive away. And he was now listening to—whom? How many? Trying hard to focus through the drug-induced haze, he forced himself to listen to the voices. Five males. Maybe six. One of them was unmistakably DIC. The men were within a couple of yards of him.

Using senses other than sight, which would clue his captors to the fact that he was conscious, he tried to get a feel for his environment. The air smelled musty and earthy. He was flat on his back, his bodyweight crushing his arms as he lay on a floor. Arms? Numb. Hands? Numb. Still cuffed at the wrists, behind his back. Legs? *Fuck!* Numb. Either he was paralyzed or his ankles and knees were bound together and tied to something so he couldn't move them. Head? A dull ache, with major brain fog.

He drew a deep, quiet breath, as clear thoughts gave way to nothingness. A few minutes later he awoke again with a start.

Ana?

Yes! Hope.

Encouraged again by his last memory of Agent Leon driving away with Ana, he clung to the hope that they'd gotten safely away. He'd happily spend the rest of his days reliving the nightmare that his daughter had been captured—as long as it ended him with him knowing that she was safe.

Dear God, let her be okay.

Voices. When last awake, he'd been listening to voices. He opened his eyes, barely making a slit in his lids. Wherever they were, there weren't many lights. Gray ceiling—maybe earthen—appeared high overhead. A bit of feeling returned to his fingers. He dug them into soft, sandy dirt.

A cave. Maybe a tunnel.

How long had he been out of it?

Absolutely no fucking clue.

"Get this done." DIC's flat, all-American accent and clipped tone was unmistakable. From the direction of his voice, the man stood six feet away and south of where Zeus lay on the dirt floor.

If I survive this, you sadistic son of a bitch, I'll kill your ass.

Slowly and with extreme prejudice.

Big fucking *if* there. He was bound like a Thanksgiving turkey, extremely groggy from whatever the hell they'd injected him with, and surrounded by at least six men. He could hear their feet moving nearby.

Beneath his body he flexed his fingers, trying to bring them back to life. Hurt like hell. Keeping his movements subtle, Zeus worked his fingers. At the first opportunity, he'd be ready for them physically. His fuzzy brain state, however, was more of an issue. Would the fog dissipate? Or was this it? Didn't seem to be clearing. His thought process was vague, his body annoyingly lax.

A foot nudged his side. A voice, sounding like it came from directly over him, said, "He isn't awake."

"Doesn't matter," DIC answered. "It's almost time to transport Barrows and I damn well want to be done with this asshole before we start that task. Hernandez is the smaller job. Delivering Barrows will make us the real money."

At least they had their priorities in the correct order. Feelings were starting to come back to his hands in a painful rush of pins and needles. Too bad his body still felt weighted and unresponsive, and his brain was still fucking mush.

A cell phone rang.

"Yeah?" DIC paused. "Wait. Repeat that."

Another long pause.

"Are you fucking kidding me? Barrows is gone? Gone where? How?"

A pause in DIC's conversation was punctuated by heavy footfalls and harsh breathing.

"Julio—get to the fucking point, you moron!"

Relief seeped through his veins, warming him, as Zeus savored the sound of DIC's apoplectic rage.

"Goddamn it! The man didn't disappear in a puff of smoke. I swear to Jesus-fucking-H. Christ, if you had a brain in that fat head of yours you'd be dangerous. You were charged with guarding him. A simple task. Simple. Barrows didn't just fucking walk out. Someone helped him and Pablo, Richie, Steve and whoever-the-fuck else you just said are also missing—*aren't fucking missing!*"

A pause.

The disappearance of Barrows—aka Agent Cox—was beautiful news. Meant Cox had either escaped on his own or been extracted. And extraction meant that Ana was with Theresa, because the Black Raven priority order for the operation meant they weren't rescuing Cox until Ana was secure.

"I don't know where they fucking are. They're probably dead, numbnuts. Why you only had four men guarding a man who is worth twenty million dollars to us is against my fucking orders and beyond my comprehension. Get out and fucking-well find Barrows! At least we have the advantage. These people don't know this area like we do."

Surprise, asshole. By now, we know this area—wherever the fuck we are—better than you can even dream. Start counting your breaths, motherfucker, because they're numbered.

Moderate relief from the brain fog, but no return of muscle control. *Fuck.* Zeus kept trying to work his fingers.

"And let me get one thing through to you. Stop thinking of this in terms of dollars, because it now means way, way more. Like your fucking life. Understand?" The thud of DIC's heavy footfalls indicated he was pacing. "We're making a shitload out of delivering Barrows. But you fucked up, and I promise you will not live to see sunrise if you don't find him."

A hard object pinged off Zeus's cheekbone. It thudded to the ground next to him. The good news: he'd felt the phone bounce off him. Feeling was returning to his body with a vengeance. The better news: his brain was starting to fire on all synapses.

Ready, Zeus opened his eyes.

DIC walked over to him, black ski mask still firmly in place. Evidently DIC hadn't unleashed enough frustration on his phone as he'd thrown it, because he stepped closer and kicked a pointy metal-tipped boot into Zeus's side. When he bent to pick up his phone, his sky-blue eyes met Zeus's gaze.

"Well what do you know? Jesus has risen," DIC said, kicking Zeus again, harder.

"Hell," Zeus laughed. "You really are a dickhead. It was a hell of a lot of work to get Barrows to you," he added, chuckling between words. "And you fucking lost him? What kind of chicken-shit operation are you running? Sounds like you should start praying to the real Jesus, instead of mocking him."

Ana—Safe.

Leon and Cox—Safe.

Nothing else matters, at least not as much as this mission is concerned.

It was a damn good thing he had that rosy viewpoint, because with his hands cuffed behind his back, and his legs immobilized, he couldn't do a goddamn thing to help himself.

DIC stared down at him, not rising to the mocking bait that Zeus had thrown to him. "Strap him down, roll the cameras, and cut off his fucking head. Then let's get the fuck out of here. If they found Barrows, they'll find this shithole too. We'll leave a warning present. Jesus's headless body, with no hope of a resurrection."

Bright light flooded the room. Or cave. Or tunnel. Whatever the fuck the dirt room was—he couldn't tell. On the wall near his right, crude red letters on a white banner declared, *We are Maximov.*

Squinting in the glare of the headlights, Zeus turned to DIC. "We know Maximov is dead." By now, he was betting that Gabe was well into Praptan and had confirmed what Stollen had told Sam. "So who the hell has you pretending to fight on behalf of Maximov?"

DIC merely glared at him.

A flag was pinned under the banner, with the initials KKK, swastikas, a lone star, and barbwire. The flag itself was crimson red, while the logo was black. Ragno had mentioned this combination of symbols the other night—*the logo of the TRCR.*

Intel from Blaze had been spot on.

Cameras were pointed at the banner and flag. In between the cameras and the flag, there was a low, dark wooden table, outfitted with leather straps that looked thick enough to immobilize an angry bull. The table surface was dark, but lighter marks indicated where a blade had slashed into the wood.

Fuck.

One man, wearing head to toe black, his face covered in a black ski mask, unsheathed a machete. About twenty-seven inches of shiny metal glinted in the bright lights from the cameras.

High carbon steel—Zeus presumed. Lightweight and efficient—he prayed.

Hope that fucking thing is as sharp as it looks.

One man untied his legs. He and three others, one at each elbow, and one at each thigh, lifted Zeus off the ground. He was still too weak from the drugs they'd given him to effectively fight them, but he had feeling now, and plenty of it. He drew his knees up to his chest and tried to turn sideways in an effort to resist them. He only managed to head-butt one of them with the side of his head and piss all of them off.

Ineffective.

They held him so that the cameras got a good view of his

face, then threw him, face down, onto the table. Before he could move, they yanked his legs down so that he was kneeling on one side of it. A leather strap crossed over his lower back and his cuffed wrists, digging into exposed skin as they buckled it close. Another was tightened over his shoulders. The final leather swatch was slapped over his head and pulled tight, giving him a view only of the tabletop. He could turn his head slightly, but there wasn't much of a point to that.

I'd prefer a bullet in the head, but they sure as hell aren't taking last requests. What the fuck is taking so long?

Zeus shut his eyes, drew a deep breath, conjured an image of his daughter's beautiful smile, and waited. His mind flashed to Sam, of the last time he'd touched his lips to hers. He grit his teeth together, braced himself for the first hacking slice into his neck, and drew another deep, ragged breath.

Come on! Fucking get this over with.

The earth rumbled. The ground at his knees started vibrating. Sounds of engines grew louder and louder, reverberating off the walls of the cave. Gunfire exploded—the fast *pop, pop, pop* of AKs in full auto mode. Turning his head slightly, as much as the head strap would allow, he watched the machete fall to the table, the blade coming within an inch of his nose before it fell flat. Men yelled, and the sounds of engines intermittently drowned out their yells.

Someone loosened the straps that had pinned his legs down, then undid the other restraints. The second he was free, he jumped into a wobbly stand, turned, preparing to throw himself into a head butt if the guy wore a black ski mask.

If the guy was a Black Raven agent, he was getting a fucking promotion.

The man was neither. He had long blonde hair, blue eyes, and a tattoo of fire climbing up his neck and arms. He wore a snug white T-shirt and a white leather vest with a black peace sign, the emblem of the Protectors of Peace.

Blaze.

Not a Black Raven agent, but definitely no need for a head butt, because Zeus guessed that Blaze's intel was the reason his head was still firmly on his neck. The mouth of the cave was twenty yards away. The cave was smoky, the air acrid with the scent of gunpowder. The bulk of the action was now outside and far into the interior of the cave, where Zeus guessed DIC and the others had run in an effort to save their asses. Two men were down at his feet. Dark red blood was pooling underneath them.

If they weren't dead yet, they would be soon, because there would be no help coming.

"Damn glad to see you," Zeus said as Blaze unlocked the handcuffs. Another round of gunfire rattled and an answering round exploded. Men yelled, and the earth vibrated with the revving of high-powered engines. "You do know we need to take as many of these people alive as we can?"

"Understood," Blaze nodded. "Interrogation first. After, though..."

"Different story," Zeus shook out his arms, then extended a hand to Blaze, glad he had enough strength to stand on his own and his hand wasn't shaking. "We gave you our word. Whether we go through regular channels, or not. The TRCR now officially consists only of the walking dead."

The desert sand will run red with TRCR blood.

A man riding an all-terrain motorcycle, his face covered in a bandanna and his body covered with sand, skidded to a halt at Zeus's side. He lifted his goggles and removed his bandanna. Zeus recognized Agent Brad Miles, lead agent from the El Paso airport contingency. "Sir, happy to see you."

"Ana?"

"Fine. With her mother."

"Leon and Cox?"

"Both fine."

Miles handed Zeus a Black Raven comm system. Zeus slipped the mic in his ear, fastened the watch on his wrist, and said, "Sebastian? Ragno?"

"Damn glad to hear your voice," Sebastian came through loud, clear, and relieved. "How the hell are you?"

"Whatever drug they gave me is finally wearing off. I'm happy to report my head is still firmly attached."

"Jesus, Zeus. If you ever put us through a night like this again..." Ragno sniffed. "Awww. Dammit. Now I'm crying. And I never cry."

"Thanks, Ragno. I love you too."

Glancing around the cave, eyes stopping on the blade of the machete resting on the table just a few inches from where his head had been strapped, his hand itched for a firearm. As tempting as it was to get into the firefight, he had a daughter to hug, and work to do. His agents and the Protectors of Peace were more than capable of taking down the TRCR and conducting a forensic search for anything that could be a clue for Jigsaw.

"Miles. There's a dickhead here wearing steel-toe cowboy

boots. He leads this faction, maybe the whole TRCR. Take him alive and interrogate."

Agent Miles nodded. "This network of caves is interconnected via tunnels. Hills surround us for about two miles. He couldn't have travelled far. We'll find him, sir."

Zeus gave Miles a hard look. "Tough guy. He'll need persuasion. Do whatever."

Translation: Torture him to within an inch of his life.

"No explanation necessary."

"When he starts praying, whether to Buddha, Mohammad, God or," he paused, "especially Jesus, call me. I want to be the one to end him and I'll damn well fly across the world to do it if necessary." Zeus gave Miles a hard glance. "Have that machete handy when I arrive."

"Yes, sir. An ATV is waiting outside to take you to a rendezvous point with a chopper."

Zeus stepped out of the cave and into the chilly, pre-dawn air. A few yards of flat desert extended from the mouth of the cave and seemed to fall away into dark nothingness. Lights from the ATV that was waiting for him shone on tall cactus and scrub brush. As he slipped into the passenger seat, the driver nodded, then gassed it.

"Sir, hold on. We're five minutes away from our rendezvous with a chopper. I'll try to avoid big bumps, but it'll be rough going. I've got to avoid some of the larger growth."

A second ATV and two all-terrain motorcycles rode as escort. The horizon was a lighter blue than the rest of the night sky, but the sun hadn't yet risen. As the ATV pulled away, his mind switched gears to the larger picture. "Ragno."

"Yes?"

"Praptan? Gabe?" Not necessarily what he wanted to talk about, but duty took priority. *Before Sam.*

"Angel and his team met gunfire on the way into Praptan. They were anticipating it. No casualties or serious injuries on our end. They extracted remains. We're running DNA analysis now, but given the details now provided by Stollen and collected by Gabe," Ragno said, "we're assuming there will be confirmation. Jigsaw gives it almost 99.999 percent probability."

"Well, what do you know? Someone else really has been playing the Maximov card—and doing it damn well."

"Could it be the TRCR?"

Zeus gripped the roll bar as the ATV went airborne and landed with a spine-jarring thud on the front wheels. "No. I heard a phone conversation. This outfit was being paid twenty million dollars to deliver Barrows. Someone else—with serious money—is pulling the strings."

"Yep. Samantha is trying to navigate a way out of the disarray that knowledge of Maximov's death will cause in the ITT. After Gabe recovered the remains, she spent the better part an hour on a conference call with President Cameron and Judge O'Connor. President Cameron wants to avoid embarrassment at any cost. Samantha and Judge O'Connor anticipate that Brier will file a motion for a mistrial. Her job will be to defeat it. Samantha is interviewing Stollen now to see if he has more information that could lead to the apprehension of whomever is perpetuating the Maximov myth. After that she is immediately heading to London so she can do damage control in the trial."

Ana—safe.

Sam—I'll fight for another chance, because I'm alive.

The rest? Details. A puzzle that I'll damn well figure out. With the aid of Barrows and Jigsaw.

Inhaling the cool desert air, Zeus relished the fresh scent of a better day that it carried. He loosened his grip on the roll bar as they reached flatter terrain. "Developments from Jigsaw?"

"We're inputting data gathered from the people and area where we extracted Agent Cox. Cell phones. Tablets. Laptops. Sim cards. IP addresses. Jigsaw is turning each puzzle piece sideways, upside down, and any which way, looking for a link to any of the perps in the ITT."

"Have we reached TRCR headquarters yet?"

"We have a location, thanks to Blaze and some of the men we apprehended earlier. We've got a cyber forensic team and some serious firepower on approach. Once there, we're doing a sweep of all devices."

"Any link so far between this event and Caller X?" Caller X, the person whose burner phone usage pattern indicated he had spoken with Duvall's mother and David Thompson, the alleged perpetrator of the drone attacks on the Miami cruise ship.

"Not that I'm aware of. Let me check," Ragno said.

The ATV rounded a small hill and arrived at a relatively flat clearing. A sleek, powerful Sikorsky waited, with engines running and rotors turning. The clearing was patrolled by Black Raven agents in ATVs. Zeus nodded goodbye to his driver, then ran to the chopper. He buckled up behind the co-pilot. Through the windshield, the horizon was turning lighter blue as they lifted off.

"Sir," the pilot turned to him with a welcoming grin. "We'll be at the El Paso airstrip in twenty-seven minutes. You'll see sunrise with your daughter."

"Great news."

"Zeus," Ragno said, her voice back to her normal crisp, clear, and efficient tone. "Barrows just informed me there is no link between the TRCR and Caller X as of yet." The plan had been for Barrows to return to Denver the moment Agent Cox stepped into the Cessna with Zeus for the ride to the DZ. By now, a little more than ten hours after Zeus had boarded the Cessna for the jump, Zeus had no doubt that Barrows and Ragno were in the office space they shared in Denver, directing the teams of analysts working under them with lightning speed and stealth-like precision.

"How much more do we need before we can identify and find Caller X?"

"From Duvall's mother and the connection to Thompson, the alleged perpetrator of the drone attacks on the Miami cruise ship, we just need to determine who called TRCR," she answered.

"We should have that soon, even if it's through interrogation." Keeping his eyes on the horizon, Zeus forced himself to focus on business, when all he wanted to do was see Ana. "Cell phones would be better, though, correct?"

"Absolutely," Ragno answered. "If the TRCR job was instituted via burner phones, we can analyze whether there was parallel usage of co-existing digital devices. Once we get that, we can run an analysis for co-existing digital devices in the vicinity of the call from the burner phone, and conduct a worldwide search for current use of the devices."

"Barrows still hasn't managed to do this for the earlier calls made by Caller X?"

"Correct," Ragno answered. "Jigsaw isn't able to trace as far back historically as Barrows would like it to go. He is modifying the program, but for now, we can't trace co-existing digital devices from the data we have relating to Duvall's mother and the Miami cruise ship bombing. Those incidents occurred more than a year ago and there are problems with doing historical analysis that far back and recreating the digital footprint of co-existing devices."

She paused for a moment, fingers clicking furiously at her keyboard. "Just pray these people weren't smart enough to strip themselves of all other co-existing digital devices—laptops, tablets, regular phones, smart watches, etc. You know the drill. We're looking for whether Caller X made calls from burner phones to the TRCR with co-existing digital devices operating at the time. Even something as tiny as a smart watch ping anywhere on the cyber grid in common with any of the other calls from burner phones, and Jigsaw will find him. It's just a matter of time."

"Something we don't have much of." The helicopter flew west to east. Daylight was breaking on the far horizon, while overhead stars were fading into a navy blue sky.

"We're aware. Zeus. I've dropped Sebastian and anyone else listening in." And she'd changed her tone to the gentle tone that she used when discussing his personal business. "Should I connect you to Sam? She asked me to break into the interview if there was news about you." Ragno's voice was in full friend mode—soft, concerned, and trying hard to guide him. "Would be better coming from you than me."

"No. I'll talk to her later. Just let her know I'm fine." What he had to tell her on a personal level would be better said in person. Not something he'd tell her when she was in the middle of an interview with a mass murderer.

"Mistake, Zeus."

"Don't think so."

"You should talk to her now, and keep talking to her. If you love her—"

"If?" He chuckled.

"Well, be as persistent as you've ever been about anything in life, and I know you—you're nothing if not persistent. Before tonight, I agreed with Angel; I thought your efforts were wasted. But," her tone became thoughtful, her words slow, "I've been the one to give her updates on your status on this interminably long night. She even broke down and called her grandfather when she learned you were missing. She'll come around, Zeus. That woman loves you even more than she knows. In my opinion, now is the time to start fighting for her."

"I am fighting for her. My way. She is scary smart and fiercely determined. I know her better now than I did before this all started. Realize now that I can't force her to admit she loves me. I can only tell her what I think of her and let her absorb it in her own due time. Which I'll do, when I see her in person."

"So until then you're giving her the silent treatment?"

"No. You're going to let her know I'm fine. When she's through with the Stollen interview, I'll call her. I'm making a prediction. All we'll do is talk about work—because she won't be the one to bring up personal issues. She and I will have to communicate about business issues until the trial ends and—hope against fucking hope—we figure out who has been impersonating Maximov. I'll keep talking to her about work, until she decides she's ready to talk about personal issues. And if she's not ever ready to do that, well..." He was quiet for a second. As the helicopter landed, and his gaze rested on the people who were waiting for him, he added, "I'll eventually change tactics. I'm not giving up, Ragno. Just trying to outsmart her without breaking my heart."

He stepped out of the chopper and ran across the tarmac, arms outstretched, as his baby girl ran to meet him.

"Daddy!"

He fell to his knees as she collided with him. Enveloping her in his arms, he buried his face in her dark hair. With his arms and shoulders shaking from the force of emotion he couldn't suppress, he squeezed her tightly as he thanked God that she was alive and safe.

Chapter Thirty-Eight

London, England
Thursday, February 10

The elevator dinged as the door opened on the fifth floor of One River Thames. As Zeus stepped into the hallway, he glanced at his watch. 1415. It felt like years since he'd been in Texas, reunited with Ana, but it was just over twenty-four hours. Now, although it was midafternoon in London, his body felt like it should be the middle of the night. Still, his adrenaline rush from Ana's kidnaping energized him. He'd barely slept on the transatlantic flight he'd just taken. Instead, he'd maintained contact with Ragno and Barrows, monitoring developments in Jigsaw, as information was fed into the program.

When jet lag catches up, it'll be a bitch.

On Wednesday, shortly after Zeus's reunion with Ana, DNA results had confirmed that the remains Gabe found in Praptan were Andre Maximov. Once Maximov's remains were identified, the judges of the ITT had recessed the trial until Friday morning. For today, Thursday, Judge O'Connor had convened an unofficial status conference for the U.S. prosecutors, defense lawyers, and Amicus counsel.

Rather than conduct the status conference at the Royal Courts of Justice, where the London phase of the ITT trial was being held, Judge O'Connor—through Sam and Zeus—had chosen One River Thames, the private building where the Amicus team was housed, as the location for the conference.

Zeus agreed with the rationale for the location. Having the status conference at the Royal Courts of Justice, a public building, would have created a media event. One River Thames was more private than the large hotel where the U.S. judges were staying. Plus, Black Raven had already secured the premises, as the team's London home base was in apartments on the seventh and eighth floors.

Walking through the long, wide hallway that led to the conference room, Zeus nodded hello to Jenkins. Glancing further down the carpeted passageway, he spotted Deal and Miles—two agents on Sam's team, along with agents who made up the security teams for Charles and Abe. Six U.S. marshals, providing security for judges and lawyers, were also present.

"Gabe, I'm on site." Gabe had flown to London to be lead

agent in charge of the Amicus team until Zeus arrived. He was in the conference room.

"Roger," Gabe responded in a low whisper.

"Ragno, I'm about to head into the conference room." He walked to a buffet table and poured coffee into a paper cup. "Give me a quick update."

"As of five minutes ago, DHS has William Peterson in custody. They're going straight into interrogation. They also apprehended a man named Christian Lawrence, who happened to be in the apartment with William Peterson when DHS arrived. Sebastian is now here, at headquarters, working with his father-in-law. Which is good, because even I can't understand some of the things Barrows tries to tell me. Sebastian's cool interpretation of Barrows-speak is going a long way."

Jigsaw had identified William Peterson as Caller X, as Zeus had been in flight from Miami to London. Using communications data gathered from the TRCR—in particular a cell phone used by DIC—Jigsaw had isolated burner phone usage on incoming calls to DIC at points in Paris and London. Jigsaw determined parallel usage patterns between the calls made to Duvall's mother, the Miami cruise ship bomber, and the calls to the TRCR. Jigsaw then pinpointed the location of the burner phone at the times the calls were made. Although the burner phones with which Peterson had made the calls were long gone, he hadn't stripped himself of all of his co-existing digital devices that had been in use when he used the burner phones. Jigsaw searched for the devices in current time. Jigsaw had located Peterson in London, in an apartment on Chancery Lane, walking distance from the Royal Courts of Justice.

As Jigsaw started putting the puzzle pieces together, Zeus had contacted the secretary of the Department of Homeland Security and the director of the National Security Agency and kept them apprised of the developments. DHS had mobilized agents—already in London as part of the ITT security team—to arrest Peterson. Interrogation would be conducted by government agents who were briefed on the classified aspects of Jigsaw, but because Jigsaw provided firsthand information to Black Raven, and not to either the NSA or the DHS, Black Raven's assistance had been requested in the interrogation of Peterson. "Your team's providing interrogation assistance?"

"Yes. We're providing strict controls on what kind of information Black Raven provides. We're succinctly laying out what we have in a manner that will encourage the suspects to start talking, but not giving them anything regarding our methodology."

"No need to tell the how and why of it." Zeus sipped the coffee, opened a peanut butter power bar that had been sitting in a basket, and took a bite as he listened to Ragno, whose calm tone conveyed underlying excitement. He felt it too, the thrill that Jigsaw—the brainchild of Ragno, Zeus, and Barrows—was putting cyber-puzzle pieces together and producing answers. Barrows was a fucking genius, and his hefty salary was worth every penny.

"I've got live camera and video feed into the interviews, so I'm seeing it in real time," Ragno added. "They will soon understand from the DHS interrogators that they have only a couple of bargaining chips. One, admit their crimes early. Two, bring down anyone they're working with."

"Either Peterson, or, what's the name of the guy who was arrested with him?" He finished the power bar in two more bites.

"Christian Lawrence."

"Sounds familiar."

"I thought so too. Getting ready to run more expansive searches. Oh. Wait. Get this: Lawrence, a lawyer, was formerly an assistant United States attorney. That fact just came in as you chewed in my ear. We're working on putting some flesh on his AUSA profile."

"Are either Peterson or Lawrence talking?" He washed down the power bar with the last of his coffee and dropped the cup and wrapper into a wastebasket.

"Not yet."

"What do we know about William Peterson, aside from him being Caller X?"

"Minimal at this point. Just that Peterson, like Lawrence, is a lawyer. Details coming shortly. Seems he retired a while back."

"Great. So they're both lawyers. What the hell? Anything else?"

"Jigsaw is still pulling the threads together. Wait. This just in—Lawrence's laptop was used in the proximity of burner phones that placed calls to the TRCR, when those calls were placed. Meaning it's becoming more likely that Christian Lawrence and William Peterson are accomplices, and now Jigsaw is dissecting Lawrence's cyber history, which...Oh. You'll love this. As of last week, Lawrence did a good bit of searching for information on you, Ana, and Barrows, at the same time Peterson was doing similar searches and making contact with the

TRCR. This confirms that it wasn't just a coincidence that Lawrence and Peterson were together today, when Peterson was arrested."

"Too bad authorities got to these fucking bastards before me."

"Given the tone of your voice, I'm glad the authorities apprehended them. Need I remind you that you can't always get away with being judge, jury, and executioner? Wait. Information is now flowing so fast I can't keep up with the items of interest." Through the mic, he heard her fingers clacking furiously on her keyboard. He could imagine her eyes scanning the numerous monitors in front of her workstation as she typed. "Holy hell. From 1992 to 2010, Peterson worked in the office of general counsel for Sullivans of New York, the company that sells insurance coverage due to terrorism."

Click. Another puzzle piece fell into place. Potential motive? Money—a lawyer's wet dream. "Hell. Peterson probably drafted the terrorism clause." The skin on the back of his neck prickled as another thought occurred to him. "Could Peterson or Lawrence be secret partners in Sullivans?"

"Zeus, you could be one of the secret partners for all I know. We have yet to discover the identities of the secret partners. Lawrence certainly has the old-family money, Ivy-League pedigree that could make such a monied background a fit. Peterson comes from humble beginnings. What I do know is, given the sparse payout history of Sullivans for claims, the company is making boatloads of money off of their terrorism coverage. Every time there's an uptick in terrorism, more companies seek coverage."

It made perfect sense. "And these guys are creating the upticks in terrorism. Either they're getting paid to do so, or they're part of the company."

"Potentially," Ragno said. "Don't forget, a hell of a lot has to come together before we can prove this theory. But we're close, really, really close. Without Jigsaw, this would take three years or more to put together. At the rate Barrows's masterpiece of a program is going, we're hopeful we'll have all the pieces tonight. Tomorrow at the latest."

Closed double doors marked the entrance to the conference room where Sam was working. He hadn't seen her since she'd boarded Raven One in Miami. She'd been headed to ADX Florence for her interview of Stollen, at the same time he'd been headed into the Sikorsky with Sebastian to rendezvous at the latitude and longitude where Martel's GPS chip had been signaling. It felt like a lifetime had elapsed, but it had only been a little more than forty-eight hours. "Alert me if they start talking."

"Will do.

"By the way, Peterson is, apparently, a serious chain smoker. Interrogators are going to enjoy depriving him of his smokes. Wait a sec." He could hear Barrows and Ragno talking. "Zeus. We're close to identifying someone else."

"How long will that take?"

"Not sure. Using Jigsaw's analysis of co-existing digital devices, we're analyzing cyber footprints from any and all devices used in the proximity of digital devices owned by Lawrence and Peterson." Her fingers raced across the keyboard as she spoke. She was telling him things he already knew, but he didn't mind. "It's a hybrid indoor/outdoor positioning system that Barrows developed. It allows pinpoint tracking of Wi-Fi enabled devices—and these days, everything is Wi-Fi enabled. Turning off a device doesn't help. The big slowdown is trying to forensically analyze historical data. We're working through it, given that we don't have to go too far back. Peterson, aka, Caller X, called TRCR several times last week—so we're dissecting that time frame."

"Keep me updated."

"Wait. Before you go in, you're not planning on revealing the apprehension of William Peterson and Christian Lawrence to Judge O'Connor or Samantha, are you?"

His hand rested on the doorknob. "The identity of William Peterson as Caller X is certainly relevant to the ITT proceeding. I'm communicating with the powers that be at the DHS and NSA on what to reveal, when. We'll have to tell the ITT something, and soon."

Ragno clicked away at her keyboard as she spoke. "Ideally, Jigsaw will reveal that Peterson was the mastermind behind the Paris metro bombings, the Miami cruise ship drone attacks, Ana's kidnaping, and other events. At the moment, however, we can't forget that Jigsaw is proprietary to Black Raven and run in the context of a top-secret government job."

"Understood."

"Unless and until you get the green light from DHS and NSA, you don't have authority to go public at this point in time with anything. Even after we have the green light, we still have to tread carefully with what we reveal. From our perspective, technical aspects of Jigsaw aren't for public consumption. It isn't in Black Raven's benefit to give away Barrows' thought processes and trade secrets."

"Agreed." He appreciated Ragno's words of caution. Given the importance of Jigsaw, and its capability to become a crime-fighting tool of unprecedented dimension, the last thing he wanted to do was to expose it prematurely in a proceeding that had been doomed for failure at the inception.

Zeus quietly slipped inside the large conference room, which had high ceilings, recessed lighting, and two walls of floor to ceiling windows overlooking the Thames. There were no drapes to close on the windows, so the glass panels remained exposed. Flat afternoon light from the overcast day filled the room. Zeus knew from his prior assessment of the building that the windows were tinted, so that no one could see into the high rise. The other walls were paneled in large squares of polished mahogany. A long rectangular table that could easily seat thirty was centered in the expansive room. In each of the four corners of the room were smaller circular tables.

Judge O'Connor and the other three judges from the U.S.—Judge Kent Devlin, Judge Amanda Whitsell, and Judge Mark Kennedy—sat in the middle of one side of the table, their backs to the river, facing the doorway through which Zeus had just entered. In dark business suits, not judicial robes, their somber, thoughtful expressions provided an immediate gauge as to the serious nature of the business they were conducting.

Robert Brier and his team of defense lawyers sat on the far right of the table, with the pretty brunette at his side. Benjamin McGavin and his team of prosecutors sat on the far left. Sam and her team sat with their backs to the doorway, directly across from the judges. Abe was on her left, Charles on her right.

"Your honors, I repeat, there is absolutely no need for a mistrial." As a nod to the informal nature of the conference, Sam, wearing a light green business suit, was sitting as she spoke. Her voice, cool and moderate yet infused with the passion she conveyed as an advocate, took his breath. Her blonde hair was in a sleek ponytail that revealed her slender neck. In the perfect world, within minutes of this conference being over, his lips would be on that slender neck, his hands filled with her breasts, and there'd be no need to talk.

However, the world was imperfect, and, given the professional nature of every conversation they'd had since he'd gotten free from the TRCR, he doubted he'd be kissing her neck any time soon.

Didn't matter.

I'll figure it out. Given what had happened in the last forty-eight hours, I'm damn thankful for the opportunity to try again.

Gabe, standing three feet inside the door to the left, gave him a nod. Four U.S. marshals, the lead members of the judicial security teams, stood nearby.

Zeus went to stand beside his brother. "Great to be in the same room with you," Zeus whispered. He added, with a touch of sarcasm, "Angel." He pitched his voice low enough that only his mic picked it up. Gabe would hear him through his earpiece.

Professional decorum didn't inhibit Gabe's wide smile, a twinkle in his green eyes, and an eyebrow arch. "Back at ya."

Gabe was a master at the Black Raven skill of ventriloquism speaking. While his voice came through Zeus's mic loud and clear, it was damn hard to detect that he was talking just by looking at him, because his lips weren't moving. With his voice as low as it could go, without an earpiece no one could have heard him. "Samantha has been countering Brier for two hours. Brier is pushing for the judges to vote for a mistrial. She's carrying President Cameron's water on this one." He arched an eyebrow. "She has certainly persuaded me. Hey, what's with Brier and his hot-looking associate?"

"You see it too?"

"They don't have the right amount of body space. I could be wrong, though."

"Right before his wife was murdered, I asked Ragno to look into it."

"And?"

"Nothing so far. Hasn't been a priority though." Zeus focused his attention on Sam's argument.

"Each event that is being tried has defendants that can be convicted, regardless of who the ringleaders were," Sam said. "The analogue in criminal law is the law of conspiracies. We can try some members of a conspiracy without having all in custody. In fact, that is often the case—"

"But not when there is no grasp on the parameters of the conspiracy," Brier interrupted, his voice loud. "Your Honors, why rush to judgment? If not a vote for a mistrial, why not close the proceeding, and reconvene at a later date? The other countries will agree to a continuance. Why not take that—"

"I disagree that this is in any way a rush to judgment, and I have the answer as to why the proceedings must continue," Samantha said. "Because the consensus of governments that created this ITT could very well dissolve it, if we lose all momentum.”

Abe handed her a yellow legal tablet. She took it and glanced down for barely a second. “As it exists in the current state, the record of this proceeding is sufficient to try and possibly convict at least one hundred twenty-seven people over the four incidents and countries at issue.” She paused for a moment for emphasis. The judges were focused on her. The room was quiet. “Conservatively, based on my knowledge of the information, I’d say I am confident at least one hundred convictions will result from the existing record. That number is based upon stipulated evidence—meaning we can drastically streamline the proceeding from here on out. But let me be clear; I am not recommending such a streamlined approach.”

Sam picked up a pen, made a quick note on the legal pad as she spoke, and pushed it to Abe. “Now that we’ve confirmed Maximov’s death, examining witnesses may very well lead to discovering who has been impersonating him. Simply put, because we were unaware that Maximov was dead, we’ve been asking the wrong questions. Also, based on last week’s motion, we’re expanding the record with additional telecommunications data in France. I am preparing motions for an across the board expansion of the record in all countries—”

“What Ms. Fairfax is admitting is that the existing ITT record cannot accommodate the new developments,” Brier interrupted. “Yes, Stollen led us to Maximov’s body, but he didn’t lead us anywhere else. Isn’t that correct, Ms. Fairfax?”

As Samantha turned to face Brier, she looked over her shoulder and her eyes found Zeus for a moment. She gave him a nod. There was barely a break in her focused expression, then her eyes found Brier. She lifted her hands and used them for emphasis as she made counterarguments. “Do not minimize the importance of learning that Maximov is dead, Mr. Brier. As you very well know—”

“Counselors,” Judge O’Connor’s tone contained a warning to behave. “Do not resort to argument amongst yourselves. You have four judges to persuade here, one way or another. You are to address the bench. Not each other. The issue is whether this seating of the ITT should be terminated. Stay focused.”

Sam turned back to the judges. “Thank you, Your Honor. No—the trial should not be terminated. However, the importance of knowing of Maximov’s death should not be underestimated.”

“No engagement ring,” Gabe whispered, as Sam continued with her argument.

"I noticed." The absence of the bling registered the minute she turned to Abe and took the legal pad from him. "Leave that issue alone."

"Could mean anything," Gabe shrugged. "She probably just needed to have it sized."

"Fuck you." Zeus made sure no one could overhear that zinger.

"You'd have an answer if you and she just had a real conversation."

"How do you know we haven't?"

"Because I know you. And I've talked to Ragno, who told me your brilliant plan to let Samantha be the one to bring up personal issues." Gabe's eye roll told Zeus what he thought of the plan. "With her, I wouldn't hold my breath. What if she doesn't?"

"Ragno?" Zeus felt like throttling both Ragno and Gabe.

"Sorry, Zeus," Ragno said through his mic. "You know Angel is my weakness, and you're a close second."

"Between you and Samantha," Gabe said, "I don't know who is cooler. You're both icebergs."

"Get outta here, Gabe. I've got this."

Gabe chuckled on his way out of the conference room.

"We've been through this, Your Honors, though Mr. Brier obviously isn't grasping the points I've been trying to make. No, Stollen had no information on who may be perpetuating the Maximov myth. When I returned to interview him after DNA identified the remains, he had no further information. What he did provide, though, were some intriguing points that should be explored further and those points should be explored in this proceeding without delay."

"Such as?" Judge O'Connor asked.

"Stollen was interviewed seven years ago. He insists that he told the prosecutor, and his attorney, who happened to be Mr. Brier, the same thing he told me Tuesday morning—that Maximov was dead and where to recover the body. Therefore, what has become an issue squarely for this court is whether Stollen is telling the truth and who concealed it. I question Mr. Brier's impartiality and believe the court must consider the advisability of his continuing role in this proceeding."

Click. Click. As Sam's argument registered, her work on the ITT trial firmly collided with the puzzle pieces that Jigsaw was assembling. *Maybe.* He needed confirmation of his hunch, though, from Ragno.

"Ragno?" Zeus whispered, his pulse doing a staccato beat as

blood coursed through his veins.

"Wait. I need a second," she said. "What Samantha just said has me doing some searches, while I'm fielding a question from the interrogation team that's with Peterson."

"Good."

"All well and good, Your Honors, but what Ms. Fairfax is overlooking is that Stollen is using revisionist history." Brier leaned forward, his voice only slightly on the civilized side of an angry yell. "I was present at that meeting. If Stollen had revealed the facts he now says that he revealed, I'd have reported it and I am insulted that Ms. Fairfax is questioning my integrity." Breathing heavily, face flushed, he paused, clearly to gather himself. "Your Honors, Vladimer Stollen is not only a mass murderer, he's a pathological liar, and—"

"Not so pathological, and not such a liar, Mr. Brier." Sam turned to Brier. "He certainly led us to Maximov's body. So, of the people who were present in the interview seven years ago..." Her voice trailed as Judge O'Connor stood, interrupting her with a wave of his hand.

"Okay, counselors. We've been at this for two hours. Take a break. Fifteen minutes. Cool off. When we reconvene, I'd like to hear the prosecutorial viewpoint from Mr. McGavin." Judge O'Connor nodded to the end of the table, where the prosecutors sat. "Mr. McGavin, I know it's hard to get a word in between Ms. Fairfax and Mr. Brier. We'll start with you when we reconvene.

"Ragno? What are you finding?"

"Still looking. Meanwhile, I'm talking to interrogators and interpreting Barrows's answers for them. Two very different streams of dialogue, trust me."

A couple of the judges and their security teams left the conference room, as did the prosecutors. Judge O'Connor walked over to where his law clerk stood, in the far corner of the large conference room, next to Judge Devlin. Brier, his cheeks flushed red from his argument with Sam, pushed his chair back. He strode to the small table closest to him and poured a cup of coffee. Turning his back to the room, he stood where the two walls of windows joined, staring out at the panoramic view of London as he took a sip.

Sam stood and walked with purpose to Brier, evidently intent on continuing their argument. Zeus's gut sent a warning signal of urgency, but from where the threat might be coming, he wasn't entirely certain. He had a hunch, however. "Stop multitasking for a few seconds. You said Christian Lawrence was formerly a U.S. prosecutor?"

"Yes."

"Tell me whether he worked on Stollen's prosecution. Need to know now."

"Give me a second."

Sam was engaged in a heated discussion with Brier. Brier gestured wildly, his jacket opening with the movement. "Gabe. Get in here."

Gabe immediately returned to the conference room and Zeus's side, eyebrow raised in inquiry.

"You aware Brier's carrying?" he demanded, not taking his eyes off the two who stood in the V of windows. Swirls of mist rose from the river. Breaks in the afternoon clouds revealed blue sky. His gut was now screaming at him not to take his eyes off Sam. At this decibel level, silent to the rest of the world but a raging inner howl, Zeus trusted his gut implicitly.

"Yep," his brother said. "Noticed his neat little Glock this morning. Evidently his wife's death has him on edge. Typically would be damned hard for a civilian to be carrying that in London, but ITT security facilitated and approved it."

Brier reached into the inside pocket of his jacket for his cell phone, and lifted it to his ear while Sam appeared to be in midsentence.

"Answer is yes," Ragno confirmed. "Lawrence did work on Stollen's prosecution. He was the government's lead attorney."

"Was Lawrence present in Stollen's post-incarceration interviews, with Brier, when Stollen claims to have told them the first time around where the fuck he buried Maximov?" With a flat-handed wave at his side, Zeus indicated for Gabe to stay in place as he started across the room, to Sam.

"Yes."

"Is Lawrence talking to investigators?"

Brier turned pale as he talked on the phone. Sam, looking coolly outraged that the man had interrupted their conversation by answering his phone, stood within a foot of him, arms folded, and tapping her foot as he spoke. They were so close to the window that they were standing on hardwood floor outside the border of the large area rugs. From where he stood, Zeus could hear the *tap tap tap* of her shoe on the wood floor.

Everything else in the room registered, but in slow motion. He was so focused on Sam, noises from others in the conference room were muted. Two of Brier's associates were still at the main table; the brunette was walking past Zeus, on her way out the door. On the far end of the conference room, Judge O'Connor and Judge Devlin were continuing their conversation. Three marshals, part of the judicial security team, were talking quietly. McGavin, the lead prosecutor, had returned to the room and was standing at the large table, thumbing through a legal pad of notes.

Zeus rounded the large conference table, putting the rest of the room to his side. The puzzle pieces weren't all there, but if his hunch panned out, that meant Brier had been instrumental in the murder of his wife. It didn't make sense. Yet. The man had seemed genuinely heartbroken upon learning the news that she'd been killed. His shock and grief had appeared authentic, even if he was having an affair with his associate. He wouldn't be the first man to have an affair, yet still love his wife.

Either Brier was a damned good actor or a cold-blooded murderer. Given what Zeus now knew about the scope of crimes in which Lawrence and Peterson had been involved, Zeus suspected Brier was the latter. And worse. The why and how of it didn't need to make sense now.

What needed to happen was that Sam had to be safe.

He walked faster as his gut screamed one thing; *Get Sam the fuck away from Brier.*

Chapter Thirty-Nine

"Interrogators gave Lawrence a phone call," Ragno said. "Presumably he made one to a lawyer—Wait."

No shit.

"DHS informs me he called Brier." Ragno's words were clipped. "Copy?"

"Copy." Lawrence calling Brier, a world-class skilled defense lawyer who'd also worked on the Stollen prosecution. Might be a coincidence. Could mean nothing as to Brier's complicity in Lawrence's criminal activity. Zeus didn't believe in coincidences.

"Perhaps just a hiring call?"

"Not making that assumption."

Brier, with his phone to his ear, glanced in Zeus's direction, eyes wide with sudden shock. Watching Zeus approach, shock gave way to wild-eyed fear. His glance flitted to the door, then back to Zeus.

Not a fucking hiring call.

Dropping his cell phone to the floor, Brier simultaneously reached for Sam and his gun. A mere ten feet away, Zeus already had his Glock in his hand.

"There's no way out," Zeus said, slowly inching forward.

"Put your weapon down," Brier yelled. "You killed my wife!"

Huh?

Someone gasped. Someone else screamed.

"Everyone, down!" Zeus yelled.

In his peripheral vision, Zeus saw the marshals dive for the two judges who remained in the room. In the mic, Gabe gave orders to Jenkins to secure the conference room. Those who were outside were to remain outside. Gabe's voice, smooth and calm, kept all on-premised Black Raven agents, and Ragno, informed of what was transpiring.

Zeus blocked everything out but Brier, Brier's laser-sighted semiautomatic pistol, and Sam—who had Brier's left arm wrapped around her neck. Brier, the same height as Sam, held her in a damn effective chokehold, which effectively shielded him from the bullet Zeus wanted to put between his eyes.

"No one will believe I killed your wife, and no one will believe you've had a mental snap, if that's what you're going for." Zeus's tone was calm, but the hard knock of his heart was loud in his ears. "Stop the bullshit and give yourself up before someone gets hurt."

"Hernandez, I won't warn you again. One inch closer, she's dead." Brier's gun, firmly and coolly grasped in his right hand, was steady on Sam's temple.

"William Peterson and Christian Lawrence are in custody." Zeus figured those names would get Brier's attention.

Hiding behind Sam, Brier harrumphed. Almost convincingly. "They have nothing to do with me."

"Not what they say." Zeus didn't give a damn whether what he was saying was true. He was trying to buy time, waiting to see more than just a half inch of the man's head, temple, or ear. "According to them, you're the mastermind. We know that the three of you have been working together for years. Actually, you and Christian Lawrence have been working together ever since Stollen told the two of you the first time where he buried Andre Maximov. You two saw an opportunity. William Peterson provided the vehicle."

Ready. Aim. Take the shot.

Dammit to hell.

No fucking head shot on Brier.

No fucking shot of any kind that would be effective.

Aiming between Sam's wide green eyes, waiting for the second he had a clear shot, Zeus inched closer to them as Brier inched further into the corner where the two walls of windows met, dragging Sam with him.

Sam filled Zeus's vision, wild-eyed as she dug her nails into Brier's left arm, the one that had the stranglehold on her neck. Her struggle was useless since he wore a tailored suit, the wool of the jacket impenetrable by her short nails.

A bullet would do the job, however. If only he had a shot.

"Let me go!" Sam's elbow found Brier's chest. He rewarded her by tightening his hold on her neck. Placing both hands on his forearm, she still couldn't wrench his arm off of her.

Move, Sam. Drop. Give me an inch.

As Brier ground the muzzle of his gun along her temple, she met Zeus's eyes with a look that conveyed stark terror and a desperate plea for help.

Drop, Sam.

As if reading his mind, she let her knees go soft. Brier was ready for the move, and merely tightened his arm across her throat, until she gagged and tried even more frantically to pull his arm from her neck.

"Your theory is insane, Hernandez," Brier bellowed, his tone loud and imperious. "Would someone please put an end to this?

He has no authority to be threatening me!"

"Sullivans of New York." Zeus inched closer. He was now seven feet away from them. "This is how it works. Sullivans sells insurance coverage to companies for business interruption due to terrorism. It's really profitable coverage. Now that Peterson and Lawrence are pointing their fingers at you, we're in your bank records. We know Sullivans has been paying you three for years to create terrorist events, to make sure their coverage keeps selling. Terrorism is big business, Brier, and the three of you cashed in on fear and made damn sure there were plenty of terrorist acts worldwide to foster that fear. You were very effective at making it look as though there were random acts of terror, by terrorists who were trying to stop the ITT proceedings. What were thousands of deaths compared to hundreds of millions of dollars?"

Zeus inched closer, hoping like hell that he was buying time by giving voice to the theory that he and Ragno had discussed in the hallway. It appeared that Brier was listening. "Through masquerading as Maximov, you've perpetuated an anti-government myth that two-bit thugs want to believe in. You learned the trade from your own clients. You use their contacts, their methods, and you've even made sure your competition gets convicted when they're of no use to you. As in Stollen's case, you made damn sure your clients stayed in jail when it suited you."

"All a crock of half-baked bullshit that will never be proven in a court of law."

Zeus moved forward another inch, as the pieces he knew from Jigsaw clicked together, solidifying a hunch in his mind. It made so much fucking sense, it had to be correct. He was putting together pieces faster than Jigsaw, but he had faith Jigsaw would catch up and prove him correct. He knew now that Jigsaw had snapped pieces together that gave him the hunch, the sophisticated program would find the pieces to prove the theory correct. Jigsaw was designed to do exactly that.

"You've been manipulating this ITT record from day one. You made sure it was polluted with references to Maximov, so that no one looked for the real puppet master. Yeah, you want a mistrial. Now we all fucking know why—because without Maximov to blame, someone smart was going to figure out you're behind all of this." Another painful inch forward. The room was silent now, everyone apparently frozen. Listening. Computing. Judging. Because what he was saying made so much damned sense, it was horrifying.

"When Stanley Morgan questioned, early on, the lack of evidence indicating that Maximov was actually responsible for the terrorist cells, you had him killed to keep him from looking for the real culprit. You tried to stop the entire Amicus team by poisoning them, because you knew they would carry on Morgan's work. You had Judge Devlin's wife killed to try to pressure the judges to stop the proceeding. You had your own wife killed to deflect suspicion so no one would look at you, you sick fuck. You tried to stop me. Used my daughter to do it. That was your biggest mistake, and not just because I'm taking this so personally I'm going to be thrilled when your balls are chained to the wall of a cell on Ultimate Exile, floating forever on the prison ship from hell. Peterson's calls to the TRCR instructing them to kidnap my daughter provided Barrows a road map leading directly to you. It's over, Brier. Put your weapon down and let Sam go."

Zeus kept his tone cool and calm, because as the pieces clicked in his mind, he felt enormous gratitude that on this cloudy, wintry day he knew that one of the men who had been instrumental in Ana's kidnaping would die. Either by his hand or, if Brier killed Zeus before Zeus managed to get a shot, by Gabe's—because the fucking bastard had no way out. Standing framed by the windows, he was quite literally cornered.

But a cornered animal was unpredictable. One wrong move and Brier would have no compunction about shooting Sam point blank.

Nothing to lose and cornered. A recipe for disaster.

Goddammit, but I need to get Sam away.

"You talk too damned much, Hernandez. See where my beam is?" The laser site of Brier's weapon now bounced in and out of Zeus's vision. "Stop fucking moving, bitch, or the second bullet will be all yours."

Sam froze, her gaze on Zeus.

"Won't matter if you kill me, Brier. You'll be dead before I hit the ground. Let Sam go, and we can talk. She has nothing to do with your agenda."

The red light found his left eye. This time it didn't waver.

"No!" Sam pushed Brier's forearm as he fired, three times, in rapid succession.

The bullets went wild, striking the window on Brier's left. As the loud *rat-ta-tat* of gunfire faded, the safety glass of the window pebbled. Thick shatter lines spider-webbed from the bullet holes. The glass broke into tiny cubes, as Brier smacked the side of Sam's temple with the gun. With a crescendo that sounded like marbles spilling onto hard floor, chunks of glass disappeared from the solid, floor-to-ceiling frame. Some fell outside, some to the wood floor that bordered the room, some bounced on carpet floor. Damp outside air whooshed into the room.

"On your left." Gabe's whisper came through as Zeus felt his brother's presence at his side.

Keeping his eyes on Brier, Zeus was peripherally, and murderously, aware of blood blooming on Sam's right temple. *Ah, shit.* Either one of Brier's shots had grazed her, or the blow he'd delivered had been enough to split her skin.

The red line of blood was steady, but there wasn't enough of it for the injury to be life-threatening. She remained in Brier's chokehold. Blood dripped into her eye. She lifted a hand to her temple, before lowering her now-bloody fingers to her line of vision.

She went limp as she passed out.

Block her out. Focus and illuminate the target. Assess injuries later.

Fuck! Still no kill shot—and Gabe obviously didn't have one either.

"Let me walk out of here," Brier said, straining to hold up Sam's dead weight and keep his weapon fixed on Zeus at the same time. His hair ruffled in the wind blowing in from the broken window at his back.

"Not going to happen, unless you let her go." Zeus inched closer. Planning to lunge, he knew Brier would likely get a good shot on him. He was too exposed. Didn't matter.

Fuck!

Situation went from shit-bad to worse, because Brier's wild expression—flitting eyes and steady weapon—indicated that the man knew he was cornered, and he was determined to get out of the situation any fucking way possible.

Brier had one out—a suicide leap through the pane-less window, to a paved walkway that bordered the Thames, five stories below. Edging backwards towards the window, dragging Sam's limp body as a shield, Brier kept his weapon trained on Zeus.

"He's gonna jump." Whispering the obvious into the mic's audio feed, Zeus's peripheral vision told him that his brother, just a foot away, was poised and ready, waiting for a signal.

It was a fucking given that if Brier went through that

window, he'd take Sam with him. Brier stepped within a foot of the open window, glass crunching under his feet, Sam hanging limply from his forearm. "On two."

"Copy," Gabe said. "With you."

"One." Holding his Glock firmly in place, Zeus visualized for a split second how he was going to get a close head shot on Brier while managing to grab Sam with his left hand. "Two."

As he took a flying leap forward, Zeus fired.

He was vaguely aware of red and gray splatter raining out behind Brier, while very aware that Brier was falling towards the window and would soon be dropping through it.

Zeus grabbed Sam's forearm with his left hand, and yanked her with all of his might out of the grip of the dead man. Zeus's forward momentum almost carried them through the window with Brier. Gabe's solid grip on Zeus's legs stopped their trajectory. Zeus pulled Sam to him, and, as Gabe yanked them both backwards, crashed with her to the floor. Safety glass crunched under him when he turned and rolled, as Gabe yanked them further into the room.

Touching his fingers to her neck, he felt for her pulse. He was able to breathe when he felt the steady beat. He cradled her to his chest and dropped his face to hers. He kissed her cheek and inhaled the scent of blood and sweet jasmine, as his body shook with relief.

Chapter Forty

Samantha's suite of rooms was a small, two-bedroom apartment on the eighth floor of One Thames Place. In between her bedroom and the bedroom of her lead security agent, there was a living room, a small kitchen, and a dining area, with a rectangular dining table that seated six. She'd used it the night before as a worktable with Abe and Charles.

Now, the dining table served as a medical examining table. Doctor Drannen, a Black Raven doctor, leaned over her, placing stitches along her hairline, where Brier had hit her with the gun, creating a several-inch split along her hairline. Rix, a Black Raven medic, worked on pulling pieces of glass out of her right arm. Rix and Drannen were working on her right. Gabe sat in a chair on the left, between the table and the windows, watching their progress.

"Wasn't that window made of safety glass?" She'd refused the doctor's offer of an oral painkiller. She winced as she felt the tip of the tweezers as Rix rooted in her arm. She could also feel the push and pull of the needle and thread in her forehead.

"Yes. Tempered, too," Gabe answered. "And film-treated for opaque qualities."

"Didn't think safety glass was supposed to cut," she muttered.

"A common misconception," Gabe said. "It still has jagged edges, especially when shot at that close range. Sort of like a buzz saw, though nothing like the shards that would have sliced you, had the glass been plain old-fashioned annealed glass."

"Why weren't you cut?"

He shrugged. "I didn't roll in it, like you and Zeus."

Focusing for a moment on the window behind Gabe, she realized that where the drapes were slightly parted, the darkness outside made the window a looking glass, where she could see what they were doing to her. She drew a deep breath, breathing in the antiseptic, and shut her eyes. She immediately opened them. Closing them made her nausea worse.

She'd first become conscious in Zeus's arms, on the floor of the conference room, with Zeus, Judge O'Connor, and Gabe looking at her. Seeing smears of red blood on Zeus's cheek, and all over his white shirt, she'd promptly blacked out again. The second time around she'd woken up flat on the blanket-covered table, her head on a pillow, with Doctor Drannen and Rix leaning over her. She'd almost lost her post-faint battle against nausea. The doctor had given her a shot that should have helped.

It did, but barely.

Gasping for air, trying to fight past the feeling that her stomach was rising into her throat, she glanced at Gabe. "Where's Zeus?"

"On his way up."

Sam straightened her features because frowning made her forehead crease, and that made the thread and needle tug harder. "Is he okay?"

"Yes." She'd known Gabe's answer, because she'd asked the question a minute earlier, as the doctor was making his first pass with the needle and thread. But she also knew these men would say they were fine, even if a bullet was embedded in them. As long as they could speak and think, answer would be, *I'm fine.*

"But there was so much blood."

"Mostly yours." Gabe gave her the same slight frown that Zeus gave when he was concentrating. "Not his."

"Talk to me." She tried to focus on Gabe's green eyes. If she looked anywhere else at him—his square jawline, his dark hair, his broad shoulders—it was like looking at Zeus, which was disconcerting, because this man wasn't Zeus. "Please. I need to focus on something. How did he put that together? Everything he was saying in the conference room. What, exactly, led him to Lawrence and Peterson? And how did he know Brier was involved?"

"You know everything I know. You heard it from Zeus. Brier went suicidal and tried to take you out in the process."

"But why?"

She'd watched Gabe with the Black Raven agents the night before. When he spoke his voice and tone carried the same authority as Zeus, and his agents treated him with the same respect they gave to his brother, yet Gabe had an easy manner and an easier smile. His easy smile, though, was apparently for others only.

Upon meeting him in person the day before, observing the contrast of his easy manner with others and the way he looked at her as though she'd done something wrong, she'd immediately gotten the impression that he didn't like her. At best, he seemed wary.

If he's looking out for his brother's best interests, I don't blame him.

She heard the door open.

"She's awake?" Zeus's voice.

Thank God.

"Zeus! How the hell did you put all of that together, and—"

"Seriously?" Gabe's arched eyebrow and marked frown quieted her.

"I'll fill you in later," Zeus said. "Best if I don't walk over there looking like this, unless you want to be sick again." She heard footsteps head towards the bedroom that had been Gabe's the night before.

Gabe gave her a headshake. "Your first thought when my brother shows up, after what he's been though in the last forty-eight hours and, by the way, almost getting his head blown off while saving your life, is to talk about work?"

"Zeus." Doctor Drannen paused, holding the needle in the air, as he glanced to his left.

"Yes?"

"Need to get that glass out of you. Rix, go get started on him. I'll pick up on Samantha, where you leave off."

"Just a few more pieces to go. Those might need a stitch or two." Rix stepped away from her arm.

She heard a door click shut—presumably the door to the bedroom Gabe had used the night before. Now that Zeus was here, she assumed Zeus would stay there.

She inadvertently got a glimpse of Rix pulling off his gloves, which were smeared with her blood. A fresh wave of nausea overcame her. She shook her head, forcing the doctor to step back for a second.

Frantic, she glanced at Gabe. "I need to focus on something other than blood."

"Here," Gabe said. Gabe held his cell phone up to her eye level. "Look at this. Doc?"

"Yes?"

"Need your confidentiality on this one. I'm not supposed to have this. I wheedled it out of a friend of mine."

"Understood." The doctor gave Gabe a smile as he leaned closer to Sam to study his handiwork. "Not a bad job, if I do say so myself."

"Samantha. Eyes here." Gabe jiggled the cell phone.

The image on the screen was a close-up of Zeus. She gave Gabe a questioning glance, which he returned with a look of Hernandez-style stoicism before tapping the screen. The video started playing, and she was immediately sucked into the gravity in Zeus's dark eyes, the underlying grim worry evident in his voice.

"*Hey, Sam. I'm heading to the DZ to rescue Ana. If you're seeing this, I haven't made it. Just wanted to tell you something I should've told you last night, when we were arguing on the plane. Instead of telling you I was done, that I was giving up on us, what I should've said was...I love you. As much as life itself. For the rest of our lives, I was never going to be more than one call away—because I was never giving up on you. I'm damn lucky that I got to be with you in these last few days and I wouldn't change one second of it.*" He gave a slight smile. "*Well, that's not true. I'd certainly change the fact that you chose to marry someone else while I was still alive.*"

The smile drifted from his lips. "*I blame myself for that, more than you though. I don't want you to regret that decision now. Well, maybe just a little bit of regret would be nice. I understand you're afraid of being with me—though I sure wish you'd have given me the chance to talk you out of that fear. You see, instead of getting angry with you, I should have just said that the simple fact is I love you. Always have. Always will. No matter what you do. You're the only one for me. And I know now that if I had a hundred years to live, I'd never give up on us. Never.*" He glanced away, then back at the camera. "*You're strong enough that you'll realize every goal you set for yourself. But don't forget to be happy, Sam. It's important. When you weren't driving me crazy—and even when you were—being with you made me happy. Just the possibility of us one day being together made me happy. I love you.*"

She glanced at Gabe through tear-filled eyes.

Gabe's eyes reflected more than a little concern as her tears started falling. "Awww. Hell. I didn't mean to make you cry. It's just that my brother's not going to tell you any of that unless you give him a reason. He might love you more than he'll ever love anyone else, but he's never going to beg." He drew a deep breath. "I just want him to be happy. He deserves to have the one woman in the world who has driven him to distraction. Your life will be better with him in it. I promise. He's the toughest guy in the world, but his heart beats pure molten gold for the people he loves. Me. Ana. You. A handful of others. You're part of an exclusive club, Samantha. Don't think you should turn your back on it. Give him a chance. Talk about something other than work. See where that takes the two of you."

"Has it occurred to you that perhaps one reason your brother is attracted to me is precisely because my first thought is to talk about work? Even now?"

For the first time, Gabe gave her the heartfelt, warm, genuine smile that seemed to be his trademark. His eyes lightened. "Holy hell. You two were made for each oth—" His eyes turned serious, his expression focused, as he touched the mic at his ear. "Zeus. Repeat." He paused. "Okay. Copy. Jenkins? I'm going to the seventh floor. Need you here with Samantha."

***

Zeus sat on a chair in the bathroom, with his arm on towels on the vanity counter, while Rix removed small cubes of glass from his left arm. The fast-paced dialogue between Ragno, Barrows, and the analysts in Denver was a good distraction from the pain. It was gratifying to hear Jigsaw prove, with data, the theory that had coalesced in his mind and which he'd voiced, as he'd tried to get a shot on Brier.

"Gabe? In position?" Zeus asked as a large pebble of glass clinked in the metal pan, leaving in its wake a gaping cut and a welling of blood. *Thank God Sam isn't watching this. She'd be out cold about now.*

"Yes."

"I'll let you know if we need to take action. Getting Jigsaw on my hunch now."

"Roger."

When there was a lull in the Denver-based conversation, Zeus broke in. "Ragno. Go private."

"Okay. Me and you."

"While you and Barrows focus on the big picture, I need an analyst to focus on a few small slices of time." Rix rinsed the cut with alcohol, then opened a fresh pack of gauze and placed it over the cut. "The time frame of Stanley Morgan's death and the cyanide poisoning."

"Good idea."

"Look for calls to either Peterson, Lawrence, or Brier that suggest any connection to those events. Morgan's death, if it was a murder, was up close and personal. Plus, the cyanide poisoning suggests an awareness of procedures in place at the Hotel Grand Athens. So far, there are no suspects for either."

Doctor Drannen stepped into the room, washed his hands, and pulled on gloves.

"Ragno. Hold a second." Zeus addressed the doctor, "How's Sam?"

"Now that I'm finished with her, she's getting her equilibrium back."

"She called Senator McDougall," Ragno said, "and her grandfather, and now she's talking to Judge O'Connor."

Upon hearing McDougall's name, Zeus's heart twisted.

Hell. After the last forty-eight hours, I'm surprised my heart—the part of it that results in emotional feeling—still exists. And even more surprised that feelings can make my chest hurt like someone's reached in for a tight squeeze. I wish the goddamned organ would just stick with pumping blood.

The doctor's eyes narrowed as he studied Zeus's arm. He glanced at Rix. "Good job. These two need sutures."

Rix lifted his hands. "My skill set runs to extracting the glass and Band Aids. Have at him." He stepped back and let Drannen take up his position beside Zeus.

"At the time of both Morgan's death and the cyanide poisoning," Ragno said, "the Amicus team was guarded by U.S. marshals. Is that where you're going with this?"

"Not necessarily." He adjusted his arm as the doctor examined the bloody mess on his elbow, which was where he'd landed. They'd hit the wood floor first and his jacket had provided no protection for the shards of glass. Sam's weight on his arm, combined with his own, had turned his elbow into a pincushion for the glass that had been everywhere.

"Can you bend that arm?"

Zeus lifted his arm and bent it at the elbow. It hurt like hell, but it wasn't broken.

"Good enough."

Zeus turned his focus back to Ragno and said, "I'm throwing into the mix the question we had when we learned Ana's kidnapers wanted Barrows."

"The question of why Barrows and why now?"

"Yep. Interesting that in the year that we've had Barrows working for us, the very first threat we've had directed against him came after I revealed OLIVER to the Amicus team." The doctor pushed the needle through his skin. "OLIVER revealed just a fraction of Jigsaw's data gathering and assimilating capabilities, but it was still impressive."

"You think someone on the Amicus team worked with Brier, Peterson, and Lawrence?"

"Yep."

"Okay, let's run with this. Assuming complicity in the three events—Morgan's death, cyanide poisoning, and learning about OLIVER—we can rule out Eric Moss."

"Correct."

Doctor Drannen did a tug, cut the thread, and started on the next laceration.

"Doubt he poisoned himself with cyanide." Zeus ignored the sharp in and out of the needle. "Plus, he was out of the picture when OLIVER was revealed to them."

"We can also rule out Abe," Ragno pointed out, "since he didn't arrive in Paris until after Morgan's death."

"That leaves us with Charles." Charles Beller, the cardigan-wearing assistant to the Amicus team.

"And Sam." Ragno's tone was quiet.

Her name in this context sliced through him. "No way."

"Jigsaw will tell us." Her fingers clicked on her keyboard. "Still want me to send an analyst down that path?"

"Jigsaw will get there eventually." He paused. "May as well figure this out now. I'm one hundred percent certain that if there is a connection—the mole is Charles."

"What makes you so sure?"

"Aside from knowing unequivocally that Sam isn't an option, I recall the night I gave the Amicus team the OLIVER database. When Barrows started talking about analyzing co-existing digital devices, I wanted to throttle him. Honest to God, that man should never be allowed to speak in public. He's brilliant, but he's got not one lick of common sense. He'd reveal his proprietary techniques without even realizing he was doing so. I shut him down that night by claiming the information was proprietary—but Charles was clued into the how, what, and why. He was more interested in the method, than in what OLIVER had produced for them. Charles asked whether a person could hide their calls from burner phones, if they turned off all their other devices."

"Turning off devices doesn't stop Jigsaw's capability of tracking them. Devices constantly communicate with the grid, even when they're off."

"I know that. Charles didn't. So I gave him misinformation and told him he was on the right track."

"Clever."

"Straighten your arm and turn it," the doctor instructed.

Zeus adjusted his position. When Drannen nodded, he continued. "Well, I wasn't thinking that Charles could have been a mole at the time. His questions were innocuous. I was just trying not to give information about Barrows' technique."

"So you're thinking that once Charles saw OLIVER, and heard Barrows explain the methodology, he alerted Brier,

Peterson, and Lawrence that Barrows and Black Raven had the capability to expose them?"

"Yep. And that's why they wanted Barrows."

"Okay."

"Last set of fresh stitches," Drannen said.

"Another thing, there might be telecom data contemporaneously with Morgan's death and the cyanide killing, but I doubt you'll see telecom data after we revealed OLIVER. I doubt he would've made a call to them after seeing what OLIVER could do with telephone calls. Besides, by then, we had all of his private phones. He wouldn't have needed a phone to do that, either. He could have done it in the proceedings last Thursday, face to face with Brier. There was a lot of time for conversation."

"Where is Charles now?"

"When Brier grabbed Sam, Abe and Charles were secured by their teams. They're both safely in their rooms. In effect—Charles is under house arrest, compliments of Black Raven, though he doesn't know it. Gabe's on it."

"Okay. I'll get an analyst looking at this."

Drannen stepped back. Zeus stood.

"Not so fast, sir."

"I'm fine."

"I know that. Sit. You've acquired an impressive collection of wounds over the last week."

Zeus reluctantly sat down again to allow the doctor to examine the stitches in his forehead. He watched Drannen's gaze shift to the purple bruise, where DIC's men had slammed the rifle butt into his temple. "Did you black out from this?"

"No."

"These stitches at your hairline are ready to come out."

The stitches from the bombing outside the ITT trial in Paris. "Go for it, Doc."

"Zeus," Ragno said. "Secretary Lindall's holding for you."

DHS Secretary Lindall. "Stay on the line with us. This call could provide parameters on how much we ultimately reveal about Jigsaw."

"Well," Ragno answered, "you know my vote."

"Yep. Same as mine. As little as possible. Results. Not method. Put him through."

Zeus strategized with Ragno and the DHS Secretary as the doctor worked on him.

Twenty minutes later, Zeus stepped into the living room separating the two bedrooms. Sam, standing by the crackling fireplace as she looked into the flames, had the Black Raven flip phone to her ear. She wore exercise leggings and a sweatshirt. Her blonde hair was scooped up into an endearingly messy ponytail. Eyeing her hairline, he wondered why the long line of stitches wasn't bandaged.

Fighting the urge to walk to her and wrap his arms around her, he reminded himself that he wasn't going there. Not until she wanted it. Not until she owned up to the fact that she really did love him. He wasn't going to budge an inch. Not going to touch her. Not going to kiss her. Not going to tell her he loved her. Even if it killed him.

Embrace the suck.

Yep.

Enjoy the hell out of this.

Chapter Forty-One

Samantha turned in Zeus's direction as she said, into the phone, "Judge O'Connor, President Cameron, may I suggest an approach that is less extreme than granting a mistrial? One that I think I can persuade others to go with, if I have a few days to do some back-door advocacy."

"Please do, Samantha," President Cameron said. With a slight nod from Zeus, Jenkins left the room with the doctor and Rix. Zeus went to the refrigerator, opened it, and grabbed a bottle of water. Barefoot, he wore a Black Raven-logo'd long-sleeve T-shirt with jeans. His damp hair was finger combed. He looked sexy and as tired as she felt. If the night didn't end with her curled in his arms, she was going to die.

In the video that Gabe had showed her, Zeus's raw emotions had been front and center. Now though, he wore his usual preternatural coolness, giving every indication that she was going to have to work to earn the right to be in his arms.

Please. Give me a hint. Make me believe we can work out. No matter how afraid I am. Please. Look like the man in the video. Like you forgive me for raking you over the coals. Like you haven't given up on me.

He held up the bottle of water to her, and she nodded, unable to tear her eyes from him.

Nope. Not a clue.

Focus.

You're on the phone with President Cameron and Judge O'Connor, for God's sake.

"First, Judge O'Connor can persuade the other judges to recess the proceedings until Monday," she said. "The court can rule without formally convening, pursuant to ITT Practice and Procedure Rule 3.3(a)(6). Judge O'Connor, I believe that if you start making phone calls this evening, everyone is so rattled they'll agree."

"Yes, Samantha. I agree with that," Judge O'Connor answered.

Zeus handed her the bottle of water and stepped away, leaving her enveloped in the fresh fragrance of woodsy soap and the pungent smell of antiseptic. A sharp reminder of his injuries. He went back to the refrigerator, took out another bottle of water, turned on the television, switched it to mute, and flipped through channels.

"Second, we can reconvene in London on Monday morning for a status conference," Sam continued. "We can let all parties make their motions and build a record from there. That will give the court time to gather facts and decide where to go. In the meantime, I'll work on a plan so that we don't lose the consensus of the countries that you've built, Mr. President. Something that enables you to paint this proceeding as a political win in the war against terrorism."

What, exactly, would that be?

Samantha had no idea.

Yet. I'll sure as hell figure it out over the next few days.

But she knew one thing. If the ITT judges conducted official proceedings in the morning, a mistrial would carry the day. Zeus glanced at her, nodded, and gave a slight smile. Evidently, her phone call with the judge and the president was more interesting than the muted news show he had on the television but apparently wasn't watching.

"Sounds reasonable to me," President Cameron said. "Ted?"

"Based on what happened in that conference room," the judge answered, "it's perfectly apparent to me that Hernandez has already been gathering facts that are relevant to the work of this proceeding. But I suspect only one of us on this phone call has the clearance to know the parameters of the job that Black Raven and Hernandez are performing. Sir?"

President Cameron's chuckle indicated to Samantha that Judge O'Connor was one hundred percent correct. "Ted. Samantha. Off the record—we're having a collision between the secrecy demanded by an extraordinarily sensitive project for which Black Raven has been hired, and the need to expose it in the ITT proceeding. Also off the record—I'll keep the two of you informed as needed. Clearance is an issue that needs to be worked through. Understood?"

"Yes," Judge O'Connor said.

"Understood," Sam echoed.

"On the record—for the ITT proceeding, I like Samantha's suggestion that we buy time. I don't like the approach of terminating the proceeding with a mistrial and I'm worried that if proceedings reconvene tomorrow morning, Samantha is correct and a motion for a mistrial will carry the day. Ted, start making those phone calls. Keep me informed."

As the president and Judge O'Connor ended the call, the click as she shut the flip phone drew Zeus's eyes to her. For a long moment, they stared at each other. The quiet of the room hung heavy between them, broken only by the sound of the crackling fire.

"Your plan sounds solid." He broke the silence with a casual nod. As though the only thing he could think of to say was about business.

As though he isn't the same man who had professed in that darn video—made when he believed his hours were numbered—to love me for the rest of his life.

"President Cameron seemed to like it." She wondered how long she and Zeus could go on talking about work. Their phone conversations since Ana's rescue—and his departure from the clutches of the TRCR—had been short and to the point, necessarily. Now, she was acutely aware, and would have been even without Gabe's prodding, that it was time to talk about something else.

If they ever would.

But I'm afraid.

Work was easier to talk about. "That theory that you threw out to Brier—"

He gave her a slow shake of his head. "Not just a theory."

"How? OLIVER?"

"OLIVER's just the tip of a highly classified iceberg. Most of which will never see the light of day. Black Raven has been working on this project with the DHS and NSA."

"Looks like our worlds have officially collided, Hernandez. President Cameron's comments just suggested I'll have clearance to know the details of your project soon. One way or another, I'm going to figure out how to get your conclusions into the record of this ITT proceeding."

"We'll see." He gave her a nonchalant shrug and took another sip of water.

"No details till then?"

He shook his head. "Not one."

"Not even the name of the project?"

Dark stoicism greeted her query. "Not even that."

"Then in due time." She shuddered. "Brier, a puppet master for terrorist acts. Pulling the strings for Sullivans of New York. You have the evidence to prove that theory?"

He nodded. "We've just received confirmation that Charles Beller worked with them."

She drew a deep breath, as though she'd been punched. "Oh. No."

Millions of questions swirled through her mind—about

work. But work would always be there. The one thing that she now knew mattered more to her than work was standing right in front of her, and until she started talking, he was going to pretend that work was all they had in common.

Hernandez-style stoicism means he damn well isn't going to make the first move. Remember—he still thinks you're marrying Justin.

She had to really talk to him—about the reason why she'd run into another man's arms—and it scared her as much as she'd ever been afraid of anything. Given what had just happened with Brier in the conference room, that said a hell of a lot.

"You feel okay?" he asked, studying her as he sipped his water.

No. I'm terrified, and I'm afraid to admit it.

"I'm fine. Thanks to you."

"Just doing my job."

"Look," she started, "I'd like to talk to you about...what happened between us."

"Go ahead. I'm all ears."

She drew a deep breath, and the scent of blood and alcohol reminded her of an urgent problem. "But first I have blood in my hair. I realized it after the doctor finished with me. I can't work the spray nozzle without wetting the stitches, which the doctor told me not to do. I saturated the bandage when I tried. Can you help me get it out? After that, we can talk."

"Let's talk first. You just managed to have a conversation with the leader of the free world and sounded perfectly fine."

"Come on, Zeus. I can't tolerate the idea of blood in my hair." Nor could she tolerate the coppery, stale smell that she couldn't seem to avoid with each breath. "It's sickening."

She gave him a slight smile, in an effort to give him a damn clue as to where she was going. It did nothing to remove his frown, but the intense burn in his eyes told her he was interested. "And our conversation is going to end very differently than how my conversation ended with President Cameron and Judge O'Connor."

He arched an eyebrow. "You think?"

"Yes." Because, thanks to Gabe, she'd seen the video of the man who she loved telling her he never would have given up. A fact that she wouldn't have known by looking at him now.

He nodded and gestured for her to walk ahead of him. In her bathroom, she handed him a bottle of shampoo, sat on the floor by the tub, rolled a few towels as cushions, then stripped off her sweatshirt, exposing her black lace bra and snug camisole. In case he had any doubt as to her intent, she stripped off the camisole, leaving on only the sheer lace black bra.

"Dammit, Sam." His voice was gravelly and harsh. His eyes were on her boobs. Her nipples responded to his gaze, as though it was a warm caress. "Not such a good idea."

"Just get over it and wash my hair, Hernandez. I want to have a real conversation with you, about us." Glancing into his eyes, she saw a bit of hope steal some of the darkness. "And if I smell blood for one second longer, I'll be sick."

"Before we go any further, I need an explicit answer from you. You're not marrying McDougall, are you?"

"No."

"My radar tells me there is a really strong possibility he's gay. Am I right?"

Her heart thudded against her chest. The look in Zeus's eyes told her he didn't need an affirmative answer from her. "Justin is my dearest friend. He's like family to me. He stood by me throughout this whole ordeal, and he encouraged me to be honest with my feelings for you, knowing there was only one possible ending. He has been as much of a champion of you as my grandfather, at great personal cost to himself."

"Why doesn't he just come out of the closet? Everyone seems to, these days."

"He hasn't been willing, mostly due to fear of how his family will react. Plus, privacy concerns. He's wanted to develop a career based on merit, without sexuality being part of it. His rationale is antiquated, I know, but I've supported him because it's what he felt he had to do. Just like he's supported me in my decisions. Even now."

"Supporting a friend in his quest to keep his sexuality private is a hell of a lot different than marrying him and being his cover."

She punched his rock-hard bicep. "Marriages based on the bonds of friendship are made all the time. Don't judge." As she braced her hands on his chest, a fresh waft of bloody odor caught in her breath. "Come on, Hernandez. Please help me get this blood out of my hair. Otherwise, I'm going to be sick. I know you want to talk, and for once, so do I. But I'd prefer to do it without puking all over both of us."

Not waiting for a reply, she leaned back so that her shoulders were against the outside of the bathtub, removing the ponytail holder so that her hair fell to the inside. As she slipped the ponytail holder onto her wrist, he knelt on her left side, turned on the water, and used the sprayer and the gentle touch of his fingers to carefully work lather into her hair from her hairline, then down. The fragrance of jasmine and honeysuckle, combining with his woodsy scent and the heat his body emanated, enveloped her. It was like crawling into a cocoon that was supposed to be her life. She leaned closer to him, enjoying the feel of his hard body against hers in the tight space. Too soon, he turned off the water.

"Wait. You're not done. Conditioner's on the counter by the sink."

"You're killing me." His tone was serious, his words almost hoarse.

She opened her eyes. His face was over hers, kissing distance away. Afternoon shadow hazed his jawline, and Samantha ached to run her fingers over the bristles, grip him behind his head, and pull his face down to hers. Not moving, she held his gaze. "It's going to be worth it. I promise."

He scowled. Getting to his feet, he stared at the toiletries on the bathroom vanity. "This it?" He held up a bottle.

She nodded. "Can you comb it through my hair before rinsing it out? Please."

"This is fucking torture. I hate being so close to you. Hate it with every fiber in my being. Dammit, Sam."

But he only hated it because he was torturing himself with not touching her intimately. And he would soon know that he had no reason to hold back.

"I told you this would be worth it." She shut her eyes, trying to calm her racing heart. "I said, please. And I know you don't hate it."

Resuming his position, wedged between the wall, the tub, and her, he turned on the water, worked conditioner into the wet strands, combed it through, and rinsed her hair with warm water. He stood and handed her a towel. When she would have stood, he sat on the bathroom floor next to her, gripping her hand so she couldn't move.

She pulled her knees to her chest as she started towel drying her hair.

"Okay. Hair's clean," he said. "Start your conversation about us. And it better be worth it. I want real words from you. A real explanation regarding why you thought it was a good idea to marry another man—whether he's gay or not I don't give a damn—when I was there, handing you my heart on silver platter.

Why you let me walk away seven years ago without even an argument. Why you were relieved when I walked away."

Maybe he was the guy who had videotaped a message of never giving up on her, but the harsh look in his eyes and angry tone in underlying his words told her he was still Zeus, and the man had never been a pushover. Heart pounding, she looked directly into his eyes, lifted her fingers to his lips and said, "I'm afraid of what I feel for you. So afraid I barely want to admit it, so afraid I thought it better to not have you in my life than to admit my fear."

His eyes softened. As a slight smile played at his lips, he reached for her and gently caressed her cheek. "Given what's transpired in the last forty-eight hours, in both of our lives, the fact that you're afraid of anything having to do with us—or me— is pretty fucking ironic."

"I know. But I am. Terrified. Always was."

"There's no need to be afraid." Eyes burning with intensity, he let his fingers trail along her neck, down her arm, and back up. "If you tell me your fears, I'll conquer each one. But first you need to admit what you're afraid of, so we can tackle it. Tell me what has you running scared enough to marry a man who couldn't possible feel about you the way I do."

Slipping the ponytail holder from her wrist, Sam wound her wet hair into a bun, pretending to herself that her hands weren't shaking and she wasn't dying inside. "I'm afraid of the strength of what I feel for you. So afraid I agreed to marry Justin, when you were working so hard to give us—me and you—a fresh start. I'm sorry, Zeus."

He shook his head. "You looked so damn happy when you were together."

It was hard to blame him, when she deserved an Oscar for her stellar performance. "Get a clue, Hernandez. I was faking. My heart was breaking. I didn't realize until that miserable night when you went missing just how badly it was going to hurt for the rest of my life."

"I'm fine. I'm here. So what are you afraid of now?" A frown-line appeared between his eyes. "You've got to say it, Sam. Admit it, and we'll think through it."

She closed her eyes, then forced them open to focus on his face. "Becoming weak."

"We'll be stronger together than apart."

Hope tried to bloom. Reality started pulling off the petals. "Love made my mother weak. I always thought it would do the same to me. The other night, though, when you were missing, I realized I don't care if my love for you consumes and destroys me. The alternative—not having you in my life at all—is much, much worse. If my love for you ultimately turns me into something weak and clingy, someone less than the ambitious, successful woman I want to be, that's a price I'm willing to pay. I just can't live without you." She drew a deep breath. "You're not my father. I don't think you'll be the drain on my life that he was on hers. And if you ultimately are—"

"I won't be. I promise."

"It's a risk I'm willing to take." She shivered, the admission being one of the hardest she'd ever made in her life. It meant she was embarking on a road of unknowns, a detour that included Zeus every step of the way.

"No risk at all, Sam. Between us, we have enough brainpower to figure a way out of any obstacle that life might throw at us. We're going to be a formidable force. Together. I promise."

"Hold me, Hernandez."

Gathering her against his chest, he rose to his feet and strode to the bed. He deposited her on the edge of the mattress, then knelt in front of her and took her hand. Brushing his lips to the backs of her fingers he murmured. "I love you, Samantha Dixon Fairfax."

Heart full, Samantha curved her hand around his prickly jaw. "Let's make love."

"Mmm. So glad you phrased it that way." He eased her leggings down from her hips, peeling them along her thighs, and past her knees. She stepped out of them. Standing, he pushed down his jeans and pulled off his t-shirt, dropping the clothes on the floor. He pushed her knees open with his thighs. Poised for entry, with his gaze locked on hers, he held back. "Say it, Sam. Tell me you love me."

"I love you. With my heart, body, and soul." Gripping his broad shoulders, she lifted her legs and locked her ankles behind his hips, but he didn't cooperate. "Come on, Zeus."

"I've waited a long time to hear this." His eyes became more intense. "Tell me more."

"I want you," she whispered. "I need you. And I'm not talking about sex. Though right now, that would be nice. I fell in love with you the moment I met you. I love you. I always will. I'll never deny it again. Never deny you. Not for the rest of my life. That enough?"

"Almost." Eyes serious, he drew a deep breath. "Answer the question that I should have asked seven years ago. Will you marry me?"

"Yes," she whispered as he arched his hips, thrust upwards, and filled her. "Yes. Zeus. Oh. Yes."

Dear Reader,

Thank you for purchasing and reading JIGSAW, A Black Raven Novel. Please help spread the word about JIGSAW by telling your friends about it and by writing a review at AMAZON, BARNES & NOBLE, and/or GOODREADS.

My stories go through a rigorous editing process, but I've learned that typographical errors can persist despite diligent editing. If you noticed any typos in JIGSAW, or in my other books, please alert me at mail@stellabarcelona.com. I will greatly appreciate your email!

Actually being in the writing chair is the best part of the writing process for me, but a close second is the interaction that I have with readers. I love to hear from you, so please like my Facebook page, at facebook.com/stellabarcelona, and be on the lookout for posts and updates on giveaways and appearances. I also can be reached via email at mail@stellabarcelona.com and you can join my mailing list at stellabarcelona.com/newsletter. Don't worry—I'm too busy to send out frequent newsletters, and I promise I won't share your email address. If you'd prefer to contact me through the U.S. mail, I can be reached at P.O. Box 70332, New Orleans, Louisiana, 70172-0332.

My website, stellabarcelona.com, has blogs that I update from time to time, some book related, some not. I'm planning to post Jigsaw "extras" on my website, so check there periodically if you want to learn more about the characters and my thoughts as I wrote the book. Please comment and let me know what you think of the posts.

Before I leave you, I'd like to share a few pages from my work in progress, *Concierge, A Black Raven Novel*. In *Concierge*, I return to my personal home, New Orleans, Louisiana. I also return to two characters you've met in my prior novels-Andi Hutchenson, *Concierge's* heroine, is Taylor Bartholomew's best friend from my debut novel, *Deceived*. Gabe Hernandez, *Concierge's* hero, is Zeus's brother in *Jigsaw*. As *Concierge* evolves over the next several months, there may be tweaks to this excerpt. I'm thankful that my tablet is not made of stone.

Thank you again, and stay in touch!

Stella

Coming in 2017

CONCIERGE

A Black Raven Novel
By Stella Barcelona

Prologue

New Orleans, Louisiana
Two years earlier

Oblivion is the answer. An absence of Andi Hutchenson. A void.

The first rays of dawn's sunshine spilled light over the murky water of the Mississippi River. As sunlight painted the sky's clouds, feathered, golden-pink brushstrokes appeared atop the dark swirls and eddies of the river. Ignoring the color of promise, Andi focused on the flow of the river's powerful currents as the water churned under the glistening surface. Sitting alone on the downward slope of the levee, she shivered in the quiet of the morning, pulled her legs closer to her chest, and rested her chin on her knees. It was her tenth consecutive morning of going to the spot on the levee where Victor Morrissey had left her for dead. This morning she'd finally made peace with her plan to die there.

No more worrying how I'll make it through one more day. No fear. No more paranoia. No more skin-crawling creeps, as though someone is watching. No more chest-tightening, feeling-like-a-stroke anxiety.

How will I get through the day?

End it. Oblivion. The only answer.

As the sun crested over the horizon, wisps of foggy mist drifted up from the water and formed lacy angel's wings, then evaporated as daylight seeped into the grayness. If angels had ever looked out for her, they'd abandoned her six months earlier, when she'd been dragged into a crevice of hell from which she'd never escape. They hadn't yet reappeared in her once-charmed and carefree life.

I'm so damn sick of feeling sorry for myself.

An ocean-going container ship glided downriver. Multi-level lights made the vessel look like a mobile high-rise building, towering high above the misty water. On her right, in the distance, the skyline of New Orleans sparkled, the windows of the tall buildings reflecting the pink and orange. If she'd ever been, or become, a serious artist, this would have been a great spot from which to capture the city, because it revealed the dominance of the river and the precariousness of the city perched so close to the mighty current.

Sure, I can sit here until hell freezes over, but I've made the decision, so waxing poetic about colors and sparkly lights is moot.

Pre-Victor Morrissey, indecision had never been a problem for her. But he'd changed that. With one violent night, the monster who never should have been given a name had changed her, and she couldn't get used to-or like- the frightened, paranoid person she'd become. Painfully aware with each passing day that the old Andi was never coming back, and not having any clue how to cope with the Andi she'd become, she'd known for weeks what had to be done. Better for everyone. Best for her.

It's time.

As the tanker glided around the bend in the river, Andi stood and stepped towards the water. A plump black river rat, with yellow-red eyes and a long tail, disturbed by her sudden movement, turned and scurried towards her then froze, it's glowing eyes locked on hers. She screamed. It was a high-pitched yell that scared even her, as though the sudden shriek was coming from someone else's mouth. The creature scurried away in tall, dark-green levee grass. When she could breathe again, she yelled, "Goddammit to hell, you damn, damn...*rat!*"

She had good reason to hate rats. Victor had left her to die on the levee, naked, barely conscious, and bleeding. Rats had feasted on her. Drugged and barely conscious, unable to move, and in more pain than she had ever imagined, she'd been vaguely aware of their teeth biting into her flesh. Since then, her nightmares had filled in the blanks that her mind had created by trying to force her to forget.

Glancing left, then right in the dim light, she didn't see anyone who would have been disturbed by her yell. *Thank God.* It was still too early for joggers, walkers, and bikers to be on this remote stretch of the levee, and by the time they got there, she'd be...gone. It would be damn stupid to attract attention, *then* go for an early morning death-dip.

Heart pounding, she walked towards the river, keeping a wary eye on the grass for more rats. The pumping adrenaline of rat-fueled fear only strengthened her resolve, because she was so damn tired of being afraid.

Face it. Everything scares the living crap out of you. There's no cure for this kind of post-traumatic stress. Except death.

Fifteen yards to go, and she braced herself for the first touch of the wet, cold water.

I hate to be cold.

In the past six months, the bone-rattling coldness that had seeped into her body and soul on the night of her kidnapping had never left.

I'll only be cold for a few minutes more. Then I'll never be cold again. I'll never BE again. Thank God.

It was a mild January morning in New Orleans, but still cool enough that Andi wore jeans, a long-sleeve wool t-shirt, a cashmere turtle neck, and her favorite pair of Luchese cowboy boots. She'd dressed for the temperature. The weight of the cool weather clothes was a bonus. It would help her sink, just in case she chickened out. She picked up her pace, absentmindedly shrugging her shoulders to get relief from the relentless, never-stopping itch on her back, along the one hundred and three cigarette burns that Victor had placed so carefully and methodically in her back.

At the edge of the levee, a swatch of flat, muddy earth led to the water. The river's edge was lined with broken concrete. She'd stared at the broken concrete slab the previous mornings and knew her cowboy boots would help her climb over the rough terrain. Where the water lapped onto the concrete, it became slippery. When her right foot slipped out from under her and she almost fell, she slowed her pace, not wanting to slip and break a wrist before killing herself.

A broken wrist would really suck.

Finally, she stepped into the river. Her heart accelerated when her boots filled with water. She turned around and almost stepped back to the shore, then stopped and swiped at free-flowing tears that burned her cold cheeks.

Keep walking. Keep walking.

She paused when the water lapped at her thighs.

God...No. Don't panic. This is it. I'll finally have peace. Remember-if there's a heaven, Dad's there. Waiting for me. I'll finally get a chance to tell him I forgive him.

Turning again to face the river, she walked three more steps into it. Strong currents pulled at her legs as she stepped further into the river. Water crept up, inch-by-inch, past her hips, waist, and boobs. Her long hair floated up around her. She could barely hear the sound of the flowing water over the chattering of her teeth. Fighting panic, she tilted her head back and looked at puffs of white clouds in the pink-blue dawn sky.

Oh God. God. God. It's really, really cold. Damn cold. Please. End this. Fast.

"Hey! What the hell! Stop!"

The distant yell barely registered. It was nothing she going to pay attention to. She breathed deeply, and then the frigid water was over her shoulders. Even if she tried to fight it, she couldn't. Her boots were lead weights, and her jeans felt like they weighed fifty glacial pounds. She'd never been that great of a swimmer anyway, and she was capitalizing on her lack of swimming ability and the notoriously strong river currents. The combination of both made her plan foolproof. She took one last deep breath, shut her eyes, and her chin slipped below the water.

"Hey! Lady!"

She turned to the sound of the voice in time to see someone running towards the water. Before her eyes slipped under the water, she saw the owner of the voice picking his way across the broken concrete, straight in her direction.

She shook her head and tried to say, 'no,' shorthand for 'no, I don't want your help, can't you see I'm drowning on purpose,' but because her mouth was under water all she did was lose all the air from her last deep breath. She breathed in frigid, foul-tasting river water and choked as her eyes slipped under the water, her last vision being of a dark-haired man as he reached the water.

Gag. Cough. Splutter.

DAMN. DAMN. DAMN.

A moment of startling clarity hit her at the same time she felt a hand pull at her hair and yank, hard. Then a strong arm wrapped around her neck, choking her. Reflex had her fighting him with everything she had, while he pulled her in the direction of the shore.

No one touched her. Not since Victor Morrissey. No one touched her. *No one.* No. One. She landed a punch in his chest, another in his face.

No! Fucking no!

He had one hand tangled in her hair and was almost pulling it from the roots, and the other in a death grip on her upper arm. He managed to pull her up, out of the water. She gasped in a mouthful of air.

"Geez, lady! Stop struggling! I'm trying to save your ass here." She clawed at his hand that was wrapped in her hair. "Shit! Don't—"

His words were lost as she fought her way out of his hold. She went under again, sucking in another deep mouthful of river water as she fought him. It didn't matter who he was, or what he was trying to do. He became Victor Morrissey, and this time, she was damn well going to win. With his arm on her neck, she bent her face down and bit his wrist as hard. He jerked his wrist out of her mouth, and reclaimed his hold on her hair with one hand while the other hand knocked her, hard, at her temple. She gasped in pain, then choked, then breathed in more water, and she couldn't get air, and no matter what she did, she couldn't get her face above the water.

Dear God, I'm drowning.

He was tall, long-limbed, and strong. He took advantage of her stunned stillness by moving, fast. He pulled her, tugged her, and yanked her to the shore. She gagged, choked, and breathed in more and more water and then, suddenly, there wasn't murky, brown water in her vision. Blessed, quiet, peaceful blackness overcame her.

Sometime later, how long she had no clue, the peaceful, devoid-of-thought blackness was gone. She opened her eyes. Crystal-clear blue eyes were an inch from hers.

The owner of the eyes had his mouth on hers. He was exhaling into her mouth at the same time the contents of her gut were roiling up. Lifting her hands to his cheek and forehead, she pushed his face away. She managed to turn her face into the earth before sour river water spewed from her mouth. She gasped for air, shivered, and more water came out of her mouth as she struggled to get on her hands and knees. She managed another breath, then another.

With her thoughts muddled, she glanced at her rescuer, who knelt at her side and was wide-eyed with worry. "Can you breathe?"

She nodded, then choked.

"You have a phone?"

On her hands and knees, gasping for air, she looked at him through the dripping tangle of her hair, understanding where he was going with his question but unable to reply.

"Do you have a phone?" he said slowly, as though he was talking to a dim-witted child.

"Of course I have a phone," she said, spitting out more water. *Who doesn't?* Then she drew a deep breath and *dammit,* her teeth started chattering, because now she was really, really cold. Not dead. *Cold.* Not the problem she'd planned on having for the morning. "But I'm not calling anyone."

His dark hair was wet and plastered to his head and neck. A lock of it fell across his forehead, as he looked into her eyes and studied her. Broad-shouldered and long-legged, he was lanky and tall, and his tight t-shirt clung to him like a second skin. He was skinny—as though he hadn't fully grown into his frame. A light smattering of morning facial hair covered his jawline and above his upper lip. If he was eighteen years old, he'd just made it, but his blue eyes-made innocent and fresh by a fringe of dark-brown lashes-had a depth that went way beyond his years.

"Wait here," he muttered, then ran along the shoreline, downriver.

She didn't have strength to do anything but sit on her butt and wonder how the hell what had just happened had actually happened. She drew her legs to her chest, wrapped her arms around her knees, and tried to absorb the fact that she was alive. She watched her rescuer leave the shoreline, approach a spot in the levee about a hundred yards from where she was sitting, and step into an area that was overgrown with tall grass. He disappeared there for a second.

No wonder I didn't see him.

He reappeared holding a backpack, some clothes, and a guitar case. In a minute, he was at her side again. What she'd mistaken for clothes was a faded blue blanket. He held it out to her. It looked like it had been in the dirt for weeks. Too cold to take it, she submitted to him throwing it around her shoulders. "Hold it here."

She looked at him blankly.

With an impatient sigh, he grabbed her cold hands and wrapped her fingers around the two edges, forcing her to hold it under her trembling-with-cold chin.

Testing her ability to speak on the words that she knew had to be said, she drew a deep breath, then said, "I should thank you. But you shouldn't have done that."

He gave her an it-was-nothing shrug and sat next to her, facing the river, with his guitar case and his backpack at his side. "It was hard as hell to get you out. *Man.* Cowboy boots in the mighty Mississippi?"

Only one of those boots had made it out of the river. Her jeans were dripping wet and cold, cold, cold. Clouds were starting to build, and what had looked like the start of a pretty day now looked like a wintry, gloomy one. Perfectly apropos.

He gave a low whistle. "You were going vertical in a big way."

She drew another deep breath and realized that her lightheadedness wasn't the reason his words made no sense. She had no clue what the soaking wet kid was talking about. "What?"

He narrowed his eyes as he studied her. "Vertical slashes on two wrists mean business. Horizontal is for amateurs. The saying is *'go vertical, not horizontal.'*"

"Never heard that one before," she mumbled, shrugging deeper into the dirty blanket while she figured out what to do next.

"It's suicide slang."

Sudden, instant nausea made her realize a few simple, life-altering truths. One-she'd attempted suicide. Two-she'd now have to live with that fact, because her attempt had failed. Three-she was actually talking about it with her rescuer and he was someone who knew about suicide slang, for God's sake. "There's such a thing as suicide slang?"

He stripped off his soaking wet t-shirt. He was young enough that he barely had chest hair, but broad-shouldered and muscular enough that he had wrecked her plan to end the horror her life had become. For a second she worried he was going to peel off his wet jeans. Instead, he just looked at her with a puzzled expression on his face. "What do you mean is there such a thing?"

"I've never heard of suicide slang."

"Lady—"

She wasn't that old. "How old are you?"

A flash of defensiveness immediately surfaced in his eyes. "What's it to you?"

"Whoa. Calm down."

"I'm calm," he said, "and I'm twenty."

"I don't think so." She studied the taut skin on his cheekbones, the bony leanness of his chest. He was muscular, but he looked like he needed some age on him before he filled out. Maybe seventeen. Perhaps sixteen. Young enough to feel like he had to answer her question, even if his answer was a lie. He bent, lifted a sweater out of his backpack, and held it out to her.

She shook her head. "No, but thanks. You put it on. Aren't you freezing?"

He gave her a small smile. "It's a hell of a lot colder where I'm from."

And he's sleeping on the levee in New Orleans. Which means he's run a long way from where home is, because truly cold climates are far, far north. "Where's home?"

He was staring at the water, his jaw clenched hard. "Someplace I'm never going back to."

Understood.

"How old are you, really?"

"Old enough to pull you from the river." He pulled the sweater over his head. It was blue wool, pilling with age at the armpits, with loose threads at the neck and waistline. As he pulled his arms through it, she saw the imprint of her teeth on his left wrist, then her gaze fell on scars on the inside of his wrists. Thin white lines rose above the smooth skin in an area where no sharp edge ever should be. His knowledge of suicide slang now made perfect sense. From the direction of the scars, she knew he'd gone horizontal. Not vertical. Hence the reason he was able to live to see another day, if the slang truly was an indicator of the correct way to end it all. She dragged her eyes back to his. He gave her a knowing nod. "And what difference does my age make to you anyway?"

"Well, what's your name?"

"Why?"

"Because you just saved my life, and I'd like to thank you properly, while I apologize for biting you."

"Pic."

"P-I-C-K?"

"Without the K. Guitar pic. Got it?"

A made-up name if ever there was one.

"Got it," she nodded, noting the absence of a last name and knowing by the wary look he was giving her that she shouldn't push for it. She bet he was lying about his age, and lying about his name. He was young, and sleeping on the levee. Either a runaway, or homeless, which made him one of thousands of young homeless kids who frequented the streets of New Orleans on there way to somewhere else. Or not.

Homeless youth had been a pervasive problem in the city for so long the individuals themselves had become invisible. They were even called 'the invisibles.'

Suddenly, this one wasn't invisible.

"I'm Andi," she said, extending her hand to his. He had no way of knowing how big of a step the handshake was for Andi. The woman who had once been a free hugger and a happy toucher, now rarely let others touch her. Usually, the people who touched her were those who she knew, loved, and trusted-and she could count those people on one hand. He took her hand with a firm grasp, and she shook his. "With an I."

His blue eyes turned serious again. "You gotta call someone. You need help."

With the words *you need*, she cringed harder than she was

shivering, because he'd just uttered the two words she'd grown to hate. "Understood."

Arms loose at his side, he shook his head. "Really. Someone needs to know that you just tried to commit suicide. You need to call someone."

"Thank you, Pic, but I'm not seeking advice, nor do I need your opinion of what I need to do."

Because dear God, in the last six months, I've gotten more than I can handle. You need to get out. Maybe you'd feel better if you went out more. You need to exercise. Exercise relieves stress and anxiety, don't you know? Try yoga. You need to start painting again-it will give you something to do with your time. You need to go to your appointments. You need to see your therapist. Are you taking your meds? You need therapeutic oils. I hear lavender oil helps with tension headaches. Maybe hypnosis will help with your nightmares. You need Ambien. I sleep like a baby when I use it. You need Xanax. It works wonders for anxiety. You need breathing exercises. You need acupuncture.

Pic frowned, folded his arms, and cocked his head to the side. "There's got to be someone for you to talk to right now, and you really shouldn't be alone. Serious help. Suicide is serious."

"Would you please quit using that word?"

"What word?"

"Suicide."

"You need to admit—"

"Stop telling me what I need to do!" If her words and tone weren't enough to shut him the hell up, pressing her fingers in her ears certainly should do the trick.

He opened his mouth anyway and, unfortunately, she could hear him. "Hey. I'm just calling it as I see it. If you can't even admit what you just did—"

"It's complicated—"

"Always is," he said. "You need a support system, and that starts with calling someone and telling them what just happened."

I have the best support system money can buy. My support network-of friends, relatives, doctors, therapists, counselors, and prescription meds-is so wonderful it led me straight here, to the river.

Looking into Pic's blue eyes, she felt for a split second the lightning bolt of clarity that had come to her when her head had first slipped under the water, when she'd known there was no

.t.
What I need is a goddamn backbone, and that obviously ...t coming from my support system, because if it were, I'd have it by now.

"You're not going to call anyone," Pic said with a frown, "are you?"

The reality was there was no one for her to call at 6:45 a.m., because the one person in her life whom she wanted to call now, and every other second of every day, had died. God, but she missed her dad with every single breath she took. Her father had blamed himself for what Victor had done to her. She'd let him, because in a way, he was culpable.

Damn, but she'd even blamed her father—and then, on Christmas day, just one month earlier, her father had died of a massive heart attack. He'd died, without Andi ever having the chance to tell him she forgave him. The aftermath of guilt and regret Andi felt brought unresolved issues that were now forever wedged hard between herself and the man who had always adored and cherished her. Her grief over losing her father and misery over unsaid words, on top of everything else, had brought her to the river.

"No," she whispered, loud enough for Pic to hear it, and pulled the blanket closer around her. She freed one of her hands, brushed away a tear, and wondered if her tears would ever stop falling when she thought that telling her father she forgave him was no longer a possibility.

"Are you going to tell anyone about this morning?"

She didn't need to think for long about that question. "Never. No one will ever know."

Because they'll never, ever stop pitying me if they know. They'll never, ever treat me like I'm normal. I'll never get the chance to be normal.

I've officially had enough pity for one lifetime.

"But you need help. Someone needs to know-"

She gave him a smile. "Someone does. You do. Dammit, but I'm freezing. And I know you've got to be as well," she stood. "Which is pretty stupid of me, because I left my purse over there," she gestured with her chin to where she'd left it, "and my car keys are in it, and my car—with a perfectly fine heater, thank God--is parked over the levee. Come on, Pic. Let's go."

He stood and shook his head. "I'm not going anywhere with you."

His face had paled and his eyes were wide. She saw fear in

them.

He really, really is young, and he's scared someone will find him. He's terrified he'll be sent back to wherever he ran from. From the fear in his eyes, that's a place as scary to him as the hell in which I live.

"Yes, Pic. You are. Because I'm going to turn into an icicle if I sit out here for one second longer. I really, really want to talk to you and I want to do it over breakfast." She didn't want to eat, but she assumed he did. "And I will not press you for information about where you've run from. Or what your real name is, or how old you really are. I trust you to keep my horrible secret about what happened here this morning, and you can trust that I won't push you to tell me anything you don't want to tell me. Understood?"

He looked like he wanted to nod, but he didn't. She eyed his tattered sweater, his banged-up guitar case, and his overstuffed backpack.

"I'm going to buy you the biggest breakfast you're ever going to eat. It's the least I can do. Hot, fluffy pancakes." Yearning replaced the fear in his eyes. "Crispy waffles, with strawberries and whip cream. Eggs. Ham. Hash browns. Fat sausage links. Whatever you want. Sound good?"

Even though he said he was twenty, she knew as sure as her teeth were chattering that he was a teenager, and a young one. Maybe sixteen. Possibly fifteen. He was sleeping on the levee, and she'd bet made-to-order, hot meals had been a premium for him in his recent history. She knew she'd lured him at the mention of pancakes, and she didn't wait for his response. With Pic's dirty blanket wrapped around her shoulders, Andi turned and walked to where she'd left her purse, confident her new friend would follow.

ABOUT THE AUTHOR

Stella Barcelona has always had an active imagination, a tendency to daydream, and a passion for reading romance, mysteries, and thrillers. She has found an outlet for all of these aspects of herself by writing romantic thrillers.

In her day-to-day life, Stella is a lawyer and works for a court in New Orleans, Louisiana. She lives minutes from the French Quarter, with her husband of seventeen years and two adorable papillons who believe they are princesses.

Stella is a member of Romance Writers of America and the Southern Louisiana Chapter of the Romance Writers of America. Her first novel, DECEIVED, was inspired by New Orleans, its unique citizens, and the city's World War II-era history. While DECEIVED introduced the continuing character of Black Raven Private Security Contractors, in her second novel, SHADOWS, A Black Raven Novel, the Ravens take flight in a cyber-thriller that was inspired by current events. Stella is hard at work on her fourth novel, CONCIERGE, A Black Raven Novel, which will be released in early 2017.

35685494R00227

Made in the USA
San Bernardino, CA
01 July 2016